No Good Deeds

PART ONE

E.J. McKenna

A Historium Press Book

First Edition published by Historium Press

Images by Shutterstock, Imagine, Promeai, & Public Domain
Cover designed by White Rabbit Arts at The Historical Fiction Company

Visit the author's page at
www.thehistoricalfictioncompany.com/hp-authors/e-j-mckenna

Library of Congress Cataloging-in-Publication Data on file

Hardcover ISBN: 978-1-962465-76-2
Paperback ISBN: 978-1-962465-67-0
E-Book ISBN: 978-1-962465-68-7

Historium Press, a subsidiary of
The Historical Fiction Company
New York, NY / Macon, GA
2024

Table of Contents

*"There is not a woman born who desires to
eat the bread of dependence."*

- Susan B. Anthony

1

It Always Starts Somehow
1893

Being a life-long killer of roadside bandits, Annie held no concern for her welfare as she travelled alone.

For many, being a 28-year-old woman alone, with nothing but old Bessie pulling her cart, would guarantee one's own death. But the world she came from had hardened her.

Though it had been many years since the name 'Schaeffer' struck the lands with dread, she wouldn't be quick to advertise its return. Wherever she could, she rented lodgings under the name 'Malone'. No need for unnecessary attention to be brought upon her in her current predicament.

A clean slate was all she wanted. Freedom. Her own life, finally.

The Southern territories were always hot, but June was a most suffocating month to travel in.

Her last few coins had afforded her lodging at a farm just over the Mississippi border. The family who took her in suggested she find work in Tinulca. It was a good day's travel, with very little cover. The prairies rolled on ahead of her, the only shade to be found were the woodlands at the side of the road. Even the birds sheltered in the pines, choosing comfort over song. It was silent except for the tumbling rocks under the wheels as her wagon trundled onwards.

Some brief movement in the distance caught her eye. At the edge of the larger hills, the flash of a silhouette darted out of sight.

A small column of campfire smoke came from the same direction. Annie readied herself against the predictabilities of desperate men. They were likely whom she was warned about not six hours ago. She didn't quicken Bessie's steps, nor feel the need to steel herself from panic. Keeping her course was as natural to her as the prickling sensation of being followed.

"Hi there, Girlie!" The unmistakable tones of a local drawled out. "You look in need of some assistance."

"Do I now? You sure about that?" She stared straight ahead and saw two more 'good Samaritans' approaching on horseback. They proceeded to flank the cart. Unflinching, and maintaining pace, she continued her journey.

"You don't sound like you're from these parts, little lady. You need to watch out, there's bad fellas 'round here."

"Thank you for the warnin', but I'll be fine."

"Oh come now, you ain't takin' us seriously, darlin'." One of the mounted undesirables sneered. "A pretty thing like you alone? You don't stand a chance." He snapped his horse across in front of Bessie, giving the cream Percheron mare no option but to halt. Annie assessed the situation with a deep breath. She felt the cart lurch as the first fellow she had encountered climbed into the back of it, stumbling over her belongings as he went.

"Look boys, I don't think you wanna do this."

"Is that right, Green Eyes?" The degenerate to her left leered up at her as he shoved a Winchester rifle in her face. "The way I see it, you're better off not fightin'. If you play real nice, we may keep you around after."

A sharp pain ran through her head, it was yanked back from her top knot by her unwanted cart companion. She was angry.

"Why don't you fellas leave her alone? She asked you nicely." A momentary stillness ran through the area as the men were distracted.

The atmosphere shifted, as did the offenders. "Move along mister, 't ain't nothin' you need worry about." Still holding onto her jet-black hair, the interloper in the wagon stepped over the seat to the foot well and squared himself up ready to shoot the have-a-go hero. This twisted Annie to fully face the rifleman. As all eyes stayed on the stranger, Annie winced through the pain in her scalp to shift her hands to the base of her skirt. She hitched it up enough to reach the knife in her boot.

"Now I ain't lookin' for trouble," the deep voice continued, "but I believe this lady ain't interested." A threatening tone fell into his throat with ease. "And I believe you need to be taught how to listen."

Annie took her chance. She kicked the rifleman's aiming arm away from her. This set it off into the face of Bessie's blocker. Next, she threw her knife into the jugular of the shooter and head-butted her cart companion. As much as it hurt, it was nothing compared to being pulled, by her hair, to the ground. Her attacker punched her full in the face, but during the grapple she grabbed his revolver and shot him through the temple. Blood, sweat, and what little brains he had, hit her like confetti.

The dust from the foray hung in the air. The tall, broad silhouette of the stranger stood still not far off.

Annie spat the remnants of her victim back on to its owner. She took the money clip, bullets, and pistol from his corpse, and rolled to sit against her cart, winded. Her head was heavy and her clothes torn.

The silhouette shifted and slowly holstered his gun. "You alright?" He started to move forwards.

"Dammit! This was my one good skirt!"

The fellow laughed nervously through the dust towards her.

"That's some impressive moves you got, Miss." The dust-fog parted to reveal a man with blue eyes. He may have been only a little older than Annie, but his life looked to have added years. He was a sizeable figure as he stood with his arm outstretched. "Need a hand?"

Annie briefly placed her hand in his. "Thank you." She heaved herself up, supported by the cart's side and winced as a lightning bolt of pain pierced her leg. "Could you perhaps point me to the nearest town with a good doctor?"

"A *good* doctor?" The man scoffed at the hopping Annie. "No, but a doctor? Sure... We ain't far from Tinulca... I could take you there."

"Thank you, Mister...?"

"Healey, Nathan Healey."

"Thank you, Mister Healey. That's most kind."

Despite the pain, Annie refused further physical help. She hopped on her good leg, grabbed the cart edges, and, in an undainty fashion, dragged herself into its foot well. She righted herself onto the seat and washed the worst of the dirt off using her canteen. Mister Healey led his horse to the back of the cart, hitched it and retrieved her knife before ascending into the driving position.

His unshaven weather-worn face told her he never really rested anywhere other than outdoors. His accent was certainly not from Mississippi. Her heritage told her there was only one reason a man like this would be this far from home. His camp might be close by, and although she could see he was an outlaw, she felt safe.

***

Nathan Healey stretched in the saddle as his mare, Prynne, sloped along the track. He was weary. Recent times hadn't been kind to the Needham Boys gang. Duke's latest endeavors, at times, were outlandish and extroverted. No one talked of the escape from Missouri after Duke insisted on getting Madsen out of jail. It hadn't sat well with many, and Nate was keen to stay out of it. He would soon be at the camp, able to rest after his latest errands. Maybe he would take some time to go hunting; clear his mind.

Up ahead were the sound of unfriendly voices. He moved Prynne to the treeline and continued in the shadows. He saw what he expected, three grifters harassing a lone woman. "Ain't a smart girl." He muttered, continuing to pursue on the back of Prynne.

He sighed. He was battered and bruised from the latest assaults fought on behalf of the gang's doctor. Nate wasn't in the mood to intervene but knew the outcome if he didn't. Why would a woman travel alone, even in the daytime around here? And how could a fellow conduct himself like that towards a lady and still call himself a man? He dismounted, checked his guns, then moved towards them, calling out to grab the men's attention.

Dumbfounded, he watched the victim burst into swift, violent action, ending the brawl as suddenly as it started. Despite her haste to remove herself from his assistance, he found her constant refusal for help almost amusing. After settling on the agreement to escort her to Tinulca, and picking through what was left of the misguided highwaymen, he offered her back her blade.

He offered her back her blade. "Here you are, Miss…?"

"… Malone."

Her somewhat hesitant introduction threw him. Suspicion crawled across his skin as he held out her weapon. "Miss *Malone*. Figure you might want it back." He passed the sticky, bloodied knife to his companion as she finished washing herself down. "Thank you. I'd be sad to lose this." She swigged a drink of water, tipped a little into Nate's hands and used the rest to clean the knife before slipping it back into her boot.

Nate noticed no feeling of unease from Miss Malone, and he was comforted by her accent. It seemed to be a mix of many and took him back to younger days when the gang travelled throughout the West. Her skills with a gun and knife, however, seemed unsurpassed, and her reactions even quicker than his own. It nagged at him.

***

They set off in silence. Annie rested after her exertions; her eyes closed, her face basking in the sun.

Eventually, Nate spoke. "You ain't from here."

"What gave it away?" She hummed.

"The voice… And that little stunt back there."

She turned to him with a wide smile. "Well, I coulda been from anywhere if I'd kept quiet."

"Are you the type to keep quiet, Miss Malone?" Nate grinned as Annie closed her eyes again with a smirk. "So, what brings you so far South, other than lookin' to win fights against robbers and rapists?"

"I recently found myself no longer in a job with my long-term employer. I needed to find work."

"But the *South*, Miss Malone? Surely there's somewhere better?"

Annie gave a short, sharp laugh. "This is as far as my money took me, Mister Healey. I gotta say it has warmer weather than the North and they are so far behind in civilization, a gal could really make a name for herself durin' these industrious times."

He shrugged. "I guess that is as good as any other reason. How's your leg?"

Annie shifted in her seat, wincing as her beaten up body groaned. "Not as painful as my head."

"That eye is swellin' pretty fast in this heat too."

"Oh I must be as pretty as a picture right now."

"I'm sure if you cover the left side of your face for a while, you'd still be quite a catch, Miss." Nate scoffed. "Though there's not much contest 'round these parts... 'less a hog is your competition."

"You know, for someone who has only just met me, Mister Healey, your familiarity knows no bounds."

The charms of his passenger were infectious, but something about her still caused him unease. "You really are quite a skillful fighter, Miss. What exactly was it you did for a livin'?"

Annie looked out across the landscape. "… Why d'you ask…?"

"Because that weren't just brawlin' I saw is all."

" You know, when I was a kid back West I saw a travelin' show with a little gunslingin' girl. She was incredible. Coulda killed a man before he even saw her comin'. I could barely pull a trigger back then, and there she was shootin' targets and throwin' knives at folk while she were blindfolded."

Annie's throat went dry. "… That right? She must be long gone now."

Nate's eyes narrowed. "What did they call her…? '*Dead Eye Annie*'… Little Dead Eye Annie Schaeffer!" he jerked the cart to a harsh stop and turned. Rage and confusion spread across his face. His hand already on the rifle as he loomed over the seated stranger next to him.

Annie raised her hands to stop the monolith of confrontation shoot her head from her shoulders. "Mister Healey, I need to explai-"

"You're damn right you do, woman! What the hell are you doin' here? I thought the last of those Irish bastards had been wiped out." He prepped the gun. "*Guess I was wrong…*"

"MR HEALEY! I ain't a Schaeffer. Not like that." Annie took a beat to be calm. Reading his hesitation she slid along the seat towards him, placing a gentle hand on the one he used to steady the rifle. She really started to dislike that gun. She looked him square in the eyes and softened her voice. "Mister Healey… I ain't been a Schaeffer for twenty-two years… I ain't one of them. Not really."

Nate looked down at the woman. Her battered face staring at him, her eyes full of sincerity. He allowed his gaze to drift to her hand as it lay on his. She could have killed him any time she wished. He didn't like being caught off guard, not many managed it.

"Please, you got this wrong. If you'd just take me to Tinulca, I'll tell you everythin'." Annie felt his grip on the rifle loosen. She became impatient. "Look, it's gettin' hot and I'm in need of a doctor. So, either you shoot me now or you get this cart movin'." With her hand still on his, she guided the rifle out of Nathan's grasp.

He slumped down next to her and picked up the reins, moving Bessie on again. With a sharp exhale he spoke again; less friendly than expected. "So, explain."

"*…Alright…*"

***

Annie brushed her skirt. "Yes, I'm a Schaeffer. Ain't exactly my fault though, is it? My father was Caley Schaeffer. I'm his disappointment. As I weren't a boy, I was a seen as a waste of time. Kept in camp with those he thought useless."

"With the women?"

Annie nodded. "But as Schaeffers we all had to be feared, and as his kid I was expected to be an '*example of greatness*'." She said bitterly. "When I was old enough to stand, I was old enough to hold this knife." She tapped the handle sticking from her boot. "It weren't long before I was throwin' it as good as the fellas. Then, when I was strong enough, I held a pistol. And when they were sure my bones wouldn't break, I fired it." She shook her head. "I was a goddamn natural."

Nate looked at Annie. His own early life wasn't much different, but at least his rat-bastard father was never sober enough to be a contender for the Schaeffers. "So, how'd you end up in the circus?"

Her stare sharpened. "*Sold*. Cal sold me. Nearly seven years old and I became Bill Smythson's most expensive attraction in the Freak Show... And I'd been there ever since... 'til Smythson suggest I start usin' my '*finer qualities*' to raise money for his show anyhow."

Nate nodded gruffly. He kept his eyes on the road, rather than acknowledging Miss Schaeffer's other undoubtedly fine qualities sat beside him. "So, you left?"

"In a manner of speakin'."

Annie looked across at her driver. His hard expression softened as he spoke. "Are you lookin' for family?"

She laughed. "Good God, no! Why would I ever do that? My Momma was the only thing I'd go get, and I heard she passed not long after I was sold." Annie picked at her fingernails. "I guess she had no reason to keep livin'..." She sniffed and continued. "Then, 'bout ten years ago I heard the Schaeffers finally got what was comin' to 'em. Big gang war or some such. Heard someone shot Cal straight through his aimin' eye in a gunfight."

Nathan tensed and cleared his throat. "Nasty business… You know the men responsible?"

Annie shook her head. "No. But I tell you what, that was the first good night's sleep I'd had my whole life. I'd like to meet that man and shake his hand."

Quiet descended on the cart until they turned in to Tinulca's dusty town centre.

"Here we are. You got a General Store, Gunsmith's, Hotel, Post Office and Church should you want to confess some sins... or you can use the jail for that." Nate nudged her shoulder.

Annie turned and clutched his arm. "I'd be ever so grateful if you didn't advertise who I am here, Mister Healey. You've proven that my last name ain't so forgotten after all."

He pulled Bessie up to the hitching post outside the doctor's. "I don't know what you could mean, Miss Malone." He said lightly. "I will happily abide by your request as long as you do me the same courtesy. Please use my formal name of '*Deleaney*'." He jumped down from the cart.

"Well ain't we a pair?" Annie was aware of how little she could see from her left eye, and her right leg was swollen and stiff.

"Now, are you actually gonna allow someone to help you this time, Miss Malone?" Nate stood beside the vehicle.

She smiled. "Don't see as I have much choice in the matter, Mister Deleaney."

He grinned and moved to lift Annie from her seat as carefully as he could. A faint floral scent cocooned her as she placed her arms around his neck. It would be both a wrench and a relief to escape her.

"Would you be so kind as to open the door for me, Miss? I seem to have my hands full."

Annie obliged and Mister Healey carried her over the threshold.

2

Played like a Fiddle
Late June 1893

There were elements of Duke's recent career choices which made some sense to Nate. Befriending the law in town kept them ahead of any news regarding their whereabouts, and it gave them some leads for some much-needed money. He enjoyed working as a Bounty Hunter. It was like the early days again, though this time he wasn't looking to take money from the desperate men he caught. That had been Duke's way in the beginning. Those 'Wanted' for crimes the Needham Boys thought victimless, were given an opportunity to buy their freedom. The rest were taken to the nearest Sheriff. Either way the gang got paid. Things turned a lot muddier as the years went on.

Nate's job now was to keep his nose clean; no extortion. He was happy to do it. It kept him away from any dramas in camp while still providing for them and earning a little cash himself. The weeks had felt strange since he stumbled into that scuffle with Miss Schaeffer. He hadn't been knocked dumb by a woman in a long time and generally stayed away from the species as a rule. He wasn't keen on making a fool of himself for anyone, but she had appeared at the forefront of his mind with each visit to Tinulca. She must have moved on by now. He chose to focus on tasks he was good at.

"I keep tellin' you, Mister, you got the wrong man!"

"So why'd you run, boy?"

"You're scary!"

"Hey! Why don't you just shut the hell up back there or I won't take you to the Sheriff alive?" Nate swung his arm backwards and hit the bound protestor. "Only reason I ain't killed you yet is my horse don't like to get dirty. I ain't keen on coverin' her in your blood." This last bounty had been more problematic than he had expected. Young men were faster on their feet nowadays, and the arrogance of their youth made them think they could outsmart an older man. But Nathan's experience and abilities with a rope put pay to that.

"You think you're doing the world a favor do you, Mister? Capturing an innocent man, and threatening death? What am I supposed to have done??"

Nate didn't much care for the chatty ones, he preferred them to accept their fate. A silent bounty made for a happy bounty hunter.

"You conned old folk outta their savins before you ended their lives, Dobson. Now shut your mouth before I put a pistol in it."

"I ain't never done nothing like that…! Besides, I didn't know that medicine was poison. That stutterin' Quack said it was good." Nate stiffened. Yet another tale about his camp's doctor. "Well then you can tell the Sheriff when we get to Tinulca, can't you?" He clubbed Dobson with his pistol and calmness fell across the rest of his journey.

He hitched Prynne outside the Sheriff's office, pulled the knocked-out Dobson onto his shoulder and lugged his delivery inside.

"This one give you some trouble, Deleaney?" The Sheriff eyed the silent gent with amusement.

"Who this fella? Nah. Young kid was all tuckered out from runnin'. Fell asleep in my arms." The lawman laughed and got up from his desk. "You must have a mighty soft touch then. Put him in that cell. I'll hope that swelling on his head don't cause memory loss."

"Might make him remember when to shut up in future." Nate threw the lump onto the cell bed and shut the bars. "He might get some strange notion that I mistreated him a little. But don't you worry about that."

The Sheriff nodded and handed over a nice stack of bills. "I'm sure he'll live, precious thing. See you again soon, Deleaney." Nate tipped his hat and left; bounty work is easy money when you know how criminals think.

"Mister Hea-… Deleaney!" Nate paused counting his earnings and looked towards the voice.

"Mister Deleaney!"

***

Tinulca wasn't so bad, though it certainly wasn't the most cosmopolitan town Annie had visited. Since the incident three weeks ago she had been somewhat stranded. Luckily, she had afforded the doctor's fee and two weeks' lodgings at the hotel thanks to the thief she looted.

She was well enough now to strike deals for various amenities in the town. Annie had food and lodging, and Bessie had a stable because Miss Schaeffer agreed to clean both in exchange. Frankly, with the things most of the clientele got up to in their rooms, she preferred shovelling horse shit to cleaning the hotel.

The little money she had earned in tips, and whatever scraps she had left from the deceased's money clip were more than a whiskey's worth, but far less than she needed to live. It seemed the only way to earn actual money in the town was to go the one route she had declined back in the mid-West. Annie was surviving, but barely. She knew her best option was to find Mister Healey and convince him to take her in. He had been spotted in town with a few companions around the Sheriff's office; outlaws bringing in criminals of all things! Their camp couldn't be far away.

She had to be smart. What if Nathan had mentioned her? The gang might not be as ready to listen to her as he had been. She would wait until he was alone before she approached him.

Annie had dreamed of independence her entire life. Now, fighting so hard to keep it was becoming impossible without help. She would propose that if provisions were made to support her survival, she could help the camp. If her suggestion was declined, she would brazen it out alone, living off her bloodline's reputation. She prayed it wouldn't come to that.

A further week passed before Annie's chance was delivered. She spotted Nathan Healey leaving the Sheriff's office and hurried towards him. "Mister Hea-… Deleaney!

Mister Deleaney!" He looked startled but walked purposefully in her direction; his hat pulled low, shading his face. She slowed to a determined strut. "Hello, Mister Deleaney. How good it is to see you. How are you?"

He towered over her. "Well thank you, Miss Malone. I'm somewhat surprised to see you here. Thought you'd have moved on by now. I see you're recoverin'. You look… well…" He felt his face redden, "That eye's almost healed now."

Annie chuckled. "I should hope so after four weeks. That fella managed a good punch, but I've been hit harder. Please, call me Annie.

"I never got to thank you properly for your help that day." Annie affected the voice of a Southern Belle, "And I would be *most* offended if you declined to let me buy you a drink." She could see a stubbled smile on Nathan's shaded face as he tilted his hat brim. "It would be remiss of me to decline. And it's Nate."

"Are you free now, Nate?"

He adjusted his hat a little more and flashed a grin. "I believe I am, Annie, after you."

***

Annie accepted his gesture and stepped in front of him towards the one saloon in town. She was dressed in men's attire; a work shirt tucked into britches. The practicalities for women to wear men's clothing in these lands also offered the addition of being pleasing to the eye of onlookers. Clearing that opinion from his mind, Nathan lengthened his stride to walk alongside Annie.

She barely spoke while they headed towards the saloon's

entrance. She was lost in thought at how to approach her proposition.

After you." Nathan's voice jolted her back to her surroundings.

"Thank you kindly."

"Seems only right as you're buyin' the drinks." He laughed as they approached the bar.

"Afternoon, folks, what can I do for ya today?"

"Beer."

"And for you, Missy?"

"I'll have a glass of your *fourth* best whiskey if you'd be so kind." Annie leaned forward and gave her most coy look at the bartender, knowing that would get at least the third best spirit at the lower price. Nate leaned on the bar and looked at her with amusement. "You know exactly what you're doin' don't you?" She stared straight ahead with a smile. "I couldn't possibly comment on that, Mister Deleaney. Ain't my fault I always stumble across nice folk willin' to do me a kindness."

He shook his head as the bartender put down the beer without word, then courteously handed Annie a whiskey more to her liking.

"No charge". She paid for the beer, and they sat at a table.

"A little early in the day for whiskey ain't it?"

"Depends what time you got up, Nathan." Annie placed her hat down, sat back in her chair and drained her drink. It was certainly more to her liking than the fourth best would have been. "Besides, I ain't never been much of a beer drinker." She slammed her empty glass down with satisfaction and sat forward, placing her hands on his drinking arm. "I really do wanna thank you for your help that day, Nate."

She gazed at him with real sincerity. It was the first time he had really been able to see quite how green Annie's eyes were. People would've cut them out of her head for jewellery if they could.

"I didn't really do anythin', Annie. You took care of the worst of it."

Annie's grip tightened. "You got me to Tinulca. And I distinctly remember you didn't shoot me in the face when you worked out who I was. Plus, you provided a very timely distraction for me to set my moves against those fellas."

There was that look again. Nate quickly lifted his arm to down his beer, leaving Annie's hands to slip back to the table. "Well, I think those fellas just had an unlucky day." He glanced at her.

"... Another?"

"…Sure."

"How's about a real one this time? Don't be leavin' a lady to drink hard liquor alone."

"Fine, I'll have whatever drink that poor fella is gonna serve you."

He half-joked and Annie sidled back to the bar.

Something was off, it kept Nate's mind sharp. His encounters with the Schaeffer Gang all those years ago made him cautious. They were savages, and Cal had been well known for being unpredictable and fiery. But there was a cunningness about Annie that put Nate on edge. He turned in his chair to check the bar. Miss Schaeffer was paying the bartender and talking casually, before returning with a forced lightness to her expression.

He watched Annie place his drink down and return to her seat beside him. "Your good health, Nate."

"*Cheers*." He waited for Annie to drink before he touched his own. The woman both fascinated and unnerved him. Annie picked up on her companion's hesitations. She hadn't been fully honest with him in either of their meetings so far, and it was beginning to get to her. "Nate, I'm in trouble."

He thumped down his glass and exhaled sharply; there it was. "Of course, you are." He glared at the table. Why was he a sucker for people in need? He was a fool. "And how exactly is this my problem, Annie?" He looked at her. "What? You thought you could bat your eyes, buy me a beer and I'd nod my head for you like that drinks monkey over there? You ain't that stupid, are ya?"

"I ain't stupid at all." Annie spat. "Despite what you may be thinkin', I ain't in the habit of wantin' help or trickin' folk into fixin' situations for me." Nathan scoffed into his drink. He shook his head as Annie continued.

"I… can't stay in Tinulca."

"Why? You already conned men outta their fortunes, have you?" Annie's face hardened to sharp edges. He had caused more of a reaction than he'd expected, and the tell-tale signs of Caley Schaeffer momentarily peeked through.

"I have no money. I can't afford to stay and I can't afford to leave."

"Then maybe you shouldn't spend what little you have buyin' drinks for unsympathetic fellas-"

SLAP.

As soft as Annie's hands were, their sting was sharper than a whip, with a noise that shut the whole bar down. Nate rubbed his cheek, fury burst forward in his eyes. He turned back to Annie as the bartender and two hopeful heroes came and stood by the table.

"Everything alright, Miss…?"

"It's fine." Annie stared at Nathan. Her green eyes were almost black.

"You need your friend to be escorted along-?"

"I said it's fine. Thank you." She broke her glare to smile sweetly at her would-be rescuers. "I'm sorry, I didn't mean to cause such a disturbance. No need for you fellas to be burdened with our trivialities."

Nate's contempt at how easily she could play a man, burned on as he cooled his cheek with his drink. The saloon went back to business as usual as the pair sat in silence at the table.

"You deserved that."

"I always do, Miss Malone." Nathan muttered. "But I don't like my good nature bein' taken advantage of. There ain't never been much of it. Even less so these days. And you are close to wearin' out my patience." He sipped his drink slowly.

Annie leaned in close. "I know what you are, Nathan Healey."

He stared daggers back. "What of it? I could say the same to you. You lookin' to blackmail me, Miss?" His expression darkened. "As you won't get outta this town alive if that's the case." He placed his glass back on the table, never breaking eye contact.

Annie rested on her hand and paused as exhaustion took over.

"This weren't how I planned for it to go." She looked at Nate with a vague desperation. "I ain't tryna do more than ask you to take me in."

"What? Take you in??" Confusion replaced all of Nate's disdain.

Annie spoke hurriedly. "I know you'll have a camp nearby; I can spot outlaws a mile off. I've seen some of you playin' Bounty Hunter to that Sheriff these past weeks."

Nathan looked around. "And, what?"

"I could be of use to you all. I can cook, clean, I could go huntin'. I'm guessin' there might be a couple of women in camp. I could teach them how to fight better, defend themselves. I'm just askin' for security. Christ! I mean I even have my own get-up. I ain't an extra mouth to feed, Nate, I'm a sure bet!"

He couldn't believe what he was hearing, it was laughable. "I know nothin' 'bout you, 'cept you're a Schaeffer." He hissed in a low voice. "You think you'd survive five minutes in camp with us when they find that out?"

"Look, you heard me out that day. If you say that you'll try and talk to 'em, I'll buy two bottles of whiskey with the last of my money and we'll celebrate. After that, if all fails, I'll be gone. You won't hear from me again."

"It ain't up to me Annie-"

"I know it *ain't up to you*, Nathan. I'm askin' you to ask the fella it *is* up to."

He sighed. This woman had proven herself already; she was tenacious and skilful and could be useful to the gang. He looked at Annie. Not only was she tired, but she was embarrassed that she had been unable to save herself unaided. Right now, her fate rested in the hands of a man she had mis-footed plenty in only two encounters.

Nate groaned, lit a cigarette and drew on it deeply. "Fine. *Fine*. I'll ask." Annie's face lit up. "You know you got some goddamn grit ambushin' me like this."

She clapped her hands, laughed and lightly punched his broad shoulder. "Thank you, Nathan. *Thank you!*"

"But I ain't guaranteein' anythin'." He exhaled the tobacco smoke and inhaled Annie's floral perfume as he turned his hostile face to her. "And you best not slap me again, Miss Malone." Annie stood and patted his back, "I ain't guaranteein' anythin', Mister Deleaney." She headed towards the barman, "Two bottles of your best whiskey please, my good man!"

***

Annie was alright… for a Schaeffer, Nate thought. She liked to push her luck a little too hard, but she did have good taste in liquor. It was late, dark outside and they had been drinking quite solidly since mid-afternoon. He didn't know where Annie had gone. He couldn't see much unless it was right in front of his face.

"You alright, Nate?" That mixed accent laughed out through the haze. "I think we best get you home before they put you in the cells."

"I'm fiiiiiine. I say when I'm done."

Annie guided the inebriated outlaw to his horse out front of the Sheriff's office. His sideways stagger and tilted angle were too much for her to handle, and she sat on the steps as tears of laughter streamed down her face. Her sides hurt, and she thought she might vomit. "That ain't your horse, Mister." She managed through the gasps for air.

"Oh." He slid off the unknown beast into a crumpled heap on the ground. "Ah, goddamn it."

Annie composed herself enough to stagger to his aid. "Here, here's yours." She attempted to help him up onto Prynne. It was futile. She was about as steady as a ship in a storm. "You sure you're gonna be okay to get home?"

"Dammit woman, I'm fine." Nate muttered as he balanced on his saddle in a mix of a slump and asleep. He kicked Prynne forward and waved in a non-specific direction as he heard that laugh behind him fade into the night.

In all honesty he wasn't even sure if he was taking the right direction out of Tinulca. Prynne wasn't best pleased with her passenger, and almost threw him as he vomited beside her. "Shit." Nathan rallied enough to squint through the moonlight and search for a landmark. He couldn't find one. He was tired. Why didn't he have a horse who just knew where to go? *"Stupid horse."* He started to doze while Prynne shuffled onwards. As he wavered in his saddle, he heard an almost recognisable voice in the darkness.

"Nate? NATHAN! You alright?? Jesus Christ what's happened to you?"

"DANAAAAAAY! My, what a joy it is to see you little brother!" He slurred with a dumb grin as the man rode towards him.

"Nate, you've been gone hours. People started to worry." "Well ain't that nice of 'em?" Nate slumped forward letting Danny take Prynne's reins, leading them both back to camp. The last sounds he heard that night, were of initial panic and exclamation. "Oh my God! He's hurt! What's happened? Where's he been…? Nathan?!"

This was followed by the fluid sensation of movement as Daniel Healey dragged him from the saddle and down to his bed.

"He's drunk."

3

Some Delicacy Required

She wanted to die. Anything was preferable to the way she felt at that very moment. Her brain was powder. Annie rolled onto her side in search of water, and quickly found herself in an empty bath in the hotel. It was still dark, she wasn't due at the stable quite yet. She hauled herself out of the bath in time to vomit back into it. The cold copper side provided some comfort for her face. With great effort, she managed to clean the mess without adding to it, then staggered to her room.

Sitting on the edge of the bed, head in hands, Annie groaned as she tried to recall the actions of last night. Other than winning a few hands at poker, there was nothing. Defeated, she grabbed the jug of water on the table and chugged its entire contents in seconds. "Jesus Christ, that's better." With the light now starting to filter through the windows, she surmised it must be almost five o'clock. She peered at the pocket watch face to try and make out its hands and forced herself into her day. She washed her face, pulled on her overalls and headed to the stables outside of town.

"Mornin', Annie!"

"Mmhmh." Was all she managed while collecting a pitchfork. Annie shambled towards Bessie's stable first.

"Mornin' sweetheart."

Bessie whinnied in return as Annie petted her. "I'm a little delicate today, but it may've been worth it. Whatever happens we won't be here much longer." She fed Bessie some oatcakes, brushed her coat, and changed her hay.

The next two hours were arduous and interspersed with Annie

dry heaving in almost every stall. Her jobs weren't ones to do when suffering from the consequences of alcohol, no matter how quickly they were dissipating. She said goodbye to Bessie and accepted a ride back to her second job at the hotel.

The mid-morning sun was beating down upon her return, and Annie was thankful the worst of the evening's after-effects had gone. She wondered if Nate got back safely and laughed at the thought of him leaving the town the previous night.

"Miss Malone! Right on time! There's been an... *event* in Room 8 that needs attendin' to post-haste if you wouldn't mind, then if you can work the rest of the rooms as you would normally that would be just fine."

"Sure thing, Mister Williams." A bucket, mop and scrubbing soap were thrust into Annie's hands by her anxious looking employer. Eyeing him with doubt, she took the stairs to Room 8 and pushed the already ajar door open. "What in Satan's Holy Hell is this?!"

As she surveyed the small room, the smell of human effluence hit her. She quickly learned that no matter how little contents were in her stomach, her body could still expel it up and outward when the need arose.

Once the horrors of her day were over, Annie bathed and scoured her skin raw. Feeling her old self again, she sat on the porch of the hotel reading '*Treasure Island*' and enjoyed a coffee. She was in a world of literary escape which she could have lived in beyond its last page.

"Miss Malone?"

***

The not-so-distant mutterings of judgemental voices hummed over Nate as he attempted to ignore the outside world. He was sure he was dying. The right side of his body felt bruised. Elephants danced a jig in his head, and the beams of flickering sunlight fighting to burst through his closed eyelids, were the punishment for his frivolity yesterday.

"Wake him up."

An unapologetic wall of cold water hit him, snapping adrenaline and his headache into full focus. He sat up on his sodden camp bed. Above him stood an unimpressed Duke Needham, arms folded. Beside him was a scowling Maw Hicks wielding an empty bucket. Through the wide doorway of his tent, he could make out a forest of snickering camp mates. Nathan covered his face from the burning light and flicked as much of the moisture from his skin as he could.

"Ah! Sleeping Beauty awakes. Good morning, Nathaniel. How kind of you to finally return to us last night, a good six hours after you completed your job for the Sheriff."

"Duke." Nate blinked painfully towards the silhouette standing above him. Small words and minimal conversation were the only way he could see himself surviving the day.

"You caused us all quite a scare you know when we saw Danny dragging your sorry ass back to camp, bruised and bloodied. That is until the smell of you hit us like a Moonshine still."

"You're lucky that wasnae horse pish, Nathan Healey!" snapped Maw; her sharp Scottish brogue attacking him. She brandished the bucket in his face and the others laughed on behind. Eyes screwed tightly shut, he pinched the bridge of his nose. "I'm sorry, all. Didn't mean to alarm you."

"Alright now everyone, give Nathan some room. Go back to your day." As the crowd dispersed, Duke rested a calming hand on Maw's shoulder. "I think he's learned his lesson, Maw, thank you." With a *humph* she turned on her heel and marched off to help her husband with his duties.

"Nathan, I'll give you five minutes, then I want a word *if you can manage it*." With that, Duke strolled back to his tent.

Nate heaved his body off the saturated canvas and dragged his feet to the campfire to pour his coffee. Slugging two cups, he poured a third and shuffled on towards Duke, muttering the odd greeting and obscenity to his friends as they commented on his appearance and the potential trouble he was in. Whatever punishment he would receive today, none would compare to the hot knives currently piercing his mind from the shrill warble of Maw's singing. She seemed to time her errands with wherever he was heading. He greeted Duke with a nod. The leader eyed his dripping friend with vague amusement.

"How's the head?"

"Well, Duke." Nate sighed, "it would feel a darn sight better if there weren't so much noise in camp." He sipped his third coffee, trying to soothe the rawness of his throat. He had vague recollections of raucous singing from the previous night.

"I imagine it would, Nathan." Duke smiled and turned to Maw.

"Keep up the good work, my dear! Always a joy to hear your songs!"
Nate winced with regret.

"Who were you drinking with last night, Nathan?"

"… Huh?"

"It wasn't any of our fine folk here," Duke gestured outwards to the camp, "they were all accounted for."

He was unable to handle the pressure of his nausea, the weight of his wet clothes, and the need to keep standing. Nate slouched, dripping against the central post at the entrance of Duke's tent. He sighed and shut his eyes. "I helped someone on the way to Tinulca a few weeks back. They'd got into some trouble on the road. They saw me comin' outta the Sheriff's office yesterday and asked to buy me a drink as a thank you. That's all, Duke."

"That's all, Nathan? *That's all?* Must have been one large and powerful drink to keep you away six hours and return to us stinking like a brewery." Nate slid to the floor of the tent and sat with his coffee, trying to get his eyes to accept the bright light of day. This wasn't going to be a fun conversation.

Duke joined him with a thunderous expression. "And what, pray tell, could have possibly been discussed in all these hours with a stranger who has been in Tinulca ever since you helped them weeks ago, hmm?"

Nate had no choice but to approach the subject of Annie now. He could always just pretend he had discussed it and go tell her that it was a no. But he was a man of his word. If their first meeting had taught him anything it was that Annie would never ask unless she was desperate. Travelling alone can be tiring for the most resilient of folk, let alone a penniless woman having to fight off jackasses on each journey.

"… They were wantin' our help…"

"WHAT?! *Our* help?? How the Sam Hell do they know there's an "*us*"?"

"She saw-"

Duke's deep deliberate scoff cut Nate off. "Oh well of course *she* did." The man shook his head and started to leave. "It makes sense now, Nathan."

"Listen, she saw us comin' outta the Sheriff's office some time back." Nate bundled himself forward to catch up with the leader and grabbed his shoulder. "She's a fighter. I barely helped her with them robbers, I just got her to a doctor after she'd kicked them to the ground. She's outta money, on her own and needs some help." Nathan felt embarrassed, Duke teased him like he was a child. "She could be useful to us. She's got skills, I've seen 'em in action-"

"Oh I bet you have!"

"I'm serious, Duke." Frustrated, Nate followed him to an unoccupied part of the camp. "Look, all I said was I'd ask. There ain't no requirement on your part to say yes."

"Hmm. Was this before or after she got you drunk, Nathan?"

"Before… The drinkin' was part of the deal if I agreed to ask you." Nate was relieved as Duke proceeded to laugh. "If she's so skilful, why does she need us?"

"Come on, Duke. These places ain't easy if you're a fella alone, never mind a woman. She's already met some of the delightful locals and soon she'll run outta energy to keep fightin' 'em."

"What's her name?"

Shit. This needed a more delicate approach than Nate had the energy to muster. Why did Annie have to be a Schaeffer?

It was ten years since the Needham Boys had a run-in with the Schaeffers in Iowa, and it was safe to say that none of them were fans of that Irish mob.

"… Well, she's been in a travelin' show as a gunslinger since she were six… They called her "*Dead Eye Annie*"."

"Mhmm? And what, then, is her *real* name, Nathan?"

Nate looked at his feet kicking the dirt. " Annie…"

"Annie *what?*"

He cleared his throat. "Schaeffer." He muttered quickly, trying to be as inaudible as he could.

A chill descended over camp and Duke bristled beside him. It was as if all sounds had been muted; not even Mother Nature dared cut through the atmosphere.

"… *Schaeffer*…" The dark calmness in Duke's voice was familiar, but very rarely had Nate been the receiver of it. "That's right. But only in name. Cal Schaeffer sold her when she were six, Duke, that's why we didn't know of her. She's on her own now. Believe me she hates Caley Schaeffer more than we do." Duke was still. His eyes narrowed. "Does she know the whole Schaeffer Gang are dead?"

"She does. She don't seem upset about it."

His friend turned to him. "Does she know it was you that took the shot that killed Caley Schaeffer?"

Nate stared back. "I didn't see it was quite the right time to mention that Duke, no."

"Is this why you're helping her? Out of some goddamn sense of guilt? How do you know she hasn't tracked us down on a course for revenge?"

Anger bubbled up in Nate; the gang had sheltered all sorts in their time, Hell! They had just risked everything getting Madsen out of prison. "She had enough chance to find this camp and pick us off the last couple weeks. She don't know we were anythin' to do with them Schaeffers endin', and she ain't sorry Cal's dead. I ain't promised her nothin', Duke, but I said I'd ask."

"Is she pretty, Nathan?"

"You know what? Never mind. She's skilful and smart. She can hunt, and said she would teach the camp to shoot as good as her. I reckon she just needs some protection is all, but it ain't up to me." Feeling too sorry for himself to entertain Duke's slights; Nathan drained his coffee and started to march away.

He was called back to finish their conversation, "Okay, okay no need to get touchy." Duke smirked. "Is she really that skilled?"

"One of the best, I'd reckon."

With an arm around his friend, Duke walked them back to a map by his tent. "Then go tell her I'd like to parley with her. But not here…" scanning the illustration of the local area for a second, he tapped his finger just up from Tinulca. "Orr Hill. Noon tomorrow. Tell her to bring her tools of expertise. Oh! And I expect you to be there with me, seeing as this is your fault. We'll head there at eleven-thirty to discuss the plan of the day… Best we keep her last name quiet until absolutely necessary." Nate told him she went by '*Malone*' most days.

As he left to dry off, Duke called out to him. "Once you've passed on that message, go up to Como. Doc has something for you."

Doc. Just what he needed.

***

Reluctantly, Annie tore her eyes away from tales of pirates, to see Nate Healey looking a little worse-for-wear. His unshaven jawline had grown wilder in twelve hours than should be possible. And though his hat was pulled low, his bloodshot eyes glowed through the shadow.

"Mister Deleaney." She mocked. "You're lookin' decidedly disheveled."

"And you, Miss, are in an implausibly good state." His deep voice was painfully hoarse as he leaned on the porch sidings for some balance.

"That's because young folk can hold their liquor." Annie said playfully as she closed her book, and sipped her coffee.

"Oh now, that ain't a nice way to talk to a fella who comes bearin' news." He removed his hat and turned to rest his back on the sidings.

"News? Already?" Annie made her way to the edge of the porch. "Is… is it good news…?"

"Well, I dunno if you deserve to hear it now, Miss Malone… Seein' as you don't seem to *respect your elders*."

"Oh Mister Deleaney, don't be callous!" Annie laughed and ran down to meet him.

"He'll meet with you." His rough voice rumbled. She beamed following her messenger as he donned his hat and moved away from prying ears.

"Now, that don't mean more than a conversation."

"Of course."

"And Duke knows a little of your story, what I had the mind to tell him anyway - about you workin' in a travelin' show - and he wants to meet you outside Tinulca, at Orr Hill. You're to bring your… *"tools of expertise"*."

Annie froze in the street. "What kind of conversation is this gonna be?"

Nate turned. "It'll be alright, Annie. He just wants to test your skills is all. And he's asked me to be there seein' as I'm the one who knows you… To a point, at least."

Annie took a deep breath and nodded. She wasn't inclined to trust anyone. But through the unkempt fuzz of his alcohol-induced tiredness, and despite how far she had pushed him at their meetings, she trusted her instincts about the man in front of her.

"Alright Nate, I'll go."

Nathan straightened up and they continued walking towards his horse. "Okay. Now, the main ways to Duke Needham's heart are bein' polite, bein' respectful, and, if you're a woman, bein' pretty." Smiling at Annie as he mounted his horse, "Seein' as you know you have that last one down, I'd work on the other two and fast. You ain't quite there yet."

"Sounds like I'll need to act sincere."

"Tomorrow at noon, Miss Malone, I'll see you there." He tipped his hat and left.

4

Annie Grab your Guns

The past 24 hours had been a struggle. Nate told himself not to drink with Miss Schaeffer again, especially if he had to endure the waste of air that was Doc Carragher shortly after. Doc had once been a medical practitioner. Nowadays, when he wasn't inhaling formaldehyde on a handkerchief, he could still manage to dig out a bullet and sew up the wound without causing gangrene.

Duke had found him pickled in an entire saloon's worth of booze after being cast out as a disgrace to his profession; found grave robbing in the name of 'progress'. He became a pharmaceutical impresario, taking to the road to sell his dubious tonics. Carragher was a hindrance more often than not, which Nate continually had to fix. The most recent job Mr. Healey was summoned to was farcical in its execution. Doc needed a stooge to convince others to part with their money. Nathan wasn't the most talented of actors, nor an eager participant. It hadn't mattered, however, as Doc had decided to partake in his daily breath of poisonous air and collapsed beside his cart.

When Nate arrived, the soak had managed to get nearly $80 in pitying donations from passers-by. It had gone far better than was to be expected, and he wondered if Doc would be better off begging.

With some money in the camp, Duke was in the best mood for the meeting with Annie.

"What're your plans here?" Nate asks cautiously. "Why did you want her bringin' her guns?"

"I want to know whether her skills really are as good as you say." Duke reflected. "And if she can hunt, she can get some good meat for Chuck to cook with. Is there anything further I should be aware of regarding Miss Schaeffer?"

"In what way?"

"Well, you've spent ample time in her *seemingly enticing* presence, is she reliable? Safe?"

"She can be a little fiery, I guess. But only if you're fixin' to make her mad."

"If she hasn't been living a life like ours, how is she prepared to work with us? Is she willing to do what it takes to survive?" Nate shifted uncomfortably. "From what she told me her life ain't exactly been luxurious, and Annie killed them attackers without any hesitation."

"*Hmm.* If she is *anything* like her father, we may need to be on guard. I'm still not convinced she hasn't just fooled you into a trap." Duke fell silent, and that was Nate's cue to stop pressing for information.

It was a clear summer's day for the activities. As the two dismounted, Duke spoke up again. "Nathan, you know this hasn't been the brightest of your ideas, don't you? Now, I'm going to chalk it up to you running around in the heat for that Sheriff these many weeks. But *mark my words*," he leaned in close, "if one thing goes wrong today, you are to shoot that woman dead do you understand me?"

Nate nodded and clenched his jaw. It wasn't *his* idea; he merely passed on a request. Duke had chosen to create this meeting, Nate believed out of some morbid curiosity to see the orphaned Schaeffer. "And what if it don't all go wrong?"

"We'll be the kindly Samaritans she needs, and welcome her into our flock!" Duke smiled with his arms open wide.

"Oh, I'm sure the rest of the camp will be just as kindly." Nate mused.

Out of the corner of his eye, he saw a familiar silhouette moving across the hills on a large white horse. Shading his eyes from the sunlight, Nate spied a guarded-looking Annie Schaeffer.

The greenness of her shirt made her eyes cut through the shade of her hat brim. That woman knew how to make a first impression. Duke started his patented Needham patter.

"Ah! Welcome! Nathaniel is this the famous Miss *Malone* we've been expecting?"

"It is."

"In that case, Miss, please allow me to help you down. That is a magnificent horse you have there."

Nate watched the most stubborn woman alive allow herself to be assisted. At least she could follow instructions, he thought as he touched his hat politely toward the compelling Miss Schaeffer.

***

Nathan's guidance for the meeting echoed through Annie's mind ever since they had first been uttered. The orders to bring her weapons to the rendezvous caused her concern. At best, this was an opportunity to show her skills to the one person who could give her aid, at worst it would be a set up. The brief discussion with Nate seemed to indicate it would be an 'audition', but she wouldn't chance it. She set her guns with full-load rounds and carried her quarter-loads in her saddle bags. She grimaced at the advice Nate had given her; be respectful, polite, and, well, *pretty*.

She dressed both '*pretty*' and understated in a green linen shirt with high-waisted earth-brown work pants held up with braces. Her hair was braided loosely under her hat, and a spritz of her homemade perfume at her neck made for a practical, yet feminine, and most humble young lady. *Nothing but the best for Duke Needham.*

It was fine weather for an outing with Bessie. Checking her location against the map she had borrowed from the hotel, Annie tracked the road around towards the top of the incline, and once there followed the sounds of conversation. She recognised the deep drawl of one voice immediately, and as she ascended the crest of the hill saw the two men leaning against a fence. The owner of the unfamiliar, well-spoken voice greeted her as both gents walked forwards. He seemed charismatic and thoughtfully dressed for a man living outside of general laws; a late-middle-aged man with groomed, silver hair, whose garments were far less tattered than those of the men she'd spotted in town. She had encountered many men like this throughout her lifetime, however, and they never held much weight with her. Con men at their best. But she knew how to play their games.

Against Annie's nature, she allowed Mister Needham to assist her off Bessie; anything not to offend. "Thank you, Sir, you are most kind." She flashed her best smile and made sure to act at ease with Duke's light, gallant kiss on her hand. He was a figure of textbook charmers. She could tell from his smarts and handle of social etiquette, that small town folk were easy pickings and why men like Nate would follow him unequivocally.

***

Duke grinned with warmth at Annie, linked her arm in his and walked towards the fence. "Now, Miss Malone... may I call you Miss Malone?"

"Or Annie, if you'd prefer, Sir."

"Not *Schaeffer*...?"

Annie stiffened and saw Nate's face drain. Needham was stony-faced, looking closely at her reaction. The world froze around her. She was trapped; Needham's arm locked tightly around her own. Even if Annie could reach the pistols at her waist, she'd be shot by either one of the men first.

She took a deep breath and continued her charm offensive. "Sir, you can call me Jimmy if you'd like, I really don't mind." Much to everyone's relief, Duke burst into a deep laugh. Nate was less amused. "*Jesus Christ.*"

"Oh *what*?! I'm just having a little fun with Miss Schaeffer that's all!" He leaned towards Annie conspiratorially. "You see, Miss Schaeffer, Mister Healey here can take life a little seriously sometimes. It's good to keep him on his toes." He winked at her and relinquished his grip on her arm.

"I can see that." Annie forced a smile. This was hard work; Mister Needham was obviously asserting his place in the engagement.

"Now that being said, Miss Schaeffer, Nathan has been telling me about your predicament." Nate bristled as he was patted on the shoulder. His patience wore thin; he didn't like being patronised for Duke's games.

"He's also told me of your skill. Said you've been at this since you were just six years old."

"Well, Sir-"

"Mister Needham, please."

"Well, *Mister Needham*, I ain't talkin' myself up, but I was at this since I were three. By the time I was six, I was *"par excellence"*!"

"Oooh, Nathaniel," he laughed, "I can see why you *like* this girl!"

Nate fidgeted. "Are you gonna get on with this, Duke?"

"Alright, alright." The host clapped his hands. "My dear, do you understand why we asked you to meet us all the way out here, alone?"

"I'm guessin' by your knowledge of my last name, and the skills Mister Healey told you about, you ain't wantin' the likes of a *Schaeffer* to just stroll into your camp." She spoke candidly. "And I sure as hell wouldn't wanna face your camp with that name without first gettin' your blessin'."

Duke grinned and looked at his friend. "She's a smart one. *Good.*" He pressed his hand lightly against the small of Annie's back and walked her further along the fence line. "Now, Annie, I don't know how aware you are of *Nathan's* skills. From what he told me about you, he hasn't had much of a chance to show off." The lack of information about today had left Nate uneasy.

Duke continued. "But Nathan here is one of the best shots I have ever known. A sharp-shooting, rope-slinging *artiste*!" Duke always became boastful about those that did his bidding, though Nate felt more than mocked by its pomp. He gave an impressed Annie a modest shrug, causing her to stifle a laugh.

She turned her focus back to Duke. "So, when the *best man I know*, with the *keenest* eye tells me he sees someone who could rival his skills and needs our help. I have to say I am intrigued."

Leaving Annie beside Nate, Duke pulled a large saddle bag from his horse, which clinked as he walked back to them. "As you could *potentially* be the next best shot in our camp next to fine young Nathan here, I thought we'd play a little game…"

The pair watched as Duke lined up bottles and tins of varying size across the different rails of fencing. "First, a simple test of your shooting skills, Miss Schaeffer. Nothing too taxing for you as you can see." He shoved the bag at Nate. "Set the rest of these up would you, m'boy?" Nate sighed and went to work as Duke explained. "I thought I'd do a quick-draw, pitting you against each other, see who can shoot these the fastest."

Nate looked at Duke with frustration. "Is this really necessary?" One sharp glance halted his protests.

"Now, Nathan, as much as I trust your judgement, I need to see things for myself. I can't just be won over by a pretty face you know!" Nate grimaced with irritation and returned to stand next to Annie as Duke held out his palm. "Your pistols, Miss Schaeffer."

" E-excuse me…?"

"I am assuming that your intelligence isn't limited to understanding why we wouldn't meet at my camp. I'm guessing there are full-load rounds in your guns?"

"Ye-yes…"

"Then, *please*, pass me your gun as you retrieve those I believe you carry for *entertainment purposes*."

Annie looked at Nate for reassurance as she handed over her only close weapons. He nodded and she went to retrieve the other bullets.

Nate watched as Duke unloaded the two six-shooters, "What is this, Duke?"

"It is our meeting, Nathaniel. And you are lucky that I'm being so patient."

Keeping his voice low, he continued his protest. "Look, there ain't a need for this. I'm sorry I got involved in helpin' someone who needed helpin', *alright*?"

"Nathan, right now you are getting on my last nerve- Ah! Miss Schaeffer. I was concerned you had misplaced your ammunition!" Duke's smile was casual though his eyes pierced Annie's soul, searching for any cracks.

"I'm sure you can understand, Mister Needham, my gun always carries the best bullets when I'm travelin' alone. It's the safest way to be." She smiled sweetly as Duke handed the gun back to her to refill, keeping her live rounds in his hand.

"I can imagine it is, Miss Schaeffer. Now, I would like you both to hit as many of those items on the fence as quickly as you can." Annie looked at Nate. He took his guns from their holsters. Much to Duke's enjoyment, both shooters were equally matched in speed and accuracy. Nate didn't like being used as a puppet; this was humiliating for them both, and needless.

"Excellent! Most impressive, Miss Schaeffer!" Duke bared his teeth in a wide, malevolent grin. "Thank you for humoring me. Nathan, you can relax."

Nate put his guns away and turned to Annie. "Nice work, Miss Schaeffer."

"Thank you, Mister Healey, I do return the compliment." He quickly moved towards Duke to avoid the distractions Miss Schaeffer's manner encouraged.

"Miss, may I ask if you have a hunting rifle on that majestic horse of yours?"

"I do, Mister Needham."

"Excellent! Nathan told me you had offered to hunt for the camp should you be able to join us. And, as we are in low supply for Chuck's meals, I thought this would be a great opportunity to see your skills in action. Nathaniel, why don't you be gun dog for the day?"

"*Excuse* me?" Nate's expression was one of outright insult. "Miss Schaeffer and I will be doing some hunting. If you could do me the kindness of collecting what we shoot it would save some time."

Nate rubbed his forehead, and looked between Duke's stern expression, and a vaguely amused Annie. "It would be my *honor,* Duke." He trudged off to ready Prynne.

***

"My apologies for Mister Healey's sullen attitude, Miss Schaeffer." Duke said. "He doesn't like being told what to do even by me, though he tolerates it, and I have to say it does entertain me greatly."

Annie laughed. "I can understand that Mister Needham." Duke gestured for Annie to return to her mare. "Please, we'll ride down the hill a little before we start, it will give us an opportunity to talk."

Annie mounted Bessie and waited for Duke to lead the way on his great black stallion.

"So, what brings you to us for refuge?"

"Well, Mister Needham, I was bein' forced to work in ways that I didn't see fit to agree to… So, I made a way to escape my situation, and have traveled as far as I can with what little I had. "I'm embarrassed to say that I find myself in need of support until I can find a way to move on with my life."

Duke stared ahead contemplatively. "You know, Miss Schaeffer, most people look to run away *to* the circus, not *from* it." He turned and smirked at Annie which she took as a cue to smile back with false amusement; he really did fancy himself above others.

"I wanted to ask you about the name "*Schaeffer*", it's not a traditional Irish name now is it?"

"No, Sir, my grandfather was German. He moved to America and met my Irish grandmother on the frontier in 1845…" Annie began to falter; she didn't like giving her life away. As it was, the only information she really had about Caley Schaeffer had been the whispers she would hear in camp as a child, or the violent tales he would retell as a means of threatening victims. She knew of his manner by bearing some of its brunt herself. And despite there always being the sensationalised stories dredged up in the press, it was likely the Needham Boys knew far more about the life of Caley Schaeffer than Annie ever did.

"I suppose we are European cousins. My family originate from English stock, for their sins." Duke smiled at her, obviously satisfied, or bored, with the undramatic story.

She looked over in the distance and saw Nate waiting impatiently on his horse, ready to play 'fetch' with dead animals. They continued a little further down the slope. "May I ask how you came to own such a beautiful horse?"

"It was gifted to me."

"Gifted?"

"Yessir, by a young foolish boy of high society back West some years ago." Annie smiled and shook her head, "He figured himself a romantic. Gave me Bessie as a way to win my affections."

"And did it, Miss Schaeffer?"

Annie raised an eyebrow to her chaperone. "No, Mister Needham, it did not." She laughed. "The only thing it did was make me fall in love with a big old horse and move on to the next town."

They came to a stop not far from where a herd of deer and elk grazed. Once again, Annie allowed herself to be assisted off Bessie and they moved quietly towards a good aiming spot. "I must say, your horse is rather impressive itself."

"Oh Atlas has been a faithful accomplice of mine for some time now." Duke mused. "So loyal in fact that he becomes quite ornery if I am so much as admiring another beast." He laughed. "He won't tolerate many others, either. Even bit our horse-hand, Tanner, once or twice." He stopped and turned to Annie. "Trust and protection, Miss Schaeffer, above all else, is what keeps this gang together. I cannot stress this enough to you." The proximity of Duke's face to hers, and his threatening tone were obvious ways to test her. She held her ground but was sure to react as expected by him, swallowing hard and nodding silently. Satisfied by her reaction, Duke turned and retrieved his gun from his steed. Annie followed suit with her own rifle, and they headed into the longer grass.

Nate had become impatient. The entire day seemed ridiculous. He couldn't help but think Duke had got lost in the idea of a new clever, pretty young thing joining their gang.

Prynne had become skittish. "There girl, we'll be done soon *God willin'*."

It wasn't long until the peace was shattered by the crack of a rifle.

"Excellent, Miss Schaeffer! Straight through the eye! NATHANIEL! Go fetch the beast, I believe it may even make an excellent pelt for Chuck to use."

Begrudgingly, Nate kicked Prynne forward towards the body of a young buck; Annie's clean shot from such a distance was impressive indeed. He dismounted and worked to heave the animal onto Prynne as Duke and Annie joined him on foot, their horses close behind.

"Nice shot, Miss." A genuinely impressed Nate remarked, winded from hauling the carcass onto his horse unassisted. Annie realised that, based on his strength, she had been wise to stay on Nate's good side. She noted not to enrage him further in the future.

After a few successful hunts, including some small game Annie dispatched with her throwing knives. Prynne and Atlas were ladened with trophies to take to their camp at Onti Lake. As the three riders ascended the hill, Nate looked eagerly at Duke to end this unreasonably long day.

Finally, his wish was granted. Duke brought the parley to a close. "Miss Schaeffer, *Annie*, it has been most fascinating to meet you. I have to say Nathan was right with regards to your skills."

"Thank you, Mister Needham."

"I think we can disregard formalities now, Annie. Please, call me Duke. I do believe we can find room for you in our merry band of reprobates." He laughed, glancing briefly at his second-in-command who had tired of the theatrics. "Do you have your own lodgings?"

"I do, they may be a little large, but I have space to store anythin' the camp may need…"

"No need to worry, Annie, it's good to know. Nathan will come to collect you from Tinulca in two days." Nate's attention piqued; why was this another errand to run? Duke continued. "That will give me time to inform the camp of the circumstances and be sure everyone is aware not to shoot you on sight should they see you." He laughed.

Despite Duke's arrogance, Annie was grateful to have got what she wanted. Today had been one of the biggest tests of her recent years, and she had passed it. "Thank you, Duke, you have been so gracious today, and I am forever indebted to you."

Nate shook his head. Annie's ability to read a man's personality quickly enough to say exactly what they wanted to hear, was quite a show when he was an observer.

Puffed up with flattery, Duke's grin broadened, and he took Annie's hand. "Oh well, Miss Schaeffer, they're all indebted in some way. But I'm sure you'll be of use to us in camp. I shall let you go on with your day. Until we meet again." Duke doffed his hat with a small, seated bow as Annie nodded farewell. She gave Nate a long look of sincere gratitude and turned towards the road.

"Nathan. A word." Duke's tone snapped Nate back from his stares. "Annie coming into camp is going to be a strain for a few. Now, I'll handle their concerns, *but* she's still a Schaeffer. And as you're the reason she is here at all," Duke held up a hand to halt the impending protests, "*you* will be responsible for her."

"What?!"

"She'll set up her things between you and Doc and will answer to you should she cause any unrest. She'll be expected to follow the rules and will explain herself to you should she break them. And you in turn will answer to me." Duke took a long, serious look at Nate as he nodded reluctantly. With a gruff voice he acknowledged his role.

Returning to Onti Lake in petulant silence gave Nate time to reflect on what was being demanded of him. He was exasperated; there had been no requirement for Duke to agree to meet Annie, nor agree to take her in. Duke's love of intelligent, pretty women had been his downfall before the day even began. Now, to keep his authority intact, he punished Nate for it. Too many hours had already been lost to Annie Schaeffer, and the last thing he needed was to nanny someone new, regardless of how captivating they were. At least he had two days to continue his life unimpeded and allow Duke to convince the camp, especially Lucky Needham, that this was a smart idea. It was a good thing they were bringing back such spoils from hunting.

5

A Warm Welcome

Annie spent her last few days alone looking for a way to ingratiate herself into what would be a hostile camp. She went out with Bessie to hunt animals to sell to butchers and trappers alike. Any money she made from them would be her camp dowry. To sweeten the deal, she managed to grab a crate of beers from the back of the saloon under cover of darkness, stashing them in her canvas covered cart.

Sleep had evaded her across those nights. She knew she was about to gain some much-needed security, but something about Duke Needham left her wary of any promise he uttered. From what she had witnessed, however, there seemed at least some form of civilised method and thought to the gang's way of life. Had it been any other band of men, she would most likely be in a shallow, unmarked grave by now.

Annie checked her belongings one final time, tied the cover to the cart's end and hitched Bessie to the front, spoiling her with a nose rub for good measure. "Well, girl, let's see where this adventure takes us." Bessie snorted in support.

With a sigh, Annie rested her head against her mare's. She reflected on her first three months of real freedom, and the cost it had come at. Though the little information she shared with Nathan had been true, it was far from everything.

She wanted to be sure that her stay in the camp was as short and uneventful as possible, and planned for as many scenarios as she could think of. She was suspicious of herself and afraid of what living with outlaws might lead to. Her similarities to Caley Schaeffer had increased with age, in part to her circumstances.

Like her father, she didn't like being pushed around. She had been taught not to stand for it. She learnt early on what befell anyone that tried a Schaeffer; she had seen to that herself more than once. She wished to be more like her mother, to harness the strength of silence and grace, and swallow the anger that could erupt inside her. With her eyes shut she vowed to make this work, to put her old life behind her once and for all.

Out of nowhere, the low tones of Nathan Healey gently addressed her, pulling her from her thoughts.

***

Nate made the most of his last few days without a tag-along. He had been more productive than ever; finding any opportunity to stay out of camp. Duke's own additional ventures to get news of the law had dragged out his opportunity to discuss the new arrival, specifically with his brother, Lucky. Nate wondered how he would react to the news. Lucky was the instigator of the fight against the Schaeffers all those years ago, which essentially ended the Irish mob; his only truly vicious moment borne from the loss of his wife.

It was time to collect Annie and bring her into the camp. He and Duke had taken time to check there was space for her to fit. Much to Nathan's satisfaction, they had asked Doc to edge further away to accommodate her. As Duke was yet to break the news to the any of the group, Nate was keen to understand the role he would play in it all.

"Yes, due to my necessity to head out on business, it hasn't quite gone to plan." Duke said quietly that morning. "But leave it to me. You go into Tinulca for Annie this afternoon, explain the rules of camp and the expectations of her. Meanwhile I'll speak to Lucky, then Maw, before announcing it to everyone. I figure the less time they have to think about it, the less trouble it will cause on her arrival."

"Do you think Lucky can face it?" Lucky had been a father to Nate and Danny long before the Needham Boys had been established. The idea of bringing back the painful memories of Martha Needham's death weighed heavily on him.

Duke became serious. "My brother has had many years to grieve, Nathan, he isn't the man of ten years ago. Of all of us, I believe he is going to be the most forgiving." Nathan nodded, trusting his friend to be right.

Duke's initial accusation that Nate had offered to help Annie out of guilt stayed with him. He didn't regret ending the life of Cal Schaeffer. If anything, he had done the world a favour; their retribution had been swift. But he thought of the little girl in that show; the name "Schaeffer" meaning less to him at twelve than it had as a man.

Having heard Annie's story, he supposed he held some pity for her situation, but she had the skills of a formidable opponent. She could be a very dangerous woman. He had seen something flash across her eyes that day in the saloon, and it whipped him back to the day he bid farewell to Caley Schaeffer. He thought it better to have her on side than against them.

Spending the morning in camp, he went fishing for Chuck, and helped Tanner with the horses. At around three o'clock Duke gave Nate the signal to make his way to Tinulca. As he left, he heard his mentor call to Lucky for a discussion.

As reluctant as he was to have to take a stubborn, boisterous woman under his wing, Nathan was looking forward to seeing Annie again. Her candid nature and good humour were refreshing, and her ability to follow instruction meant that it would be unlikely he would need to do much watching at all.

He arrived at the hotel expecting to see her on the porch as he had done earlier that week. Envisioning a bright-eyed figure beaming with relief to see him. He was surprised to find the place deserted. Nate walked to the back of the building and discovered Annie standing with her back to him. She appeared deep in thought; her posture was far removed from her usual bold confidence. He couldn't help but notice her appearance, her prairie skirt fell flatteringly from her waist, down over her hips and pooled in the dust at her feet. Her loose hair lightly brushed her shoulders as it swayed in the warm breeze, it was an image that wouldn't be forgotten easily. As Nate stood alongside her, he saw that her eyes were closed, and a tense expression pulled tightly at her face. "Annie…?" She opened her eyes and forced a faint, kind smile.

Seeing her this way, he felt he was witness to a rare moment of vulnerability. The true Annie Schaeffer stood before him. No bravado, no swagger, not even a sly comment. Just a strong, smart, woman looking to him for help. "You ready to go?"

***

Annie was quiet as they hitched Nate's horse to the cart and climbed into the vehicle. The next few hours were out of her control. All she could do was keep herself in check.

"You sure you got it all?" Nate asked, eyeing his passenger.

"There ain't no comin' back here."

"Yeah, I got it all." Annie turned and sighed. "I weren't really expectin' this to come to anythin'."

"We're folk of our word, Annie… for the most part… And this is what you wanted weren't it?"

"It was…"

"Well then." Nate took the reins and moved Bessie forward. Under normal circumstances, he would have relished the relative quiet of his companion, but Annie Schaeffer was not a woman of few words. He waited until they were out of Tinulca before speaking again. "So, Duke has given me the honor of informin' you of the rules in camp, and what's expected of you."

"Okay."

"You'll be helpin' in and, eventually, outside of camp. Unfortunately, freedom comes at a cost and we all work to put in for that."

"I understand."

"Dependin' on what jobs you end up takin' outside, half the money you get is given to the camp, the rest is split equally between whoever helped you."

Annie looked at her hands in her lap, and nodded. "Seems fair."

"While in camp, you're to help Maw and Chuck around the place as needed. Eventually Duke'll see you be escorted to go huntin'." He looked at Annie, her face was blank as she listened. He pulled the cart over and cleared his throat. "You alright?" She looked up at him.

"I dunno how good an idea this is, Nate."

Nathan smiled at her concern. "It's a little late for that, Annie, they know you're comin'."

She knew he couldn't understand her struggle; the grip she had on the more agreeable aspects of her personality were strained most days. Thrusting herself into a world that could shake them loose completely made her twitchy. "It ain't gonna be a good welcome is it?"

"Well no, you're a Schaeffer." Nate chuckled. The fact that despite her quietness she still didn't project an ounce of fear was admirable. "But listen, you're to answer to me in that camp d'you hear? Anythin' you do outta line is to be justified to me, and I pass that on to Duke. You're my responsibility, Annie. That means I ain't gonna let you mess anythin' up." He leaned close to her; his sincerity gave her some reassurance. "And there ain't gonna be anyone who'll mess with you neither. Not that I think you'd need my help in straightenin' 'em out." He winked.

She laughed like she had been holding her breath. "Thank you, Nate. I would've preferred it not come to this. If I hadn't needed help, you'd be free of it all."

He leaned back and began to move Bessie forward. "True," he teased, "but at least I get to watch a group of unhappy folk havin' to be amicable to a newcomer."

Lightened by the conversation, they continued towards Onti Lake as evening approached. Nate took the longer route to be sure Annie was ready for what may lie ahead.

As they reached the track to camp, irate sounds filtered across to them. Nathan briefly squeezed Annie's shoulder as her instincts kicked in. "Calm down. Ain't no need to get kicked out for fightin' when we just got you here."

Unseen, they pulled Bessie up to the farthest, most shaded hitching spot. Duke was holding a sermon by his lodgings, shouting over the din of objections. "Aren't we a group of people who *care* for others in need? Not all enemies are dispatched with such haste!"

"COURSE NOT! WE'VE STARVED 'EM OUT!"

The crowd began to jeer in agreement. "No goddamn Schaeffer deserves that kindness!"

Nate sighed and looked at Annie. "You ready to make some friends?"

With a dry laugh, she waited as he stood in the wagon and signaled to Duke. The crowd turned as the speech maker marched over to the cart. Annie took that as her cue to retrieve the stock of beer from the back of her cart.

"Ah! Miss Schaeffer, welcome!" a tense Duke Needham smiled as she jumped down from the cart. "Please excuse the noise. Your camp mates' passions run high this evening."

"Good evenin', Mister Needham. I wouldn't expect anythin' different, given the circumstances. But I thought I'd bring a peace offerin'."

The beer crate tinkled as she raised it.

Nathan took them from her and Duke looked on, delighted. "I hope you haven't spent all your money on this, Annie?"

"Not at all, Sir," her face stretched into a playful grin, "I wouldn't want to spend my donation to the camp's funds." She handed a small money pouch to the leader.

He turned to his scowling throng. "You see folks? Here is someone ready to *contribute!* Chuck, please relieve Nathan of those drinks. Pass them around. I'll make sure this donation is locked safely away." Duke pocketed the small bag of money as a disgruntled-looking woman scowled beside him. "Annie, Maw here will help you set up your lodgings next to Nathan. I believe you are aware of the rules?" Duke leaned close to her. "And that until we can trust you, you'll be answering to him."

"Yes Mister Nee-"

"*Duke*, I insist."

"Duke. I understand. Nate was very clear on your expectations."

"Excellent!" Duke clapped his hands. "Mrs Hicks, please do Annie a kindness and show her to her space. I shall get Chuck along momentarily to assist in moving your things. Nathan, I have some business to discuss with you."

Nathan looked at Annie with Maw glowering beside her. He nodded a warm encouraging goodbye as he turned to leave. "Now behave yourself."

"I will Nate."

"I weren't talkin' 'bout you." He teased, bumping Maw Hicks with his side.

"Dinnae push it Mister Healey!"

Nathan chuckled as he followed Duke into the camp, leaving Annie with a decidedly sour-faced Maw.

***

Annie looked at the stout ball of fury. Her sizeable arms folded across her ample bosom, and the dark glitter of her beady eyes protruding from her surly face, told her that this woman wasn't to be taken lightly. Smiling at the squat, solid statue, Annie awaited her instructions.

"Grab what ye can 'nd follow me, *Miss Schaeffer*."

Annie loaded herself up with as many essentials as she could and followed the manic wiry hair of Maw through the judgemental stares. Conversations ceased as she passed. Annie held herself straight; jaw set, her gaze locked forward, and strutted purposefully through the den of wolves, to the open pitch space, allowing the whispering and not-so-subtle comments to be spat towards her as she went.

Maw stopped at a hitching post to the left of her spot. "You're to set up here, next to Mister Healey. Ye can tie up your nag there."

"Thank you, Ma'a-"

"I guess some things dinnae change. It dinnae surprise me Mister Needham were so taken in by you, but I thought Mister Healey were better than that. I always thought he let his *mind* make the decisions."

Annie stood, amused by Maw's comments as she eyed the Schaeffer girl with repugnance and stepped up to her.

Had they matched in height their noses would have touched. "Ye best know now that I'm no' impressed by bonny faces and flutterin' eyes, *Miss Schaeffer*, and I've never been afraid of your name."

"Good to know, Ma'am." Annie loved to goad bitter folk, forgetting her promise to behave already.

"Ye best mind your goddamn manners, lassie! *Aye*, ye must be feelin' pretty chuffed with yoursel' havin' them two won over." She flung a hand over towards Nate and Duke, deep in conversation outside what Annie assumed to be Duke's quarters. "But this camp only runs 'cause we look oot for one another. And I never heard of a Schaeffer lookin' oot for anybody but a Schaeffer. *I'll make sure you earn your kip here*." With that, Maw turned on her heel and marched away.

Annie felt the rest of camp looking at her; happy to drink her beers she noted, but wary of the woman who brought them. She placed her load down, laughed bitterly, and issued a short salute to her observers as a driver appeared with Bessie and the cart.

"Thank you, Chuck I presume?"

"That's right, Miss Schaeffer! It's actually Peter Hicks, but I seem to do all the cookin', so everyone calls me Chuck." Annie was pleasantly surprised by the jovial man's civility towards her. She smiled as he lumbered his life-worn body down from the cart and shook her hand. "Is that alright for you there, Miss? You need any more help?"

"No, no thank you, that's perfect. And thank you for not

thinkin' on every way you could kill me while I sleep." He laughed and looked around at the camp. "Oh, don't worry about 'em, they'll come 'round." He turned back to Annie and patted her reassuringly on the arm. *"They just like to give folk a scare."*

Annie laughed at his naivety. "I'm guessin' you ain't had much to do with the name 'Schaeffer', Chuck?"

"… It ain't so much that, Miss. My Bonnie – *Maw* - does the judgin' for us both. She's more knowin' of those things. I worked in the Big House for most of my life, cookin' for the guards. I saw some of those attached to your – errr, *heritage*, but I figure if you ain't crossin' me, I ain't got issue." He smiled warmly and thanked her for the beers, indicating he would have to get back to readying the supper. Annie thanked him again and turned to look at her living space for the foreseeable future.

Grabbing a beer from the crate by Chuck's wagon, Nate took a moment to survey home. After the initial protests, everyone had quietened down, knowing that this was Duke's decision, and Duke's decisions always stood. His eyes fell on Annie's silhouette as she kept to herself, lighting a small oil lamp and setting about building her lodgings alone.

The side of her cart hinged open and became a wall of her structure. The canvas cover popped up in an arch, creating a roof across the length of the wagon, and connecting to a larger rectangle frame which was staked into the ground. *"Looks like I shoulda got into travelin' shows."* Nate muttered looking with envy as the large shelter took shape with three canvas covered walls, roof, and skid flooring.

"Mister Healey!" Chuck greeted him cheerily; his ruddy face glistening from the stroll back from delivering Annie's belongings. Nate raised his bottle. "Chuck."

"Duke tells me that Miss Schaeffer will come in handy for huntin' for meat stocks?"

"Eventually." Nathan reminded him. "She's gotta earn that trust first, but I figure it won't be too long before you can ruin a perfectly good bit of meat she brings you." He swigged a drink as

his disgruntled sister-in-law, Clara, appeared beside him.

"I don't see why *she*, of all people, is gonna get the chance to go out huntin' while I'm stuck here guardin' nothin'." Nate laughed into his beer. "Because she ain't gonna go off shootin' her husband with buckshot."

"Hmpf." Was her reply. "Well, it don't seem like there's many folk happy about her presence. Your brother ain't gonna be best pleased at your decision when he gets back. And I ain't lookin' to fix that neither."

"Now Clara, Annie ain't even done nothin' to you." Nate pointed out. "But feel free to keep away from her. I think the two of you on the same side could overthrow Duke." She raised her eyebrows with mild intrigue as they looked on at Annie.

"Well, I will be grateful for the help, Mister Healey." Chuck lowered his voice. "I must say, she seems most pleasant, given her family… *but I ain't gonna be quick to tell Maw that…*"

Nate smiled and nodded in agreement. Replacing his empty bottle with four full ones, he headed towards the lake where Duke informed him Lucky would be. He was keen to ensure that his father figure was coping.

"You look thirsty." He said as he sat beside the old man on a fallen tree trunk.

"Thank you, Nathan…" Lucky held the bottle in his hands for a while. "… So, she's a Schaeffer?"

"Apparently." He said, sympathetically. "But she don't know nothin' more about them than anyone else really… P'raps less." He couldn't tell if that reassured Lucky, but the last thing he would ever want to do is break the old man more than this life had done already.

"We can't be held responsible for the names we're given, son." Lucky sighed and took a drink. "You know, I did my fair share of bad in this lifetime, and Martha's death was a result of that." His grey eyes glistened sadly as he stared into the water. "Annie's still got so much life ahead of her, I'm glad she wasn't with those monsters longer than a few years. The Schaeffers weren't people who should have had the responsibility of children." Nate nodded. "You gonna be ok?"

"Yes. I just needed some time. I'll make my acquaintance with the young lady tomorrow; she doesn't deserve any hostility from me." He looked up at Nate and drew out a kind, familiar smile. "Thanks for the drink."

The pair sat undisturbed, reminiscing about their lives to this point, until the moon shone on the lake, and the din of voices behind them murmured into the night.

6

Onti Lake

July 1893

It had been four months since Annie had used her lodgings. Before that, there were always people on hand to help fix things in place. Every performer helped every other, and she missed that family beyond measure.

Building her quarters alone was a lengthy process, and she was conscious of how lavish they seemed compared to some others in camp.

It was very late by the time the basic structure was set and a beer-soothed Nathan Healey checked in on her. "Looks good, Annie. Think I've been in the wrong business all these years." They stared at his own raggedy tent; its doorway ripped and fraying, adorned with badly patched areas that let in the weather. "Perhaps, if you'd spent less time connin' folks, and more time learnin' to juggle, I'm sure you coulda made quite a name for yourself."

He smiled. "Duke said that you're to stay in camp for a while, get to know everybody. Try not to rile 'em any further." He winked. "You're to work for Chuck and Maw Hicks."

Annie rolled her eyes. "*Great.*"

"Now Maw may be a bit of a battle-axe, Annie, but she ain't gonna bite ya… Well… maybe just once." He walked to his tent. "If you ain't workin' you find somethin' to do in sight of everyone." He turned back to her. "Oh! And you're to keep your tent open whenever you ain't sleepin'."

Annie looked at the doorway that faced Nate's lodgings and

turned to him playfully. "But what if I'm dressin', Mister Healey?"

He paused and looked at her; momentarily caught off guard by her flirtation. He cleared his throat awkwardly. "I'm guessin' it wise for you to keep that private too… Goodnight, Miss Schaeffer."

"Mister Healey."

Annie's first night in camp was sleepless. She stared up at the roof as she lay on her canvas camp bed. The soft hum of slumber around her reminded her of those she had left behind, and what may have transpired from her actions to escape.

She pulled some parchment and a pencil from her belongings, sat on the floor, and by low lamplight proceeded to compose a letter to her oldest friend.

Dearest Sally,

I trust you are well, and our cousins are still with you. How is work? It has been so long since we last spoke, and I was unsure if you would still be with the same employers. I am sorry that I did not say the farewell that you deserved, but I feared that it may be too difficult to depart if I had. I know you would have tried your hardest to talk me out of it.

I am well, at least for now. I am daring to venture into unknown lands in this great country! I have met a band of travelers that are helping me in my adventure. I don't know how long we will be in company, but at present it is amicable.

Send my love to all our cousins. Please write to me using the name and address provided. I miss you terribly.

Much love, Sister.

Setting down her pencil Annie re-read the note with sadness before placing it in an envelope. She would pass it to Nate to post and hope that it wouldn't cause harm to its receiver. Deciding that sleep had evaded her, she continued Deer unpacking.

At sun-up, she awoke stiff and confused having fallen asleep mid-work. She was so used to waking early to start her chores, that it would take a lot to shake it off. Annie went out to see Bessie and feed her a handful of carrots she had picked some days earlier, then stood to assess her new home in the cool haze of dawn. It was quite beautiful in its stillness. The site was on the edge of some thick woodland by a large lake; far back enough from the water, and away from the nearby roads to be easily hidden from prying eyes. Across the water was a small, tented settlement where a Lumber Mill was taking up residence. No doubt, Duke had got the men to scout the workforce prior to landing here, but their business was left to itself, as was the gang's.

The tents in the Needham camp seemed spaced out with thought. Ahead of her, past a communal fire and some rudimental tables with seating, she could make out Chuck's food wagon. It seemed well stocked with canned goods and garnished with a recently killed deer hanging from a frame. Around that were the tents and shelters of her fellow campmates. To her right, she could make out the long silhouette of Nathan Healey through the breaks in his tent; asleep on his back, seemingly fully clothed, arms folded across his chest. It gave his manner a look of seriousness that made her laugh.

Thinking back to her arrival, she realised that the group's ages varied wildly; obviously these people had been brought together by unplanned circumstances and adopted into the fold for some reason or other. Most likely beneficial to Duke's own ends.

Gentle bird calls were beginning, signaling the start of a good weather day. With a deep breath, Annie returned to her tent to change into some practical clothing.

By the time the rest of the camp had stirred, she had set about arranging a make-shift practice space using some items she had from her performances. There were two wooden panels decorated with hand-painted red targets which she used for knife throwing, and one metal silhouette of a man for anyone willing to learn how to shoot someone dead, she thought disparagingly.

"Miss Schaeffer, I presume?" An older gentleman with white hair walked towards her with two cups of coffee. "Good to meet you, my name is Lucius Needham, but everyone calls me Lucky… Because I'm not." With a chuckle, he handed her a cup and shook her hand. Over his shoulder she noticed that some of the earlier risers, most noticeably Maw, watched intently as the exchange took place.

"Good mornin', Mister Needham. Thank you." She raised her coffee cup and proceeded to drink. "I don't believe I saw you yesterday."

He smiled. "No, I was at the lake side, enjoying the peace from the rabble. Please, call me Lucky. I must say it is a treat to have a distraction large enough for the whole group, so that the wearier of us can slip away." He nudged Annie with his elbow and grinned, though his eyes didn't follow suit. Lucky had some similarities to Duke, though he was smaller both in height and build. Obviously older, his demeanour was far less determined, and she guessed he had always been the patient one of them.

"I'm glad I could be of assistance to you, Lucky." She took another drink as he stood next to her, looking towards the smattering of watchers. She heard Nate cough himself awake, and saw his shadow sit up and stretch.

She continued. "Your camp is quite lovely. I must say it has been some months since I slept outside, and with all the tall buildins springin' up back home, the vistas ain't quite the same."

"Yes, against all its other failings, at least the South still has the scenery to win us over." They looked at each other pleasantly. Annie hoped Lucky could influence the rest of the camp into relaxing their resentment towards her.

Lucky continued as they saw Nathan stroll sleepily towards them. "I hear you've got the unfortunate blessing of being nannied by Nathan, here." He joshed.

"I figure he ain't such a stern task master." She smiled deeply at Nate as he greeted them.

"Ain't this a little early to be plannin' against me, you two?"

"It's never too early for anything, Nathan." Lucky laughed. "Anyway, I best be on with my day. It was nice to speak with you, Miss Schaeffer, and don't mind these louts, especially this big one." He patted Nate on the back as he left.

***

Nate and Lucky had reminisced into the late night. He felt great relief that the old man was able to work through whatever he felt about having a Schaeffer in the camp. It had been a long time since they had snatched a moment like this. Not since their ridiculous escape from Missouri. Lucky had grown more reserved than his usual placid self and Nate knew the decision to cause such commotion to save Madsen sat poorly with him. Now, with Annie's presence, another choice outside of his control had been made. Nathan couldn't help but feel this latest betrayal had been his doing. The two men agreed to keep Annie in the dark about the Schaeffers' exact influences on Lucky's life; she didn't need to apologise for something she was never involved in.

"You trust her, Nathan?"

"She ain't given me a reason not to."

"Good. I hope she never does. I'd like to believe we can all get over her unfortunate affiliation quickly. A rose by any other name, as they say."

Nate smiled. He and Danny had been fortunate to have been taken in by Lucky and Martha at such an impressionable age.

His life had been on a dangerous path, and without them he would surely have been hanged years ago. They had taught him to read and to understand the actions of others. He had learnt to question the world around him and come to his own conclusions. It had been the makings of a good life before the money ran out. Nate doubted how many others in the gang had been so blessed prior to joining the Needham Boys.

The pair finished their final drinks and returned to the main camp. Most of the inhabitants had decided to slink off to bed, nursing their displeased feelings in private. He bid goodnight to Lucky and crossed towards his own dwelling.

He saw that Annie was still working away at her bulky tent by lamp light and should have passed Duke's message on to her hours ago.

Having finally relayed the information she needed; he made his way to bed. He rolled onto his back and turned his head. Through a gap in the canvas, he saw Miss Schaeffer retire to her lodging, pulling the canvas door down as she went. It wasn't long before the thin beams of light reaching through the gaps in the tent snapped to black as her lamplight was extinguished.

Nate stared up at the sagging canvas roof of his humble covers and thought of Annie's grace under pressure today.

He sighed; the drink had taken effect, and he resigned himself to sleeping in his day clothes. Judging by Duke's plans, this might be the last time in a while where he wouldn't be out under the stars. He would make sure Annie was clear on her duties before he left. Her confinement to camp for the next few weeks meant he would not be bound to watching her as much as he had expected. *"More's the pity."* He thought as he drifted off, smiling at their last exchange.

It was still early but the muffled sounds of conversation began to increase as Nate woke; he could make out Lucky and Annie exchanging pleasantries. Rubbing his face, he eavesdropped on the conversation before going to join them. It was a relief to hear the two getting along, and it reinforced his respect for Lucky, considering the pain he must be reliving.

***

"Annie." Nate nodded as he stood beside her, "Sleep well?"

"Not as well as you by all accounts." She teased. "You seemed quite serious as you slumbered."

"It's a serious business," he looked down at his rumpled clothes, "though I don't think Maw will appreciate my current appearance."

"Yeah, she likes to think she's in charge, don't she?" Annie mused, looking on as the ball of fury fired a barrage of commands towards one of the slovenlier men loitering about. Nate snorted with amusement.

"If she didn't, we'd be in a far worse state. And she can bully Campbell Madsen as much as she sees fit as far as I'm concerned." He looked at his neighbour's set up. "Looks like you kept yourself busy last night, you unpacked already?"

"I am, I even set up a practice space behind the tent."

"Nice work, Miss Schaeffer, that could prove useful. Listen. I have some scoutin' work to do for Duke away from here for a few days." He turned to her with seriousness. "Remember what I said to you yesterday? You're to stay here and do as is asked of you." He could see the frustration on Annie's face.

"You don't need to be treatin' me like a child, Nate, I ain't lookin' to cause any problems."

"Well, don't rise to none neither." He looked around camp. "There's some folk that will push you every chance they get, just keep your head down."

Annie leaned back on her hip, arms folded and a sullen look on her face, "Don't patronize me, Mister Healey."

"Alright, alright I just wanna make sure I ain't gonna have to come back to any mess you've caused is all." His joke didn't seem to land as she glared out across camp. "…Okay well fine, I gotta get outta here soon, and seein' as you don't have anythin' goin' on I recommend you go ingratiate yourself with Chuck and Maw."

Annie's head snapped back to him. "As you're out anyway, would you mind postin' this?" She handed him her letter. "Seein' as *I ain't able to leave* and I don't know what we put as a forwardin' address. *Please…* I don't know if it will even reach my friend."

He nodded stoically and stowed the envelope. "See you soon, Annie."

She twitched a frosty farewell nod and moved herself towards the others. Nate shook his head at her obstinance; he wasn't happy about having to be a minder or being sent away from that task so suddenly. Nor did he appreciate the insolence that shot across her when he was just doing his job. He grabbed some food from Chuck's station, and left the camp, deciding it best to escape any further interactions with the changeable Annie Schaeffer.

"Maw!" Annie called brightly to the matron, "I am reportin' for duty this mornin'."

Maw looked sternly at the grinning Schaeffer who had so rudely interrupted her scolding of the man Nate identified as Campbell Madsen. "So ye've decided to join us, eh?" There was nothing else to criticise Annie for seeing as she had spent the night building her quarters alone.

If it hadn't been for the fact that she was a Schaeffer, Maw might have even admired Annie's focus and tenacity. "Follow me, I'm sure we can find ye plenty to dae." She slapped Campbell Madsen once more for good measure and led Annie away from the uncomfortable stares of that man, towards the water, and the other fastidiously working people in the camp. "Seein' as ye can put that monstrosity o' a tent up on your own, ye must be able to dae a better job than these preenin' princesses when it comes to cleanin'!"

Annie smiled and nodded at two workers busy scrubbing shirts and dishes clean. Or one of them was at least. They looked up at her with boredom.

Maw shoved an empty pail into Annie's hands. "Here, put those *delicate hands* to work and find me when you're done." She sighed and sat between the two others on the edge of the lake.

"Hi there."

"You're the Schaeffer girl!" the younger of the two acknowledged, "I'm Dotty."

"Nice to meet you."

"Marie Bassett." The older of the two said, with a slightly curt tone.

Marie was glamorous for a woman living outside; she rouged her lips, and her white-blonde hair glistened brightly as her curled, bundled locks shone in the sun. She looked older than Annie, though much younger than Maw, and her sharp blue eyes spoke of a worldly knowledge beyond boys and their guns.

Annie shook hands with both and began to pick up soaked

clothes to wring out. "So, this is the glamorous lifestyle of a Needham Gal, huh?"

"Oh yes," Marie beamed, "we're the envy of everyone in society!"

"Well I am *highly honored* to be allowed to join you ladies!" The three laughed as they continued in their labours throughout the morning.

Both Marie and Dotty were smart, and both had faced their own troubles before joining the Needham Boys. Their backgrounds made them open-minded to the situations of others; Marie was sharp-witted, sharp-tongued, and determined, while Dotty, still in the earlier years of adulthood, was somewhat of a hoper. Annie found she was getting to know two women who could hold the world in their hands if they wanted, but they were smarter than that.

"Leave the bickerin' and destruction to the men, and we'll build it right once they're done." Marie smirked.

Annie enjoyed their company. They had given her some useful information about others in the camp, while she managed to stay quiet about her own life. It was past noon by the time the chores were finished, and with raw, stiff hands Annie took to the communal stew pot for some lunch. She stood by the bubbling mixture, realising how few people were around.

"They're out workin'." A young voice said. "You're new." Annie turned her head towards the voice and saw a brash-looking boy with thick, dark brown hair looking up at her. "I'm Mikey."

She smiled and nodded. "Annie."

"Lotta people seem unhappy 'bout you bein' here, Annie." He smirked in a way only the youthful can; as if he had been the first to discover some great secret.

"I don't doubt." She sighed and leaned against the edge of the table; her arms crossed.

Mikey eyed her mischievously, "They're sayin' you a bad person."

Annie's eyes twinkled as she looked at the boy; she was still trying to decide whether or not she'd like him. "How old are you, kid?"

Mikey drew himself up to his full height which, much to Annie's dismay, wasn't far off her own. "Fourteen."

She smirked, "I didn't realize that was the age where a boy becomes the authority on every person's perceptions."

"It ain't exactly difficult to see," Mikey placed his hands on his hips, "folks here ain't exactly quiet on the matter of you." Annie nodded. "Can't argue with you there… What about you?"

"*Me?!*"

"D'you think I'm a bad person?"

Mikey paused with a great deal of dramatic intention; his brow furrowed as he rubbed the invisible stubble at his chin. "Well… You a Schaeffer aintcha?"

"For my sins…"

"I been told stories 'bout them. They weren't good folks… *Buuut…*"

Annie laughed at his pondering. "Now Mikey, do you think Nate would allow anyone *bad* to come here?"

He looked up at her with amusement. "No," he laughed, "Nate don't even like good folk much. He ain't 'bout to bring in a badun!" He looked over at her horse. "Besides. Ain't no big bad woman callin' their horse *Bessie*!" He snorted at her mare's name, and Annie chuckled. Maybe she was going to like this kid after all.

7

Getting Acquainted

Annie was unguarded often. Like most of the men, Nathan had been sent out regularly to follow up on leads or other less innocent errands. Despite some of the disparaging stares or hissed comments toward her, she had generally been left alone by the others during their comings and goings. She made it clear she was smart enough to not cause trouble, and it was no one's concern if she was the victim of it, which made the promise Nate had said to her the day she arrived so hollow now.

She spent her days unnaturally gracious, allowing herself to be berated. The pressure of forced pleasantries took its toll on her, however. But as she was outnumbered by a bunch of ruthless, angry, and somewhat desperate people, she didn't see it worthwhile to end her life by being herself.

Sleep still eluded her. Having been a lone wanderer for the past 3-4 months, the continual bustle and hum of the camp was proving difficult to ignore, and the tasks she was being handed were far from exhausting when compared to performing, practicing and the relentless travelling she had been used to her whole life.

One night, she noticed that there was a stillness in the camp; no arguing between drunken poker players, no campfire songs – almost all the men were out on a job to rob some unlucky folks. Those left behind had retired to bed early, and it seemed that Duke was otherwise engaged with Marie.

She stepped out of her tent, shivering against the chill of the clear July night; the dew-laden grass caressing her feet indicated a change in weather may soon be upon them. Nate was away yet again, and so, with the advantage of the diminished moon, she decided to take a closer look at the life of the man she had put her dependence on. Waiting in the shadows to make sure the night patrols were far off, she slipped inside the yawning opening to his meagre shelter and peered across the small collection of trinkets he kept beside his bed. In the minimal light she could see a framed photograph. On closer inspection, she could faintly make out a matronly figure seated in a chair, holding a bundled babe; her expression strong and determined, but with a soft sadness to it. To her left was a young boy no older than five; his face telling a far more honest story as a figure stood behind them all, almost shadowed; his features difficult to make out.

"Healey <u>1867</u>"

Placing the picture back with care, and a little guilt, she reached across to another frame closest to his bed; in it wasn't an image but a short piece of writing that she had difficulty making out. She dared to light a lamp, keeping its light low as she hunched over to make out the beautifully cursive handwriting;

> *And yet, through rosied eyes I see,*
> *You have made a sinner of me,*
> *And as I try to keep from your fates*
> *They slake my soul as would good wine.*
> *And thine own destiny shall be mine.*

She smiled. "Well, you old dog, you do have some joy in your life after all." Relieved to find his softer side, at least once anyway, she shut off the lamp, and shuffled away from his quarters. She chose to enjoy the sensation of the cool grass between her toes, and softly made her way through the uninhabited areas of the site. "People'll think you're crazy creepin' about in your nightgown." Annie stopped. Ahead of her in the trees was Clara Healey; rifle in hand. "Considerin' what most of them think of me already, 'crazy' is a step up."

"I guess so." Clara smirked, "What you doin' out here anyhow?"

"Camp's quiet." Annie shrugged. "I can't sleep, and it's probably the only time I can move around here without Maw shovin' some kind of shovel or other godforsaken thing into my hand for work."

"I'm Clara by the way. Danny's wife… Nathan's sister by marriage…? I guess you're feelin' a little *itchy* doin' that stuff."

They shook hands and Annie walked with her companion along the scout route. "Yeah, but I ain't exactly gonna get given a rifle to protect y'all am I?" Annie hopped through the bracken and stones that stabbed at her feet. "Jesus I'm regrettin' this walk now. Maybe I am crazy."

"You know, considerin' the reputation of the Schaeffers, I was expectin' some wild-eyed hag, not some pretty young thing who wouldn't say boo to a goose."

"Believe me, Clara, if it were up to me I'd have that goose strung up, plucked, and roasted by now, never mind '*booin'*' at it!"

"You really wanna be tellin' me stuff like that, Annie? I *am* holdin' a gun after all." Clara stopped and faced her, her hand lightly rotating around the rifle. "And I find you out here in the middle of a dark night, quietest it's been in camp furra while… Shufflin' around without makin' a sound?" She shifted the gun to alleviate some of its weight in her arm.

Annie spurned the idea. "Clara, what makes you think I am that stupid?"

"Nothin'," Clara sighed, "I was just really fixin' to dislike you, and I can't. I guess Nate was right; you and I could probably give old Duke a run for his money."

"I don't think anyone wants that." Annie joked. "But maybe we could cause some noise once I'm allowed outta this place for a goddamned second."

"I know exactly what you mean. I ain't been beyond the borders of camp since I had a little… *accident* a few months back."

"Accident?"

Clara gave Annie a sheepish look as they approached her large tent. "I might've nearly made myself a widow durin' a bounty stick up back West. Didn't think Danny were gonna speak to me again." She grinned. "And, well, the fellas ain't trusted me with 'em since."

Annie laughed in disbelief. "Jesus, Clara, you ain't supposed to shoot your own fellas!"

"*Well*, he got in my way…!" She chuckled. "But I figure I better not push my luck for a while. Nate wouldn't allow it anyway."

Annie nodded. "I guess he don't need two hot-headed women causin' him troubles. He don't seem to enjoy it that much."

"Oh I don't know, Annie, I think it's one of the better perks of his job. Goodnight."

"Thanks for not shootin' me."

"You got better clothes to die in than that, Miss Schaeffer."

8

Dead Eye Annie

Her first ten days had been particularly solitary. There had been a mixture of responses from people in camp, and Annie had been the very example of courtesy and respect to those around her, even if they were unwilling to reciprocate. She had near enough met, or at least seen, every member of the outfit now; many, such as Campbell Madsen, she had only caught glimpses of as they had been sent on scouting missions for Duke. Her only experience of Madsen had been the great dislike he stirred in her from his furtive and slithering looks, as well as the extremely low opinion Nate had of him.

Her toughest opposition had been Daniel Healey - Nathan's younger brother, who obviously knew the wrath of the Schaeffers first hand; Maw Hicks - though Annie began to feel that it was her demeanour to everyone, which was in such stark contrast to the kindlier nature of her husband, Chuck, and finally a fellow named Sam Clifford. Mister Clifford was an angry man, and today was the day he decided to make Annie's acquaintance to point out that she had outstayed her welcome. "Aren't ya done with us yet?"

"Excuse me?"

"I *said*, aren't ya done with us yet?" Sam held a somewhat formidable figure as he squared up to Annie. His shadow loomed over her; arms folded, itching for a fight.

She chose a sweet disposition in which to address him to get a reaction. "Mister Clifford, I know we ain't spoke since I arrived, but I don't think this is how one usually starts a conversation."

"Don't backchat *me* girlie!" The camp stared towards Sam's tirade at a rather bemused Annie. "I Don't trust *damned*

Schaeffers! You're all the same! You think I believe your *lies* about not bein' one of 'em do ya?" Annie was finding it hard to take the man seriously; his whiskered cheeks were reddening and with every venomous sentence, a small shower of whiskey-scented spittle fired out the corner of his mouth. "Ain't no reason for you to be here. I'll find out your game and then you'll be gone, one way or another!"

She watched, perplexed, as Duke stepped in to diffuse the situation; he caught the frantic man's hand as it raised to strike.

"What are you doing Sam?!" he wrenched the man's arm down and pinned it at his side.

Sam Clifford turned to Duke and immediately refocused; looking ashamed as he saw his leader's thunderous expression. "She's up to somethin', Duke. I can *smell* it."

"The only thing we can smell, *Clifford*, is the stench of alcohol on your breath!" Duke turned to Annie as he loosened his grip on his friend. "My apologies, Annie, Sam hasn't been properly house trained."

Sam replied with a petulant huff. His head was lowered but from under thick eyebrows his eyes glared, locked on Miss Schaeffer.

"Could you excuse us for a moment, I will deal with *this* and then I would like a word with you."

Annie nodded. "O-of course, Duke, happy to help however I can."

Duke shoved the meaty shoulder of Mr. Clifford and marched him towards a distant edge of the lake's shoreline, which proved unsuccessful at drowning out the din of a severe reprimanding.

"Drunk moron's been gettin' worse for some time now." Marie Bassett sidled up to Annie, shotgun in hand from her patrol shift. "He was in for a surprise if he'd picked a fight with you though. I'm guessin' you'd silence him pretty quick. He must be gettin' dumber too." The shapely blonde eyed Annie with indifference. "Good thing Duke came in to save you both." She sniffed with a smirk. "Shame. I was kinda lookin forward to you bein' here to kick shit up."

Marie sashayed off to continue her patrol as Duke reappeared, red-faced and exasperated. He strained a smile at Annie. "Miss Schaeffer, my apologies for Sam Clifford's suspicions. I'm afraid his loyalty to this group can sometimes surpass his rational thinking. As I'm sure you're aware, your last name can cause some… adverse reactions."

Annie nodded. She had been expecting this since her arrival, and now Sam was done it felt like a storm had cleared. "It were only a matter of time 'til someone gave in to their feelins, Mister Needham." She suggested. "I can't think how hard my presence has been for some."

"Yes, and about that…" Duke put a heavy arm over Annie's shoulders and walked with her around camp; his cigar smoke intertwining with his thick silver moustache as he spoke. "You have, *so far*, proven yourself to be a hard worker and kept out of trouble." he drew on the La Reina stogie. "But folks are still intrigued about you." They stopped walking as Duke turned Annie by her shoulders. "It seems, *Miss Schaeffer*, you are a little reluctant to share your life with them."

Annie felt uncomfortable. "I don't like to bore folk with my life, Duke, I'm sure they'd be bitterly disappointed to learn that I ain't Cal Schaeffer." She felt the pressure on her shoulders as Duke squeezed them with irritation. He forced himself to it play off as friendliness. The cigar in his mouth belched smoke straight into Annie's eyes.

His morning seemed littered with uncooperative people. "You see, Annie, *that's* exactly what we want them to understand. That you are very different from your father, and it's an attribute you should want to parade through the streets." They took up their promenade once more. "From what Nate told me, it should be an excellent opportunity to have someone like you here. A chance for *entertainment*!"

"I can see why you'd think my skills might be of use," she scowled in confusion, "but I don't see how my life in a world that excites children is quite so complimentary to you all."

"Miss Schaeffer, aren't we all just big children?" Duke grinned at her as he gripped the rolled tobacco leaves in his hand. "I believe, as a *thank you* to the camp's hospitality, you might want to put on a little spectacle this evening. Maybe we can set up a space around the campfire for you to show off some of the skills that kept '*Dead Eye Annie*' employed all those years, hmm?"

Beads of cold sweat rolled down Annie's spine; she didn't want to become a performing monkey. The idea of this band of outlaws, thieves and killers watching a woman perform ridiculous stunts was humiliating, but there was no one to fight her corner on this. Even if Nate was there, he would probably see it as a good idea, and she knew it was a test of her '*loyalty and trustworthiness*'. She forced her best false, most flattering smile. "Oh *of course*, Duke! I would be happy to!"

"Good!" Duke slapped Annie's shoulder with satisfaction. "I'll tell Chuck and Maw you will be indisposed for the rest of today and get them to rearrange some space… Oh! and make sure it's as if you were in front of a paying audience – Full regalia if you please."

"Full regalia?!"

"Until this evening, Miss Schaeffer!"

***

Six days sleeping rough was enough for any man, but Nathan welcomed the peace of nature. He always slept better away from the never-ending commotion of camp life, and the stars provided a soothing innocence for him to settle under. But, alas, it was time for him to return. Prynne was tired and would need to be rested back at Onti Lake, and his provisions were gone.

He had delivered Annie's letter early in his travels, adding the forwarding address to the back. He had not really thought about her situation beyond its immediacy and realised she may have left a lot of people behind when she ran.

Whatever Annie left, she certainly wasn't eager to return to;

this Sally must be very important to risk being found, he thought. As well as keeping his hand in playing Bounty Hunter, Duke had requested he go listening for information about their escape from Missouri. And since they no longer had their man, Tom Kelley, hidden within The Fitzgerald Gang, he had to scout any news on their movements too.

With what he had learned, he was sure it would appease Duke enough to ease up on his travels for a while at least. Nate had been accompanied through some of his trail thanks to Danny and Kelley, though he would have preferred to not have to hear their choice comments regarding the latest newcomer.

"A *Schaeffer*, Nate? What the hell were you thinkin'?"

"Ah! C'mon, Danny," Tommy teased, "havencha seen the girl? There's some *very obvious* things Old Nathan was thinkin' about!" The young Irishman laughed as he made various gesticulations in the firelight.

"Always got your head in the filth, don'tcha, Mister Kelley?" Nate scolded. "Maybe you'da been better off left spyin' on the Fitzgeralds for us 'til they caught you out."

"Oh cheer up, you old fart!" Tommy contested, "I don't care how much of a psychopath her Daddy was, if I had someone like that willin' to do *anythin'* for some safety, to hell with it, I'd give her some options!"

"That right?" Nate scoffed. "Doubt Dotty would be so impressed hearin' you say that." That quieted Tommy for a while.

"I wonder how she's survivin' in that place. Fancy you leavin' her unprotected from Maw and Madsen." Danny chuckled. "I guess she mightn't be much to worry about if Maw finishes her off before we get back." He looked at his brother. "How's Lucky doin' with it all?"

"Fine... I *guess*... He made his introductions on her first day. Seemed pleasant enough. In fact, he's the one outta everyone bein' a goddamn grown up about it all."

"So what happened, Nate?" Tommy enquired. "I mean, the Schaeffers were legends among the Irish lads, but I didn't know anythin' went down between you."

"One of Cal's men killed Lucky's wife." Danny answered bitterly.

Nate lit a cigarette. "We were workin' the bounties 'round Rock Valley in Iowa. Picked up the wrong fella I guess." He shrugged sadly through the smoke. "Gave him a choice – pay for freedom, or get brought in. He just spat at us and gave us all the usual blusterin', that we'd be wise to let him go. We took him in, got paid and left. Turns out Caley Schaeffer bust the fella out and then came for us. He weren't a fan of folks *disrespectin' his brothers* as he put it." Nate's eyes glistened in the firelight as he sucked heavily on his tobacco. "Bein' feared for so long had made him more dangerous than he'd ever been. Lucky tried to talk them into an agreement." He exhaled and looked at Tommy; a deep, sad rumble enveloped his voice. "Cal found the idea *insultin'*, so one of his men shot Martha without even a pause. They robbed what we had and left."

"We had nothin'," Danny spat, "just didn't like the fact some outfit were quicker than his dumbest gang member."

"I ain't never seen Lucky like that before or since. I guess his grief got the better of him. We rounded up a coupla smaller groups who were sick of the Schaeffers too, and we all hit 'em. *Hard.* Only folk that refused were the Fitzgeralds. Duke never forgave 'em."

"Nate got Cal through the eye!" Danny boasted proudly of his brother.

"Jesus Christ, man, I had no idea." Tommy Kelley sat back. "Yeah, well neither does Annie. So don't go shootin' your mouth off alright?" He glared at both of his companions. "She ain't been a part of that world since she were a kid, and she don't need to know what that world has done to us." The two opposite him nodded, and all three decided to take that opportunity to turn in for a night under the stars before going their separate ways.

The light was fading fast as Nathan turned down the final track towards home. He was looking forward to passing on his news and rewarding himself with some hard-earned liquor.

"Nate! Glad you could join us again." Clara greeted him from her patrol post.

"I'd be back sooner if I didn't have to go out earnin' for the rest of you." he taunted as he passed on Prynne.

"Hope you ain't fixin' on gettin' shut eye," she called after him, "Duke's puttin' on a spectacle!"

Confused, Nathan approached the opening to the camp to see a lot of activity in its centre. A large space had been created with a seating space facing one of the campfires. He hitched up Prynne and removed her saddle, quizzing Tanner as he came to manage the mare. "What's all this?"

"Duke wanted a little party for Annie I guess." He shrugged. "They've been workin' on it most the day. I reckon it's to distract from the fuss our camp clown caused."

"Fuss?"

"Oh just Sam's last braincell snappin'. Started threatenin' Miss Schaeffer, Duke dragged him away and he's been in a mighty sulk ever since."

"Well I guess if anyone was gonna be first to kick up a stink it was gonna be Sam. Miserable bastard." Nate's sigh had the slightest hint of amusement in it. "Is everythin' else alright?"

"With Miss Schaeffer and camp?"

Nate nodded to Tanner. He'd been gone for days and was finding the dramatic switch around in camp disconcerting, especially now there had been this to-do.

Tanner shrugged. "She ain't really made much of a mark I'd say. I think we're almost disappointed. She just stood there and took it from Sam. I ain't really spoken to her. Seems to have made friends with the girls well enough." Tanner looked across to Annie's tent. "She's been keepin' to herself when she ain't workin'. Can't say many folk have tried to change that, 'cept maybe Mikey. Probably workin' out how to rile her up, seein' as he's managed to do that with everyone else."

Nate was relieved Annie had proved herself trustworthy. "When was that nonsense with Sam?"

"Just happened this mornin'." Tanner chuckled. "The fool accosted her like some bitter old fishwife. Started rantin' at her about somethin' or other, don't really know. It's Sam so it didn't make too much sense. He was probably still drunk from the night before." He sniffed, "And I'm guessin' that's why this show is goin' ahead."

With a heavy groan of aged bones, Tanner gathered Prynne's horse tack and shuffled off to store it as Duke appeared. "Ah! Nathan! Welcome back Kiddo!"

"Duke," He greeted his friend with a look of confusion, "what the hell's all this? I go out on jobs, and you turn the camp into a circus?"

"Ah yes, I suppose there's been a couple of changes." Duke admitted as they walked together back through camp. "I felt that everyone needed a helping hand to *warm* to Annie quicker. She hasn't been too forthcoming about her circumstances so far, so I suggested she show off her skills."

Nate felt uncomfortable; he hadn't seen even a glimpse of Annie since he got back, and the camp was beginning to look more like a stage for ritual sacrifice than frivolities. He didn't understand Duke's motives beyond showing off. "And Annie's fine with this?"

"Of course, Nathan! She's more than happy to do it. God knows we can be a bit starved of entertainment around here." "I guess it'll be somethin' to talk about for a while." He muttered, thinking Tanner's theory was right. "You know what's best for morale."

"I would love to say I do, but Campbell was the one who suggested it."

Campbell. Of course. Madsen's favourite pastime was to irritate Nate; he obviously hoped this suggestion would be humiliating for Annie, and in turn cause some problems.

Nate laughed dryly. "*Good Old Madsen.* Duke do you wanna hear this information I've been out gettin' for you or not?"

"Of course, son, we have much to discuss. Grab a beer and come with me." Nate took a bottle from the crate close by and sighed as he looked across to the light glowing out from Annie's closed tent. He hoped the evening wasn't a bad idea.

***

"Full Regalia." Annie muttered, kneeling in front of her show trunk. She carefully took her costume from its resting place and unfolded it. It had only been a few months since she last wore it, but she never thought she would need to again.

The costume consisted of a structured cream one-piece bodice with capped sleeves, adorned with black piping along seamed corset channels which held the shaping steels in place. There were black fringed shorts that stopped just above the mid-thigh and cut high up at the back, white hose for her legs, and black kid leather slippers.

She also wore full length arm gauntlets painted with beautiful interflowing images of nature; day and night; both serene and terrible. They had been designed by her oldest friend, Sally, a woman who had been with the show before Annie; tattooed from toe to tip, and a contortionist. She had kept Annie safe as a child. Annie looked at her reflection in her small, mottled mirror. Through the warm glow of her lamplight, she finished tucking her hair up, checked her makeup and fortified herself, determined to command the crowd.

Duke had agreed to allow her to take Bessie out for a run bareback along the lake's shoreline, under the watchful eye of the patrol all afternoon. The fact that she hadn't had to do menial chores or face the scowl of Maw, as well as Maw having to take on the additional bind of changing the camp space around at the request of Duke, had been the highlight of her week. She felt this one-time-only show was a small price to pay for that.

The increased noise outside her tent told Annie that most of the gang were settling in, expecting quite a performance, seeing as Duke had made sure all of them would attend. He really was going out of his way to ensure the spectacle Sam made of himself this morning was extinguished from memory, she thought.

"Miss Schaeffer?" A tired voice called from outside her tent. Annie pulled her doorway aside to see the older, pink-faced man looking slightly irritated as he held a bridle and reins. She smiled. "Tanner."

"I have the kit you requested, you need me to set her up too, I suppose?"

Annie smirked at his huffy manner. "Yes, thank you Tanner, and if you could put Bessie behind my tent that would be perfect."

"Anythin' else? Some sun rays in a jar, perhaps?" "Not right now, thank you. I ain't got much use for 'em at present." Tanner nodded. "In that case, I'll struggle on with this."

Nathan looked across at his neighbour's tent as he got changed; her door was closed, and he could see the flickering of light as Annie moved around readying herself for this evening. He wondered what might have changed from her early work, what he could loosely remember of it anyway; the wise-cracking mini gunslinger calling out into the audience. Perhaps it wouldn't be so different. Smirking, he stretched, lit a cigarette, and went to join the audience, figuring he would talk with Annie after the exhibition was over.

He found himself a spot next to Dan and Clara.

"Nate!" Mikey scuffed his heels as he sauntered over to him.

"Mikey. I hope you ain't been causin' trouble for Lucky this week?"

"Didn't see the point," he shrugged, "didn't figure it'd get seen what with Fat Man Sam's loud cryin' this mornin'. What's all this about?" He waved his hand vaguely towards the cleared space. "Duke said somethin' about Annie bein' a performer in a show or somethin'. Is she a magician?"

"Aye! I am *sure* there's a fair few magical things she can do, Mikey Lad!" Tom Kelley piped up behind them. "I bet there's some stories!" The men in earshot laughed and Clara punched Tommy hard in the gut. Nate managed to stifle his amusement and told Mikey to get sat down.

He shot a look at Tommy who was already trying to cosy up to

Dotty, and they both raised their drinks to welcome him back after a long week away.

"Healey!" Nate's mood dropped as Campbell Madsen greeted him.

"Campbell. I believe we've all got you to thank for this ridiculous idea?" He dropped his cigarette end on the grass and took a beer from the hand of a passing Marie.

"If you think keepin' the morale of the people up is ridiculous, then sure." Campbell patted him on the back. "I missed you, Healey. Thought the wolves had got you. Looks like they have anyway."

Nate bristled as Campbell looked him up and down with amusement. "Well, I'm glad to disappoint you so bitterly, Madsen. Feel free to remove yourself from my presence 'til you learn to come to terms with it."

Much to Nate's dismay, Campbell settled down next to him just as Duke stepped up to make a formal introduction. "*LADIES AND GENTLEMEN!* I thank you for attending tonight for what promises to be an evening of fun and free entertainment-"

"THE BEST KIND!" Tanner shouted from his seat on the ground.

"Quite." Duke continued. "Tonight, our newest addition to the family has *very* sweetly offered to put on a little show as a thank you for our kindness!" There was a mix of dry laughter, groans and the odd explicit comment from Tommy regarding his expectations for the evening. Duke gained control of the crowd again. "I hope you will all join me in welcoming the Wonder of the West, *DEAD EYE ANNIE!*" The crowd cheered as the show began.

Hiding in the relative darkness behind her tent, Annie had gone through her prep with Bessie. The mare's role would be small, but Annie had still taken the time to braid her mane and tail with black ribbon. "I'm sorry girl," she patted her, "I didn't figure we'd do this again, but here we are." She sighed as she heard Duke begin his introductions, and mounted Bessie, moving through the shadows to make her entrance from behind the crowd, "*Just one more show,*" she whispered, "*then we won't be trussed up like this ever again.*" Bessie snorted with understanding as Annie fed her a sugar cube to sweeten the deal. She kicked her trusty horse forward to pick up pace before greeting the crowd. She shifted to her feet on the mare's back, just as she had so many times before.

The orchestral sounds of '*The Gal I Left Behind Me*' crackled out from an old, small phonograph Annie gave to Duke for the occasion. As the group drunkenly whooped and clapped along with the ditty, Annie started towards the stage. Nate heard genuine gasps from some of his campmates as they spotted her arrival. He turned his to see a figure standing tall and proud on her horse; arms outstretched as she passed swiftly through the crowd like the figurehead of a ship through the waves. She swiftly ducked into a handstand as she arrived at the allocated space, balancing on one hand, waving with the other; her shapely legs pointed above her, all while on the back of her huge horse.

Taking a deep breath, Annie shifted her body into a descent. Her legs stayed arrow-straight and pointed ahead of her as she rotated her hips lithely, and gently lowered herself onto the bare back of Bessie in side-saddle position, before gliding – arms above her head – to land feet-first on the ground. Ever the professional, she stood there a moment to allow the applause to die down.

Nate sat in stunned silence looking at the woman he witnessed brawl against, and kill, three men in under a minute; the woman who shot dead wild animals with such precision they had been able to make some decent coin from the pelts. Now stood in front of him, bearing a number of unexpected arm tattoos, made up and tightly cinched so all her form was visible. Her legs enticingly on show were adorned with leather scabbards holding her knives in place, and a bandolier with pistol holster caressed her hips. Feeling slightly breathless, he took a large swig of beer as the hollering from Tommy and some of the others pierced his eardrums.

Annie moved to pass Bessie's reins to Chuck, and he led the mare away as she began her welcome. "Good evenin', folks! Thank you for such a *raucous* hello!" She saw the dumbstruck, unkempt face of Nathan Healey staring out from the crowd. "Are you fellas looking forward to bein' impressed by a lady without havin' to *pay extra*?!" The men cheered and laughed. "And *LADIES*! Are you ready to let a woman show these fellas that we *are* the better sex?!" The women of the camp roared with boozy competitiveness, even Maw happily joined in. "Now before I start, I'm gonna need the *bravest, strongest* fella in the audience to help me."

Nate watched Annie's face stretch into a mischievous grin as she sashayed her way through the group. His eyes followed her figure as she stood in front of Mikey; her features glowing in the camp's lights. "Mikey, what say you help me out this evenin'?" Mikey blushed and cringed with embarrassment. *"Do I have to?"* He looked at Lucky who, leaning against a tree further back, smirked and gesticulated to get a move on. Nate shoved him forward a little.

"Fine!" he announced with a grumble, though his face couldn't hide his smugness at being asked.

Annie steered Mikey by the shoulders to the centre of the space and looked at him seriously. "Now, Mikey, you're gonna be one of the stars of the show tonight, so you should practice takin' a bow!" He rolled his eyes and hid his face in his hands as the gang jeered him on.

Annie tutted and shook her head. "Don't tell me you ain't never been taught how to bow!" She placed one hand at the back of his neck, and one hand at his stomach. "You just bend in the middle, see?" She hinged Mikey back and forth three times as the congregation applauded for him. "Okay, okay that's enough now," she joked as she stood Mikey upright and pulled his hands from his now red face, "don't want you thinkin' this is your show! But you are gonna be my trusty assistant tonight." She grinned, *"And* your first duty is to help me do some quick-shootin'."

At this, Mikey's interest in the evening piqued. Annie picked up some old tin plates from a pile and handed them to him. The pair proceeded to work as a double act with Mikey surprisingly obedient to every instruction he was given; tossing the plates as high in the air as he could, and Annie would shoot them with speed. Lucky looked on at his ward with immense pride. At the end of the quick-draw section, Mikey voluntarily bowed in the most flamboyant way he could.

"Alright, Mikey," Annie said. "It's time to pick another person outta this group." She turned the boy so that they both had their backs to the crowd. One of them occasionally glanced over their shoulders as they conferred. Looking to one another, they gave a sharp nod, turned back to the front; eyes sparkling with mischief, and Mikey went to fetch Tanner. "*NOW!*" Annie continued over the din of raucous drunks, "Tanner here is gonna be of *great* help." She shook Tanner's clammy hand. "Come over here, good sir."

"What're y'doin'?" He protested as Mikey helped wrestle the lightly intoxicated Tanner over to her large target board. "I ain't a young man!"

"We all know that Tanner," Annie joked as the crowd heckled unsympathetically, "this ain't gonna hurt whatever it is today that's causin' you to grumble. And it *certainly ain't* gonna make you feel younger!" She thanked Mikey and moved him behind her. "In fact," she teased, "I need you to do what you do best and stay. Perfectly. *Still!*"

With a flash of silver from her leg, Tanner yelped as a knife pierced the fabric on the inner thigh of his trousers. "I guess we know which side he dresses on now at least!"

Her showmanship was boundless. Nathan found himself whooping and cheering with the rest as he watched this bewitching entertainer rapid-fire all but one of the knives she carried, straight at Tanner, until his aging body was framed by her blades. She leaned and whispered something to Mikey as the crowd hooted and hollered, and the kid ran off toward Chuck's wagon.

"*BUT THAT AIN'T ALL, FOLKS!*" Annie sidled up to Tanner; the gun belt and holster gently swinging against her hips as she walked, "I'm gonna need to take this for a moment, Tanner." As she removed his hat Mikey returned with a small apple. "Thank you, Mikey, I'll swap you."

She stuck Tanner's hat on Mikey's head and placed the apple on Tanner's. "Now... This is *very* important, Tanner," She toyed;

her voice low and soft, "you best stay *stock still*. This is a small apple; it can make things a little more difficult." She turned to the audience. "And despite what the ladies tell ya, fellas, *SIZE MATTERS!*" A loud cheer went up from the women of the camp, but none of the gents were hurt for long as they watched Annie slowly pull a long scarf from her prominent cleavage. "*Ain't exactly a family show.*" Nate heard Clara quietly chuckle through the whoops, he smirked into his beer, not seeing a problem with that.

Annie bent down and mentioned something to Mikey as they both looked in Nathan's direction. "Now, for my final trick of the night, I'm gonna need a hat from the rabble out in the crowd…" "Nate, I'm needin' your hat for Annie."

Nate looked at Mikey's face, flush with what now seemed more excitement than embarrassment; the boy was having the time of his life seeing Tanner pinned helplessly.

He gave Mikey a cheeky smile. "Oh well I don't know about that, kid, I ain't too happy about the idea of it bein' that near Tanner!" He looked over at Annie as she slinked back into her hip; arms folded, and an eyebrow raised. He laughed along with the crowd and handed Mikey the hat.

"Thank you, Mikey," Annie said, as the kid returned, "you keep hold of that for now, but I need you to do me a favor…" she unwound the scarf that was wrapped in her hand, "I need you to tie this like a blindfold and cover my eyes alright?"

"*WHAT?!*" Tanner cried, very much stuck in his position. Annie gave a look to the crowd and knelt down. "And once that's done good and tight, I need you to stand me up to face Tanner, d'you understand?"

"Yes." Mikey answered succinctly; apparently matured temporarily by his responsibilities.

"Now I gotta be *exactly opposite* him alright? Otherwise, I might split somethin' other than the apple." The crowd laughed as Mikey nodded with utter sincerity and tied the blindfold around Annie's face. "You alright there, Tanner? You ain't lumbered off, have ya?"

"I ain't enjoyin' this!" He yelled.

"Don't worry now," Annie joked in the dark, "one way or another it'll be over soon!" She straightened up and let Mikey shift her to where he believed was the right spot. She felt out the divots she had made previously and distracted the audience by finishing her commands to her assistant. "Now Mikey, you still there?"

"I am."

"Good! I need you to come stand *right* next to me, okay? Because as soon as I throw this knife, I need you to pass me Mister Healey's hat."

The crowd fell silent as she held her hand up for hush. She could hear the quiet whimpers of Tanner, and the excited breathing of Mikey. The smell of firewood and alcohol wafted through on the summer breeze, and she slowly slid her hand up her leg to grab the blade of her final knife. As she exhaled, the knife left her hand. She instantly grabbed for the brim of Nathan's hat from Mikey's expectant hands and flung it forward. She lifted her blindfold when the crowd leapt to their feet roaring in disbelief. Tanner's face was hidden from view by Nate's hat, which hung from the knife she had thrown to pierce the apple.

"GET ME OUTTA THIS GODDAMN THING!!" Tanner shrieked over the crowd.

Annie and Mikey scurried to him, removed the hat, the apple on the knife, and the knife sticking through Tanner's trouser leg. He tumbled out back to his place on the floor, snatching his own hat back as he went.

"LADIES AND GENTLEMEN! A BIG ROUND OF APPLAUSE FOR TANNER!!" Annie applauded the protesting old man through the racket of laughter. She turned to Mikey, took back the knives, and handed him the apple. "AND ONE FOR MY MAGNIFICENT ASSISTANT!" The din of the delighted group erupted as Mikey took three dramatic bows at Annie's request, then waltzed back to his seat with the swagger of a man.

Nate was beyond impressed by the woman before him and roared along as Chuck brought Bessie back to the space.

"LADIES AND GENTLEMEN! THANK *YOU ALL* FOR BEIN' A GREAT AUDIENCE! I *AM* DEAD EYE ANNIE! GOODNIGHT!" She donned Nate's hat, leapt on to Bessie effortlessly and rode off into the dark.

*****

Annie hitched her mare at the paddock a little way from the revelries and started to unravel the ribbons in Bessie's long mane and tail. "There girl," she cooed, "I think we'll be alright now." She looked across to see people singing and drunkenly dance around as others sang; the scene was beginning to resemble something from a Renaissance painting of Greek festivities.

"Maybe she ain't so bad after all." A drunken Danny slurred, "She's certainly impressive, and I think Mikey might be a little taken with her!"

Nathan smiled watching the kid enjoying a beer and dancing with Marie. "Maybe we should help get that boy his beauty sleep if he's wantin' to impress Miss Schaeffer in the mornin'." He drained his fourth large bottle of the night and watched Danny stagger off. Nate took another drink from the crate at Chuck's station and sat at a vacant table, looking out at his friends cavorting around the campfire, full of songs and high spirits. As loathed as he was to admit it, Campbell's plan had been a good one, even if his reasoning behind it had backfired. He sat taking in the bliss of this moment, it felt like the old days before their journey South. He sighed contentedly and sipped his drink.

"Your hat, Mister Healey." Annie Schaeffer's gentle voice made him turn to see her alluring figure saunter towards him still in her performing garb, including the knives she had prized back out of the target before any fool could do themselves an injury. He took the hat from her outstretched hand as she joined him, sliding herself onto the tabletop; her thigh closely in line with his shoulder. "Thank you, Annie. Weren't sure if I'd ever see it again." He held it in his hands.

"It's part of my show," she said with a glint in her eye, "I always pick the hat from the best-lookin' fella in the audience and wait until after to hand it back. Gives me a reason to talk to 'em." She gave him a friendly nudge with her hip. "*Just don't tell Duke it ain't him.*"

Nate laughed a little sheepishly, turning his hat over. "Oh I won't, don't you worry, Miss Schaeffer." He cleared his throat, trying his hardest to keep his eyes on her face, "That were some impressive stuff up there, I enjoyed it."

She raised an eyebrow. "You *enjoyed* yourself, Nate?" She teased. "Be careful, you ain't a man used to enjoyin' himself by all accounts. I don't want you to hurt yourself now!"

"Alright, alright." He agreed sardonically. "You know, I think you might've won 'em over and in just two weeks. It's taken others a helluva lot longer."

Annie smirked as she looked at the celebrators. "I'm guessin' they don't have quite the same get-up in the costume department as me though."

"Well, no, you have got 'em beat on that. I didn't realize your arms were…"

"Oh these?" Annie rubbed the material. "No, it's just decorated covers to *look like* my arms are tattooed." She unhooked them from the cap sleeves of her bodice and rolled them down. "I've had them about ten years." she explained. "We – *Sally* and I – thought it would add somethin' to the show." Nathan studied Annie as she stared sadly at the balled-up fabric in her hands. "Sally painted 'em for me," she sighed, "she's such an artist."

"Is she the lady you wrote to?"

"Yeah. I hope she's alright."

Nathan gave Annie's hand a rough squeeze of reassurance. "If she's half as fiery as you, Annie Schaeffer, she ain't got nothin' to worry about."

"Thank you, Nathan."

Nate admired the work; the detail was precise, "You show lot are impressive folk."

Annie's laugh waved over him with familiar warmth. "Yes,

well, you don't get far in a travelin' show if you ain't!"

"Even with fake ink up your arms." He teased.

"I weren't employed to be covered in tattoos, Mister Healey." She grinned. "… don't mean I ain't sportin' some somewhere."

He stopped and looked at her. "*Really…?*"

She smirked at his overly eager response. Unless he frequented side shows he would not have met many women that would be tattooed. "Oh, come on, Nate! You can't be in a show without gettin' somethin' done." she exclaimed. "It's a rite of passage! I just don't have mine on show, *it ain't ladylike*." She winked at him. Not knowing where to look, Nathan went back to watching the crowd, and sipped his beer with a shaky hand.

"I tell you what…" Annie said as she jumped down from her seat and bent down to lock eyes with him. The familiar scent of flowers hit him like a train, and she grinned mischievously, "if you keep practicin' enjoyin' yourself maybe you'll get to see 'em one day." With that, she dumped the hat on his head, pulled it down over his face, and stole his bottle.

"Hey!" he called, "I thought you didn't drink beer!"

"I said I *don't drink it much*," she retorted, "I still drink it!" She waved the bottle above her head as she glided towards her tent to change; her tightly laced silhouette slinking side to side.

"You can put your eyes back in your head now, Nate," Clara's mocking voice and a fresh beer broke him away from his view, "'less you can see through canvas."

"Very funny." He said, and raised the bottle in thanks. "How's it been, Clara?"

"Well," she said, settling on a seat next to him, "I think Annie's a little bored, but Sam put pay to that this mornin'." She took a drink.

"Yeah I heard about that." He looked over at a subdued Sam; sulking at a distant campfire alone. "You think he'd be over it by now."

Clara smirked. "A man who lived off notoriety only to find he ain't even important enough to be killed by a Schaeffer man, then don't even get a rise outta Annie?" Clara chuckled. "Considerin' what a dumbass mad man Samuel Clifford is, I'm surprised he only ranted at her. Maybe he knew she'd drop him in a breath if he did more."

Nathan turned to her. "What is it about this gang that seems to pick up pig-headed women?"

"Just lucky, I guess," Clara joked.

The camp revelled long into the early hours; the tension brought by Annie's arrival was finally released and the gang made the most of it. Even Annie joined in the socialising, answering questions from the likes of Tommy about quick-draw techniques. At one point, Nate saw his brother and Clara taking a moment to enjoy the music and it made him smile to see them still happy. He even spotted Annie dancing with an inebriated Mikey before he rushed off to vomit and be sent to bed by Lucky. He was heartened as he turned in for the long rest had been hoping for since returning home.

9

Stir Crazy

With the celebrations spilling over into the early hours, the hostilities towards Annie had been forgotten, mostly thanks to the alcohol. Members of the gang she had yet to speak to came to get to know her better and she learnt a great deal about some of them. Dotty opened up about a lost love which had led her to camp.

Previously known as Mae-Belle Johnson, she had started an affair with a young farm hand who worked on her parents' farm back West. When the two were discovered, they escaped, but her lover sent her on without him. He saved her from the horrors of his lynching at the hands of her family. It wasn't long after that she had met Marie.

Marie Bassett had been a Madam in a saloon, took Dotty in and taught her to pickpocket men when the girls were keeping them otherwise engaged. This is how they became part of the Needham Boys; Duke offered them a place within his camp, most likely because he was more than enamoured by Marie. The gang became family, and the Healey brothers were like older siblings to Dotty. Annie looked across at Nathan's tent. For all his irritability and seriousness, Nate genuinely cared for these people. The way they spoke of him, the way he protected them, even against other gang members at times, made him a greater man than he would admit. She understood the attractiveness of this group's closeness. If it wasn't for the suspicions that arose in Annie whenever Duke spoke, or the way she had been kept at distance by them all initially, she could see herself falling for the enchantment of this lifestyle herself.

Annie started the following day early as usual. Working on minimal sleep, she dragged her sorry, slightly hungover self around behind Maw like a well-trained dog. She knew there would be payback for the labours she had avoided the previous day. First, she was made to clear up the mess left from the festivities of the night before; various glass and debris littered the entire site. Once she had worked up a sweat doing that, she was told to take the offal from Chuck's butchering, separate the useable pieces for stock, and bury the rest. The smell from it was enough to make a sober person turn green. Annie wrapped a bandana around her nose and mouth to filter the worst of it. Chuck stated that normally he would take the task on himself, but Maw insisted with great glee that Miss Schaeffer was more than capable.

Once finished, a remorseful Chuck asked Annie to sharpen his knives. She took them to a table near the centre of camp to stay in full view of everyone, as deemed necessary by the rules laid down to her.

She hummed lightly as she ran the whetstone across each rust-stained blade until its edge shone brightly again. She poured all her concentration into the task; anything to keep her mind from thinking about her confinement. As pretty as the views were, she wasn't used to staying still this long; at least in Tinulca she had freedom to roam.

Putting her feet up on the table and lowering her hat to shade her eyes, Annie pulled her own Bowie hunting knife from a scabbard on her hip. She inspected the large steel blade with maternal love while slowly sliding the whetstone up its edge with care and precision. The polished ram-horn handle needed attention; its layers were peeling with age, but the steel was still as bright as the day she had bought it. The banner of Celtic sister knots engraved on the sides kept the memories of Sally close in her mind.

"There ain't nothin' in this world like watchin' a woman tend to her blade so lovinly." Annie looked up from her task to be greeted by a lascivious sneer.

"Mister Madsen," she said coolly, "how *nice* of you to finally make my acquaintance."

She watched with distaste as he sat himself on the table next to her feet with a rasping laugh, "Oh, Miss Schaeffer, you seem to have gotten yourself *most* comfortable with wit like that!" He sucked his teeth as he unapologetically perused Annie's body with slow, unblinking eyes.

She raised an unimpressed eyebrow at his pathetic attempt at intimidation. "Is there somethin' I can help you with, Mister Madsen?"

"Oh, there are a lot of things you could help me with." He leered as he leaned forward towards her. "But I am here today to offer somethin' to *you*."

"And what, pray tell, could that be?"

"It seems that there is still a little mistrust among the gang as to your intentions while you stay with us. Duke is always *such* a suspicious fella."

"That right?" Annie continued sharpening her blade, making no effort to look at the man in front of her.

He placed a boot at the corner of her seat. "Now, last night which, not to brag, were my idea, really did go a long way to soothin' those feelins."

Annie rolled her eyes. "Oh, well thank you for that!" He ignored her sarcasm and continued. "But, you see, there's some very deep connections against the Schaeffers that run strong here, Annie. And it takes more than a few circus tricks and a... *stimulatin'* outfit to fully accept you as one of us. Now me, personally, I ain't got quarrel with your daddy's gang. Sure, they were a little violent, but it were violent times. I like to see them as opportunists."

"Has this got a point, Mister Madsen?" Annie hadn't ever wanted to get back to chores more in her life. The chatter about Caley Schaeffer's 'opportunistic' lifestyle aggravated her almost as much as Campbell's smarmy conduct.

He put a hand to his chest humbly. "My apologies, Miss Schaeffer, I digressed. What I'm sayin' is that I'm somewhat of a confidante of Mister Needham's. He trusts me totally." "Good for you." She placed the whetstone carefully on top of Chuck's knives.

"*And*, I've kept a very close eye on you since your arrival and thought that you ain't lookin' for trouble. I know you're a good girl, I can make Duke see that."

Madsen casually lifted her braid from its resting place across Annie's shoulder and twirled it in his oil-stained fingers. Fury filled every sinew of her. She chewed the inside of her cheek to keep calm; her body tensed as her tiredness was tipped over the edge by his final action. His blatant leching, the patronising phrasing, and his obvious want to be owed something, snapped Annie. She stood up, slamming her knife's blade into the table, dangerously close to Campbell's crotch. Her knuckles glowed white as she gripped its handle.

She leaned in, her face contorted with utter contempt, kissing distance from Madsen's thick black moustache. "I ain't a good girl, *sir*," she purred threateningly, "I am an *exceptional woman*. If Mister Needham needs further proof that I am worthy to keep around, he can come tell me that himself, rather than sendin' his greasy lice-ridden little ass kisser. I don't need the like of you providin' false promises to get what you want outta me. You think you're the first fella to try and trick me...?" She stood up and looked down her nose at him; her eyes dark, her voice low and menacing. "You're just the first fella to survive it. Good day, Mister Madsen."

She levered her blade from the tabletop, taking a large chunky splinter with it, and marched toward Chuck to deliver his freshly sharpened knives.

***

Nate's deep sleep had been filled with strange dreams of moments from his life – a wild-eyed little girl in a tweed outfit, blindfolded, firing bullets into targets, the death of Martha Needham, the burst of red out the back of Cal Schaeffer's skull, the crackle of lawmen's gunfire as they escaped Missouri. He woke with a start. Breathless and unnerved, he went to wash his face and hack away at the forest sprouting from it. As usual, Annie was already working on her tasks for the day and he watched her finish clearing the detritus from the previous night, then be sent over to Chuck for one of the worst jobs at camp. He got a coffee and went up to Maw Hicks who looked on with some amusement at the scene she'd orchestrated.

"You know, Maw, I'm here to protect Annie as well as keep her in check." He joked. "What you've got her doin' could be seen as torture."

"Which bit?" She smirked, "The chores or her havin' to work so closely with mah Chuckie?"

He laughed into his coffee. "Well, both, I'd say." To her credit Annie was working hard without complaint. Even if she was suffering from slight over-indulgence from the previous night. It was entertaining to see the woman wrapped up like a bandit in her mask. Her determination to be busy did cause problems, however. Nate still needed to check in to see how her week had been. He had spoken to her less since she'd moved to the camp than when she lived in Tinulca.

"Nathan, my boy!"

"Mornin', Duke."

"I think last night was quite a success." His grin was mirrored by the lightness in his voice; there certainly seemed a lot less strain in his deportment.

Maw snorted. "I'm no' surprised the lads have cheered up after everythin' of *that lassie's* was on show."

Duke gave Maw a playful squeeze at her waist. "Oh, Maw, you can't fool us. I spotted the crack of a smile when you watched Tanner pinned to that board!"

She grinned. "Eh, aye, who wouldnae enjoy that?" She bid them farewell and headed off to make Chuck some coffee. Duke turned to Nate. "How are you, son? You rested?"

He eyed his friend with distrust. "Why?"

"Daniel and Sam have some more bounty work outside Tinulca."

He sighed. "Ain't I supposed to be guardin' Miss Schaeffer? Why d'you need me to play nursemaid to everyone?"

"Oh now, Nathan," Duke slapped an arm around the man's shoulder, "Miss Schaeffer has been nothing but amicable, she's no threat to us."

"And what about the threat to her?"

Duke laughed off Nate's concerns. "I think you know she has no fear of that. Besides, I need you to go on this bounty. You're the only one that can keep the boys in check."

"Are we collectin' the bounty, or convincin' them to pay us off?" Nate grumbled.

"Oh to collect for the Sheriff, Nate, *for the Sheriff...* I still believe that keeping in his full sights is preventing us from being noticed as anything more than do-gooders. But..." he confided quietly, "if the bounty has the cash to pay you all handsomely, you can always let him go. I don't think we have need for the Sheriff much longer... Shouldn't take you long!"

"*Fine.*"

The job the men were sent on was a joke. The bounty in question wasn't one man, but a small group of angry, disenfranchised workers who had taken to robbing their boss of his possessions and profits. They were holed up in the woods north of Tinulca, and desperation had made them quick-tempered and violent. The boys took the odd nick with a hunting knife while trying to round the men up, and Sam wound up with a black eye, which no one other than Mr. Clifford seemed upset by. Once Nate had managed to pacify the self-appointed leader, he learned that they had stolen trinkets and coin worth close to $1,000. Considering the reward was worth the same as half the stash, a deal was in order, which Nate suggested at gun point. The Needham Boys headed back to town and explained to the Sheriff that they had been ambushed by the wanted men who then escaped. Thankfully, the shiner on Sam's eye was good enough proof for the lawmen.

By noon, the trio returned to camp, accompanied by a good amount of cash, and the incessant complaints from Sam about his injury.

Nate put the camp's cut of funds in Duke's tent and went looking for lunch. As he headed towards Chuck's wagon, he saw Annie at the centre table doing everything she could to ignore Campbell Madsen's harassment. She so was intensely maintaining a rather magnificent hunting knife, that she hadn't noticed Nathan. The same couldn't be said for Campbell, who flashed a sly grin as he sat unnecessarily close to Miss Schaeffer. Nate watched the conversation carefully; Campbell wasn't above telling Annie about the gang's history with her father, just to cause a problem.

He gritted his teeth and stalked around the edge of the camp, trying to get a better view of them both as Campbell occasionally glanced back in Nathan's direction with a malevolent sparkle in his eyes.

Suddenly, Annie's head turned sharply to Campbell. She shot out of her chair and slammed her knife between his legs. Nate jolted and made his way quickly forwards ready to stop anything worse happening.

He let Annie march off before addressing Campbell. "Enjoyin' yourself, Madsen?"

"What, *brother*? Disappointed you didn't ride in as a white knight and save your precious Princess?"

Nate's day had been frustrating enough without having to now diffuse an infuriated Annie. "I ain't keen on jackasses like you tryna push buttons 'round here is all. She don't need your inputs."

"*Ohhhh,* I plan to give her more than *inputs*, Healey." Madsen's lips peeled back to show his tobacco-stained teeth. "I think it might be just what the girl needs to put her fire out."

Nate squared up to the man and glowered. "Just keep doin' what you're doin', Madsen. I've always wanted to string you up since the law couldn't manage it." He strode off to Annie, away from Campbell's raucous laugh. The man was more rattlesnake than human.

***

Nate found Annie at the back of Chuck's station scrubbing used plates left over from lunch.

"I ain't sure what them pans have done to ya, Annie, but I doubt they deserve such a beatin'."

Slamming the last of the dishware down with a crash, she turned her thunderous face to him. "What d'you want Nathan?"

"A hello would be nice for a start." He snapped. "*Hmpf.*" Annie was in no mood for pleasantries. She had been humiliated, judged, ogled and ignored. She was amazed that she hadn't got herself killed considering how close she had been to ending some lives, and now her patience had surrendered to her anger.

She picked up the basin of dirty water and dispensed it towards Nate, grabbed an empty pail and flounced towards the lake.

"*ANNIE!*" He marched after her. "Don't be actin' like this at me. I ain't in the mood."

She threw the empty bucket at the lake's edge and spun to face him; the crazed look of Caley Schaeffer creeped through her features. "Oh! You ain't in the mood, huh?! I am *so sorry,* Mister Healey, I hope I ain't caused *offense!*"

Nate took a deep breath to stay measured and walked towards her. "You need to calm down, *right now.*" His eyes followed her as she paced back and forth like a caged lion. "You shouldn't be lettin' folks like Campbell Madsen get you riled. It's what he wants."

She stopped and stared at him in disbelief. "You think *Madsen* is capable of gettin' me like this?!" she snorted scornfully. "I have spent more hours locked up in this one goddamned place than I would've got for robbin' a stagecoach. I have been playin' the docile little servin' girl; smilin' sweetly, *takin' crap* from these *people…!*" She sidled up to him; too angry to raise her voice beyond a soft, menacing tone, "I have done everythin' I was told I had to do. I even played the dancin' monkey for their entertainment, and still, I get shit from them."

"You gotta understand, Annie, there's a history between us and the Schaeffers-"

"*A HISTORY THAT AIN'T MINE, NATE!*" She exploded. "I can't be held responsible for the lives that sonofabitch destroyed!" She sat on a nearby boulder, breathless; her head in hands to regain control of herself.

Nathan turned to see some of the camp watching on gleefully. He waved them off, knowing this wouldn't help Annie's cause. He could see her tiring from her outburst. "You done?" He asked lightly as he sat beside her.

She exhaled into her hands, ran them over her face and into her braid which pulled on her scalp. She unpicked her hair and allowed the thick waves to flow behind her like a long shadow. "I guess." She sniffed, turning to wince a smile at her companion. "It's been a long coupla weeks, Nate."

He nodded sagely. Her face returned to that familiar softness with a hint of strain. "I take it you hadn't figured it'd be so hard bein' stuck here?"

"This is the longest I've stayed in one place since I were six years old. And at least most of the folk I were with my whole life didn't wish me dead."

Nathan sighed. "They don't want you dead, Annie. They're just..." he looked at his hands, trying to find the right words to describe his friends, "... they're protective is all. And when somethin' new happens with a link to bad feelins, it can be hard to change their minds." He gave Annie a gentle look.

"I ain't expectin' to be treated like one of you." She said mildly. "I just need a new view. This lake ain't so pretty after a while." Nate couldn't help but laugh. All fire and fight from her had evaporated as fast as it arrived. Her impatience was somehow endearing when it wasn't trying to rip out his throat. The lowering sun enveloped her in an aura of orange as she looked out across the lake. He could see why men took great pleasure in her company, and why they managed to underestimate her at every turn.

"I'm bein' wasted here." She turned to him with a determined expression. "At least let me go huntin'. The carcasses some of you bring back ain't even worth skinnin'!"

He patted her hand and got up to leave, filling the abandoned pail to take back to Chuck. "I'll see what I can do but, Annie, don't expect too much right away. Folk seem impressed with you, and you've won 'em over for the most part. But it's gonna take time and outbursts like this ain't gonna help your cause. You need to keep a lid on it and come talk to me if you got troubles, *and*," he raised his hand against her protests, "if I ain't around, leave a note. I'll see it. Maybe get good rest, tonight."

"Fine."

He walked back to the camp with the pail; a little annoyed by the group's reluctance to let Annie in. She hadn't shown any interest in the more criminal aspects of their activities, which wouldn't be such a problem if she could provide food and pelts. She could certainly handle herself in the wilderness and could keep everyone well fed for months. Then again, there were none he could trust to escort her and bring her back alive, and he felt that Duke wouldn't be too worried about that. Perhaps she could start using those targets.

"Is Miss Schaeffer alright, Nate?"

"She's fine, Chuck, just needed a minute. I'm gonna have a word with Maw, tell her to rest Annie for a while. Give her the chance to show some of the folk how to throw a knife." "Sounds like a plan. Maybe we can get her out huntin' too. The amount of buckshot in some of this meat is ridiculous." Looking towards the lake, he saw Annie marching defiantly back into camp. She really was a force to be reckoned with, and he admired her for having kept her anger under wraps for so long. He knew that he had broken his promise to her more times than was respectable, and he found it odd that Duke had kept him so busy away from the duty he had bestowed originally. Once she had stormed into her lodgings, Nathan made his way to Duke to discuss her employment.

"Seems like all Schaeffers have a temperament." Duke smirked into his cigar as Nate approached him.

"I'm guessin' you ain't too impressed with that scene?" "Nathan, that woman has been here nearly two weeks without a bad word uttering from those pretty lips. She has kept her head down. Campbell was just playing with her, but I've spoken to him, and he knows he took it too far."

"Campbell Madsen is, and always has been, a jackass."

"We all can be, kiddo, but I'm assuming that you came over to talk about Miss Schaeffer, and *not* Madsen?"

"She's gettin' bored, Duke. She feels wasted scrubbin' plates in this place…"

"She's been an *asset,* so Chuck told me."

"Yeah, well." Nate lit a cigarette. "I'm sure Chuck ain't been ungrateful for the help, but even he's askin' for better meat in camp. I ain't been around much to hunt and let's face it, few of the others are either interested or any good at feedin' folk."

Duke turned with a bemused expression to Nate. "And you want me to put her on her horse, rifle in hand, and believe she's just going to ride out of here without issue, under the supposition of *hunting?*"

"Not on her own. I'm just tryna offer a solution to avoidin' further dramas."

"When it comes to ideas for Miss Schaeffer, I think it best you keep them to yourself, Nathan." Duke's eyes glinted with childish teasing.

"So let her start teachin' folk. She's got everythin' set up; she's shown everyone what she can do. She don't even need to leave camp. We've got some spare knives somewhere."

"I'll think on it, Nate. Take some rest, Tommy wants you up at Edgenest Estate tomorrow afternoon and you're looking tired."

***

Annie lay on her bed and stared at the photographs beside her. Both images were of the showcase's performers; one from her early days, the other taken a year previous. Sally had barely aged, though her tattoos had increased. Looking at herself staring out from the images, Annie sighed; the wild-eyed child in a cutesy prairie costume fired a rebellious glare back. The darkness of the Schaeffer family pierced the image, and she could feel that stirring inside again. Her Schaeffer side hadn't ever really left, but she had learned to control it. The showcase had used her most fruitful skills to protect them on the road, but Smythson's departure from this earth had been a glimpse of what she was truly capable of. Being stuck here was, as Clara put it, making her itchy, and the constant distrust from those around her was an invitation to shake her control loose.

"I don't get adults arguin'."

A tired but cocky voice brought Annie back from her daydreams. She sat up. "Recovered after your antics last night have you, Mikey?"

"I'm perfectly fine... Sun just got to me through the day is all."

"... *Uh-Huh.*" Annie smirked as the kid shuffled into the shade of her tent. "Come in why dontcha? Don't wait for the invite."

"Why were you arguin' with Nate?"

She smiled. "Oh now we weren't arguin', Mikey, I was yellin' at him. Nate was just lettin' a lady yell. It were a good example in how best to survive a feral woman. You'd do well to remember that for when you're older." She eyed him suspiciously. "Is there somethin' I can help you with...? You hidin' from someone?"

"Duke's tryna give me lessons Lucky set." Mikey mumbled, scuffing his shoes at the ground.

"In what?" Annie scoffed.

"I dunno...! I... don't wait 'round to find out..."

He trailed off as Annie rolled her eyes. "Look, I keep my doorway open 'cause I have to, but that don't mean you can just come over here and talk to me when you're meant to be doin' somethin' for Lucky. What if it were somethin' real interestin'?"

"It's never interestin'!" he looked up at her incredulously, "'sides, Duke don't put effort in findin' me when I have stuff to do for Lucky, and we both sorta agree I done it. Anyway, Lucky's too busy workin'. But you're here and you seem to have interestin' stories I think you should share."

"If I had a choice, I'd be out workin' too."

"Is that *you*??" Mikey was staring at an illustration of Annie that had been made to advertise her act on posters in the towns they toured. She awkwardly removed it from the wooden side of the wagon. "A very flatterin' drawin' of me, yes. I were younger then…" She gently thumbed the edges of the yellowing paper and looked at the young 21-year-old beaming out at her; the more sellable points of her body emphasised, her costume more revealing than it was in reality and tattoos were drawn up her arms. She was standing on the body of a dead man as if he was a trophy kill. It saddened her.

"I's gonna say! You ain't half as pretty these days, you're gettin' old!"

"Hell, Mikey! Way to make a woman feel good about herself!" She punched the kid's arm hard and he laughed.

"What's it say on there?"

"What? Your young eyes not able to see the words?" Mikey looked down sheepishly. "I- erm… Well, readin' ain't my thing."

Annie looked at him pityingly. "Sounds like you should start takin' those lessons from Lucky, huh…?" She cleared her throat and dramatically flicked the poster so it would stiffen, and then started to read.

"Smythson's Traveling Vaudeville Showcase Presents… The Devil of Dakota The Incomparable Knife and Gun Wielder The Intimidating Dead Eye Annie Schaeffer"

"What does '*intimidatin*' mean?"

"It means she can scare folk if she needs to, Mikey." Nate's silhouette blocked some of the orange sunlight as he appeared.

"Nate! What was it Tommy was sayin' 'bout Annie's *special*

magic yesterday?"

Nate marched over to the smirking teen and escorted him out of the tent, "Mikey, why don't you actually go do whatever you're meant to be doin' for once? You might end up learnin' how to be an even bigger pain in the ass!" He stifled his laugh and forced a serious glare at the boy's cheeky face as Mikey said his farewells.

"That boy is far smarter than he wants us to believe."

"So it seems. Though I don't see why Tommy should be discussin' my *special skills* in the first place..." Annie sighed. "Look, Nate, everythin' earlier… it just finally got to me."

"I know. Listen, I talked to Duke-"

"Was he mad?" Annie stood to return the poster to its point of display.

"Not overly. He's seen you manage everythin' for the last couple weeks without issue, plus he's got more pressin' matters to worry about. I suggested that you start trainin' folk on how to throw knives and such. He's thinkin' on it, I'm guessin' it'll be a yes. Now it ain't huntin', but it's a start."

"Thank you, Nathan." That signature Annie smile was haloed by the glow of summer light in her surroundings.

"You're welcome." Aware he was staring, Nate cleared his throat and gestured to the small photographs behind her. "That the folks you traveled with?"

"Yeah," Annie picked the two small photographs from the wooden wall by her bed and walked over to him, "taken 'bout twenty years apart." Her eyes were locked in a loving gaze at the images, a warm involuntary smile spread from her lips.

"I recognize this feral lookin' creature!" Nate joked as he pointed to infant Annie glaring out from the early image. "That can't've been far off the time I saw you as a kid."

"It's probably about a couple of years into that life by then. Still spendin' most days tryna run off, kickin' punchin' and bitin' Smythson whenever he punished me for it." She laughed bitterly. "I'm surprised you survived."

Annie looked at him with some amusement. "I were still a

Schaeffer then, Mister Healey. It would take more than a weak-punchin' string bean of a man to break my spirit!"

"So, what did?" He joked.

Annie pointed at a woman in the photograph seated on the ground, limbs tied in knots, in front of the young gunslinger.

"Sally." The volume of Annie's voice faded as she explained. "If Smythson had his way, he would've made sure I got wilder and more dangerous as I aged. Anythin' to keep the *money rollin' in*. If it weren't for Sally, I'd be dead by now… probably at the end of a rope." Nate looked at her. He knew that whatever Sally had done to get Annie to salvation was capable of unravelling if the conditions were right.

"I regret every day leavin' her behind." She smirked. "Don't think she'd get on so *amicably* with Maw though."

The beige canvas of Annie's lodgings gave a warm tone to the inside and the space was heavy with the familiar floral scent that could be so very distracting. Her belongings were inherent to a performer in a travelling show; the poster she had been showing Mikey beamed out flirtatiously towards him from its home on the wagon siding above her bed. An old empty barrel beside that held her lamp, accompanied by a well-thumbed book and a spritz bottle he believed must hold the perfume she insisted on wearing all the time.

Between the barrel and the tent's doorway sat a large, red-stained wooden trunk with brass metal fastenings that he imagined held more keepsakes from her years as '*Dead Eye Annie*'; and at the foot of her bed was a small, dark-wood upright cabinet that held her regular attire.

He turned his gaze to her and smiled. "I'm sure you can hold your own without her, Annie. She's brought you up well." He slapped her shoulder a little too casually as he left. "Get some rest."

10

We all Carry Ghosts

Annie looked up. The dense trees stood unnaturally tall, and what little of the grey sky she could see was filled with the screech of birds as their black outlines darted across her view. There was a strange metallic sheen to everything around her as if the light reflected off every surface. She looked down and saw the ground swell with dead leaves until she could barely see her raggedy shoes. Her body felt heavy; her heart ached as it tried to punch its way out of her chest with every determined thump.

"ANNIE!"

She drew her sleeve across her nose and looked ahead of her. A boy of 17 stood opposite, held at the elbow by one of the gang. He was so much bigger than her, she thought; his face was streaked with tears, and with his lip trembling he tried to beg his way out of it all.

"ANNIE! For shit's sake what are you doin'? This is the *asshole* that robbed ya, right?" Annie sniffled and looked up at her father; his eyes were practically black, and his thick dark hair crawled out from under his hat. She winced as his grip on her left shoulder almost cracked her collarbone. *"So stop bloody cryin' about it,* and be a goddamn *Schaeffer!"*

She looked to her right. The green eyes of her mother flicked between Annie and Caley. "Cal! She's not ready... Maybe you should just show her once more… she-she's only-"

"Shut the hell up, Lizzie! She's gotta learn sometime." He shook Annie violently, and she yelped. *"No one* messes with a Schaeffer, girl."

"Cal! He's just a *boy*! He didn't know better!"

The pain in Annie's shoulder dulled as her father marched over to her mother, grabbing her tightly by the throat with one hand; his knuckles white against her blueing skin. "You goin' soft on me, Lizzie?" He menaced through gritted teeth. "You think you can speak on these matters, eh? You think *my child* is goin' to show up this gang?" He twisted his body to look at Annie. "That's not goin' to happen now, is it lass?" Annie shook her head, gasping for air as she held back tears.

Her father effortlessly dragged Elizabeth Schaeffer one-handed towards their daughter; her mother's eyes bulging and bloodshot as they rolled back into her head, her mouth gaped for what oxygen she could reach.

The noise of her father's demands, her mother's gasps, the boy's whines of fear, the shriek of birds in the trees and Annie's own sobs filled her ears. The world spun. She couldn't make out any detail and thought she might vomit.

"*ANNIE!*"

SLAP.

The sharp sting of Caley Schaeffer's backhand whipped across her face sending her to the ground, was instantly replaced by the rib-cracking *thud* of the Irishman's steel-tipped boot in her midriff. "Get up. *Get. Up. NOW.* I don't want your mother dyin' before it's done."

"Mister, I-I'm sorry! I didn't mean nothin' by it! I-I was just bein' dumb… I-I didn't know it was your-"

"Then why'd you do it, son, eh? You think pickin' on a little kid is the action of a big man?"

"P-please! Little girl, Annie… I-"

"*DON'T YOU SAY HER GODDAMN NAME…!* If you wanna be a man, you gotta accept your fates. The only reason you're not dead yet is 'cause *she's* gonna take your apology *the Schaeffer way.*"

Annie had pulled herself up from the ground. Every piece of her screamed with pain. She looked across at her mother trying desperately to loosen the vice around her neck, then she turned her gaze to the boy ahead of her. His face morphed into that of Caley Schaeffer. Through the din and arguing, the cries and whoops from the men, Annie stood tall, raised her pistol, and pulled the trigger.

She found herself sitting bolt upright in bed; her hunting knife thrust forward into the darkness. As she caught her breath, the chill of night crept across her sweat-drenched skin. Carefully placing the knife back under her pillow, Annie wiped her brow with trembling hands, and sat quietly in her tent, straining to hear any noise beyond her own heartbeat. All was still. She heaved herself out of bed, stretched her aching limbs and peeked outside; it was a clear night, and the moon shone brightly on the lake. There was movement in the distance from people on night patrol, but it was otherwise peaceful. Many of the gang were either snoring soundly or out on their own errands.

Her nerves were shot, and she needed to wash that memory from her mind. She grabbed two blankets from her trunk and walked to the lake's breakwater, picking through the darkness. She took her time, focusing on the textures her steps encountered, from the silky fronds of grass to the chalky shoreline. The roughness of the wooden jetty was warm under foot compared to the dew-soaked ground by her tent. Placing the blankets at the edge, she closed her eyes and inhaled deeply; lifting her nightgown over her head, allowing her hair to tumble over her bare shoulders as her garment dropped softly to the floor. She took a moment to stand naked in the moonlight, looking out to the blackness of the lake; the horizon seemed to stretch back forever. She stared down at her reflection in the water. Having been in the summer sun of the South these past months, she noticed significant changes in her skin tone; there were definite lines between the exposed and covered parts of her body; her hands much darker than the paleness of her stomach. Reaching to ease the tightness in her shoulders, she felt the raised scarring of the whip marks on her back.

She stepped forward, curling her toes over the jetty's edge before sitting down to place her legs in the lapping water, then slid herself into the cool, welcoming arms of Onti Lake. As she sank into the darkness, she felt the light stir of fish around her. Upon resurfacing she ran her hands back over her hair, looked towards the camp, and swam out as far as she could.

She had no idea how long she had been out, and she didn't care. The moonlight bounced all around her like a spotlight as she floated peacefully, contemplating if she really needed to return. Eventually, the very edge of dawn glowed on the horizon, and she decided that a naked runaway wasn't going to get far.

When she finally closed in on the jetty, she saw a slim figure standing by her belongings. "You know that isn't the safest place to go swimming, Miss Schaeffer!" Lucky Needham stood at the edge chuckling to himself.

"I'm pretty sure the fish are more scared of me kickin' them than anythin' else."

"I have no doubt that's true."

"This is the cleanest I've been in weeks, Lucky," she said lightly, clinging to the jetty's leg so as not to drown, "and I ain't been eaten yet, so I figure I'm alright."

"I would be more concerned that those lumber men across the way would try to gather you in a net." Lucky smiled and turned on his heel, walking to the end of the jetty, waiting with his back to her as she hauled herself onto the wooden slats, wrapped her blankets tightly around herself, and joined him.

"What are you doin' sneakin' about at this time of night, scarin' swimmers anyhow?" She teased as he hesitantly turned to look at her, "I thought you'd be retired from night watches by now." "Less of the age-related insults, young lady, I'm spry for a man of my age and I could shoot you if necessary!" The lightness in his tone as he reprimanded her caused them both to laugh. "The only downside of getting older is there seems to be many more ways to be disturbed at night. *Ablutions* included."

"I sincerely hope that ain't the reason I shouldn't go swimmin' in there." Annie teased as they moved towards a tree just on the shoreline and sat on the grass at its roots.

"I can't speak for the rest of those terrors, but you're safe from me at least. In actuality, I got woken up by Tommy and Nathan returning from some work." He nodded towards the camp, "Tommy is never particularly quiet when he's here, and he always likes to celebrate a job done well with a few drinks and a song, much to everyone's distaste at this hour. So, I took a walk and saw your… *Items.*" He gestured towards the nightgown in Annie's hand as she held the blankets to her with the other, "Why were you out there? I thought you may have done something drastic."

"I had a bad dream." She shuffled in her blankets and looked down at her toes. "This place brings up some old things I don't like, and it ain't helped by people already decidin' who I am."

Lucky nodded sympathetically. "It must be tough." He calmly looked out towards the water. "You've done well so far, keeping your head down."

"Don't have much choice, Lucky. It ain't like y'all gonna allow me freedoms to come and go as I please, is it?"

"You know, life brings pain and challenges at different times. What makes it difficult is that pain might hit when it seems no one else is suffering." Lucky picked at his fingernails and sighed. "It comes to us all sometime. The trick is to have people you can trust to help."

"Must be nice for those that do." Annie muttered.

"Annie Schaeffer, you do forget yourself." Lucky gently reprimanded. "You are here because you had help from my boy." Annie froze. "Nate is… and *Danny*…? They're-"

"*Adopted.* It's a long story, but yes." A small twinkle hit Lucky's eyes. "Long before all this, it was just the boys, Martha and I… *Until*… Gambling, Miss Schaeffer, is a dangerous vice. Especially when you ow money to the Fitzgeralds. If it hadn't been for my brother, we may not even be here. He worked for them as a younger man..." Lucky swatted away his thoughts. "That's all done and gone now, anyhow. We are where we are." He turned to Annie and winced a smile. "What I'm trying to say, Annie, in a *very* garbled, round-about-way, is that you can only play the hand you're dealt, and you have played yours with elegance, and certainly far more successfully than many of us can compare to."

She didn't say anything. Lucky's kind words were just whispers on the breeze to her. He didn't know what she had done, and if any of them did, she would be back in that lake with a bag of iron tied to her ankles.

"You know," Lucky mused, "Duke said Domhnall Fitzgerald always spoke highly of Cal Schaeffer?"

"I bet he did."

"Said he was a man that got things done. Didn't care of the consequences to anyone else, as long as he got what he needed from a situation."

"Sounds about right."

"Fitzgerald wanted to be like him."

Annie turned to Lucky with a look of disgust. "Well, that's a horrific thing to hear. But, as awful as that fella might be, he ain't ever gonna be Caley Schaeffer." She scoffed. "Hell don't create two the same, 'less there's a bloodline." Annie's dream had shaken her. She knew her restlessness came from something far darker than sleep deprivation.

She felt a warm hand on her shoulder. "You shouldn't worry, Annie," Lucky reassured her gently, "you're a good woman. You keep your head and manage each hostility with grace. Don't fool yourself into thinking you're your father."

The sincerity in the old man's eyes comforted her. He had been through a lot it seemed, and yet he still managed to find the goodness in people. She smiled sadly pulling herself up to leave.

"Thank you, Lucky. G'night."

"Good Morning."

Annie rose late after returning to an undisturbed sleep. The swim had removed some of the excess energy she had, and her talk with Lucky had given her perspective. The respite from the Hicks's incessant chores brought relaxation for the first time in weeks. After a futile attempt to rake a comb through her damp hair, she decided to tame the ever-expanding waves with a loose braid. She changed into a grey striped cotton blouse and navy riding pants; their wide leg styling kept her cool in the increasing humidity. She donned her hat and made her way out to grab a coffee, glancing across to Nathan's tent she could see her neighbour had safely returned from his legally ambiguous adventure, and she smiled as she moved towards the campfire.

"Good Morning, Miss Schaeffer!" Duke greeted her lightly as he joined her en-route to the coffee. "You seem well rested today."

"I am indeed. I slept soundly at last." She collected the pot and poured for Duke first.

"Thank you my dear, tired out from your ravings perhaps?" He grinned at her playfully as he sipped from his cup.

"Oh, well-"

He waved his hand to silence her. "Don't worry, Annie, no harm done, especially as you seemed to aim your rage towards Mister Healey." He joked, "Besides, I understand how Mister Madsen can cause upset among some of the camp; he's felt the sting of Marie's hand many times. I have spoken to him, and he apologizes."

Annie nodded and sipped her coffee, hoping that her irritability didn't show through.

"You seemed quite vocal about the part you're playing here, young lady."

"I think y'all could benefit from my abilities more." She shrugged.

Duke stood back and studied his latest addition to camp. Being the great dramatist he was, he rubbed his chin in false contemplation. "*How about* we get you teaching your skills...?" It took all of Annie's strength to keep a straight face, "I mean you've got your space up and ready, and it would be most useful for all the family to be as competent as you and the Healey brothers."

"That is a fantastic idea, Duke!" Her thinly veiled compliment seemed strong enough to camouflage her sarcasm, judging from Duke's smile.

"Excellent, Miss Schaeffer! You can start today. I shall make everyone aware."

***

"Jesus," Nate whispered through gritted teeth in the dark. *"How do I even get convinced to do these things with you?"*

"Ah shut up, Healey, just move through here." The pair scrambled as quietly as was possible up and out through a coal chute at the big old sugar plantation house outside Tinulca. Thanks to his persistent attempts at charming housemaids, Thomas Kelley (as he referred to himself while courting), had managed to seduce one into providing useful information about her cantankerous boss, and where he stashed his most expensive items. She had let them in late in the evening to rob the house, but their escape was far more difficult, as a large clattering from the kitchen brought the Head Butler to investigate. Their only option had been the coal chute.

*"What a goddamn **oaf** you are, Kelley!"* Nate hissed as he wriggled free of the chute's doors with difficulty; pulling the loot *and* Tommy out after him, "Why were you even *in* there?!"

"I had to thank that lovely girl for her help somehow didn't I?" Kelley grinned; his teeth almost glowing against the coal dust covering his face. "And I'm guessin' I'll not get to be seein' her again." He chuckled, slapping Nate's arm as he scurried towards their horses.

"Can't you keep it in your pants for one goddamn second?" Nate caught up with him.

"Relax, old man! Just 'cause you can't remember the way under a skirt doesn't mean you have to stop everyone else's fun!" "I think you'll find *you* did that when your *whimsical Irish ways* made her swoon, Thomas." Nate laughed with his friend as both men tore across the lands of Mississippi by moonlight. As intense as the evening's exploits had been, Nathan enjoyed working with Tommy. If nothing else, they always got a good story from whatever ridiculous plan he came up with.

"Hey! We got a good haul, and Duke was more than happy to let me set this up." He called from his horse.

"Yeah, well, Duke ain't the one covered in goddamn coal!" Nate grumbled as the stench of soot leaked out of his clothes. "And I got to have a little fumble thrown into the mix."

"Strange how you don't pursue Miss Dotty in similar fashion." Nate chided.

The two slowed their horses as the entrance to Onti Lake appeared through the darkness. It was late, nearer morning now, and Tommy's exuberance from the evening hadn't diminished as the pair descended from their mounts, split their share of the take and went separate ways. Tommy immediately headed for the whiskey, ensuring he woke as many of the nearby sleepers in the process. *To be young again.* Nate thought.

He looked around, those who had been disturbed by Tommy's welcome settled back down as a drowsy Maw shoved him towards a distant area of the lake to drink his booze away from the gang. Depositing the camp's share of looted trinkets, Nate looked across to his neighbour. There was no light or sense of movement. He was surprised Annie hadn't been disturbed by Tommy's antics, maybe she was finally used to the strange hours the Needham Boys kept. He heaved himself towards his bed and slumped down. The distant sounds of Tommy singing played on the light breeze around the site, it reminded Nate of happier times of his own. He reached across to the framed poem and read it quietly to himself.

Sighing, he opened the back of the frame and looked at the photograph he hid there; a faded image of him and Louisa; the author of the verse. She was a woman he felt he had mistreated so easily. She had known Marie in Iowa, and after a torrid affair, Louisa told him she loved him. She was young and silly, and he was uninterested in her attachment to him. Even in that image, his face showed his apathy. She was just a good lay, and an admirable ornament on his arm when he wanted. He had always kept the note as a lesson to be better, to be the man Martha and Lucky had expected him to be. Giving the image one final lingering stare, he removed the items from the frame and crumpled them in his fist, crept to the closest campfire, and dropped the bundle into the embers before returning to his tent and looking across towards

Annie's own dwelling. He had been better to someone that deserved it for once; maybe he had turned a corner.

He pulled his coke-infused garb from his body, stripped down to his union suit, and lay on his bunk. His skin felt thick and leathered from the coal, he must get washed tomorrow he thought.

***

Nate lay still as the daylight pawed at his closed eyes. If anyone thought he was awake they would no doubt want something from him, and he wanted to enjoy a well-earned lie-in. His shoulders were bruised and stiff, and his skin almost sticky from the coal residue they had scraped their way through in that constrictive chute.

He was undisturbed for some hours, maybe people finally felt he deserved a rest, though it could also be due his present lack of grooming. The air around him hung with the stale odours of hard work. He needed to wash, change, and feel human again, but his weary body fought all urges to get up.

Finally, hunger overtook his need to rest so he pulled his aching frame up out of bed, and sloped towards the inviting vapours of Chuck's miscellaneous concoction. *"I must be starvin' if that's encitin'."* He muttered.

"MR HEALEY!" Nate had barely reached for the ladle when an astounded Maw Hicks marched towards him. *"WHAT* in the *hell* are ye doin'?!"*

"I'm gettin' somethin' to eat, Maw, if that's all the same to you?"

"Not like that you're no'!" she grabbed his plate from him and shoved him towards his lodgings. "Honestly! Wandrin' around in your skegs… Folks are eatin'!"

"I know! I'm tryna be one of 'em!" he laughed along with his fellow bystanders out of over-tiredness, and snatched his meal back, downing the hot mush as fast as he could. He smiled and handed the plate back to the scowling Maw.

"Get yourself in that lake right this instant, you *reek*!" his sister protested.

"Oh, don't you start, Clara! Can't you go pick on Danny instead? Or are you used to *his* stink?"

"*GO!*" Clara shoved Nate in the chest with a laugh and the two women watched, arms folded, as he shuffled to collect a blanket and a change of clothes before being motioned to take himself to a more secluded area of the lake to bathe.

He trudged towards an edge not far from the site and peeled his union suit from his body. Even at arm's length the smell emanating from it was potent. "I should just burn this." He grimaced as he flung the ripe garment as far from himself as he could. He placed his blanket and fresh clothes on a boulder near the water's edge, took his ragged bar of soap and dipped into the lake, the water stung like icy hands, causing him to shiver as he attempted to scrub himself clean as quickly as he could. He looked back towards camp to try and focus on something other than the cold reducing his manhood, and in the distance, he saw Annie organising the practice area. Her behaviour seemed lighter than he had seen since that night of drinking at the Saloon in Tinulca. She almost skipped as she tended to her duties and carried herself proudly as he watched Clara greet her.

***

By noon Annie had pulled the training equipment together from her show trunk and made sure all the targets were ready. It wasn't long before Clara appeared, a bundle of throwing knives in her hands. "I hear you're finally open for teachin', Annie?"

"That's right, Mrs Healey," she grinned, "though I'm surprised to see you here, I thought your ability to scrap with a gun would be enough."

"It never hurts to be subtle sometimes," she shrugged, "and if I run outta bullets I have another option."

"Well, as true as that is, and as sure as I am that all them bullets would end up in Danny's arm, have you ever thrown a knife other than in an argument?"

"Not that I can recall, but that must count, surely?"

Annie laughed and removed the knives from Clara's hands, placing them on the ground by her targets. "Judgin' by your already *sterlin'* reputation as a gunslinger, I think it's safe to say no, it don't count." She picked up a small crate of what looked like wooden daggers and dropped them at Clara's feet, she then opened a small jar of red ink and began to dip the point of the tips into it, placing each painted plank on the ground. "You ain't gettin' *near* a blade until I know you can hit a target with these." Clara looked at the wooden toys with horror. "*These*?! I ain't a child, Annie."

"Then stop actin' like one and pick it up!" She laughed as a disgruntled Clara begrudgingly collected up the nearest plank. "Now, once I've seen the red ink *hit* that target, and *more than once,* I'll maybe hand you a real piece of steel." "This is ridiculous," Clara snapped, "it's just throwin' a knife." "Okay then, throw it." Annie stepped aside, hands on hips with a know-it-all expression as she watched Clara fling the prop, blade-first, with a force that stuck the slat sharply into the soft earth two feet away from its starting point.

She looked from its landing point to a sulking Clara.

"Shut the hell up, Annie."

Annie smiled. "I said nothin'… but you're about six feet short and the only way you'd kill someone with that is if the fella ran at you, tripped over it and broke his neck." Laughing, Annie walked over to the dispatched training knife, wrenched it out of the sod, re-dipped the end in ink and handed it back to her trainee. "Are you ready to actually *listen* to me now?" She teased.

"Fine."

"Well that'll be a first." Nate joked as he greeted the pair, fresh from his ice bath in the lake. He leaned against the large tree beside Clara and lit a cigarette as he grinned at Annie, interested to watch how she'd begin teaching her stubborn equal.

Returning the smile, Annie continued with her lesson. She exhaled sharply. "Okay, Clara, first we gotta sort the way you're standin'." She grabbed Clara by the hips, kicked her right leg forward and twisted her slightly. "There. Now take the blade like this." Again, Annie manhandled Clara, thrusting the wooden knife into her hand, placing the blade between her thumb and forefinger. "Okay bend your legs a little, try to relax."

"*Relax*? I hope the fellas you been with like it rough, I feel like you shoulda taken me to dinner first!" she looked at Nathan. '*Relax*', she says."

"Hey!" Annie clicked her fingers to gain Clara's attention. "He ain't needin' to get involved in this." She turned to Nate now accompanied by Danny, both chuckling. "Don't you be two be causin' ruckus, else I'll send you packin'. In fact," she collected the bundle of knives and thrust them into Nate's hands, "keep a hold of these, and make sure Clara don't throw 'em at me."

Swallowing his laugh, Nate stood up straight with and saluted. "Yes, Ma'am." He teased as she shot him a look before turning back to the job in hand.

Afternoon bled into evening, and with a lot of tough coaching from Annie, Clara finally proved herself worthy of taking on a real knife. The commotion and laughter of the day had drawn a crowd, and the practice area now looked like the scene of a massacre. Red ink splatters decorated the grass and dotted the soft pine target. The breeze was picking up and with it came spots of rain.

"Alright, Clara, this is your last chance today. The light's goin' fast and the wind's pickin' up. You ain't ready for fightin' new weather conditions yet. Here," Annie handed Clara the gleaming steel blade, "set it up, and throw it."

The stillness of the audience was only marred by the rustle of leaves in the tree Nate leaned against. His hands rested on his belt as he and his brother watched on. Stepping between the Healeys and her student, Annie placed a gentle hand on Clara's shoulder, leaned close to her and gave her voice a warm, reassuring tone.

"You know what you're doin' now, Clara. Just take your time, focus on where you want the knife to go, breathe out and throw it."

Annie backed away to give her room and held her breath.

Clara locked her determined gaze on the target ten feet away, checked her stance, drew in all the air her lungs could hold. Controlling the exhale, she raised her arm, and released the blade. A metallic flash whipped through the air, and with a dull *thud* stuck in the target, close to its centre. The faces of both student and teacher lit up with triumph. With relief Annie grabbed her friend in a victorious embrace as the crowd around them responded with applause and back pats. Annie broke from the group to retrieve the blade, sheathed it with the others, and passed the bundle to Clara.

"Here. You got the basics, just keep practicin', and don't be usin' them on folks that irritate ya."

"I ain't promisin' anythin', Annie." She joked, winking at her husband. "Thank you."

"I didn't do much really."

"I still think you owe me a meal!" Clara called as she left to put her new weapons away.

"Nice work, Miss Schaeffer." Nate walked up to her as she cleared the mess, a deep smile stretched across his stubbled face. "Though it was probably wise to keep those knives from her 'til enough witnesses gathered." The rain was starting to come down more determinedly, and the pair walked to relative shelter as they talked.

"You gotta know who you're dealin' with." She confessed. "A lotta you are pretty stubborn folk, I'd probably have to treat y'all the same. I'm sure the fellas wouldn't mind bein' grabbed by a lady."

He looked out towards the camp as they stopped under the awning of his lodgings. "No I don't think they'd mind at all." he laughed.

Annie smiled at him. Her guard was uncharacteristically low as she looked at the figure in front of her. His weathered face held the shadow of a man who hadn't shaved in days, and his blue eyes smiled out playfully from under the shade of his hat. "You ain't such a curmudgeon you know, Mister Healey?"

He shifted a little closer, his arms folded across his chest. "That right?"

"I think you just like to *seem enigmatic*." She said, flirtatiously grinning up at him.

"Great work, Miss Schaeffer!" Lucky Needham brought the world back into focus. "Really, great work."

"Thank you, Lucky," Annie smiled as the three huddled in Nate's quarters, "I'm just glad someone wanted to learn somethin' from me."

"You're a talented lady, Annie, they would be fools not to take the opportunity to hone their skills. I think you'll be kept quite busy going forward, judging from their responses. I know Mikey will be looking to get taught."

"Well, he should focus on his *proper lessons*, first." Annie smiled.

"HEY! *Schaeffer*! You ain't so impressive." The three turned towards the entrance of Nate's tent, and saw the bulky frame of Sam Clifford, bottle in hand, wavering slightly on his feet. Annie felt the two men beside her tense up.

"Sam," Lucky stepped out of the tent, "get out and do some goddamn work." Annie was taken back by Lucky's harsh tone, she had never heard him raise his voice in all her time confined at camp.

Nathan began to step from their shelter as Sam struck up again. "*All* pally now with goddamn *Schaeffers*, eh, Lucky? I don't think it right."

"Shut up, Sam." Nate calmly readied himself to shut the fool's mouth.

"It ain't *natural*. I seen 'em all playin' nice with you, Schaeffer, you ain't foolin' the likes of me. You don't deserve a welcome here. Not for what your daddy did."

Annie took a deep breath and pushed out into the rain. "Cal Schaeffer upset a lotta folk, Sam, I ain't surprised he did the same here."

"Well that was the mistake he made, weren't it? *Killin' Martha*

Needham." Sam laughed maliciously as Nate snatched him by his shirt collar. "He never upset no one again after that, ain't that right, Nate?"

"You shut your goddamn mouth, *right now*, Clifford, or God help me I'm gonna shut it permanently."

Annie looked from Lucky's pained face, across to Nate, who was wrestling with the idiot. As she sidled up to Sam Clifford, she drew herself to her full height, still some inches shorter than the drunk in front of her. "Were you there, Sam? When all this happened?" She looked at him calmly, the struggling relented as Nathan stared at Annie in astonishment.

"No. I weren't. But tha-"

"Well, I weren't neither. And it would do you good to remember that when you see me next. I can't help what that prize-winnin' asshole did to folk, just like you can't help bein' a prize-winnin' asshole yourself." She removed Nate's grip from Sam's collar; her eyes locked defiantly on her target. "Now," she exhaled, "I suggest that you listen to what Lucky says and make yourself useful by draggin' your sorry ass outta here and doin' some goddamn work." She remained static; jaw locked with anger as Nathan shoved Sam away, knocking the bottle from his grasp. Lucky sighed, placing his head in his hands.

"I'm sorry, Lucky." She looked at him softly.

He looked up. "Did you kill her…?"

"… No, but I-"

"Then you have nothing to apologize for." He forced a smile. "My dear, we can't be blamed for the actions of others. Sam Clifford is a drunk, ex-gunslinger; bitter because one of Cal's men shot him in the ass rather than worry about killing him. I have had quite enough of him lately. You *are* welcome here, Annie. Mister Clifford, on the other hand, is starting to be questionable." The old man patted her hand and went towards his bed to calm down, leaving Annie to stand alone contemplating Sam's revelations.

"What in the hell is wrong with you??" Nate's anger had taken charge of the situation as he held the drunk by his throat against a

tree a distance from camp. "You think that was a good idea? You feel *better* now?" He let go and Sam dropped to the ground to catch his breath. Nathan paced in a circle, hands on hips, unable to look at his friend.

"I-I'm sorry, Nate," he coughed, "I just find it a little sour y'all fraternisin' with someone like that, I mean, Marth-"

"Martha Needham was killed by a gang of soulless, outlaws *twelve years after* Annie left!" he roared over the sounds of solid rainfall. "We did what was needed, there ain't no more to it." Breathless from his irritations, he forced himself to calm down. "And considerin' you weren't even with us then I find it interestin' that you feel the need to protect them that were. Stop drinkin' and get outta my site 'til I can stand to look at you."

Annie stood in the rain where Nate had left her. Her solitary figure seemed defeated. She wrung her hands as she stared at the ground. Her clothes, now drenched, clung to her and as he approached her she seemed small. "Come on, Annie, you should get outta this weather."

Her eyes were full of regret as she looked up at him. "Lucky's wife… Your-" she whispered.

"It don't matter now."

"It obviously does, Nathan. He's been so kind to me, and now I find out that Cal… I dunno, maybe you shoulda just left me outside of Tinulca."

"Well I didn't. You're here now, and you ain't got a reason not to be. Sam don't know what he's talkin' about." He grabbed her shoulders and smiled. "You ain't a woman to take notice of *any* man, Miss Schaeffer, let alone a drunken moron like Sam Clifford, so stop actin' like you are. Get yourself outta this rain before you catch somethin'." She gave a short laugh and nodded at him, but something bothered her. She stopped as they walked back towards shelter, "Why are you so keen to drop this?"

"What d'you mean?"

"I don't need protectin' from truths, Nate."

"I know Annie, I-"

"Caley Schaeffer was a tyrant. The only thing he enjoyed in his life was hurtin', maimin' and killin' folk. Without reason beyond he could."

Her voice dropped to a rasp as she looked down, rain pouring from the brim of her hat. "You know I shot my first person dead at six years old? It was my goddamn birthday. I think I had almost the worst childhood imaginable at the hands of that man. The only thing I ever got from Caley Schaeffer were tortured into learnin' these *skills*." She raised her hands and stared blankly at him. "I would trade them *any time* to go back and have a life."

Nathan felt an anger on Annie's behalf that had nowhere to go. She carried the burden of her family's legacy as well as the pain of her own life as a young Schaeffer. He had ended the life of the man that had caused this, but in doing so had no way of making him truly answer for his crimes. But Nate was younger then; still angry, and Martha Needham was a mother to him. Caley Schaeffer was better off in the ground.

He gently patted her arm, and she winced a smile. "I told you the first day we met I wanted to shake the hand of the fella who put Caley Schaeffer down." She looked sadly at him. "I guess I already have."

<h1 style="text-align:center">11</h1>

<h2 style="text-align:center">Fine Weather for it</h2>

The following week at Onti Lake passed without further comment from Sam. He preferred licking his wounds to adding to the camp's current perception of him. Annie was kept busy with both improvements to the gang's skills, and with regular chores as bestowed on her by Maw and Chuck Hicks.

As time lurched rapidly onwards, her nights had become less restless, and with her varied days, camp seemed less suffocating. She found herself alone a lot less in the evenings now she had been embraced into the group of Clara, Marie and Dotty.

"But the *romance* of it all," Dotty gushed, "travelin' from town to town, meetin' new folk, livin' a life of fun and wonder!"

"Have you *been* to a travelin' show, Dotty?" Annie smirked.

"No, but I've read about them."

"It ain't the romance you read in books."

"Was there at least... *someone?* You would've met so many people, I can't possibly believe that you've *never* held some fella close to your heart."

Annie's cynicism softened. Dotty's need for the romanticised idea was perhaps to comfort her from her own experiences. But she was putting her hopes on the wrong person. "Dotty, the only thing I have ever loved is my horse, because she ain't never let me down." Annie laughed. "Other than that, love ain't ranked so highly on my list of life's choices." She propped her leg up on the table and swigged from her whiskey bottle as the last light of the day burned orange behind the horizon, the trio laughed.

"Now I *know* you ain't tellin' me you're a..." Marie snorted.

"I ain't ever been in love, Marie, I'm still a red-blooded

woman. You of all people know you don't need to be in love to get your itches scratched. And I've had my share that's needed scratchin' in my time." The ladies raised their whiskey bottles in agreement and drank heartily.

"I still can't understand how you don't believe in love." Dotty sighed pityingly.

Annie leaned forward, a little drunk. "Listen, darlin', when you've been dragged up by a fella that beats you 'til you kill someone, then at the age of six he sells you to *another* fella that beats you. And *then* when you come of age *that* fella will try to beat you or bed you, or hire you out to *others* that wanna do the same…? There ain't much room in my little flint of a heart for love." Annie owned another gulp of her drink. "Didn't say I don't believe in it though." She grinned, sitting back in amusement.

"*Jesus,*" Marie whispered, "at least I had a care for the girls in my place."

"Now don't get me wrong, ladies," Annie hiccupped, "I ain't got anythin' against makin' money from life's carnal desires. Only problem I have is that we don't get to choose the buyers." The group cackled. "Believe me, if I could select who pays me for the pleasures of my company, I would not have ever darkened your doors." She swigged another large dram of amber liquid from its bottle, allowing its burn to coat her throat.

"I don't think you'd have a shortage of money in this place." Dotty teased.

"They look at all of us like that. They're fellas livin' outdoors, it don't take much for 'em to go animal." Annie laughed when Tommy Kelley made her point for her. He walked past and offered some obscene invitation to the group, causing Dotty to blush and let her eyes follow him as he left their table.

"I dunno if I should get concerned about this." Nathan Healey stood by the three ladies; his clothes dirty from the day's efforts. "Can't ever be a good sign when you three're sat around together cacklin' like witches. Shame Clara's on watch, she'd bring the cauldron!"

"Sit down, Nate,' Marie cooed with a slur, "we're talkin' about *carnal desires.* Maybe you'll remember somethin' 'bout it from your dusty old past!"

"Very funny." He grumbled over the tipsy laughter. "I'm goin' to bed."

The next morning Annie rose early to help Tanner change the water for the horses. She gathered the empty pails by the trough and gambolled lightly through the camp towards the lake's edge. Life felt a little easier now she had been given the chance to show her usefulness, but she kept reminding herself that this was just a temporary stay. She was still stuck financially and would need to find a way to start making herself money to get out and move on with her life before it was too late. She sighed, attending to her work with a song she and Sally would sing as they mucked out the horses.

As her voice trailed off from the song, she felt a presence close by.

"Mornin', Annie." She jumped from the deep tired voice of Nathan Healey appearing behind her.

***

Having finally accepted Annie, the camp had settled into a calm, regular routine. Even Sam had finally realised that he should start pulling his weight.

Lucky agreed to help Doc take a shipment of tinctures up to a small-tented community that was growing into a fully-fledged town. They had convinced Nathan to act as protection should their small act go wrong, which it inevitably did. Nate hadn't liked dirtying his hands in these types of cons, but Lucky had confirmed the medicines were no worse than snake-oil, and no one would get hurt. He felt obligated to Lucky after the dramas Sam had kindly bestowed on them all.

"Let us do the talking, Nathan." Lucky reassured as he shoved him into a cramped spot within Doc's small wagon. "You stay hidden, and we'll call on you if needed." Nate begrudgingly agreed and wedged himself into the small space between the crates.

The day unravelled pretty much as Nate had expected. Once word got out that a Quack Doctor was selling another so-called "*Miracle Cure*", some local men appeared to extinguish the situation. They had apparently been taken for fools by the same inebriated doctor, who had neglected to remember. Nathan had come prepared for such an event and produced his Repeater as he faced a town square full of angry people. The trio made their escape, weaving and swerving haphazardly away. Doc drove, while the more over-zealous men of the town chased after them. Once they had dodged the rainstorm of bullets, the three men made their way back to Onti Lake, taking their time to double back to keep their trail cold.

By the time they wearily arrived in camp, the sun was low.

"*Why* am I still dumb enough to be part of these goddamn farces with this *damned fool?*" Nate's humiliation stung him, he wasn't a fan of being made into a joke, and he had been surprised that Lucky had wanted to be part of this particular job at all. Doc slowed the cart near the horse paddock, and Lucky chuckled. "Oh hush up boy, that was fun!" he clapped his hands. Doc shrank away from Nate's glare, jumped down from the cart, and shuffled towards his tent.

"*Yes*." Nate's sarcasm pushed through his gruff voice. "I love bein' part of a moronic idea that leaves us runnin' for our lives. We must do it more often."

The sunset over the lake was almost gone as the two unhitched the horse from Doc's wagon.

"Annie seems to have settled now anyway, *despite* Sam's best efforts." Lucky said.

"He won't be causin' more trouble, I made sure of that."

"Yes, well, let's hope not." Lucky slapped Nate's arm and went towards Chuck's wagon in the hopes of some food. The sound of laughter carried on the air as Nathan threw the cart harnesses over a stump near the grazing horses. Looking towards the centre of camp he saw three silhouettes deep in conversation at a table, their voices raised in high spirits and alcohol.

"... *I can't possibly believe that you have never held some fella close to your heart...*"

As he walked towards them, the occasional the husky tones of a whiskey-driven Annie Schaeffer holding court floated on the air.

"*...only problem I have is that we don't get to choose the buyers!*"

On his approach, he witnessed the romantic skills of Tommy Kelley in action.

"Ladies. Annie...! you've got some fair bit of Irish in ya, dontcha? Would either of you other lovely ladies *like some*??" Tommy blew a kiss at the three before heading towards the campfire.

"Jackass." Marie mumbled with a chuckle.

Nate immediately regretted stopping to talk when he quickly became the target of their teasing. Before Marie could make him feel any more inadequate, he said his excuses and headed for bed. The tipsy laughter behind him gave him some comfort. Annie had finally loosened up, and the responsibility of teaching others to improve their fighting skills had brought a new energy to her he'd not seen before. He smiled as he sat on his bunk. She had been an asset to the gang in her own way; she had even helped teach Mikey to read and write. The kid had become a more patient student for his new teacher. Nathan laughed, *can't blame him*, he thought as he turned in for the night.

He woke to a chill in the air. Opening one eye, he caught a glimpse of Miss Schaeffer at work; her walk brighter and, if it was possible, more winsome as she passed his view on her way to the lake; four empty buckets in hand, humming as she went. He briefly relaxed back into his bed, readying himself for the day. It had been some time since he was free from commands. The situation in camp was much better than it had been in a long time, and everyone now seemed to be contributing somehow. Maybe he would actually get a day of freedom.

Annie's humming became more structured, turning into a song which accompanied Nathan as he dressed. Through the noises of a bustling camp, he could make out some of the lyrics.

"Oh, hard is the fortune of all womankind, I'm always controlled, and always confined..."

Nate stopped dressing to hear her better. He hadn't heard many soft songs living in this camp. The most he knew had been altered to more profane lyrics and sung with drunken, reckless abandon. Nate followed the melody to the lakeside, and in front of him was a woman focused on her work; her eyes closed as she sang. Her black hair cascaded in waves down her back and whipping behind her in the breeze, the light gave her face a warm radiance, and her voice softened as her song came to an end.

He greeted her and smiled. "That's a pretty tune to start the day."

***

"Jesus, Nate! You scared me!" Annie caught her breath as she handed him two full buckets of water ready to carry to the horses.

"You nearly got a full face of cold water!"

"Wouldn't be the first time." He escorted her back to the horses. "Weren't you drinkin' last night?"

"I was." She grinned.

"How're you *alive* this mornin'? The others're a mess." He laughed.

"No *pace.*" She explained. "You can't be hurlin' the stuff back like water, you gotta at least enjoy it. Them ladies ain't got their pacin' right."

"Is that so?" He placed his buckets next to Annie's. "I don't recall you doin' much pacin' back in Tinulca."

He stood at one end of the trough, and helped tip the stale water onto the grass as she teased him. "Do you recall much of that night, Nathan?"

"... Well... *No.*" Her laugh echoed through camp as she poured the fresh water.

"I'll tell you what," she confided quietly as she petted Bessie, "I thought I was gonna die that next mornin'."

"Ha!" Nate stood on the other side of Annie's horse, feeling at least a little vindicated.

"Ah! Nathan! Here you are, and good morning, Miss Schaeffer."

"Duke." Nate nodded. "Everythin' alright?"

"Fine, yes, but listen I was wondering if you could go out hunting today? I understand few have had time to get supplies recently, and Chuck's running low again, and I *cannot* face having to hear his complaints further."

Nate sighed, he wasn't sure what his day was going to entail, but he had hoped to have made that decision himself. "Alright."

"Oh! And take Miss Schaeffer here, will you?"

Annie gawped, Duke must have made a mistake. Judging by Nathan's expression, he thought the same. "… Are you sure?"

"*What?* She's got a good eye and the perfect horse to carry large game. She's being wasted here, son, let's get her doing some *real* work." He smiled at Annie. "Better make sure you change first, Miss, that skirt isn't practical for hunting."

"Sh-sure, Duke. Right away." Dumbstruck, Annie turned and hurried to her tent.

Nate eyed his friend with confusion. "What's brought this on? Why the sudden change?"

"There's no reason for Miss Schaeffer to have to stay here all the time, and quite frankly I'm tired of Sam's mutterings. I cannot be bothered to deal with him causing another outburst."

Nathan laughed. "So you're happy to sacrifice *my* safety for a quieter life?"

"At this point, Nathan, *yes*." Duke sighed. "You know she isn't a problem, just take the day. Go out to better grounds than here." He slapped Nate's arm in thanks and marched back towards the campfire.

By the time Nate had saddled up, Annie returned dressed the same as the day she'd met them at Orr Hill, and armed to the teeth. The anticipation of escaping the camp's confines had her working at double speed. "I picked up some food from Chuck's wagon on the way. Better to have somethin' to eat on the move." She jabbered excitedly and set about saddling Bessie before Duke could change his mind.

"It looks like it rained a little last night," Nate looked amusedly at his rushing companion, "there should be some good huntin' today."

"Okay, so *let's go!*"

The pair journeyed North from Tinulca, riding up towards more wooded areas. Tanner didn't exercise the horses much, if at all, and it was clear Bessie needed it. Annie barely touched her mare's sides before she shot off ahead of Nate in an impromptu race. The landscape blurred past, but Annie whooped and laughed as the pressure of detention lifted. She let go of the reins, stood tall in her stirrups and raised her hands above her head, waving her hat like a flag.

"ANNIE! Slow down! What are you doin'?!"

She sat back in the saddle and halted Bessie sharply, her expression wild as she turned her horse to face her escort. "I'm enjoyin' myself, Nate. *FINALLY!*"

"You're scarin' the animals away, that's what you're doin'." He slowed Prynne to meet her. "C'mon, we're nearly there."

They turned off to higher ground where the grass grew tall and lush, and the varied meadow flowers would be perfect for an abundance of grazing animals.

As they set up, Annie raised a question that had hung like a cloud since Sam's outburst. "Why weren't you gonna tell me about killin' Cal, Nate?"

Nathan's body stiffened. He had hoped that this conversation would never happen, especially while out alone with the unpredictably tempered woman holding her rifle at close range. He tightened his grip on his gun. "I didn't see how it would change matters." He lied.

"Way I see it, you were fixin' to save your own ass when you realized who I was that day, thought I'd come back for revenge, huh?" She shifted her body down onto her belly, "… I can understand that." She muttered bitterly. "Though you shoulda known the Schaeffers well enough to think one woulda come back harder and sooner than *ten years* if they wanted to find you." Nathan looked at her lying in the grass next to him. "What was done was done, I don't see how it would help our cause either way if you knew." They both knew he was full of horse shit. The truth was he found himself enjoying the company of a Schaeffer and he didn't want it to change if she discovered he was the reason her father was dead. He wasn't prepared to have to shoot the woman, but he couldn't be sure that he wouldn't need to.

"Okay, Nate," Annie eyed him incredulously, *"whatever you say.* I'm sure you trusted me the moment I stopped you from killin' me."

"Well, you can have a pretty compellin' way about you when you want."

The rest of the morning was taken up by the pair making light work of some small game. By lunch, they had managed a good collection of rabbits and wild turkeys, before deciding to head towards heavier woodland hoping to find larger game grazing in relative shelter.

They settled against a large tree on the edge of the woods for rest and refreshment.

"You over the excitement of these views?" Nate teased as Annie fought with a can of meat, "I mean, grass is grass, but I s'pose there's somethin' about it bein' on a different bit of ground that's appealin'."

"Shut up, Nate." Annie hissed as she struggled on with her can.

"Just 'cause you get to come and go, you take life's luxuries for granted." She stuck her tongue out at him childishly as the can's lid finally relented to her will.

"Oh yes, I am most definitely *so weary* of life's luxuries." He looked down at his clothes; scuffed and muddied from hunting. "I'm just upset you didn't bring the fine wines."

"You know what I mean." Annie spluttered through a mouthful of food. "Freedom is the biggest luxury of all, I ain't had much of it in my lifetime."

"I guess so," he smiled, "but this life ain't easy, Annie. This world is determined to box us all into the same thing. All toilin' for someone else, no one bein' allowed the life they want."

"Come on, Nathan, there's always been rules."

"Not really, not like now."

Annie put her can down and looked at him with bewilderment. "Are you tryna tell me that once it were *fine* to shoot, rob and kill folk? 'cause I'm pretty sure that's always been frowned upon." He looked offended. "You know what I mean. There was a time where things were settled... *Privately...*"

"You mean, with guns and an eye for an eye? Yeah, we both know how well that works."

He shook his head. "You sound so different from the others."

"Yeah, well." She huffed as she returned to her meal. "Sounds about time you got some fresh eyes in the group."

"Never thought I'd hear a Schaeffer callin' for law and order. Even Louisa wouldn-" he stopped himself.

"Who's Louisa?" Annie asked, already pretty sure it was the owner of that framed poetry.

"Just someone I knew a long time ago." He sighed sadly and lit a cigarette. "Just someone I shouldn'ta let follow me." Annie smiled at him sadly as she packed up their leftovers. "Folk ain't all made to think the same."

"I know." Nate looked at her. "I guess I kinda broke her. She threw away the chance for a good life, and I weren't interested. She deserved better."

Patting his knee, Annie turned quietly. "You know," she whispered, shifting onto her haunches; rifle butted to her shoulder, "I don't believe it when folk say, *"it's better to have loved and lost*". I ain't ever loved and I really don't think I'm missin' out." With a **CRACK** of her rifle, and the distant thud of her target, she pulled herself on to her feet. "I mean, there's enough pain in this world through other means, I don't need more."

Nate watched as Annie slung her rifle over her shoulders and walked over to the large body of a deer with one pristine bullet through its eye.

"ARE YOU GONNA GIVE ME A HAND WITH THIS OR WHAT, MR HEALEY?"

***

"Looks like we got a good haul, Annie. Maybe you ain't such a pain in the ass after all."

"You can't mean that Nate," she chided as they headed back, "I have a reputation to uphold in that camp. I can't have people seein' us return and you not havin' your usual, sullen expression."

"Funny. You're lucky your horse has got so much on it, else I'd leave you out here for the wolves."

"If you were smart, you'd just take Bessie and leave me anyway." She joked.

"As good as Prynne is, I ain't able to control her and tussle with your beast."

"Prynne?"

"Yeah, I thought she suited it." He patted his mare affectionately.

"Don't tell me she's named after the woman from that book. How d'you know about stuff like that?"

"Lucky and Martha. They forced me and Danny to learn all sorts when we were kids. I think it was the only way they could get us to behave." He smirked. "Readin' was the easiest thing to get me into. Martha had that book, and I snuck it away one day. I dunno… Just somethin' about that story stuck with me. That family livin' defiant against everybody. I guess it's kinda silly." He shrugged embarrassedly.

Annie looked at him with great admiration. "You really like your insolent women don't you, Mister Healey?"

"Ain't no better kind, Miss Schaeffer." He grinned out towards the horizon.

The pair continued along the main road to Onti Lake, talking comfortably as they went. Their friendship had grown quickly. Annie very much enjoyed the time she spent in Nathan's company, and it scared her. She was not a trusting person, yet this man could drop her guard without her noticing.

She was so confused by his life, well-read and seemingly wise in so many ways, yet his unyielding defence towards less righteous men seemed misguided. She didn't question it, this was his whole world and people do strange things for their families, she reminded herself with a shiver.

Something about the stillness of the landscape made Nate uneasy. He hadn't seen anyone for most of their journey home, and the quietness felt unnatural for the time of day. As they turned onto the familiar track for camp, they were greeted by the guns of an angry Clara Healey, Sam Clifford and Thomas Kelley.

"It's us!" Nate yelled as hunters halted. "What the hell is goin' on?"

Clara lowered her weapon. "Some folks have been *sniffin'* around here this afternoon. Duke reckons they're law. We had to take a couple of them out."

"*What*?! How did they know…?"

"No idea," Tommy escorted the two back to the camp, "but you're the last back, Duke wants us all to lay low tonight."

Annie watched as Nate quickly dismounted to greet Duke. "Nathan, m'boy! Thank goodness you both made it back. We were just waiting on your return."

"What's goin' on? *Law men?*"

"They've been nearby, but not been here." Duke reassured. "Campbell spotted a couple and got rid of them, but the rest aren't too close. No one is to leave the camp until we're sure it's safe."

"Okay." Nate turned to grab his rifle from Prynne before Duke stopped him.

"No, Nathan, get some rest. We have the night covered, just be ready tomorrow. You and Miss Schaeffer seem to have had a successful day." He smiled as Annie approached.

"Is there anythin' I can do, Duke?"

"Oh no, my dear," he patted her lower back, "you and Nathan have done *exemplary* work today. Rest up. But thank you."

Nate watched as Duke went to catch up with the patrol. "The law, Nate?" Annie grew concerned, maybe her letter had caused someone back West to pick up her trail. She still hadn't heard from Sally.

"It's a long story. It ain't for discussin' now." Nate turned and took the young deer from Bessie, transporting it over to Chuck.

"Take good care of this, Chuck, Miss Schaeffer ain't gonna be impressed if you ruin it." He turned a strained smile to Annie as they went to grab some stew. The camp was quiet except for the faint caterwauling of Tanner drunkenly singing *"She'll be Coming Around the Mountain"*. Most people had taken an early night in case any company arrived uninvited.

After they finished their meal, both walked together towards their lodgings. "That was a pretty good day." Nate mused.

"Oh, you have *no idea*. It's so good to get out and breathe somethin' other than stew and camp smoke."

Nate laughed, he hadn't thought about it that way. "I enjoyed ridin' with you today, Annie."

"You gotta be careful with enjoyin' yourself, Nathan. I told you, you ain't used to it. Besides, people will start to think you ain't a misery." She teased.

Nate had felt a connection to Annie recently. He had to admit he was enjoying harmless attention from someone like Miss Schaeffer; it brought back some ardour to his personality.

He turned to her with a boyish confidence. "Well, I recall bein' told by someone close by, that if I practice enjoyin' life, I might get rewarded." A deep, knowing grin stretched across his face.

Annie stared at his blue eyes. Her skin grew warm. She had never expected such a familiar sentence to utter from the man, nor the expression on his face; it was like looking at a different person.

She folded her arms and leaned into her hip. "So you were," she said coolly, controlling her eagerness. "Good evenin', Mister Healey," she purred.

"Good evenin', Annie."

She slinked back to her tent and Nate's eyes followed her every step. Her hair was messy from the day, her clothes marked with mud and grass stains. "*It's been a long time.*" He thought. Hearing himself made him wince with embarrassment.

Inside her tent, Annie lit her small oil lamp. The light caught on a full bottle of brandy she had never bothered to open. She grabbed it and headed to the doorway, just in time to see Nate removing his hat and gun belt, rolling his aching shoulders; fatigued from the long day.

"You know," she spoke low and softly, "I've been savin' this for a celebration. Seein' as it's still early, and I got to have a life today, I thought I might open it, if you'd care to join me?"

Taken back by the invitation, Nathan stumbled. "I-I dunno, Annie, I shouldn't."

She shook the bottle coquettishly. "You sure? It's *real good.*" Nate fought against the adrenaline trying to kick him forward. He had never been offered such a blatant invitation by someone that wouldn't charge him for the pleasure.

He swallowed hard. "I-err, I gotta keep a clear head in case anythin' happens with the camp." He heard himself say, much to his own frustration.

Annie drew out a long, deliberate sigh and looked at the bottle. "*Okay.*" Her green eyes glimmered seductively. "How about we just don't drink the brandy?" She turned slowly and walked back into her tent.

Nate stared, frozen, his mouth hung open like some dumb-headed kid. He looked around and found that no one was paying attention, busying themselves with patrols or quietly resting. He turned back towards the space Annie had occupied. Her tent's doorway summoned him with the warm flickering lights from inside. He was hot and breathless. He ran his finger around the back of his suddenly stifling shirt collar, cleared his throat and stepped forward.

12

A Trip to Town

Nathan stretched slowly. He was well rested and calm. The enclosure of Annie's lodgings meant a lot of the noise from the camp was considerably muffled. The intact canvas walls kept him warm and dry as the soft patter of rain drummed overhead. He had no idea of the time, but the daylight glowed through the fabric around him as it undulated in the breeze. He looked at the woman asleep next to him, a sprawl of black hair covered her face and most of the pillow, and he was surprised to be awake before her. The camp bed wasn't designed for two he thought, as he stirred the leg planted to the floor that had supported his weight while he slept.

He moved stealthily so as not to wake Annie, quietly grabbing whatever discarded clothing he could find; managing to pull his on pants, shirt and boots in relative silence. He turned back to her with the glance of an awkward teenager. It had been a long while since he had spent the night in such sweet company.

Annie shifted onto her back, and the blanket rose and fell gently with her breathing, caressing her curves. Nate felt ridiculous, both for the uncomfortable mood crawling through him, and the youthful desire to return to the covers.

As he drew a deep breath in a futile attempt to focus, the heady scent of her perfume hit him. *"For god's sake grow up."* He grumbled and forced his body towards the exit. Peering out from the door, he snuck as inconspicuously as he could to his own lodgings. He took a moment to gather his thoughts, allowing a short reminiscence of the evening to play through his mind, before changing quickly and making his way towards Duke's tent, with what he thought was a casual gait.

"Here he comes! The Great *Casanova* himself!" Tommy shouted as Nate found himself in front of a mob of men sat around Duke's tent, all smiling and jeering at him.

"Good work, my man," the Irishman continued, "I'm impressed you've still got it in ya. We were all beginnin' to worry you'd forgot how things worked!"

"*Alright, keep it down, will ya?*" Nathan hissed, taking a coffee and a pat on the back from his brother. "The whole camp don't need to know, Kelley, we ain't all like you."

"You're right," Tommy goaded, "if it'd been me, I'd have been on that *weeks ago*! And Tanner owes me five dollars now!"

"Would it be alright with everyone if we continued with our *discussion*?" Duke interrupted sternly. "Nathan, as happy as they all seem to be with your most recent achievements, we *were* talking about our next payday."

"What's the hit?" Nate mumbled, his eyes catching Miss Schaeffer as she meandered to Chuck's wagon for breakfast.

"The bank vaults in Tinulca. You aren't getting any more work through from the Sheriff, are you?"

"*... No...* But... we ain't done somethin' like that in a long time."

"We need to get enough in the coffers to get gone." Duke put down his notebook and looked at Nate. "This isn't our home any longer... Shame," he sighed, "I rather liked it here. But I doubt those men from the Timber company across the water will keep quiet once they have the law around."

"How'd they find us?"

"I'm not sure," Duke frowned, "but after Madsen got rid of the nearest ones, everything went quiet. No one has seen them since. I think we're safe, *for now*, but we need to move on. We've got a place in mind. Tom, go and tell everyone to start packing up." Tommy made his way through camp, subtly for once, while the rest were given their duties for the robbery.

"Nathan. A *word*." Duke waited until the rest of the men

dispersed before standing and clamping his arm around Nate's shoulder, walking him towards the lake's shoreline. "How did Miss Schaeffer enjoy hunting yesterday?"

"Fine." Nate shrugged. "… *Why?*"

"How's her aim? I hope that she hasn't found her ability… *dwindling* while being cooped up here."

"… Seems as deadly as ever, certainly got some good meals ahead of us from her kills."

"Good! Good… I need you to bring her with you to Tinulca. Help us out today."

"*What?*" Nate halted in his tracks, snapping around to face his friend.

"You said her skills were still as deadly as ever, correct?"

"Well, *sure,* but-"

"Then don't you think we should get her using them for as many things as we can?"

Nate tensed. "*Duke*. She ain't gonna wanna do this. It won't go well for any of us if we drag her into somethin' she's never wanted a part of."

Duke rolled his eyes. "We aren't going to have her *up front* with us, Nathan." He gripped Nate's arm with a thick, patronising weight.

"No! *She'll act as lookout*. There's a building opposite the bank, she can get up on the roof from the back of it, and just watch out."

"… And what if she needs to warn us of anythin'? Throw stones and hope they hit the window?"

"It won't come to that. Just go tell her to ready up and meet us in Tinulca."

"*ME?!* This is your goddamned idea, why me?" Duke responded with a withering look. With a clenched jaw, Nate agreed and sloped back towards the group, staring over at Annie as she packed up with Marie. Seemed he couldn't even have twenty-four hours of enjoyment.

"Alright, Big Man?" Tommy slapped Nate's back. "How's the energy levels?"

"They're *fine*, Tommy." Nate snapped as the Irishman smirked at him. "Why?"

"Just checkin' you'll be awake enough to get this done without any problems."

"You worry about yourself, Kelley. I ain't the one that *gets distracted* on jobs." He glared, thinking back to the debacle with the coal chute.

"Listen, I'm headin' to Tinulca now to meet up with the lads, get yourself along once you're done with Miss Schaeffer!" He jostled his friend.

"Go on, get outta here, you damned deviant!" Nathan joked and shoved Tommy away.

He made his way towards Clara as she returned from seeing his brother off.

"Mornin'." She eyed him slyly. "… Fun day yesterday?"

"Don't start." He grumbled as they sat down. A childish smirk played at her mouth while she cleaned the camp's guard rifle. "Is there gonna be anyone in this place who don't know about the last twelve hours of my life?"

"No." She snorted. "Take it from me, a quiet night with a full camp ain't the best night for romancin'. Just so you know… *For next time*."

Nate shuffled in his seat to alleviate some embarrassment and leaned forward. "Look, enough of my day yesterday, what happened with the law?"

Clara sighed and placed the gun on the table. "All I know is Campbell was comin' back to us from god-knows-where, and he heard some fellas pryin' about us in Tinulca. He tracked 'em for a while and put 'em down. He came back here and alerted the camp. We sent out scouts to round up everyone, but Duke said you and Annie were probably too far away to be an issue." She shrugged. "I'm guessin' so if you had no troubles yesterday."

Nate was frustrated. Missouri had been a mistake; the men had to risk everything to break Campbell out of jail, because "*It's all of us or none.*" As Duke put it. Before then, they could have all continued living relatively undetected, taking money from folks who didn't miss it, at least not miss it for long. Their escape from Missouri had been a huge song and dance, and for the first time in his life, he found that he had been made notorious. He didn't like it. "Every time we try to get back to life somethin' stops us."

"Yeah, well," Clara huffed, "one of you better come up with a smart move quick. Once the law knows two of their men are missin', they're gonna get real sniffy."

Nathan sighed and stood. "I know. Look, Duke's uncomfortable. But he says we got a place to head on to, so go ready yourself to move."

"Alright."

He squeezed Clara's shoulder affectionately and grimaced as he made his way towards Annie's tent; out of ways to delay the inevitable.

***

The shuffle of hushed movements had roused Annie from her dozing. On opening her eyes slightly, she had seen Nate pulling on his clothes to leave. She smiled to herself and waited for him to leave. It had been one of the best days she could remember, and its outcome had certainly exceeded any expectations of how she originally intended to spend her evening.

She took her time to dress. A grin spread across her face, accompanied by a light, satisfied chuckle at the sounds of male bravado jeering in the distance.

As she went to grab some coffee in camp, the knowing looks directed at her, and sniggers from Dotty and Marie at the campfire merely emboldened her.

"Looks like you found a fine way to spend your evenin'."

"Nights are long when you're hidin', Dotty," Annie shrugged, "and I can't think of a better way to pass the time."

"If you like *old grumps*." She teased and cast her eye across to the group talking and laughing by Duke's tent.

"There's nothin' wrong with an older man, thank you Dotty." Marie chastised her lovingly as they drank their coffee. "Duke is talkin' of packin' up and movin', so you might wanna think about closin' down the firin' range today. I can give you a hand if you need."

"Is this because of what happened yesterday?" Annie gripped her coffee cup.

"Yup, I reckon those goddamn assholes have been followin' us since Missouri." Marie spat.

"Why?"

"Nate ain't told you?" Dotty shuffled closer to her friends. "I guess he's been a little preoccupied, *especially last night*." Annie's companions' mouths twitched smugly.

"Things went wrong. The boys had to get Madsen out of clink. He'd been picked up because of…" Marie faltered and shuffled, "well, it's said he forced himself on a girl… I just hope Duke is right to trust him. Anyway, we all packed ahead of time and got ready to run. The boys all went off and got him out and then, I dunno. But *the Law* say they took a woman hostage to get out of town. Then we met up in Arkansas." Marie looked down at her coffee and shook her head. "I can't believe that's true. All I know is we had to get outta there fast and now those rat bastards're on our heels."

"*Ladies*!" Tommy scurried up to them, giving Dotty a quick and affectionate squeeze at her middle. "Busy day today, you should start movin' those beautiful backsides into action!"

"Here, Annie." Marie pulled something from her cleavage, "I almost forgot, this letter came for you a coupla days ago. I ain't seen you to pass it on." Annie took the browned envelope.

Sister A, C/O N. Deleaney, The Mission,

Tinulca Station Mississippi

"The *Mission*??"

"Yeah," Marie shrugged, "It's what Duke calls us. We've used it for years. He always likes to think of us as a sorta life raft, always says folks are welcome. It has the added use of keepin' people from thinkin' we're bad news. Says it helps us keep a *low profile*." She smirked. "Be a damned sight easier if the boys remembered how to actually keep a low profile."

"I guess." Annie felt it was all a little odd. Nothing about this group came across as charitable; from the regular burglaries, to Doc and his medical cons. She felt that, maybe, with Duke, Marie wasn't so wise.

"Thanks, Marie." She turned the letter in her hands and walked quietly back to her quarters, her heart started to race. Sitting on her bed, Annie opened the envelope and carefully pulled the thick parchment from its home.

My darling Sister,

It is so good to hear from you after so long. I was afraid for your safety, though I told myself that you would be fine, you are not a woman that can be easily detained.
I wish you had not left without farewell, though I understand your reasons for it. I wish you had spoken to me of your plans but, as you say, I would have tried to convince you to take a different path.
I am still with the cousins, they have been in turmoil since you departed. The death of our uncle shook us all to the core, and we had many people asking questions regarding the circumstances. For now, the "well-wishers" believe they have spoken to all our uncle's kin. It is such a shame that none of us were awake to witness the brutal robbery that took place upon him that night. Those who acted out this deed must have some true hate in their heart to cause such a death. I trust that this has not followed them into their future, and that they have found peace.

The family is going east to establish themselves more permanently in New York. I hear they are fans of morbid entertainments there. I insist that you cease writing to us further, as the nature of your departure has been very much a concern to strangers. I am glad you have got people to travel with - a Mission of all groups! Something I would never expect you to live amongst. I hope that they are nothing but a good influence

Two items lay in the envelope. One was a vivid illustration drawn by Sally which depicted Annie and her best friend together. The sky above them was bright and clear. Sally had drawn herself comically standing on one leg, the other bent over her head, her raised foot holding a paintbrush to a canvas. Her white-blonde hair is tied in a bun, and a wide smile stretched across her glowing face. Annie was shown standing rebelliously; her eyes shone with a pearlescent vibrancy. She was firing a gun which expelled vines and flowers that enveloped the entire page, surrounding the two figures and merging with the tattoos across Sally's skin. The second item was a silver-plated locket that Annie had misplaced the night she left. It had been her mother's. Her initials "EM" stamped on the front surrounded by a filigree pattern. Inside was an image of her mother before the life of a Schaeffer ravaged her; her features so similar to Annie's. She stroked the image as a single tear fell from her cheek onto the engraving inside; 'Elizabeth Malone' shone out from it. Annie's hands felt an unfamiliar roughness on the back of the pendant and turned it over finding a hastily scratched message there, '*DO NOT LOSE YOURSELF*' it read. She grasped the locket in her fist and held it to her chest. Suddenly feeling a presence, she fired her eyes open, glaring towards the figure watching in her doorway.

"You alright, Annie?" Clara looked at her with concern. "You need a minute?"

"No, Clara, what is it?" She roughly rubbed her face.

"With everyone jumpy and lookin' to pack up for a quick getaway, *and* as you have the most obnoxious of all the tents, I thought you'd probably need the most help." She smirked.

"It's alright," Annie smiled as she stood up and attached the locket, tucking it into her blouse, "Marie said she'd give me a hand

and you got all your own stuff to pack up."

"Alright. I'll go see Danny off. Make sure you holla if Marie ends up sittin' around fannin' herself more than helpin'."

The camp was a hive of activity, a lot of the gang had been corralled the previous day to keep everyone safe from potential capture, but now only a handful of the men were around. Annie started to miss the peace of hunting with Nathan as her ears were filled with clattering pans and Maw marching around dolling out orders.

"So, what do you need help with?" Marie stood at her doorway, a fan gently wafting past her pristine face. Annie stifled a chuckle.

"I guess you could start foldin' up some of the lighter things in here…" she gestured towards the blankets and bedding, "I'll go take down the targets."

"Don't be ridiculous." Marie snapped the fan shut and marched in. "Don't be thinkin' that just because I don't choose to dress like *Mikey*, I can't do more than fold sheets!"

"Alright, *m'lady*," Annie bowed, "I am humbly regretful for my assumptions."

"That's better." Marie smiled.

"You can start helpin' me with the targets then. Seein' as they'll need to go in the cart first."

The pair set to work.

"What's your deal, Marie?"

"In what way?"

"You don't look like a woman that really belongs here, you know? I mean, you just seem like you should be above this life."

"You of all people should know that it's dangerous to make assumptions based on looks, Annie." Marie sighed as the pair shoved the last target into the cart. "You could say I weren't from this life… But I certainly ain't above it… I guess Duke just offered somethin' more freein' than managin' girls in a saloon." She kept her eyes on the blankets as she folded them and shoved them in a spare crate. "I doubt my husband misses me… Maybe misses the saloon girls, they did bring in the money for him.”

“You mean you-”

“When I left with the boys, I got all the girls outta there, too.” Marie stood tall and beamed at Annie. “No doubt some of them went back to it. There’s little for us ladies to do in that town… I hope they’re safe is all. Only Dotty came with us; she’s like a little sister to me and I weren’t leavin’ her.”

The pair continued to pack up more cumbersome items when the light *thud* of steps came towards them.

“Mornin’ Ladies.”

“Well, well, *Mister Healey,*” Marie turned and slinked into one hip, crossing her arms, “I wonder what you could possibly be doin’ here.”

“Mrs. Bassett.” Nate cleared his throat. “May I have a word with Miss Schaeffer in private?”

“I guess you mustn’t have had your fill of *conversation* yesterday, huh?”

Nate sighed and pinched the bridge of his nose. “Can you just get outta here? Please?”

“There’s the man we all know and love!” Marie cooed as she sauntered up to him and gave his cheek a gentle pat. *“She’s all yours, darlin’.”*

***

“G’mornin’. You seem a lot less relaxed than I’d expect.” Nate’s stomach lurched as he looked at Annie folding blankets with a smirk.

“Yeah. Listen, I need you to come to Tinulca with me.”

“… *Now…?*”

“Yep.”

Annie put the last blanket into her wagon and stared at Nate. He fidgeted where he stood, keeping his look away from her. Her gut dropped. *“Why?”*

"Well…"

Annie suddenly realised that only Tanner, Mikey, Lucky, Doc and Chuck were left in camp with the women. "*Where're all the fellas, Nate…?*"

"… Tinulca."

Annie had known already, she knew from the moment Marie was asked to leave. But she had hoped she was wrong, and it was taking all her strength not to explode. "*Big party happenin' there, huh…?* Well, I ain't interested."

"Annie-"

"I got packin' to do." She slammed shut one of her trunks.

"Listen, we just need you to keep an eye out."

"Just? *JUST?!*" The glare from her darkening eyes shot through him. "First I ain't trusted to even be a guard, now, **I'm good enough to rob with you?!**" She snorted and shook her head.

"You ain't robbin' shit. You're keepin' watch, that's all. From a roof across from the bank."

"The church school? You want *me*, to climb on top of a buildin' *full of kids*, and just sit there?"

"… I'm guessin' you'll need some kinda… protection for yourself if-"

"If it goes wrong?"

"… *yeah.*"

Annie marched up to him. The shining emerald green now non-existent from her eyes. "And what happens if I refuse to sit on the roof of a *goddamn school* with a gun, and play *lookout* huh?"

Nate swallowed. "It ain't worth askin' that. I doubt Duke assumes you'd decline."

"Then he ain't such an observant leader. I'd like to know exactly what my lookout job is, if you're all in that bank, and the law turn up, and I'm the only one *with a clear shot at them.*"

Nate hated this, it would have been far easier for them to fight their way out like they usually did, rather than get Annie roped in. Far easier on his patience, at least. This whole debacle was draining. No need for pleasantries when the clock's ticking.

"I guess you'll have to shoot them, Annie." He spat through gritted teeth, picked up her rifle and shoved it into her hands. "I ain't got time for this. We gotta go. *Now.*" They stood in silence for what seemed like eternity. Nate had handed her a weapon and, in his haste, forgot to check if it was loaded. It slowly dawned on them both as he readied his hand over the pistol on his hip. "No need to shoot me today, Mister Healey," Annie picked up the box of bullets from the barrel beside her camp bed, "I don't keep this loaded."

Nate slumped as she looked at him with disappointment and roughly shouldered past him. "Guess I better do what my guard says."

The journey to Tinulca was excruciating. Nathan didn't try to engage Annie, he just let her ride in front, pushing Bessie harder than necessary; her anger getting the better of her.

It wasn't until they could see the town on the horizon that he caught up and got her to stop. "You'll want this." He pulled out a spare ragged kerchief from his saddle bag and handed it to her.

"*Just in case?*" She hissed.

"No." He sighed. "Look, if you see folks gettin' too interested in the commotion at the bank, just cause a distraction. However you think best."

"What if that's me goin' to the Sheriff's office and tellin' 'em you're in there?"

Nate's head snapped up. He looked at her properly for the first time since the argument began. A sad smirk played at the corner of her mouth as she handled the cloth he gave her.

"I'd say that might put a bit of a dampener on things."

"I ain't gonna kill anyone, Nathan."

"I ain't askin' you to. You'll do right, whatever you decide." He hoped that wouldn't include her running off.

They said their farewells, agreed to meet back at camp, and went to enter the town from different points.

Nate hitched Prynne close to the back of the bank, as discussed, and followed the low chatter from Duke. The group looked up from their huddle as Nathan appeared at the entrance to the alleyway by the building.

"Where the hell have you been, Healey? Woman troubles?"

He shifted his glare briefly towards Campbell Madsen before greeting the men stifling their laughs.

"Did Annie come with you, Nathan?"

"Yeah, Duke, she's makin' her way to the school now." Nate clenched his jaw. "Did you know it's a school?"

"Hmm? Oh! *Well...* it's fine, they're all inside. It isn't like we're bothering *them*, is it?" Duke slapped his friend's arm and they all peered out from their hiding place.

Annie stopped Bessie two roads away from the school. "If somethin' happens, girl, I ain't lettin' you be near it." She patted the mare heavily and slipped from the saddle, loaded up the rifle, packed herself with more bullets, and shoved the bandana into her blouse until she needed it. She made her way towards the school as nonchalantly as she could; not easy as a woman in men's clothing, carrying a rifle.

She pulled her hat low, exhaled sharply and wound her way through the twisted route before arriving at a secluded and narrow pathway with the light tinkle of piano floating through it. It was deserted, obviously underused as she fought through sharp thorny weeds towards the sounds of small voices singing hymns. She stopped short of her destination and looked up at the buildings with a sigh.

"What the hell're you doin' Annie?"

The schoolhouse had a large window at the back, and the gap between it and its neighbouring structure was too tight for her to fit. The building next door only had one window which was fogged up from mould or green algae. It had an overhang from its back door which, with a jump, she reached and hauled herself up, stepping carefully across dilapidated tiles; almost putting her foot through it in places. There was a structurally sound crossing point, and Annie deftly leapt onto the school roof, before making her way to the front; crouching to keep her head below the line of the school's large sign. She hoped the music from below drowned out her footsteps. Leaning against the back of the signage she wrapped Nate's bandana across her face and peered over the edge, waving towards the small speck of faces by the bank.

"Took her long enough. Well, better late than never." Duke grumbled as he saw the silhouette move above the school. "You boys ready? You know the plan?"

With a sharp nod, the men readied themselves for their mission, shouldering their spare saddle packs as Duke sauntered into the crowd. Casually keeping his head down, he opened the establishment's doors, raising the cloth over his face as he entered the lobby. He was quickly followed by the rest of the men bursting through the doors, bandanas up and guns drawn.

"Softly and tenderly, Jesus is calling
Calling for you and for me..."

Annie shifted uncomfortably trying to ignore the sweet voices below her, as she watched the men marching towards their goal. There were a few people around, but it was after the working day had started, so most folks were either back home, at school, or at work.

"Come home, come home
Ye who are weary come home..."

She cleared her throat and placed her rifle to her shoulder, peering through the scope to see the commotion beginning through the bank's window, before Sam pulled the shutters almost completely closed save for a small gap they could use for lookout.

"Though we have sinned He has mercy and pardon
Pardon for you and for me"

Then she heard a scream.

"Madam, *Madam!*" Duke cooed forcefully. "There's no need for such dramatics."

Nate rolled his eyes. It's a little hard for the lady to stay calm when a large group of men had them at gunpoint.

"We don't come here to *harm* you, no, not at all!" Duke began his orations as if conducting a sermon. "*No*. We understand you hard working people are just as in need as us. We aren't here to take your *meagre* earnings. *We're here for the vaults.*"

The heavy hand on Nate's shoulder was his cue. He went up to the bank man, his shotgun pointed through the bars. "Mister, it'll be a lot easier for all of us if you just do what we ask." The teller stood perfectly still, save for the shaking; his face now a milky white.

"Are you the man we need to unlock the vault?"

The man swallowed and managed to blink his bulging eyes.

"Because, *if you ain't…*" Nate leaned his elbow on the counter and pushed the double barrel almost up the teller's nose. The woman who screamed began to sob.

The scream had drawn some attention from passers-by, who now lingered outside the building. Fortunately, the children hadn't noticed as they continued to sing. Two braver men in the street gingerly approached the bank, putting their ear up against the door. Suddenly, there was animated panic; the women hurried away to safety, the eavesdroppers headed towards the Sheriff's office, and others ran towards the Gunsmith's.

> *"See, on the portals, He's waiting and watching*
> *Watching for you and for me."*

"*This is takin' too long.*" Madsen hissed.

Nathan drew back the shotgun and slammed the butt of it against the bars.

"*You heard the man!* **WAKE UP!**" The bank teller was sweating.

"You got family, Mister? *Wouldn't you like to see 'em again today?*"

Nate watched the teller look desperately across to the sobbing woman at Duke's feet. It didn't go unnoticed. Campbell moved over to her, pulled his pistol from his hip, aimed at the woman, and drew back the hammer; his eyes locked on the man behind the counter.

"Alright, a*lright!*" The teller's voice wavered. "Just, *please.*"

Nate laughed bitterly. "Mister, you coulda avoided a lotta this if you didn't wanna be a hero in front of your *good lady wife.*" He wandered over to the doorway and loomed over the man as he let him through. "*Heroes always die.*" He grabbed the man's collar and shoved him towards the basement steps that led to the vaults, followed by Danny and Sam.

"What the hell is takin' them so long?" Annie fidgeted at her post. The crowd was expanding outside, and the children's singing was lessening as the commotion started to distract them. She surveyed the area below her. "*Distraction... A Distraction.*"

Annie spied the stack of hay by an empty hitching post. Above that was a small, lit kerosene lamp. She had to be smart; if she shot it too early, the law wouldn't be on the scene, and she would be found. Too late and someone besides the gang could get caught in the ruckus.

The vaults were cool compared to the main floor of the bank. Nate shouldered his shotgun and relaxed in the shade letting Danny keep watch at the stairs while Sam entered the first room.

"Now don't think about lockin' him in there, *Mister Hero,*" Nate leaned on the pale, sweaty man and brandished his pistol in his eyeline, "my friends and me mightn't be too happy about that." Sam marched out with the first filled saddle bags, handing them to Nate and swapping them for empty ones, waiting expectantly beside the second vault.

"Haven't you got enough?!" the teller whined desperately. "These are people's *things, their prize possessions!*"

"Then they should take better care of 'em, not have 'em sit in the dark, gatherin' dust." Nate shoved the man forward, and he dejectedly unlocked the door.

It wasn't long until the Sheriff arrived. "*THIS IS THE TINULCA SHERIFF! GET OUT HERE NOW!*"

Annie saw that the bank was flanked on both sides by local law men and militia. Those not armed rushed to the safety of the schoolhouse below her. She watched one of the Deputies march up to the door and try it, which made her laugh. *"Well they ain't gonna just let you in are they?"*

Through her scope she saw distinctive movement in the bank, and the quick flash of Tommy Kelley's face at the window. It was now or never.

She twisted to her left, took aim, and shot the kerosene lamp from its hook. Flames spilled across the hay; they instantly began to lick back up towards the pole that once held the light. She heard multiple exclamations as she ducked down and hurried her way back across the roof. She chanced leaping down straight in front of the school's big window, hoping all the activity out in the main street would be diverting enough to stop anyone noticing. She shouldered her rifle, ripped the bandana from her face, and walked purposefully away from the scene she had created as people cried out in panic behind her.

Nate had heard the call of the Sheriff upstairs, and it wasn't long before Tommy and Duke joined him by the vaults. "Time to go." Duke muttered as Sam appeared out of the second vault. "Mister Bank Teller, do you perhaps have an exit down here for us to depart from?"

"Where's…?" Nate asked suspiciously, noting Madsen's absence.

"He's guarding up top until we get out." Duke followed the unlucky employee to a small back door used by staff and those wishing to access their vaults unseen. As a thank you, Duke handed the man a stack of bills before turning to Nathan. "Go call him down, son."

Nate grumbled his way back towards the stone steps. *"HEY! DUMBASS! WE'RE LEAVIN'!"* He waited at the base of the staircase; his gun ready should anyone break through before they got out. *"What the hell is he doin'…"*

Suddenly, the teller's wife screamed again, then Madsen appeared quickly, hurrying past him. His eyes creased in what looked like a smile. "Time to go, *sourpuss.*"

As they clambered quietly out of the basement, they heard men break into the front of the bank. Smoke and flames billowed upwards to their left; the men rushed towards their horses.

"*Good work, boys!*" Duke called putting the additional saddle bags on Atlas. "See you at home!" The men split up and went their own complicated, pre-agreed exit routes. Nate hesitated when he got to a viewpoint of the school's roof. No Annie in sight, and no one paying much attention to the building at all. He sighed with relief and kicked Prynne on.

***

Annie sat and stared down at the river while Bessie drank. She had spent the best part of the day away from camp, away from Tinulca, letting the peace and stillness of her surroundings forget her actions. She sighed. Duke was frustratingly smart; he had made sure she was useful for their cause today, but far enough from any of its spoils to stop her making a run for it.

She started to grind her teeth as she thought about the gall Nathan had to ask her to be lookout. She'd been used, lured in by the simplest of human desires, and it stung her. "*Annemarie Schaeffer, you absolute fool.*" She shut her eyes and played with her pendant. "*I guess we got similar weaknesses, mother.*"

Stretching her back, Annie ran her fingers under her shirt to feel the scars that sat between her shoulders. "*Perhaps I ain't meant to move beyond that life.*"

A wet pressure nudged her head, Bessie had decided that it was time to go.

Nathan had taken up a watch at the entrance to camp as the rest finished the final pieces of packing up. It was getting late, and the gang were moving out when it got dark, "*With or without Miss Schaeffer.*" Duke had confirmed.

"I dunno, Healey, you finally get a girl to see you naked and she runs off." Campbell Madsen's voice crawled over Nate's skin as he stood beside him with a cigarette hanging from his mouth. "Least she looked first." He muttered. "Considerin' women don't

157

even wanna be near you, I can't see how you can make comment." Madsen chuckled and belched a large cloud of stale smoke into Nate's face. "Oh I do *just fine*, Healey."

There was something sinister in his grin that pulled a question from Nathan. "What happened back there, in the bank?"

"We *robbed it*, Nate, or is your hick brain too small to hold that information?"

"Why did that woman scream again?" He turned to Madsen with a scowl, "There were no reason for her to scream. Not at the end."

Campbell chuckled and took one final drag on his cigarette before he threw it to the ground. "Some women get hysterical around *real* men, Healey. Their emotions get the better of 'em." He nodded back towards the entrance through the trees. "Speakin' of hysterical women."

In the dwindling orange light of the day, Annie careered through the woodland, thundering Bessie up to her tent without slowing, calling out to the watchmen, or raising a greeting to a single member of the Needham Boys.

13

The gang journeyed west through the night, back into Arkansas. They hadn't spent much time in the state when fleeing Missouri, but Tanner had spoken of an old water mill he knew about from his younger days. It had earned him a spot up front in Chuck and Maw Hicks's wagon to give directions. Not that anyone trusted him much, but he was their only hope, and he was happy to keep up the guesswork if it meant a break from riding his old mule of a horse.

Nate and the rest of the men swapped watch points throughout the convoy as they trudged carefully through swamp-like paths and rocky river crossings. Annie trailed at the back of the group, partly due to the size of her cart, but also due to her being an additional support should they need defence. She had begrudgingly agreed to the position, too angry to argue, and it gave her a good excuse to keep back from them all.

She had stayed silent when she returned from Tinulca. The only real effort she made had been when she forced herself to politely converse with Duke when he came to thank her for her good work within the robbery, handing her a small cut of the take; twenty dollars. She had taken it reluctantly. The whole enterprise had made her feel dirty, and Duke's smile only added to her humiliation.

Nate was sullen throughout the trail. The unpredictability of Annie's nature was wearisome, and he allowed himself to indulge in some sulking from what little conversation he had with her that day. It didn't stop him try at least to coax some form of acknowledgement or reaction from her when he did fall back to the tail end of the gang's caravan. But she was stubborn, and any flicker of a look in his direction was masked by the night's shade. Only making the odd grunt of acknowledgment to the posse when they switched, he sat stewing in his saddle thinking about how quickly things could change. His liaison with Annie seemed unreal now; the memories were as if they were someone else's, and he didn't want to dwell on it. He felt he had let her down, and knew she felt the same. He thought back to reaching for his pistol during their argument before heading to Tinulca. The disappointment in her eyes wasn't even the worst part, it was the resigned acceptance that poured out from her stare. The look of a woman who had learned never to assume anything more from someone than the threat of being shot. He took to grinding his teeth when he ran out of cigarettes, and whenever the thoughts gnawed at him too much, Nate would shift back up the line to get Annie out of view. He didn't like silence; it gave him too much time to brood over questions he normally drowned out with busy work. Long night trails mocked him.

It took the group many hours to cross through to their final resting point, but when they arrived it was somewhat of an idyll. The stone building was abandoned, but not fully in disrepair; its foundations were sturdy, and large parts were dry inside. There seemed to be a battle between nature and man as the ivy from the forest floor crept up the exterior, and a tall red maple grew through its centre.

With plenty of space for everyone to rest, and the multiple levels to the building, there was opportunity for privacy. It had only one way in or out to the land; a thin roadway with a small wooden bridge over the river. To the back of the building was vast woodland, in front was a pond-sized lake that the old mill's stream led to. Inside the building they found sealed bags of grain, perfect for the horses, as well as old sandbags and wood scraps that the men could work into sturdy barricades. The river and pond made for a make-shift moat, which would funnel any unwelcome visitors into a narrow route, unless they ventured through the forest behind. Annie kept herself camped in the grounds. The humidity of Arkansas was inescapable both indoors and out, and she preferred to be closer to any potential breeze in this instance than locked away from it. It also meant she could keep her distance from the others, and re-focus on the whole reason she joined this group in the first place.

The bulk of the gang chose to keep sheltered, and sleep on the ground floor of the mill. The upper floor was split into two for Duke and Lucky, and the middle floor was split into three; the communal space – wherever wasn't taken up with gears and machinery for the mill – was predominantly used to store ammunition and any dry goods. That level was also home to two small closed-off spaces – once offices – one now given to Nate, and the larger to Danny and Clara. The outside of that level was wrapped with a small wooden walkway that once must have been used to check on the mill's wheel.

Once everyone had settled, the camp collapsed into an exhausted slumber.

14

New Views

August 1893

Annie had slept amongst the belongings in her cart, too tired to set up her tent. It was afternoon before the group were fully rested. The heat and humidity burned down on her as she blearily made her way to the throng who were being roused to action by a weary, but commanding, welcome from Duke, choosing the base of the red maple as his stage. "… And a big thank you to Tanner for guiding us here. We have shelter, privacy, and the makings of some fine protection!" The crowd mumbled their approval at Tanner being of benefit for once.

"Thank *you*, Duke." Tanner drew himself up and grasped his braces smugly. "There's a town called Boulderhead close to here. Used to deliver to it back in my youth… Some fun, fond memories from them days I can tell you!" He chuckled filthily. "Why, there's this one place, where the gir-"

"Yes, Tanner." Duke interrupted. "Folks, we have some work to do before the day ends, and we'll need to build barricades at the entryway." Duke continued to dole out instructions before escorting Tanner away.

Annie watched with petty amusement as Nate Healey fidgeted, annoyed at the job he had been issued and the partner he was lumbered with. She smirked when Madsen slapped the man on the back when they shuffled into the shadows of the mill to find items for make-shift fortressing.

Her smile didn't last long. Turning back to face her wagon, Annie remembered she would have to struggle on with it alone while the sun bounced sharply into her eyes from the murky lake Mikey now excitedly frolicked in.

"Need a hand?" Danny asked while she worked on the arduous task of staking her spot. His face creased with what seemed to be an uncomfortable smile as he patted Bessie.

"Shouldn't you be helpin' Clara?"

"There's barely room for both of us in there without tryna unpack 'round each other too." He coughed a small laugh. "And her exact words to me, as I recall, were *"If you don't get outta my face Daniel Healey, I'll throw you out this window!"*, and I ain't good at flyin'."

Annie grinned. She really did like Clara. "Sure. The more help I get, the quicker this monstrosity is up." She leapt up on to her cart and handed Danny one end of the heavy canvas roll. The pair worked with eventual synchronicity building the structure, and Annie realised this had been the most time Daniel Healey had ever spent in her presence, though the number of words he spoke to her had not increased by much. She watched him tie off the last rope in silence with a troubled frown.

"Come on, let's get Bessie up to the rest of the horses."

They walked in silence to the paddock. She couldn't understand why Danny had bothered to join her if this was how he conducted himself. The Healey brothers were frustratingly difficult to read. With Bessie settled, she turned to leave. "Thanks for your help, Danny. I appreciate it."

Danny gave a short, serious nod and kicked the edge of his boots. "… You should lay off Nate a little, Annie."

"Excuse me?!".

"Two days ago you weren't nothin' but sugar, now one thing changes and you're prowlin' 'round like a wounded cat."

Annie folded her arms with a clenched jaw. "It might seem like nothin' to *you*, Daniel Healey, but some of us ain't so willin' to be part of a bank robbery. *Nate knew that.*"

Danny lit a cigarette and sighed as he sat on a tree stump near the horses. "My brother is good at a lotta things, but women ain't one of them." He scoffed and shook his head. "But even he ain't dumb enough to go against the wishes of one if he had a choice."

"Nate had a choice," Annie stomped up to him, "he coulda left me to pack."

"You think he *wanted you on that trip?*" Annie shrugged.

"Jesus Annie, the last thing he'd want is the girl he lay with skippin' along to danger with him. You think he asked you for *him?*"

"*I. Weren't. Asked. At all.*"

"How long you been with us?" Danny was getting irritated.

"I don't see how tha-"

"And how long's Nate been here, huh?" He glared as she chewed the inside of her cheek. "*This is his family.* He always steps up for 'em. Unfortunately, you and he put him in a tough spot with regards to Tinulca. That's the trouble with bein' the oldest – there's no one makin' the mistakes before you. He just wades in and hopes for the best.

"But you can be sure that if there'd been need for you beyond lookout, he'd've stood against it. Stopped it. He's always the first to step forward. He'd step in front of a movin' train if it meant everyone else were safe."

Annie pulled up a small beer crate to sit on. "Yeah. Well, you gotta say that stuff, you're his brother."

Danny looked back towards the mill to see Nathan tramping around building defences with Madsen. He smiled. "You're right. I am his brother. And I wouldn't be alive today without him."

"Everyone has a story like that 'bout someone." Annie muttered.

"Look. All I'm sayin' is you need partners in this camp. And they don't come better Nathan Healey." He threw the butt of his cigarette on the floor, slapped her shoulder, and stood up. "So go choke down whatever pride's rattlin' 'round in that husk you call a soul and get back on side with him."

***

Despite their journey and the long day leading to it, Nate didn't sleep well on arrival. Partly because he slept on nothing more than a few bust sacks of grain under his bed roll, but mostly because he was still annoyed at the whole Schaeffer debacle. He flounced to get comfortable and failed, wrenching himself up out of his cramped office-bedroom he shuffled towards the camp's dry stores for tobacco. He took his pack of smokes out onto the old walkway, lit one up, and decided to take in the sights. The place really was quite lovely, he reluctantly admitted to himself. The distant, golden haze of morning mixed with the rare sound of a totally silent camp soothed his gloom. With a lighter step, he patrolled the whole gangway, checking for any rot in the wood. None of it was treacherous, though he would be sure to get someone to fix the less sturdy areas.

"P'raps Madsen could do it..." he pondered through his cigarette. *"Sure hope he don't fall through and break his neck."*

He chuckled to himself, rounded the corner, and walked towards the door into his room that overlooked the front of the camp, towards Annie's cart. From the gangway, he could see her outline scrunched between her life's possessions. Her mood would need to improve quickly to make life bearable for everyone; she wasn't the warmest person when she was friendly, let alone when she felt she had been wronged.

He turned into his room and looked dejectedly towards his temporary sleeping arrangements, then forced himself to get some shut eye before the busy work began.

After a couple more hours of uncomfortable sleep, he found himself almost completely seized up on the ground. With great effort and loud groans, he managed, slowly, to heave himself upright.

"Christ I'm gettin' old." He muttered as the blood returned to his muscles and he was able to rigidly hobble towards the stairs. "You alright? Sounded like a bear was killin' you in there."

"What you doin' awake, Danny?"

"I got disturbed by some terrifyin' noises," Danny smirked, "so I decided I better check my brother ain't bein' murdered."

"I was just gettin' up." Nate grumbled. "Sleepin' on floors ain't exactly comfortable."

"That's a depressin' look into my future."

"You won't have a future if you continue to rile me like that." The pair made their way downstairs quietly, with Danny playfully shoving his brother to hurry him up. "*Listen. I'm gonna snap them fingers off if you don't quit!*" Nate hissed, once away from their sleeping camp mates. He twitched a smile and turned towards Chuck's wagon. "Not everyone has a woman happy to set up their sleepin' area for 'em."

"Well, why change the habit of a lifetime? You've always had talent for beddin' 'em then completely pissin' 'em off." Danny's laugh soon faded as his brother glared at him. "She really is a stubborn ass ain't she?"

Nate shrugged and grabbed a tin of coffee. "She got cause, I guess. Just gotta wait 'til she gets sicka ignorin' everyone, then maybe she'll be more willin' to actually listen about what went down." He started to relight the previous night's hastily cobbled campfire and brew a pot of coffee. "But I can tell you this, I ain't walkin' into that viper pit. Not today. I got enough aches and pains without earache on top."

The brothers sat in the sun, quietly discussing how to fix up their new home and the supplies to be purchased using their latest cash boost, until the rest of camp stirred. It wasn't long before Chuck had cooked up a large pot of oatmeal, despite it heading much closer to noon, and everybody's tiredness started to evaporate.

"*GOOD MORNING, ALL!*" Duke called from a window at the very top of the building, "*What a glorious day this is. Come meet me by the maple!*"

The Healeys laughed as they dragged themselves towards the slowly congregating throng. Nate made his way inside, towards the shadier corner of the ground floor, and leaned against one of the supporting beams, Lucky joined him with a nod.

"Well now, people," Duke began, "I would like to commend you all on your tireless efforts to get here in one piece over the last day or so. *Yes, it was a slog*, but I think we can all agree it was for the best." Nate spied Annie shuffle in quietly, late, with a sullen pout smacked across her face.

Nate zoned out when Tanner started recounting one of his 'glory days' tales no one asked for. His eyes drifted towards Doc Carragher who was looking decidedly bug-eyed, pale, and clammy, nibbling nervously at his fingers, obviously running out of whatever kept him going.

"... Nathan, you go with Campbell and start collecting spare items that will work, everyone else, go help Maw and Chuck sort this place. The fun starts tomorrow. Tanner, I think you and I should take a tour of the nearby town you speak of so fondly." Nate groaned. He grabbed Tommy's arm in passing. "Hey, wanna trade with me?"

"Nice try Big Man, but I can't think of *anyone* better suited for such manual tasks." The Irishman chortled before chomping into an apple. "I best make meself available to assist our young maidens in fixin' up their cosy beds!"

Nate kept his grip on Tom's arm, took the apple from his hand and happily took a huge bite of it before throwing the rest to the ground. "*You* can go searchin' for stuff to fix the walkway upstairs. Go find Danny, he'll see you right." Nate grinned and patted his friend's face. "*Off you go now, Mister Kelley.*" Tommy sighed and headed off upstairs in search of Daniel Healey; his manner more than a little dampened.

"HEALEY!" Nate's amusement quickly left him as Campbell Madsen's hand thwacked down on his shoulder. "Looks like we got a job to do."

"*So it seems.*" Nate grumbled as the pair walked towards some of the discarded materials piled at the back of the mill.

"Why so cranky, buckaroo? Is there trouble in Schaeffer's heavenly gate?"

It took all of Nate's might not to ram the broken roof beams through Madsen's sneering grin. "It's been a long couple days. I ain't slept much, and you would do well to mind your goddamn tongue." He shoved the pile of wood into his camp mate's arms with such ferocity, it knocked him backwards.

"Oh ho ho!" Campbell steadied himself and watched Nate lug a couple of solid sandbags onto his shoulder. "Sounds like you're needin' somethin' to tire you out then! Maybe a wrestle to the death with that wildcat is just the ticket."

"Can you just, *for once*, shut that trap of yours and do the work you're given?"

The pair made their way out into the bright afternoon sun, with Nate taking a detour to Chuck's wagon for basic tools. "Chuck! Will you make a supplies list? We'll get stocked up soon as we can."

"Sure thing, Mister Healey."

"Oh! And see if you got anythin' to straighten out Old Carragher. Looks like he's outta whatever crazy juice he's been huffin'." Chuck nodded with concern and went back to prepping a meal for the evening.

"That Doc is our own reaper if you ask me, Healey." Madsen muttered.

"I didn't."

"Always out of it. Hands shakin'. I dunno how he's still alive let alone not killed any of us."

Nate huffed and rolled the bags heavily off his shoulder. "Well, I am more than happy to donate you to his medical practices. See if he can prove your concerns right." He shoved the small caddy of tools into Madsen's hands. "Go start puttin' the defenses up 'round the entrance. I'll get more scrap to use as barriers." His eyes were drawn from Campbell's boot-scuffing across the front of the mill, to his brother assisting Annie. "*What're you doin' Danny…?*"

"HEY! GROUCH!" Nate was hit with a flick of slimy water. "Quit lollygaggin'! Duke ain't payin' you to stand around!"

"Duke ain't payin' me at all." Nathan wiped the gloopy liquid from his cheek and looked amusedly at Mikey. "Y'know that thing is probably riddled with cholera?"

"Aaaahhh, you worried about me *Nathaniel*?"

"Nah, kid, just prayin' that you get it and I get some peace at last. C'mon, get outta there, Marie'll have a fit you runnin' 'round, stinkin' like whatever's died in that pond."

"Alright, alright old man." Mikey pulled his naked self up onto the grass with a laugh. "Just tryna pass time."

"For god's sake, Kid! Where're your clothes?" Nate followed Mikey's finger to a pile over by a dead tree "You really don't care do ya?"

Mikey shrugged. "Just as God intended. Don't wanna ruin my things, besides, no one noti-"

"MICHAEL NEEDHAM!" The beetroot face of Maw Hicks came thundering into view, triggering Mikey to sprint in the opposite direction. "YE GET BACK HERE RIGHT NOO, YE WEE NAKED HEATHEN!"

Nate continued his work with the barricades, trying desperately to keep Madsen as far off as possible by sending him to the back of the mill to add blockades there.

Danny had spent a long time talking to Annie, and Nathan didn't like it. His brother hadn't been so quick to welcome her as Nate, and this was looking decidedly amicable. He scowled and made his way back inside the old mill.

"Done." An exasperated Mr. Kelley dropped some scraps of wood unceremoniously by Nate's feet.

"*Good.*" He pondered a couple of huge, broken Mill cogs propped up by the wall then saw his brother coming through the barn doors and beckoned him across. "How heavy d'you think these are?"

"*Wha??*" Tommy looked to Danny. "Has he gone batty from the sun? You'd never lift 'em, lad."

"Not on my own." He looked to his bewildered friends and an unwelcome understanding fell across their faces. "Look like they could work as extra barriers, good to shoot from. Ain't no bullet gettin' through 'em." He kicked the rusted spoke of one with his boot, causing some of it to crumble to dust. "… *Well… most of it anyhow.*"

"I'm not helpin' with this, I've nearly died *twice* shorin' up that thing up there." Tommy Kelley's protest fell on deaf ears. "C'mon fellas, there's two of these, we can roll 'em out no trouble."

His two assistants glanced at each other, unamused. Nate also rounded up Sam and Campbell.

"There ain't equal bodies, Healey, you expect us to do *all the work?*" Madsen goaded as they arrived at the huge gears. "Well, you can take Kelley too, *seein' as you're all so weak.*" Nate laughed.

The five men weren't methodical in their process. With a lot of contesting grunts and complaints, they quickly worked up a sweat, finding the objects too heavy to roll with the spokes diggin into the dirt.

"*Ohhhh great idea, Natey-boy!*" an exhausted Tommy puffed, affecting a very bad redneck accent. "We sure gone done get this done in no time, folks, *YESSIR!*"

"Shut yer cock holster, *you… potato eatin'… halfwit…*" Nathan strained as he and Daniel kept forcing their wheel forward, "or… god help me… I'll kill you… *once I get my breath back.*"

Eventually, with much sweat, scowling, and the additional joy of Mikey's taunting encouragements from the side, the men shoved the great iron pieces in place – right at the front of the mill's entry wall. All five stood gasping; too breathless to sling insults any further, choosing to leave Nate to admire their hard work.

***

"You boys made a great effort of that now, didn't ya?"

Nate jumped. The last few hours had worked well to keep him distracted from everything else "Least we know they won't shift if there's a need for 'em." He pulled his sleeve across his brow and cleared his throat awkwardly.

The pair were rooted in silence. Nathan was too tired to move, and too stubborn to speak again, especially when he saw Annie fidgeting, finding little to distract herself with.

"You know, your brother's got some stones on him." With crossed arms, she leaned tentatively against one of the recently placed cogs and looked at her companion with vague amusement. "Not asked so much as the time o' day of me since I arrived, and then to tell me to lay off the sulkin'…? *Bold.*"

Nate laughed and kicked a couple of stones from under his foot. "Had to happen to him someday." He looked at Miss Schaeffer staring her piercing eyes through him. "I saw him pokin' the bear with a stick."

"*And you didn't come rescue him.*" Annie shook her head playfully. "What kinda brother are you?"

"*A smart one.*" He grinned. "If he's big enough and dumb enough to get himself in trouble with Annie Schaeffer, that's his issue."

"Yeah, well, Healeys seem most skilful at it… It's lucky I like his wife." Annie stood beside Nate and nudged him with her shoulder as she lit a cigarette. "Lucky for you both."

Nate nodded with a laugh and looked out towards the world; he guessed this was as good an apology as he was going to get. "I'll get her to pass on Duke's messages in future then." He chanced a side-eyed glance.

"Don't push it, Mister Healey," she mumbled through her cigarette, "it's a thin edge you find yourself on." She pursed her lips in a tight smile and exhaled her tobacco smoke.

"Excellent! What excellent work you've done, Nathan." Duke clapped his hands in victory. "This place looks like a fortress."

Annie rolled her eyes.

"Let's hope it ain't necessary, Duke, but at least it's there."

"Indeed. We shall be able to enjoy a few libations tomorrow evening with such safety around us now."

Annie sighed and started to make her way back to the main building.

"Miss Schaeffer, you've done some excellent work of your own of late. *Proven yourself.*" Duke's hand gripped her shoulder tightly to turn her back to face him. "The way you conducted yourself so *admirably* during our last adventure in Tinulca," he grinned in a way that told Annie he was riling her, "and then the absolute focus you showed protecting our merry band on our journey here. *Marvelous.*"

"Thank you, Duke… I guess, I were just doin' as I was told." She shot a sharp but lukewarm look at Nathan.

"*EXACTLY!*" Duke declared exuberantly as he escorted her back to the mill, his hand sitting snugly at the small of her back. "And as such, I believe you've earned the right to roam without concern. Please deem yourself free of Mister Healey's watchful eye." He laughed. "And I thought you would like to take your first watch tonight alongside Tom Kelley in celebration."

Both Nate and Annie gawked at that invitation, but Duke continued regardless. "I also recommend you take a trip into town tomorrow. Wonderful place. Full of many sights. Until then, I believe we have all earned a quiet, restful evening." He tipped his hat with a jovial half-bow and sauntered away.

***

"Looks like you're free of me." Annie said to Nathan as they walked further into camp.

"I could say the same to you. Pity. I was startin' to get used to your particular brand of crazy."

"Not sure that's true."

"I ain't sayin' I like them outbursts," Nate shoved her playfully, "just that I'm gettin' used to 'em."

"Well I ain't gone nowhere," Annie teased, "I'm sure you won't have to wait long for them to reappear. *And then you can learn to love 'em.*"

Nate felt the charge between them spurring again. "So, you're finally useful in this camp, huh? Makin' it onto the watch patrols?"

"That's right. I better go get some rest, seein' as the first one's tonight."

"*That's a shame.*" He murmured to her, watching her walk towards her tent.

"Yes, it is." She turned back to him with a furtive look before slinking away.

The late afternoon's glow through her canvas hadn't made it easy for Annie to rest prior to starting her more trusted responsibilities. Although the gang had the luxury of a permanent structure to dwell in, the most communal activities still happened outside. The bustle of the others was still very much in range of Annie's ears, not to mention the constant barrage of admonishments Maw was dolling out to Mikey. Eventually, failing to get any semblance of rest, she got up, splashed her face with tepid water and went looking for Tommy.

When dusk finally fell, Nathan joined his brother on their walkway.

"What's next, Nate? Are we all just gonna live here 'til we're grey and old?"

"I don't know," Nate chewed on a small splinter of wood, "I think our plan is to settle a while, then... Well... I guess make some cash...? Maybe back to bounty huntin'."

"I don't see how that's possible after Tinulca." Danny muttered.

"*Or Missouri.*" Nathan added.

"What was Duke thinkin'? Madsen weren't worth that. And alright we got a good haul in Tinulca, but it won't last and I ain't a fan of bein' on anyone's posters. I know Lucky ain't comfortable." Nate sighed. "Maybe we could send Tommy out as a carpenter, he ain't done that bad of a job on this." He struck his foot against some of the stepped repair work.

"Only if folk want to pay an Irish slowpoke. Clara said the man took a cigarette after each hit of a nail."

The pair laughed.

"Mister Kelley!"

"Well, well, Miss Schaeffer. I believe I have the delightful honour of escortin' you on this fine evenin'?" The Irishman stood and bowed deeply, nearly losing his cigarette as it casually hung from his lips.

"So it would seem." Annie looked up and saw the Healey brothers in light conversation on the walkway.

"Tanner said it's a big town." Nathan propped a scuffed boot up on the gangway siding. "There's bound to be work, maybe we can send Mikey out to the stables, clean some shit rather than cause it for once."

"So," Tommy handed a rifle to Annie with a cheeky grin, "you've finally got us all on side then. Even Danny Boy thought he'd have a chat, eh?"

"And you, Tommy? We ain't had much conversation since I arrived." The pair started off towards the edge of the barricades.

"Ah, well," he exhaled the final scrag end of his cigarette and dropped it to the ground, "despite appearances, I'm *shrewd*, Miss Schaeffer. I like to see how people go about their days. And as you were the daughter of that old bastard, Caley, I thought it might be a more adventurous watch. But seems you're more of a riddle than I thought."

"In what way?"

"It's wise to be careful of pretty women who can kill as easily with a glare, as with weapons. Though what made me warier is that you never used your skills for anythin' better than a spectacle."

"What d'you mean?"

"Nate told us how you killed them three men the day he met ya, but when you come here, you're just a sideshow!" He stopped and laughed. "Now. Don't get me wrong, Annie, I *very much enjoyed* it, but with your background, how come you didn't want to be somethin' more?"

Annie stood stony-faced. "I were six when I got sold to some asshole. The folks in that show were my family and I loved them. I weren't interested in bein' somethin' *notorious*. I didn't want a life that were about ransackin' towns or *robbin'* banks, and the only folks I've ended have been those that have done me *wrong*. I'm a survivor, Tommy. Not someone who romanticizes my sins by believin' they're my only option."

"Well, whatever happens, it ain't gonna be decided tonight." Danny opened a large bottle of whiskey and laughed as he caught his brother's gaze meander to where Annie and Tommy patrolled.

"Tell me if I'm borin' you, Nate." He teased. "I don't want to be keepin' you from apparently important matters."

"Very funny." Nate mumbled through into the whiskey bottle.

"So, I guess I missed the fact you can kill a man with your words, too." Kelley laughed and slapped Annie on the shoulder. "Cheer up, I'm just playin' with ya." The pair turned back towards the mill to tour the rest of the grounds. "But I better warn ya, you know Duke'll expect you to pull your weight. He wants the best marksmen workin' with him. Includin' you, Annie."

15

Civilisation for the Uncivilised

The exertions of the last two days finally hit Nate. His limbs felt weary as he and Danny finished the bottle of whiskey by lamplight.

"Boys?" Duke stepped out onto the gangway. "Looks like we're going to be settling here for a while, I want it to be worth everybody's time." He placed a heavy hand on the shoulder of each brother. "Daniel, go hunting with Sam tomorrow. Keep him off whatever hooch we have left for the evening. Try to get some big game."

Danny nodded to Duke and shot an exasperated look at Nate. He knew the day would be taken up with Sam Clifford complaining about various injustices done to him throughout his lifetime, and then somehow bring it around to being Annie Schaeffer's fault. "Sure thing. I best get my beauty sleep then."

"*YOU NEED IT!*" Nate called as his brother made his way to his room.

"Nathan," Duke sat in Danny's vacated seat, "it seems we are getting low on various supplies. Chuck mentioned you asked him to make a list. The ammunition stocks could do with a refresh, and Doc is apparently short on a few specifics."

"*Hmmm. How surprisin'.*" Doc Carragher had been shivering and useless for most of the day – more useless than usual.

"Yes… Anyway, I'll need you to find someone to get at least some of these items, Miss Schaeffer perhaps, and you can collect the rest." Duke handed over the scribbled notes and a map of Boulderhead. "I want you to meet Lucky and me in town in the afternoon, there's a small bar down near the market square. We need to sit down and really think about what we do now."

"Why? Ain't things alright here?"

"They are, *for now…*" Duke's brow crumpled slightly, and he cleared his throat, "But it pays to be prepared. That Tinulca money won't last forever, and we need to get something solid." Nate lit a cigarette and shifted uncomfortably as he looked out into the night. Duke could be vague at the best of times, but his manner of late was confusing. "So, no more bounty huntin'?"

Duke guffawed loudly as he stood to leave. "Oh, Nathaniel, you always were a joker!"

Annie patrolled the boundary lines with purpose. Though she was now deemed an asset, she was eager to go into town and make herself some money. She could finally make enough to go to New York or beyond, start over again. However, she didn't trust Duke. Something about him never sat comfortably with her, and Annie was sure he would make it impossible for her to move on. He had only ever agreed for her to join them, not to leave.

She still felt restless when Clara came to relieve her of her post. As dawn was yet to break, she forced herself to get some sleep before her day of living.

The sun was high by the time Annie emerged, skin sticky from the humidity. She had pulled on her least grime-laden clothes and went to get some water to drink from Chuck's wagon.

"Aaahhh M-M-Miss Schaeffer." Doc Carragher shuffled towards her, his pale face gleaming in the sunlight. "I believe there is s-some congratulations owed to you, that you a-are f-finally free to roam out of camp?"

Annie eyed the clammy medic with suspicion. So far, her dealings with the man had been minimal; he favoured the sweet caress of his laudanum to the company of people. "*Doc.* To what do I owe this specific good mornin'?" She took a long, slow sip of water, timing how long it would take the man to make his proposition. He wasn't known to speak much unless it was for his own ends.

"Oh! Nothing, n-nothing at all, my d-dear… I was just wanting to congratulate you… A-and…' Annie smirked behind her drink as he continued; his stammer becoming more pronounced with each word towards his question, "… A-a-and I w-was wondering what you p-planned to do with your f--ree time?"

She sighed, placing her cup heavily on Chuck's table. "I ain't quite decided yet. I need some money, might go huntin' and sell what I find. It would be nice to explore the surroundins a bit. I ain't never been in Arkansas."

Doc's face lit up. "Oh! W-well! If you need *funds*, and the ch-chance to e-explore, Miss, I-I believe we can h--elp each other."

"Oh, you do, do you?"

"… I-indeed," Carragher mopped his brow with a grimy handkerchief, "y-you've a g-great t-talent for-er-for p-performing. You m-may have seen th-that I sell t-tinctures to locals."

"Like a Quack, huh?"

"No. I-I am a s-skilled doctor, M-Miss Schaeffer. Th-these are *r*-remedies!"

Annie leaned back and crossed her arms with amusement. "Of course, Doc. Please. Go on."

Doc huffed as he shoved his filthy cotton brow-mopper back into his pocket. "I-I'm sure you have seen M-mister Healey as-ssist me selling these w-wares…?"

"Perhaps."

"W-well, he isn't so… *Q-qualified* i-in the – errr-… *W-well*… In the a-*art of selling*… I-I thought that *y-ou* might wish to assist?"

"You think my ability to shoot targets is suited to this kind of work?"

The small man paused. "W-well, not *that*, M-miss… Y-you also have s-certain *ch-charms, q-qualities* that Mister Healey l-lacks… Q-qualities th-that would l-likely make the s-sales o-of my wares far easier… They say you catch more flies with h-honey than with vinegar."

It was a couple of hours before the energy of the day finally got too strong for Nate to fight. Now his room was arranged, the space wasn't overly cramped, and it had been good to have solid walls and ceilings to shelter in finally. Living in a tattered tent for such a long time had started to wear him down. Even one night of sleeping in the draught-free room had put him in a brighter mood as he made his way down to the camp.

Looking at the ground floor of the mill, he noted the ingenuity of his friends. Maw and Chuck had managed to split the space into three – the Hicks's 'room' had been made from a large stack shelf pulled lengthways from the back wall, a roof and front covering had been made by draping the canvas of their tent over the top and down. The same had been mirrored on the other side of a small back doorway for Dotty and Marie (though Nate was certain Marie would be spending her evenings with Duke).

With the time nearing eleven o'clock, he could feel the humidity reaching into the building. He gave his lungs a moment to adjust to the air's thickness then made his way towards Chuck's wagon. Annie was suffering Doc's company, and as Nate approached, he could hear the man's struggles to recruit her.

"I hope you ain't likenin' me to vinegar, Doc." Nate cast a large shadow appearing behind the man; irritation slammed across his face.

"Oh! W-well, M-M-Mister He-Healey." Doc tried to dig his way out., "Y-you m-must admit, y-you a-aren't a sh-showman… I believe that maybe M-M-Miss Schaeffer here could b-bri-ing a-a-a softer -errr- m-more a-attttractive approach. F-fellows won't be as ready to d-disagree w-with s-such a f-fine lady."
"You think?" Annie began. "You sayin' I'm only good for battin' eyelids, Doc?" She glanced at Nate and saw him trying to stifle a smirk.

"N-no, just that y-you have…" Doc's eyes darted in panic, trying to find any way out of this conversation.

"*Womanly skills*?" She pushed.

"Erm…"

"Why don't you go back to your poisons, Doc? Annie ain't

interested… You ain't, are ya?"

"No I *ain't*, Mister Healey." She grinned.

"W-Well." Doc huffed and shuffled away. "I-I can see this was a f-futile use of my t-time. There was n-no need for insults." The pair laughed as Doc headed towards his sales cart.

"God that man makes for a sad figure sometimes, don't he?" Annie said watching Carragher slump away.

"Yeah," Nate sighed, "he ain't a bad guy… 'cept for the fact he may've killed some folks on accident. He's good when he's sober… Or, at least when he's taken just the right amount... How was first watch?"

"Fine. *Borin'*." Annie admitted as the two walked towards the horses. "Which I s'pose is for the best. I'm just gettin' ready to find my way to Boulderhead. I need a wash, I feel all… *gritty.*"

"I'll ride with you." Nate smiled. "I got some things to attend to. You can go get some supplies while you're there." "Hey, I'm a free agent now, Mister Healey," Annie teased, "I don't need to be runnin' errands."

"I gotta meet up with Duke and Lucky, discuss some things. I ain't got time to go shoppin'." Nate handed her a list of ammunition which needed to be restocked, and mounted Prynne. "I'll take you to the gunsmiths, you're on your own from there. And don't go flyin' off into the countryside like last time." The pair rode casually in to Boulderhead. It was odd for Annie to be around such hustle and bustle again after so long. The scene felt almost comical as the town rose out of the farmland's horizon. Nathan sighed heading in to the cramped, cobbled streets. He looked at Annie. "God, I hate these places."

"Why? Look at it! The opportunities here!"

He scoffed. "Yeah. Opportunities. Opportunity to get trampled by crowds. I ain't missed this stuff. Throwin' up brick buildins, freezin' the landscape like that forever. Nowhere for quiet."

"Oh hush up, there's two ways you can look at this world. *One,* you can see the chance for learnin' somethin' new and takin' advantage of the changes to better your situation. Or *two*, you can be a curmudgeon 'bout how the way things move forward, makin' an unstoppable, inevitable thing your enemy. Personally, I go for option one."

"I never pegged you for a Townie, Annie Schaeffer."

"I ain't. I just know I can make a lotta money off some dumb rich folks here."

They halted outside the gunsmiths and Nate produced a money clip and a map of the town. "Here. You'll need this. And I want some of that money back." His grip stayed tight on the bills as Annie went to take them from him. "This money is for *that list only.*"

"Of course." Annie smiled sweetly and snatched the $30 out of his hands.

"Alright, take care, and don't cause any trouble."

"As if I would."

"See you back at camp."

***

Annie looked down at the bills in her hand as Bessie fidgeted underneath her impatiently. She looked towards the thick door of the premises and back to the items. Pocketing the cash, she opened the map of Boulderhead, scanning it for useful establishments. She made a note of the large Gin House Hotel, pulled her hat from her saddlebag, placed it on top of her tumbling knot of hair and directed Bessie onwards.

The large stand-alone building loomed over the centre of town. The white brick structure stood three stories tall, with a wrought iron balcony encircling the first upper level. Annie hitched Bessie and made her way to the doors. All revelries stopped as the bar gawped at the grimy woman stepping inside. To her right she saw a collection of gambling options, including more than one poker table. At the only table with a spare place were two ruddy-faced older gents; their robust shapes confused by her appearance, and a third, younger man who seemed keen to know the scruffy customer better; eying her as she made her way to the bar.

"Excuse me, my good man." Annie hailed the barman who was in quite a hurry to try and move her on. "May I ask if you have the facilities for a woman to bathe?"

"Women's rooms down the hall." The barman gestured frustratedly towards a dark corridor to the side of his bar. "It's a dollar for an hour. You gotta fill it too."

"Well, that is just fine." She made her way past the surprised looks of scantily clad residents; beyond the noises of their satisfied customers howling out from behind locked doors, and onto the final door marked 'bath', which may as well have been outside.

Despite there being a window onto the back delivery yard for the saloon, and the vaguely dishevelled ambience of what was most definitely the saloon girls' usual shared bathroom, there were still womanly touches that made the old Tinulca hotel look like a slop trough. There was a large wooden modesty screen with a faded frieze peeling from it, which Annie pulled across the window. A tray lay across the bathtub, which held a large decanter of gin, a crystal jar filled with scented bath salts, and a couple of fat cigars that were probably for the gentleman callers. Once the bath was full, Annie lowered herself into the perfumed water, leaned back and lit a cigar.

She soaked in peace, with the distant sounds of pleasure and drunkenness floating through the walls. She lay there for as long as her time might allow, until the water started to match the murky hue of the pond at the mill. With great reluctance, she forced herself back into her dirt-laden clothes, pocketed two more cigars for good measure, and made her way to the poker tables. The same group of gamblers she saw when she arrived, still sat with a vacant seat. "Excuse me, gentleman, may I join your game?" She beamed at them.

The youngest of the three men leaned back and stared at her coolly while one of the older fellows blustered. "Ladies aren't permitted to play at this table, *Madam*, it is unseemly."

"Well it's lucky I ain't particularly ladylike, ain't it?" She grinned and leaned on the back of the spare chair. "Now, I have money, and it ain't like you're full to the rafters at this table, so I'm guessin' that you're just afraid to lose to a woman."

"Let her play." A soft southern accent came from the distinguished gentleman. He waved a hand smoothly and the men stood until she was seated.

"Thank you, you are *most* accommodatin'." Annie locked eyes with the enchanted man opposite and swished her hips into the seat. He was smooth-faced and well groomed. His shock of blond hair was slicked into a fashionable side parting, and his eyes were a piercing ice blue. His tailored clothes were expensive, and the chain of a platinum pocket watch peaked out from his waistcoat.

"I'm Luther Cowley, heir to the Cowley Textiles empire. The fellow to your left is Charles Rathbury, and the *blowhard* ready to pop with sheer affront to your right, is Ernest Langton."

"It's a pleasure, gents." Annie looked across the expectant faces of the three men. "Annemarie Malone."

Mister Cowley dealt the cards as the players added their chips to the pot. "So, what makes you so eager to gamble with us fellows at this table, Miss Malone?"

"You were the only fellas sittin' at it, Mister Cowley." Annie purred. "I gotta say, I was a little surprised you were all still here by the time I returned from my wash."

"I felt there were some fine reasons to wait around a while." A mischievous smile played on his lips.

Over the course of the next hour, Annie proceeded to gamble with the funds entrusted to her. She was a good gambler, and an even better card counter; the benefit of being brought up in a show with a magician. She was careful not to bet big or win overly often, sure to lose only small amounts. Finally, Messrs Langton and Rathbury were bust and took their sorry selves to the bar to drink, leaving Annie alone with the overly confident Luther Cowley.

"Looks like it is just you and I, Miss Malone."

"So it would seem."

"Why don't we make this our last hand?" He rotated the deck through his fingers.

"Why? Are you tired of makin' small bets like a girl?"

"Oh on the contrary!" Cowley chuckled. "I would just rather spend time in your *enticing* company without the need of cards. Let's make this interesting."

Annie folded her arms. "Go on."

"If you win, you can have all the money on me, and that includes this watch." He pulled the ornate timepiece from his vest pocket; its platinum shell glistening in the sunlight streaming through the window.

Annie moved her eyes slowly from the watch up to him. "And if I *lose?*"

Cowley rested his head on his finger and thumb, gazing at her serenely. "Let's not see it as you *losing*, Miss Malone. I think you would be quite comfortable should I win."

Annie placed the unsmoked half of her bath cigar between her teeth and lit it. "That depends on what your proposition is, Mister Cowley." She stared at him as she extinguished the match with a flick of her wrist.

He placed his hands on the green cloth-covered table and leaned forward. "Should *I* win, I would like to take you out on the town. I assume you are new to this place? I could escort you around the sites, buy you dinner, perhaps furnish you with more… *suitable attire…?* Perhaps you keep me company after." Annie smirked behind a pillow of smoke. His assumption that she would entertain such a proposition was all she needed. "So you wanna to take me out, buy me dinner *with my own money*? I don't think I've ever treated myself so well!"

"I wouldn't put it like tha-"

"I tell you what, Mister Cowley," Annie pulled the cigar from her mouth and sat up, "I ain't so concerned about losin', 'cause either way I'm gonna get my money back."

Cowley was eager. "*What makes you say that?*"

"You're a good poker player. I've been watchin' you make small bets or fold when you probably had good cards. You wanted to get to this point, it's been your plan all along."

"*Smart girl.*" He licked his lips.

"And it's exactly what I wanted too. You see, judgin' from all you rich fellas sat around this table, you were the only one not dulled by age and matrimony, and you weren't shy in lettin' your face show it. I figured I could get you on your own eventually, and you'd be easy to make a nice bundle off. You seem like a fella that would rather bet everythin' and look triumphant, than step away from the table right now."

Cowley laughed and sipped an expensive gin cocktail. "My, you are a clever little hellcat aren't you, Miss Malone?"

"And up until your proposal, I weren't lookin' for more than winnin' all at this table. But you've made it *so much more desirable* to take everythin' you own... I ain't a fan of robbin' someone 'less they know it's comin'. So here it is. If you win – and may I point out that it'll be because I *let* you - you may buy me a meal *here*, and I will escort you to your room. But I will knock you out, tie you to the furniture and take it all, includin' that fancy little outfit you got on. What d'you say?"

Cowley's laugh was brash and loud. 'Modern men' never believed her when she spoke the truth, because they never believed a woman was capable of the things she stated. The only people who ever believed her were the likes of Nathan Healey; a man who had been so imbedded into the darker sides of the world that he knew better than to underestimate the female of the species. And with Cowley's complete audacity to win a free lay with her, it was personal.

"Very well, Miss Malone, let us continue. *All in.*" The game played out as Annie wanted. She was able to lose to the boisterous, uppity dullard, knowing that the additional riches she would take from his room would be a great reward.

"Well, Miss Malone, I feel you're almost happier to have me win." Cowley swaggered off to order the best food on the menu. Once Annie had endured a meal and downed a large glass of good wine with such a vapid, patronising man, she allowed herself to be led by the hand to Luther Cowley's room.

"Here we are, Annemarie," he opened the door for her, "I feel, considering the circumstance, removing formalities makes sense."

"Of course, Luther, I-"

"Oh! No, no, my dear. I'd prefer you to continue to address *me* formally. There's just something about the way you say it." He leered at her as he closed the door and stepped close behind her, stroking her arms. "You are so different from the girls here," he gripped her shoulders, "*stronger.*" He held her close and buried his nose into her hair; his hungry southern drawl was like nails on a blackboard. "So many girls are simpering waifs." He let go of Annie and walked towards the bed, with his back to her he unbuttoned his trousers, "They would faint at the idea of gambling let alone the wager we agreed to. But you? You're something else."

"You can say that again, Mister Cowley." Annie pulled the pistol from her holster and stepped softly towards him. "I can be pretty honest too." She bludgeoned Cowley with the butt of her gun, directed his limp body onto the bed and proceeded to strip his room and himself of all his valuables. She grabbed a large, empty holdall and filled it, then used his braces to tie his wrists to the headboard.

"*Oh sweetheart,*" she sighed sarcastically, "you're just... *Awful.*"

Cowley's room overlooked the main street, and its French doors opened directly onto the balcony without obstruction. Annie walked to the secluded side of the hotel shaded by its neighbouring building, separated by a side alley. She looped the handle of the bag over her arm and shimmied down the balcony pillar. As she landed in the alleyway, her attention was drawn to the brick wall opposite. Staring back at her from a Wanted poster was the crudely drawn face of a very familiar man. Whomever had pasted the poster had done a slapdash job, and Annie was able to peel it away from its place to give it closer inspection.

WANTED:
LEADER OF THE NEEDHAM BOYS
Marmaduke Needham
For Armed Robbery and Jailbreak

50 years in age.
Approximately 5 feet 10 in height, lean build, silver hair.
First caught the attention of Missouri Lawmen for aiding
criminal Campbell Madsen in escape from jail.
Last seen in Tinulca, Mississippi robbing bank vaults
$1,000 REWARD BROUGHT IN ALIVE.

Casually, Annie folded the poster, slipped it into Cowley's holdall, and made her way back to Bessie. As she tied the bag to her saddle, she noticed a man leaning against a balcony strut close by, eyeing her shiftily while he picked his teeth.

"Them Needham Boys ain't worth the piece of paper that's printed on."

"Excuse me?"

"You a Bounty Hunter? Don't reckon I seen many girls off playin' Bounty Hunter." The man shifted his weight from the pillar and slithered his way to Annie as she mounted her horse.

"What makes you think I'm a Bounty Hunter?"

The man looked up at her from under his flat cap, a decidedly dark grin crawled out behind his toothpick. "Why else you takin' a poster off a wall…? 'Less you know 'em."

Annie looked down at the man. "Perhaps I collect them… Is there somethin' I can do for you?"

"You *sure* you ain't a Bounty Hunter? You got a *very familiar face* to me." Bessie tried to pull her head back from the man, when he patted her, but he gripped her bridle tight. "You're dressed as badly as one."

"I ain't no one. But I tell you somethin', if you don't get your paws off my horse, I will shoot you as if I were a Bounty Hunter."

The stranger lifted his hands from Bessie and held them up. "No offense, Miss… Those are mighty words from someone who ain't no one." He waggled his finger at Annie. "I know who you remind me of! I remember seein' somethin' 'bout a missin' person. Sounded very similar to you. Name o' Schaeffer. She's been missin' since the violent, robbery of her employer some months back. Read all about it in a newspaper up North." The fellow stared at her for what seemed like a lifetime. "Tragic."

"Yes, well… As much fun as this is, might I suggest in future you refrain from approachin' women you don't know, and keep your hands to yourself 'less you should get 'em cut off."

"Mind how you go, Miss," the man tipped his cap, "it's dangerous to travel alone in these parts, even in such a *well-to-do town*."

Annie '*harrumphed*', turned Bessie away from the stranger and made her way in the opposite direction; the feeling of eyes on her stayed until she turned out of sight of The Gin House Hotel.

Not only had Annie avoided losing any of the petty cash she had been issued throughout the afternoon, she had, in fact, more than quadrupled it thanks to the wares she liberated from Luther Cowley. She hocked it all at a less than reputable market in town. To celebrate, she treated herself to some new and very flattering clothes from the tailor, before heading to the gunsmiths. Overall, it had been an extremely lucrative day, she thought as she made her way back home.

Returning to the mill in high spirits and high fortune, Annie hitched Bessie at the paddock and went to unburden herself of her purchases. She chose to keep her new clothes until any chores she might need to do were completed. Under Maw's instruction, Annie proceeded to deliver the restock of ammunition to its stores in the communal space by the Healey's rooms. She also took the opportunity for a peace offering by returning the bandana Nate had issued her in Tinulca. His quarters seemed almost homely compared to what he had been living in at Onti Lake. He had brought his camp bed in from his tent which took up the full length of the far wall. Beside it, he had a small wooden chair that doubled as a table for a lantern; she placed the triangular cloth on it and turned to leave. As she did so, she spied a small ramshackle desk close to the door that led out onto the gangway. The tokens and photographs she had seen before were displayed, though the frame that once held the affectionate poem was glaringly absent.

***

It was after one o'clock when Nathan had completed his errands, and as he finished tying the last pack to Prynne, a poster caught his eye. A close inspection showed it was a list of the Needham Boys' names. At the top of the poster was a sketch of what looked like Duke if he had no moustache. Nate ripped it from its nailed post and balled it in his fist before marching towards the bar.

As agreed, Duke and Lucky were waiting in the ramshackle tavern, sat in a dark corner towards the back of the room. The building was across two floors, judging from the sound of festivity tumbling down from upstairs. The small, lower floor was reserved for hard drinkers only.

"Beer," Nate barked at the barman.

"You look tense, son," the barman said in a friendly tone.

"Perhaps somethin' more *pleasin'* than beer is required, huh?" He nodded to the staircase. "All fun 'n' games are up that staircase. Steps to heaven the fellas call it."

"Just get me the beer." Nate slammed some coins down on the sticky bar top and grabbed the bottle unceremoniously, choosing to ignore the mutters that followed him towards the back of the room.

"*Will you cheer up, brother!*" Duke hissed. "Names are nothing. We haven't used our full names since leaving Missouri."

"And a fat lot of good it's done us!" Lucky spat back, folding his arms. "I can't *believe* that we went along with you for Madsen. *He isn't a good man.* We were fine with our racket. Bounty work wasn't badly paid. And now *bank robbery?*"

Lucky's face reddened as Duke waved his protest away. "You've done none of that for nigh-on *ten years!* What the hell were you thinking?"

"You seen this?" Nate threw the paper ball into the centre of their table and slumped into the vacant chair. "Mentions Tinulca *and Missouri.*"

"Thank you for your imperfect timing, Nathan." Duke took the paper and opened it carefully. He smiled. "I really wish they didn't draw me so incorrectly. How offensive that man's face is."

"You ain't takin' this seriously at all are ya?" Nate muttered into his beer before taking a long, angry swig from the bottle.

"I will when the Marshalls do." Duke chuckled as he looked at the two men opposite him. "Oh come on, boys, they've used our full names, they only have *my* description and that's obviously been given from some old sheriff back from our bounty days. The picture doesn't even look like me."

"*One. Thousand. Dollars* for you, Duke." Lucky whined. "Five hundred for each of the rest of us."

"Brought in alive." Duke cooed at his brother. "And that isn't going to happen. We aren't worth anything to them lifeless. The Marshalls know the Bounty Hunters won't bother with that amount of people if they have to bring them in alive." Duke crumpled the poster back up and playfully threw it at Lucky's face, making it bounce off his nose and back onto the table. "No one's coming for us."

"Least Annie's not mentioned yet." Nate muttered taking the poster back and shoving it in his pack.

"Yes, well…" Duke's mood quietened, a shadow flickered briefly across his expression before his whiskey glass blocked it.

"So what now then? It's clear we ain't goin' back to bounty huntin'." Nate complained. "Are we gonna have to move on again after all that goddamn work we done puttin' that camp together?"

"*No,*" Duke said lightly, "no, we're all good there. No one goes to that mill; you can see that from how run down it is. No, we are to stay put, make some headway with the right people in this place. It's a big town, full of people happy to show off their wealth. Dotty can get herself in as a maid somewhere, we can get some protection work from those people too. Then, when we're in, pick out some of their least favorite heirlooms for ourselves, and get gone in a couple of months." Nate and Lucky shook their heads with disappointment.

"We won't last a couple of months." Lucky sighed. "There's plenty of people around this country that could give the law more information on us. *Happily.*"

"Will you two cheer up." Duke laughed with exasperation and stood to head back to the bar. "I almost miss the days when you threw your money away at the card tables, brother. At least you were more chipper then."

Nate looked at Lucky sitting in his defeat. "Maybe Duke's not totally wrong." He attempted. "I mean, we're sat in here, ain't no one given us a second glance."

"*Hmmm.*"

"… And you know rich folk don't pay no mind to wanted posters. If that's who we're headin' for, then we might be fine. No one has linked me and Tommy to that sugar house back in Mississippi, no mention of that on here at all."

"I just wish we never got Madsen out of that godforsaken jail. Made no sense to me."

"Yeah, well…" Nate took a long drink of beer; draining the bottle. "That makes at least two of us."

***

As dusk fell, camp buzzed with anticipation. People started setting up for a night of frolics as per Duke's instructions while he and Nate were in town. Maw and Chuck worked happily to prepare a feast from the large deer that Sam Clifford and Danny had hunted down in the woods, Tanner was tuning his banjo; Tommy was trying to convince Dotty to teach him how to dance and making her laugh with his over-obvious blundering. Lucky, who had returned early from town, was sitting with Marie and Mikey trying to teach them both to read.

Clara tended the horses while Danny took a watch, and Madsen - who should have been guarding towards the woodland at the back of the mill - was making a beeline towards Miss Schaeffer as she enjoyed a moment by herself.

"I hear *Doc* tried to recruit you this mornin'."

Annie sighed out a long line of cigarette smoke to keep calm.

She had had enough of men providing their uninvited conversation today. "Indeed. What of it?"

"Thought it might be a good idea. Might make for a bit of fun havin' a *sauce box* dressed all pretty, bound up in them dresses nurses wear. I'd be sure to put myself in more danger if you were fixin' me up."

Annie grimaced an impatient smile at him. "I'd be sure to send you to the great beyond as *slowly* and *painfully* as I could, Madsen." She took another deep inhale of her cigarette and huffed it out. "*Alas*, I turned his request down."

"Shame…" Campbell leaned against her, the edge of his moustache lightly grazing her neck, "But, I'm always here for you to practice changin' dressins."

Annie stubbed her cigarette out roughly on the dead tree she leaned against, and at glared at the man as she spat by his feet. "You disgust me."

"Ain't you dressed all fine." Clara eyed Annie with amusement from her seat as Miss Schaeffer joined her on a chair beside the mill's large double doors. "Where'd you get those clothes?"

"Boulderhead." Annie shrugged and looked at the view. "Got myself a treat after a little streak of luck at the poker table. Maybe you should join me next time and we can take the whole town." Clara laughed and lit a cigarette, its glowing embers illuminating her face. The sky was beginning to darken now, and the camp had exhausted its tasks waiting on the return of their wanderers.

"Maybe you and I will need to go out as a scoutin' party if those boys are much longer."

"And leave this place wildly under defended, Clara? I don't like the idea of leavin' it in the hands of Sam and Campbell." "Hey! We still got Danny, thank you."

"Oh Jesus don't make it worse." Annie nudged her friend.

"God you sound like Nathan." Clara shook her head with a laugh. "Just 'cause you two are *close* it don't mean you have to become him."

"IT'S THEM!" Danny called from the front watch point and

waved towards the two men trotting back into camp.

"Aboot bloody time!" Maw marched towards them. "Where the hell have ye been? We were gettin' ready to start withoot ye!"

"Aaah, Maw," Duke jumped down as he handed Atlas to Tanner, "you'd never do that to us." He put an arm around the squat woman and jostled her shoulders before moseying into the celebration that was laid out before him. "Excellent work everyone!"

As Nathan struggled with the parcels tied to Prynne, his gaze drifted towards the silhouette of Annie Schaeffer making its way towards him in the dwindling light. From what little of the day remained he could make out a small smile, as she shifted to help him.

"You took your time shoppin'." She took a couple of the larger parcels from his arms. "You tryna become a lady of leisure?"

"Oh, I don't think I'm in danger of that any time soon. Not with Duke in charge." He huffed a short, bitter laugh as he juggled the last packages into his arms and the pair made their way back to the main congregation. "Besides, I ain't got the hips for them dresses."

"No, I s'pose not." Annie eyed him cheekily. "I don't think the tailors got enough of one fabric to cover that frame of yours neither."

Nate stopped and enjoyed the decorations the gang had created in his absence today. Dotty and Marie had fashioned fabric streamers from ragged clothes and tied them to Chuck's wagon as well as branches of the trees; Chuck and Maw had made one huge campfire to roast the deer on. The place glowed warmly and, for the first time in a week, Nate relaxed fully.

Annie looked across to the group congregating around the smaller campfire as Tanner picked up the banjo. "Go on, go enjoy yourself. I'm sure you've earned it, somehow."

The celebrations echoed through the night, long into the early hours. Annie had stayed back from the group; she had felt uncomfortable joining in the bawdy saloon songs. Each person took turns in teaching the rest one of their own tunes; this wasn't her family, and she wasn't going to let herself forget it. As the booze flowed more freely through the night, she retired towards the front of the mill, and took watch.

Nate spied Annie's chosen retreat. He finished the drink in his hand and replaced it with two short bottles of whiskey before making his way over to the woman leaning on the gear barricades.

"Miss Schaeffer, you seem to be without a drink."

"I didn't think there'd be much left by now." She teased, taking the bottle from Nathan's hand. "I ran your errands for you, Mister Healey. The restocks are already safely tucked up inside the place."

"See? You ain't always a pain in the ass." He played. "Any chance you have some money left for me off the back of it? Or did you somehow manage to spend *exactly* thirty dollars?"

"Oh well, now," Annie turned fully to face him. She casually propped the camp's rifle against the make-shift wall and slowly pulled the full billfold from her pocket, "I *was* gonna give you this, but after that most *insultin'* comment…" she stepped closely to him and her perfume swirled through his alcohol-dulled senses, "I figure maybe I should keep it, *by way of apology.*"

Nate took the money from her grip and looked down with surprise at its heft, "How much is here, Annie?"

"Thirty dollars." She stated matter-of-factly. She leaned back again, the nearby camp light spilling a warm glow onto her as she pulled a cigar from a spare cartridge pocket on her shotgun belt. Nate was suddenly aware of Annie's appearance. Her boots had been cleaned and fixed, the pants she wore were newly tailored; clinging to every part of her legs and waist lovingly, held up by a leather belt cinched at her waist. A new, bright blue paisley shirt wrapped her torso tightly as it tucked into her waistband, and the shirt collar was open to reveal an old locket. All of this was framed by the tumbling locks of long black hair that fell around her neck and shoulders.

As distracting as she looked, Nate grew concerned about the way she may have obtained her new garments. "You look like you've had a productive day. How d'you still have all thirty dollars, plus the ammunition and...?" He gestured towards her.

She exhaled a large cigar cloud and smiled smugly. "I had a *very* generous benefactor in the form of a man named Luther Cowley. I didn't want for nothin', he even bought me lunch."

Nate stood beside her, his broad frame as close to Annie's body as was decent in public. "That right?" He took her cigar from her and drew on it. "And did this *Luther Cowley* just so happen to be in the Gunsmiths where I left you?"

Annie looked out towards the darkness, a mischievous grin played across her face. "Only if the Gunsmiths turned into a poker table at The Gin House Hotel." She swigged her whiskey.

"*You gambled with the camp's money*?!" He hissed. "I took a bath first," she took her cigar back, "*then* I gambled with the camp's money."

"*Jesus Christ, Annie*, what if you'd lost?"

"I never lose, 'less I plan to, Nate. Just so happened, Mister Cowley was a lucrative man who thinks with his pecker, and I was able to take all he had and make a fine pot of money for myself in the process. He might be able to be tricked again by a pretty face. Maybe Dotty." Annie playfully puffed a short plume of smoke her friend's face as he glared at her with a mix of irritation and amusement. "Don't be sore, Nathan, it ain't cost this gang a single penny and I left with my dignity, *and virtue* intact."

He laughed. "Your *virtue*? You're a lotta things, Annie Schaeffer, but I don't think virtuous is one of 'em."

Annie moved her face close to Nate's. She could feel his warm whiskey-scented breath stroke her skin. "I can be anythin' I want for the right situation." She purred.

16

Unwelcome Visitors

"So what now?" Annie asked. "You were a mighty long time in town yesterday. I take it you three put some wheels in motion to get back to livin' again?"

"Not exactly." Nathan shuffled uncomfortably. "Duke and Lucky spent most of their time bickerin'. Duke has some ideas about workin' for the rich folks in town. Maybe as coach guards or somethin', 'til we're trusted enough to grab their riches and hightail it outta there."

Annie looked across at him from the opposite end of his bed, she was far from impressed. "That ain't much of an idea. He can't think livin' in this crumblin' buildin' until *whenever* is good enough."

"We've lived in far worse."

"That ain't an excuse, Nathan." She reached down to her newly tailored pants and pulled the neatly folded poster from its back pocket. "'Specially when your fame's followin' you here." Nate knew what would be on the poster before he even unfolded it.

He sighed. "Yeah, that were what most of the bickerin' was about. I found another one listin' every one of the Needham Boys on it, 'cept you."

"Well I ain't one of the Needham Boys, am I?" Annie stepped out of bed and stretched. It was the first time Nathan had been at a distance to appreciate the view of her fully undressed. The chain of her locket glistened in the morning's light creating a border where the tan on her neck faded gently into the pale skin that was usually covered. The scars across her back glanced out from behind her curtain of hair, reminding him that she never spoke much of her life before these last months.

Following her curves downwards his gaze lingered on the artwork that encircled the very top of her right thigh; the tattoo was of a lace garter holding a long revolver and Bowie knife. Both weapons had intricate designs 'etched' onto them; the knife's blade was decorated with triple spiral illustrations, while the butt of the revolver showed an oak tree whose branches sprawled onto the gun's barrel, morphing into fanged serpents. The artistry was as beautiful and fearful as the woman it adorned.

"I can tell you one thing though," she chuckled, pulling on her clothes; her voice snapping Nate out of his gawking, "I don't know what I thought his name were, but I never had him pegged as a *Marmaduke*."

Nate smirked. "Him and Lucky were from good stock 'til their Pa lost everythin' to some railroad asshole. Still, had enough money and class before that to give the Needham sons pretty uppity names."

"No wonder they go by what they do." Annie snorted in amusement as she buttoned her blouse. "Shame they ain't got no one who can help 'em out right now."

"I can guarantee they burned those bridges long before I knew 'em." Nate laughed as he continued to watch Annie dress. "Maybe you could speak to your *generous benefactor*, get him to help us out." He grinned.

"Very funny. I'd rather not have to associate with Luther Cowley again, *as rich, and handsome as he was*, he ain't my type. Besides, I don't think he'd feel too favorably about me after the way we parted."

"The man can't be that sore 'bout losin' at cards, can he?" "I think he ain't a fan of bein' knocked out, tied up and stripped of all he carried in his room." Annie shrugged and turned to leave.

Nathan shook his head and smiled to himself, lighting a cigarette as he got up to dress, *that woman really ain't to be trifled with*, he thought. Once clothed, he left his room to check the recently delivered munitions and bumped into Danny in the hallway.

A childish smugness played across his face. "Mornin' Nate."

"Mornin'."

"*Good night?*"

"Be quiet." This wasn't the first time Nathan's dalliances had faced teasing from his brother. With Danny being five years Nate's junior, it made for some awkward morning-after encounters in their younger days. Even though he was married now, Danny couldn't let his older brother's private life pass without mockery.

As Nate checked the bullet stocks, he found that there was an excess surplus. Though she liked to pretend that she was separate from the gang, Annie looked after them. He pocketed the ammunition he needed and, stubbing out his cigarette on the stair's banister, headed for the ground floor with his brother.

"That Schaeffer ain't as sour as she likes to make out, is she?"

"Not by my reckonin', Danny, no."

The pair walked out towards the grounds together. "What's all this talk from Duke about laborin'? Lucky was complainin' about it between drinks last night."

"Ah I dunno," Nate grumbled. Annie's questioning around it mixed with his brother's concerns left him more than a little uncertain, "he was talkin' loosely. I just hope he's got somethin' more formed today."

"He better. Lucky said 'bout them posters goin' up. I ain't lookin' to get to know the law folk any more than we already have done."

Nate nodded and looked around the grounds, Danny went to help Tommy fix equipment in camp.

Annie had already changed - she had pulled on her grey cotton blouse and wide riding pants, having managed to wash the worst of the grime from them a few days earlier. Nate's eyes glinted with amusement seeing her stifle more than one yawn as she fed the horses. He went to check in with Sam Clifford on watch, then headed off to find Duke to discuss some ideas for survival in more detail than he had managed the previous day.

Duke was on the very top floor of the mill, sat at a desk, looking over a map of Boulderhead and its surrounding areas dotted with large private land holdings; making notes.

"Looks important." Nate greeted him.

"Seems to me that the old bustling town of Boulderhead is somewhat of a draw for the wealthy to hide their last few dollars in." Duke waved his friend over. "See? There were a lot of cotton plantations around these parts. So much has fallen on hard times since The Panic, but Tanner mentioned that there are a couple of families who managed to make it out alive."

"That's all good, Duke, but how're we gonna work that? Ain't like we've got any name safe to spread about here. And I can't see any of us farmin'." Nate laughed at the very thought of the men being of use with a shovel. "You can barely get 'em to go huntin' most days. They ain't ones for toilin' the lands."

"We aren't going to be *farmers*, Nathan." Duke walked towards one of the windows that looked out across the front entrance. "I spied The Gin House Hotel in town yesterday, before meeting up with Lucky. It is one of the more *up market* establishments. I think one good evening of socializing should get us in with the right crowd."

"Might be worth takin Marie and Dotty with you," Nate pondered, "Annie mentioned there's a fella hangin' 'round that might be won over by a pretty face. Could prove a useful in."

"*Good to know…*" Duke scowled towards the view from his window. Nate followed his gaze. A short distance from the entrance, a lonely figure sauntered happily towards Campbell's watch post, the distant sound of tuneful notes floated from him.

"*Who the hell is this now…?*"

***

Annie leaned against one of the horse's hitching posts and sighed. She had kept the news of her small Cowley fortune to herself, and

Nate didn't seem to ask questions about additional cash when he got the full $30 back. She was stuck. The $20 she got from Tinulca, alongside the funds she liberated from Cowley would barely give her enough to live if she got herself a train ticket even halfway east to New York. Even then, she would have a long search for Sally. She had no way of knowing where to start; Sally had been very clear to avoid getting back in contact and finalised it by leaving no forwarding address.

Bessie's boxcar ticket and the storage for her meagre possessions would eat even further into the costs, and without a cart at the other side of her journey she couldn't hope to travel far.

"The cart."

She whined as she looked back to the monstrosity. It was her home, her transport and her storage box. The thing was not going to be easy to get out of the mill's grounds without notice, and Annie had a very real sense that Marmaduke Needham was not a man who happily let new members of this group suddenly up and leave, especially if their last name was Schaeffer. No, she would have to stay a little longer and work hard to make enough money so that the lesser cut she gave to the camp wouldn't be questioned when she pocketed the rest.

As she turned to make her way towards the coffee pot, she saw Lucky sitting at a table with Marie who chided a bored-looking Mikey.

"Good afternoon, young sirs, Mrs. Bassett." Annie beamed at them. "How're the readers gettin' on?"

Marie flicked her fan back and forth frustratedly. *"Slow."* She huffed as she looked at Mikey picking a divot out of the table.

"Would be a far easier task for me *at least* if I were able to have time to do this without Mikey here."

Lucky clenched his jaw. "Maybe you could ask my dear brother?" He snapped. *"Maybe* you could spend your time with him slightly more productively than you currently do." Annie and Marie exchanged a mix of shock and amusement as the teacher slammed his book shut.

"I'm sorry my dear," Lucky sighed and patted Maire's hand, "you're doing perfectly well. Perhaps Dotty could assist a little too?"

He looked towards a distracted Mikey whose gaze wandered towards a dragonfly that hovered close by. "But I fear this one may be a lost cause, Miss Schaeffer." He flicked a quick grin at Annie, held the book and stood up. "I was wondering if maybe you would be brave enough to take on the *mighty* challenge today?"

Annie groaned. She wasn't a patient woman, and if Lucky's tolerance had faded in trying with Mikey, Annie's had no hope of surviving. She nodded reluctantly and took the book. "As long as I'm allowed to hit that kid with this when he ain't payin' attention."

"I'm sure it won't be *as* bad with you, Annie."

"As opposed to time with me, eh, Mikey?" Lucky teased.

"Exactly!" Mikey slapped the old man's arm lovingly and hopped off the chair. "C'mon, Annie, we got book learnin' to do." The two started to walk back to Annie's tent, Mikey almost skipping as they went."You think I ain't gonna teach ya, don'tcha,

Mikey?"

"Course!" The boy laughed. "Learnin' is borin'. And you ain't borin' from what I've seen."

Annie laughed as they stepped into her tent. "Okay, look. I did my dues for this borin' stuff. And believe me, you don't wanna be a dumb fella when you're older. Ladies ain't interested in dullards."

Mikey sat and thought on that point for a moment and nodded with some seriousness which made Annie's mouth twitch. "Alright, Schaeffer, you may have a point… But I got smarts up *here*." He tapped at his temple.

"Ain't worth a penny if you can't prove it on paper, Michael Needham."

"*Fine.*"

The boy surrendered.

"I tell you what," Annie pulled a small collection of flyers from her performance trunk, and sat beside Mikey on her canvas bed, "we can read somethin' a little more interestin'." Mikey sat up, took the top piece of paper from Annie and started to try and speak out the words as his fingers ran over the text.

An hour passed. Annie coerced Mikey into reading by breaking up their lesson with conversations about her time with the Smythson show. Some of the more enjoyable stories at least. Mikey pulled a small bar of chocolate from his trouser pocket and turned it sheepishly in his hands.

"Where'd you get that?"

"Snuck it." He mumbled. "Saw Nate drop some things off last night, Chuck pocketed it first and then I took it from him." Annie laughed "Mikey!"

"He ain't gonna say nothin'. The man weren't s'posed to have it anyway, Maw's always tellin' him." Mikey broke the candy into pieces and shared some with his teacher.

It had been a long time since Annie had eaten anything as luxurious as chocolate. The sweet confection melted and swirled around her tongue thickly, and she pressed the shrinking square to the roof of her mouth to try and slow its demise.

"*This is good.*" She muffled a whisper through her mouth of cocoa.

"And it's worked to shut you up 'bout readin'." Mikey blustered through his own full mouth. "See? *Smarts.*" Both Annie and the kid suddenly stopped as they heard a voice singing on the breeze. It seemed that the whole camp was straining to hear it. Something about the tone and pitch of the unknown voice was familiar, but Annie couldn't place it. All she knew was that her mind told her to get Mikey inside.

She reluctantly swallowed her candy and spoke with firm calmness. "*Mikey.* I think we're done for the day. Get yourself inside, all quietly now. P'raps go look for Nate. Tell him we got company."

***

Mikey followed Annie's instructions exactly. He stepped out of the tent and walked with stilted, overthinking steps towards the entrance to the building; too tense to look back towards the singing stranger.

> *"Oh! make her a grave, where the sunbeams rest*
> *When they promise a glorious morrow;*
> *They'll shine o'er her sleep, like a smile from the west*
> *From her own loved island of sorrow!"*

"Nate!" Mikey called running up the stairs towards him and Duke descending from the top floor. "There's a fella out front! He-"

"We know, kid." Nathan placed a heavy hand on the boy's shoulder. "Get everyone inside, get 'em up top, and keep yourself in there too." Mikey nodded with wide eyes and scurried to his task. It wasn't long before Clara, Danny and Tommy appeared at the munition stocks.

"Who's on watch?" Duke barked.

"Sam and Madsen still I reckon." Nate muttered nervously. He marched to his room and started to pick up a small collection of his weapons.

"Now, now, hang on boys." Duke tried to calm the rising panic as those not wanting to fight rushed past those clambering for bullets. "It's one *man*. Let's not get itchy fingers yet, he's singing. Probably just some lost drunkard."

"HEY! FELLA!" Madsen kept his rifle raised on the young man while he swayed merrily to the final note of his song. "You best turn around now. This ain't your home, and no one wants you here."

"Ohhhh now," the man cooed, "you don't know that mister! I might be y'all's guardian angel. *Save you from worse fates.*" The man's gaze rolled up towards the middle floor of the mill where Nate, Danny, Duke and Lucky were standing.

"What you want then, huh?"

The stranger opened his arms wide and took a few steps back. "I AM HERE TO DISCUSS A RETRIEVAL!" He continued to stare beyond Madsen, and grin like a marionette.

Annie stayed in her tent listening carefully to the chatter unfolding. She knew that voice; that same smug know-all voice from Boulderhead, and she knew what he came for. As quietly as was possible, she collected up all the guns she could carry and loaded them, then proceeded to pack herself with spare ammunition.

"What's he talkin' about? Retrieval?" Danny muttered. "The fella's insane."

"Annie." Nate said flatly. "He's come for Annie."

Annie stepped outside of her lodgings and walked towards the two men at the front of the mill, much to the glee of the stranger.

"Well, as nice as it was to hear a serenade from you, I have to say I shan't be accompanyin' you."

Madsen looked quickly at Annie. "Who is this joker?"

"No idea. But you might as well step back, Madsen. He ain't interested in talkin' with you."

Madsen tightened his grip on the rifle and backed up slowly. "No problem. Just means I can get you *both* in my sights."

The grinning menace stepped closer to Annie. "Miss Schaeffer, I presume?" Annie nodded sharply. "My oh my, how much more *fittin'* you look now than when I saw you yesterday. All guns and grit. Just as we would've hoped."

"*WHAT DO YOU WANT?*" Lucky called from the gangway.

"*WHY, THIS SWEET THING RIGHT HERE!*" The messenger replied. "*SHE'S BEEN CALLED FOR!*"

"By who? Ain't no one alive as I see that would want me."

"Ah sweetheart, don't do yourself down with such talk." Annie flinched back and pulled her pistol as the man reached to stroke her cheek. An echo of rifle clicks behind her followed suit. He raised his hands and chuckled. "Oh ho-ho! You are a most *desirable character*, Miss..." He turned his attention back to the gunmen in the building, "*LEAST DOMHNALL FITZGERALD THINKS SO!*"

The Healey brothers ran for more ammunition as Lucky headed to Tommy and Clara standing on the walkway that faced into the forest. "He's a Fitzgerald. *Keep watch.*"

The two exchanged glances. "Be alert, Clara," Tommy muttered, "them lads roam in packs. He won't be alone."

"I don't know any Domhnall Fitzgerald." Annie spat.

"Oh but he knows you, and that's all that matters."

Annie shuffled, pushing her gun into the man's chest. "How did you know where I was? This ain't nowhere near where I started."

"Fitzgeralds have ways, *Miss Schaeffer.* More eyes and spies than a church gossip… *AND WE GOT A GREAT RING O' ROSES 'ROUND THIS PLACE just for you.*"

"Who told you about me? *TELL ME!*" Annie pushed. Her rage began to burn in her gut, and she could feel her hand squeeze tighter on the trigger.

"Let's just say snakes don't just slither in grass-" A burst of red lightly fluttered onto Annie's face. With a confused hand she gently touched her fingers to her cheek and checked them. *Blood.* It was the sound of the man's body hitting the ground that brought her back to the world.

Before she could process what had happened, Annie heard yells and screams from the trees around them. Instinctively she dove for the cover of Mill gears Nate had put up front. Madsen joined her.

"*What the hell did you do that for Campbell?*"

"ME? That weren't me, you ungrateful bitch!"

The attackers sprawled out from the trees and tried to flank the front entrance between Annie and Madsen at the front line who managed to pick off a couple with fast headshots. To her right Annie saw that the horses had broken free and scattered. Bessie thundered away as one Fitzgerald member tried to grab her mane; a primal noise erupted from Annie as she used her shotgun to obliterate the would-be thief's legs from under him.

Nate and his brother quickly returned from the ammunition

stores, back to the walkway outside, and picked off a few of the runners advancing from further back. Running to check on the others, Nate found Tommy and Clara shooting almost blindly into the shadows of the forest as the bullets whistled back towards them. Below them on the ground was Sam Clifford, fighting back ferociously, almost laughing with a rekindled love of gunslinging, calling up to the others where to aim.

"CLIFFORD! GET YOUR ASS INSIDE!" Nate yelled down to him. *"THIS AIN'T NO TIME TO START THINKIN' YOU'RE TWENTY AGAIN!"*

Lucky joined them at the back of the house. "I'll help while he gets inside. Get back around the front."

Downstairs, Maw had got hold of an old, big game hunting rifle and started to help cover Annie and Campbell as the front became overrun. "AYE! Take it ye nee good bastards!" The gun was unwieldy in her hands, and the two were concerned she would cause more damage to them than the enemy.

As Annie thought to reload her rifle, she looked above the parapet; the Fitzgeralds weren't stopping, even if they had been injured in the crossfire. *"How many of these assholes are there?!"* She yelled, scrambling to fire off the bullets she had left.

"GET INSIDE!!" Duke called from the walkway above, as he continued to shoot.

Madsen stood and rushed back past Nathan as he came to cover Annie. He took her shoulder, but she shook him off and switched from her empty firearms to her pistols.

"Annie." Nathan's voice sounded distant as she focused on making every round count. *"Annie, we gotta go."* She felt him drag on her collar and she backed her way quickly towards the doors, her ammunition depleted.

The men heaved the double doors shut and lifted the huge log bar across its brackets. They stepped back to catch their breath, as the sound of bullets pattered against the wood.

"That should keep them out for now." Nate panted.

"You know what would get them gone?" Madsen piped up.

"*HER!*" He grabbed Annie by the wrist. "She's the only reason we're in this shit storm. Throw her out that goddamn door and be done with it."

Annie tried to wrench herself from his grip. "Get your hands offa me you goddamn sonofabitch!" She punched him square in the jaw and he let go. "Ain't my fault they're here, I dunno how they found me."

"ALRIGHT!" Nate roared. "Will you both just get the hell away from each other and fight them that are outside? Madsen get upstairs and help Danny out front with Duke. Annie…?" He looked at her with a pang of regret. "Just… Just get to the back room with Clifford and fire from there. There's plenty of Fitzgeralds in the trees." He shoved two boxes of bullets in her hands and marched up to the next floor.

Annie clenched her jaw and took her orders. With her guns restocked, she joined Sam Clifford in the cramped room, shuffling from the door to the edge of the broken window opposite him. "Ain't this great?" Clifford cackled. "Finally some action!"

"*What?! Are you crazy??*"

Sam had forgotten himself in the gunfight, he was almost civil to Annie. "Been a long time since I had to think!"

"*I can see that.*" She muttered to herself.

"But, these Fitzgeralds," he continued, oblivious to Annie's slight, "they don't stop…! Makes for some fun practice."

Out of the corner of her eye, Annie spotted the flash of a figure sprinting away from the other attackers. She was almost certain they were looking for a way in, and with the rest of the Needham Boys' fighters spread sparsely across the mill, it could be the end of their defence. "*Shit.*" Annie shoved her rifle into Clifford's hands. "Take this, and don't bust it."

"Where the hell are you goin'?" Sam watched as she kicked the rest of the glass from the windowpane and hopped out into the weeds.

"I'm gonna get the last of 'em."

Annie used her revolver to clip at the heels of the runner. It was enough to make him change track and dart back into the trees, but she wouldn't let up; she stopped running, raised her shotgun, and fired. The man crumpled in place. Annie dropped the gun down to her hip and sighed. Eventually, the firing lessened behind her, and as she turned back towards the mill, everything went black.

***

As the dust settled, the men removed the barricade from the double doors and headed outside to check the destruction.

"Well," Danny sighed, surveying the mess, "that certainly passed the time today."

"Bloody Fitzgeralds." Tommy spat. "Damned bastards followin' us here. Why the hell did they do that?"

"Schaeffer." Madsen muttered, a dark bruise forming at his jawline. "Godforsaken woman's a curse on us all. Wouldn't be surprised if she led 'em here herself."

"Don't talk stupid." Lucky snapped at the man. "She hates anything to do with that life."

"*Really?*" Madsen sidled up to Lucky Needham. "*So where is she right now?*"

"What're you talkin' about?" Nate shook his head. "She's inside."

The men looked back towards the mill as the gang filed out and set about clearing the grounds of corpses; Sam Clifford was the last to emerge.

"Sam, you seen Annie?"

"She went outside."

Nate marched up to him. "Whaddya mean she went outside?"

He looked down and saw Annie's rifle in Sam's hands. "The door was locked. *She was with you.*"

"I know." Sam shrugged as he handed the gun to Nate. "She leapt straight out the window, ran off."

Nate felt sick. He marched his way around the building for any clue as to her whereabouts. *"Annie! C'mon, Annie, this ain't funny!"* When he rounded the corner to the front of the mill again, he checked in with Clara. "Did you see Annie outside durin' the fightin'?"

"No, why?"

"She ain't here."

Clara's face greyed, then Tommy called out from the woods. Danny, Clara and Nate made their way towards him.

"I found somethin'." He handed Nathan Annie's shotgun. "But… She's alive, right?" Clara enquired hopefully.

Nate looked out to the edge of the entryway's horizon. "Not for long."

17

Hell Hath No Fury

Annie was floating. Her body swayed under another's momentum, and there was great pressure on her front as she struggled to balance with her hands and feet tied. A shooting pain in the back of her head stopped her from opening her eyes. The strong smell of horsehair and sour skin told her she was in the company of the Fitzgeralds, and probably better off unconscious.

"How much further before we stop, Smithy? The boys need their wounds checkin'."

"We gotta get as far as we can tonight, it won't be long before they're missin' this little gyp."

The group cackled, and Annie shook at her own foolishness; she should have never separated herself so far from the mill. Now, at least five Fitzgeralds had her.

The air had cleared and cooled, making it obvious that they were heading towards more northerly terrain through back trails. Finally, the urge to understand her predicament surpassed every warning sign her body screamed at her. As she opened her eyes, the combination of pain and dizziness overwhelmed her, causing a cascade of vomit.

"WHOA! What the Hell?! Smithy, looks like your passenger's awake." Annie's transport halted.

"Ah, *shit*! You better not've got that on Whipper, he'll kick your pretty head clean from your shoulders."

Annie coughed a sickly laugh. "I'll make some nice furniture outta him if he tries." The group jeered as the man known as '*Smithy*' gave her a clout in her temple with the butt of his shotgun.

"C'mon, we'll set camp here. I wanna get this bitch off my horse before she paints him further."

Annie returned to consciousness when she was unceremoniously dumped against a tree, her hands and feet still bound. Her vision was blurred, and her head swam as it tried to focus on the scene around her. She blinked slowly, taking deep breaths to stop the nausea and clear her vision. The group had stopped in a dense forest. They had set up a fire, and four of the five men sat around it; the fifth was patrolling nearby. Two of them were performing surgery on their gunshot wounds, muttering obscenities about those that caused them. They turned to look at Annie, and one made a comment that made the group burst into grotesque laughter.

The comedian stood and hobbled his wounded way towards her. He was a lumbering oaf of a man with a leering grin protruding from a tattered nest of a beard. He was wider than he was tall, and the smell that emanated from him brought the world into sharp, hideous definition.

"*Jesus Christ* you're like a walkin' snuff box nobody wanted." Annie complained, stopping the deviant in his tracks.

The man swigged his drink then flung the bottle towards her face, shattering it against the tree. Shards of glass nicked her cheek. "You got a lotta nasty things comin' outta such a pretty mouth." He stood over her, looking down over his gut; his hands suggestively clasping his belt buckle. "But I got a way to keep you quiet that we can all enjoy, darlin'."

She twisted her head up and narrowed her eyes. "You put anythin' near my mouth and I'll bite it off, *Sasquatch*." The man wiped his face hungrily and chuckled. "Big talk, little girl." He bent down to face her, and ran his hand over her jaw, gripping her chin tightly. "You'd be smart to behave. We don't wanna mess up that face o' yours permanent."

"*ELI!*" The patrolman walked up to Annie's admirer. "Keep it in your pants. *Domhnall* wants to meet her first. He don't want no one doin' anythin' that could stop her cooperatin'. After that, you can do what you want with her."

Still holding Annie firmly, Eli turned to his friend. "Calm down, Smithy, we're just havin' fun, ain't we darlin'? Though I am lookin' forward to seein' what else those lips can do beyond talk." Eli ran a fat, dirt-crusted thumb over Annie's lower lip.

In a flash she lunged forward and bit down hard. She glared unblinkingly at Eli. His expression turned from shock to horror to excruciating pain as her teeth buried deeper into his flesh. She could feel the panicked digit flailing in her mouth. With every jolt the man gave, she clenched harder. The warm, metallic taste of blood and earth coated her tongue and the red liquid dribbled out the corner of her mouth as she made sure not to swallow it. *"AAARG! GET HER OFFA ME! GET. THIS. BITCH. OFFA MEEE!!"*

The other men fought to prize him away from her vice-like jaws, but Annie stretched her face into a wide, malevolent grin, and with a **crunch**, Eli fell backwards onto the ground; one thumb less than he'd started the day with. She spat it out and snorted her saliva into a ball of bloodied phlegm to join the lifeless appendage on the ground beside her.

With an unnervingly placid expression, blood streaming down her chin, Annie looked at her captors. "May I perhaps bother you gentleman for a sip of water?"

***

"Danny, take Tanner and go round up the horses, they won't've gone far." Nathan marched towards the house with Clara in tow; his guilt and sense of urgency mixed into a formidable concoction.

"They did all this for Annie? *Why?*"

"She's a Schaeffer, Clara. Domhnall knows she's a Schaeffer."

"But how? And how did he know where to look?"

"I don't know."

Clara waited as Nate entered his room, placed Annie's gun down carefully and picked up every weapon he could carry;

loading them all and filling every available pocket with spare bullets.

"All his life Domhnall wanted to be Caley Schaeffer," he spat, "he's a rotten man."

"Nathan!" Duke appeared at his doorway as Clara left to collect ammunition for the men. "I just heard. I'm sorry, son, but… she's as good as dead now."

"Annie ain't dead. Not yet. *You know that,* Duke. Fitzgerald'll try and recruit her first. He ain't gonna let someone like her pass him by." Nate couldn't understand what he was hearing from the man. "And I ain't gonna leave her there."

Duke stepped towards his Lieutenant. "And how do we know she won't be amenable to his proposal?"

Nate stared. "You say a lotta crazy things, Duke, but that one's enough to put you in the hospital." He pushed past the leader and hurried back out towards the paddock where his brother and Tanner had managed to get all the camp's saddled horses back.

"We've lost the spares." Tanner sighed as Nate patted Bessie sadly before loading up Prynne.

"Tommy," Nate unravelled a map, "you were with 'em long enough, got any idea where they might be takin' her?"

"There's a sort of old settlement place that I think fur runners used. It's abandoned now… Well, apart from the Fitzgeralds…" his nervous chuckle died as Nate's glare burned into his temple. "… She's there. *But* you're not gonna like where it's at."

"I don't like where any Fitzgeralds are," Nate mumbled, "just tell us where it is."

With a shaky finger, Tommy pointed to a small spot on the map. "It's called Sugar Oak… *Missouri.*" The Healey brothers tensed up. "It'll be a day and a half's ride all told, and that's before we run into the fellas in that place. But she'll be there."

"*Missouri?*" Danny mounted his horse. "You gotta be shittin' me. We can't just ride in there."

"It's right on the edge, lads, we'll be right. No one patrols that border, why d'ya think them boys use it?" Tommy went over to meet Clara as she appeared with a bundle of bullets. Nate looked on gratefully seeing his brother and Tommy sit into their saddles. "Listen, I ain't about to get more people caught up in this business, I can get it done. Then, at least if I'm caught it's only one of us."

"No offense, lad," Tommy chuckled, "but the law won't get a look in. That's a Fitzgerald fort these days. You need all the help you can get."

"Are you *certain* she ain't nowhere else?" "*Certain*…" Tommy's voice flattened. "It's where they take all the women…"

***

Annie's three rescuers rode until their horses fatigued. They had made good ground by combining main road travel and shortcuts through trail tracks, but the need to rest finally won out. It was two o'clock in the morning when they hitched up and prepared a fire. As the adrenaline from the day's exertions had long worn out in the others, Nathan took watch.

"We'll get her." Danny passed him a cigarette and leaned on a tree next to him.

"She would've been better gettin' killed." Nate shook his head and dropped the barely smoked cigarette to the ground. He had no appetite for anything but getting Annie before she reached the Fitzgerald outpost. Now, he had to admit that wouldn't happen. Danny cleared his throat and stared out into the darkness. He knew the levels of depravity the Fitzgeralds were capable of from the reports Tommy had come back with. Clara had also confided in him during their courtship days, having been witness to it; the Fitzgeralds had a penchant for indiscriminate violence and rape.

"Listen, if anyone's gonna survive this safely it's Annie. They're in for a world of hurt if they try to cross her."

Nate huffed a short laugh as he looked at the slowly dying cigarette at his feet. "I guess I should feel sorry for the bastards."

There was a maudlin quiet over the Fitzgerald Gang as they rose before dawn to move on to Sugar Oak.

Eli woke Annie with a hard kick to her stomach. "Wake up, *Princess*."

She looked up and laughed at the man cradling a blood-stained hand bandaged in a ripped shirt. "You got gangrene yet?"

In a moment of anger, Eli pulled a gun from his holster only to be stopped by Smithy. "Eli! For Christ's sake! You wanna explain to Domhnall why we're bringin' him a corpse instead of a Schaeffer? *Calm down.*"

Eli looked at his friend, sighed and re-housed his pistol. He glared at Miss Schaeffer sitting smugly at his feet. "That's right, Eli. *Listen to your beau.*"

Annie shivered. She was dehydrated; her mouth tasted of thumb and her guts and head ached. Her clothes were torn from being dragged from the mill.

She had no idea what the day would bring, nor how she would escape it. But from what she'd overheard the night before, there were at least twenty men at the outpost, and she was in no state to fight any of them.

Time passed randomly as she drifted through consciousness. Eventually the echo of voices muttering close by became clearer.

"Wakey, wakey!"

A sharp, burning sensation pierced her shoulder as a cigar pushed into her skin. With a yelp Annie went to punch the culprit, but found she was tied down to a chair; the ropes wrenched her muscles.

A rough, strong hand gripped her face tightly. "I sure as shit hope this ain't been a waste of our time." Smithy glared, leaning close to Annie. "You really know how to piss folk off." "It's one of my best qualities." She joked through her squashed face. "*How's Lady Eli?*"

"Gettin' patched up." Smithy shoved her back. "Don't pine too much, he's comin' back. I know how eager you are to see him." He turned to the men by the door as they all left the building.

"Domhnall's coach'll be here soon. Make sure the boys are doubled on watch. We don't want anythin' goin' wrong, 'specially while he's here."

They left Annie tied up alone. She looked around. The dilapidated room had once been a school. She had been placed on a raised stage where the teacher would conduct lessons; sat right in the centre, like a reward. She noticed her gun belt and knife scabbard on a desk beside a small, broken window to her left. Under it was a ripped-up mattress decaying on the floor. The only thing keeping it together was its multiple stains. Ahead of her was the only door, and either side were windows too small to break out through. She could make out a large number of Fitzgerald's men moving around outside, and there were too many to pick off with what little weaponry she had.

It wasn't long until she heard the sound of coach wheels, and light greetings between men. The door creaked open and in walked Smithy, Eli and a new face; Domhnall Fitzgerald.

The Needham Boys were about two hours' ride from their target when Nathan stopped and pulled out the map to make a plan of attack. "We've gotta be smart, no runnin' off alone. This place is fairly open but as Tommy said, they'll have more men on lookout.

"If we place ourselves out in these points, with the range we got in this group, I reckon we can rush them successfully."

The men nodded in agreement.

"Look," Nate continued, "we're right on the edge of Missouri, so no wastin' time. Whoever finds Annie first, get her out and away from there fast. Anythin' goes wrong we'll meet back here."

***

Domhnall Fitzgerald wasn't what Annie had expected. The man was old, lean and withered in appearance. He was as showy as Duke in his attire, but the sharp whiskers poking violently from his chin, and the constant watering of his eyes told her it was nothing more than a disparate show.

The man's joyful smile revealed yellowed teeth as he approached his guest. "*Miss Schaeffer.* It is truly an honor to meet you. I hope you are being treated well?"

"The accommodation leaves a little to be desired." She sniffed and stared towards the two men she'd endured for two days. "And I ain't impressed with the lack of *caterin'* in this establishment."

A throaty chuckle emanated from the host. "According to poor Eli here, you managed to get yourself a snack."

"I couldn't stomach it. I weren't sure where it'd been. I still can't get the taste out my mouth."

Fitzgerald walked over to her with a canteen. "I never figured a Schaeffer for a joker." He fed her some stale water and eyed her face carefully. "You know, I wasn't sure the newspapers had it right at first." He cradled her head and pushed it backwards, his bony fingers digging tightly into her skull. "You see, some of my boys told me about an awful robbery of a show man up in Illinois. Mentioned a missing person. One of their ageing stars named *Annie Schaeffer.*" Domhnall grinned at her as he released her from his grip. "The fellas showed me the paper. Terrible how he went. Big fire, stomach sliced. His guts melted to the floor." Fitzgerald shook his head and tutted. "Folks didn't even see him at first. He was just a charred lump of human coal…Well, seeing as it wasn't us that did it, I figured maybe that particular Schaeffer wasn't just a name to draw crowds."

Annie grew impatient. The water had sharpened her sense slightly, but Domhnall's talk needled her. "Are you goin' somewhere with this, Fitzgerald, or did you wanna tell me a story I already know?"

"You know, I always *liked* Cal Schaeffer."

"Then you obviously never met him."

"Unfortunately, you're right in that regard." Domhnall pulled a sarcastic pout. "Though having one of his descendants in my presence will do quite well."

"It's always nice to meet a fan." She winced an irritated smile.

"You want my signature?"

Domhnall stared determinedly at her. "I *want* to give you an opportunity."

Annie laughed and shook her head. "Why is it that folks keep offerin' me *opportunities*? None of 'em ever seem to be in my favor."

"Judging by your skillset, you could be infamous. We want to give you that chance."

"How delightful." She spat.

"It's a shame we had found you with that band of *misfits*." Domhnall shook his head. "So much wasted time that could've been lucrative for all of us."

A great cloud of anger started to swell in Annie's mind, and Domhnall Fitzgerald edged ever closer to its centre. "WHAT DO YOU WANT, FITZGERALD?? Why must every man be some goddamned orator? Just spit it out. I only have one life on this earth, I'd rather not wait around listenin' to the likes of you spewin' bullshit for hours!"

A brief look of surprise flashed over Domhnall's face before he grinned. "I want you to work for us, Miss Schaeffer. Say yes and I can guarantee that my boys won't harm you. You'll move freely in these lands, and have the right to end any man who touches you."

Annie sighed and looked down at her feet, "I can already end any man without you, thanks."

"But now, you can bring back your father's legacy once and for all."

She wasn't sure what caused it, but a quiet laugh started to build inside her. Eventually, Annie couldn't hold it and she threw her head back, bellowing out a hellish cackle.

She slammed her gaze on the gang's leader. "Lucky Needham said you always wanted to be Caley Schaeffer. And you think that by collectin' someone who had the misfortune of comin' from his bloodline is gonna make up for that?"

The three men in front of her shifted warily.

"You *think* you're as feared and depraved as him?" She smirked with a vicious, crooked smile. "You think ruinin' womenfolk and robbin' stagecoaches is anythin' darin'?" She leaned forward, her skin burning against the ropes; her eyes darkened like the sky on the brink of a storm. "A wizened old fool like you don't scare nobody, and a wizened old fool like you with a bunch of lunk-headed outlaws? *It's pathetic*." She spat on the floor. "Caley Schaeffer didn't need that. And I can tell you right now, Caley Schaeffer wouldn't wipe the shit off his horse with the likes of you."

Domhnall sighed and rubbed his hands calmly. "That's a no then?"

Annie sat back with disgust. "It's a no."

"Well, that is a shame." Fitzgerald turned to leave and gave a sly smile to his escorts. "But at least every man here can tell the story of how they bedded a Schaeffer." Domhnall patted Eli's shoulder as he left with Smithy. Stepping into his stagecoach, Fitzgerald called out to the men. "*IT'S A NO!*" A raucous cheer went up, and he left.

Nate watched his companions move into position undetected. The mood of the outpost was calm but alert. As the posse waited for a signal to begin the attack, Nate used the scope of his rifle to figure out where Annie was. He noticed the stagecoach parked by a crumbling stone building. That's where she would be. Suddenly, the door to the shack opened and out walked Domhnall Fitzgerald. On entering the coach he called out and the throng of men caterwauled with lascivious needs, leaving them momentarily distracted. It was all the trio needed to take advantage.

Sounds of gunfire started in the distance.

Eli moved towards Annie with a lecherous look on his face. "Bet you're wishin' you were nicer to me now, Schaeffer."

"Bet this would be a lot easier with all your fingers." She goaded.

He took her hunting knife from its scabbard on the table, used it to rip open her blouse, and lightly dragged it across her throat, knocking its blade against her locket. "What's this?"

"Don't you-"

Eli clicked it open and looked at the image inside. "She's almost as pretty as you. Think I'll keep this *for those lonely nights*." Annie began to struggle as Eli tore the chain from her neck and pocketed the jewellery. "Don't be makin' any moves you're gonna regret, darlin'." He placed a hefty knee on her lap, and using his good hand, sliced through the ropes that bound her upper arms, leaving her wrists and ankles tied.

"If you can't find your pecker, fat boy, I'm guessin' you left it in Smithy's mouth."

Her chiding had gone too far. Eli grabbed her by her hair and slammed her face-first into the rotting wall. "Oooh sweetheart, this ain't gonna be pretty. And neither will you be once I'm done." He salivated into her ear. "If only I could trust you on your knees, but you made it clear that mouth's off limits."

Annie didn't hear any of that. The force with which she had been flung knocked her back into a 14-year-old memory. She was in a dark side alley late at night. There was a pressure of her body being squashed against the wood sidings of a saloon. She could hear laughter and the untuned tinkle of a piano through the wall. Her arms were pinned overhead by a man twice her size, and a good four times her strength. The sharp, rough splinters dragging across her cheek encouraged her to push them deeper into her skin as if to focus on something other than what was happening. With each cheer from the saloon, and forceful thrust from her attacker, she grew angrier knowing the final piece of her soul was being taken from her. As he focused less on her struggles, she managed to wrench an arm free and reach for a large, discarded whiskey bottle standing empty on some old crates. She swung behind her, hitting the man hard enough for it to break against his temple. Back in the crumbling school room, Eli the oaf was taking his time as he switched between one-handed fumbling at his britches, and hard punches to Annie's back, or cracking her head into the wall with frustration.

With every blow to her spine, and every slam of her head, her memory grew clearer of the man in the alleyway. Gripping the neck of the bottle in her hands, she lunged over him, pushing the jagged end down into his eyes; twisting and gouging as he screamed.

Annie's eyes ripped open. With her hands still bound behind her she felt for Eli's gun while he fumbled. In the foray she found its handle protruding from the holster, forced back the hammer and squeezed the trigger, shooting the bullet through his calf and into his heel. He collapsed to the floor. Blood pooled underneath him as he searched for his weapon, but Annie had held on to the gun as he fell.

She sat herself on the floor and looked at him with a venomous stare. "Don't you go dyin' on me now, Eli, we've only just started." She managed to thread her legs through the loop her bound hands made and hopped towards the discarded knife, placing the gun on the desk. After cutting through her ankle ropes, Annie walked over to her bleeding menace while she sawed through her wrist bindings. She stomped down hard on his arm, breaking it against the stone floor. *"Wake up, Princess."* Eli screamed in agony as, free from her constraints, Annie retrieved her locket and placed it in a cartridge pocket on her gun belt.

She picked up Eli's pistol and pointed towards him. "You know why I ain't like Caley Schaeffer...? *I'm.*" She fired the gun straight into Eli's left kneecap. *"Careful."* Another round in his right kneecap. *"Who."* One to his left thigh. *"I."* One to his right thigh. *"Hurt."* The final bullet was saved for between his legs. The man gargled a final gut-wrenching note and passed out. It wouldn't take long for him to bleed to death.

The gunshots outside grew closer and more hurried, but to Annie they were as quiet as rain on a canvas roof. In a trance-like state she wrapped her gun belt around her and tucked the surplus gun in the waistband of her shredded pants. The door flung open in a panic.

"Eli! You gotta get out here-" the dirt-covered face of Smithy stared at the mass on the floor and looked across to where a feral Annie stood. "YOU GODDAMN WHORE!"

As he lunged at her, she dug her knife deep into his shoulder and used it to level him to the ground. Before he even realised he was down, Annie was kneeling on his chest, pummelling his face with her bare hands; her knife still in his shoulder. Smithy struggled to reach her throat to stop her, but she grabbed his hair and slammed the back of his head into the stone repeatedly. She took her knife and stabbed wildly at his torso before she slid off and crawled to a dark corner.

The three gunners had managed to end the lives of a lot of Fitzgeralds before the rest tried a sharp retreat to safety. As the others finished their battles, Nate heard a terrifying noise from where Annie was imprisoned. He rushed ahead and smashed open the door. Horrified by the scene before him, his gaze moved from the corpses, towards a creature that resembled the woman he knew; her shirt ripped open to reveal blood-soaked undergarments. Her eyes were black, and where her skin wasn't bruised or bloody, it was deathly pale. Almost catatonic on the flagstones, she hugged her knees, her bloodied hunting knife still in her hands.

"Jesus, Annie." He whispered. Suddenly the body with barely a face gargled. Its hands tried to claw at some invisible lifeline as its lungs filled with blood; the skull was as good as gone. Nate raised his gun and, with a grimace of sympathy, pulled the trigger just as Tommy appeared.

"What're ya doin' shootin' a corpse?"

"He weren't a corpse." Nate swallowed his sickness and stepped towards the wild animal beyond.

"You shouldn't oughta've done that," It whispered, "he would've gone eventually."

"C'mon, Annie, let's get you home." He wrapped her in his jacket and gathered her up.

Annie looked up into the hardened, worried face of Nate, and heard Danny speak. "You're alright now, Annie, and we got Bessie back too." She sighed, exhausted. The warmth from Nate as he carried her to his horse helped her relax.

"Duke don't need to know about what happened here." She heard him say shakily. She was placed in the saddle and he sat behind her to stop her from falling. Finally, she collapsed back onto him and fell asleep.

18

Nate didn't speak on the return journey unless it was to stop the convoy to check on Annie and feed her provisions. He was certain she was unconscious. Her most perfunctory needs of eating and drinking happened mechanically all while her eyes remained closed; her body barely responded. The posse didn't stop beyond that, it was imperative to them all that Annie be returned and watched over in safety.

The mood was sombre, they had all seen the carnage at Sugar Oak, and none of them recognised the being that caused it as it slept in the saddle of Prynne.

It was night when they arrived back, much to the relief of the camp.

"DOC! You better be goddamned sober. *I am in dire need of your assistance.*" Nate called as he hitched up and carried Annie to his room, his comrades in tow.

"O-o-of c-course… Oh my! W-what has the poor girl b-been through?"

"More than enough." He grumbled, carefully placing the unconscious Miss Schaeffer on his bed. "She'll need a lotta care I'd have thought."

"Y-yes, indeed, Mr. Healey."

As Doc Carragher assessed the situation, Maw Hicks hurried into the cramped space, forcing Tommy, Danny and Nate backwards towards the door. "Och, my! The poor wain…! What can I do, Doc?"

Nate stared, helpless, while they looked carefully over Annie.

Doc's manner became serious. "Get cloths, blankets, warm

water and… Th-there should be some morphine in my stores. *Hurry.*"

"Aye. Right away." Maw turned to the group of onlookers. "I think we'd do better *wi'oot the audience.*"

Nate's companions nodded and stepped out of the doorway as Marie and Dotty arrived to receive their orders. Time crawled by as Doc carefully eyed his patient while waiting for the return of his assistants. Eventually the convoy of women returned with supplies, shoving past the audience.

Nathan stood against the doorframe, unable to look away as the nurses carefully removed his jacket and the remnants of a blouse from Annie. An alarming amount of bruising was daubed across her entire upper body. They ranged from plum tones, through to the darkest black, stopped only by rope burns and cuts she had. His friends stood behind him, and all three men had to turn from the painful sight as Doc's team worked.

"*Jesus…*" Dan whispered, and Nate clamped his eyes shut. Clara arrived with warm water, placing it by the bed before turning to the men in the doorway. "C'mon. Y'all need rest." As she passed Nate to leave, she squeezed his arm softly. "*You too.*"

"I will. Thank you. All o' you." He turned his back to watch over Annie as the men and Clara departed.

"O-only a rib or two seems broken, M-mister Healey." Doc muttered from his place at the bedside. "All this – *a-as awful as it is* – i-is just superficial. She'll heal." He placed a needle in Annie's arm and her body relaxed instantly. Having tended to his duties, Doc let the women wash the blood from Annie's face and hands, which revealed that almost none of it was her own. Beyond the bruising, Miss Schaeffer resurfaced.

"I cannae fathom how only a coupla ribs are broken, nothin' else, not even her jaw. There isn't even a tooth missin'." Maw whispered to Nate. "They made thisun *strong.*"

"They certainly did." He managed a small smile of relief.

"We won't be able to shift her ferra while, Mister Healey."

"I had no intention of her bein' moved, Maw, don't you worry."

Annie's carers removed her gun belt and the remains of her riding pants in order to clean and bandage her as needed. As Dotty carried the belt towards the desk, a small, silver locket dropped from it. She handed it to Nate. "The clasp's broke."

He ran it through his hands, "I'll get it fixed. Thank you, Dotty."

The relief of his friend's wellbeing slowly loosened the tension in his muscles, and Nate found himself exhausted. He made his way outside, forcing himself to ignore the quiet, concerned stares of his camp mates. He sat alone at a table, stabbing at the gloopy leftovers he picked up from Chuck's stew pot.

"You boys did well."

Nate huffed a small, bitter laugh through his nose as Lucky joined him. "Don't see how killin' a bunch of fellas, even if they are Fitzgeralds, is doin' well."

"You saved Annie, you brought her back. And by all accounts she'll survive just fine."

Though he knew Lucky's words were meant as comfort, the whole business had shaken Nate. Annie's creature-like attack had been vengeful and deliberate, at least by the looks of one of them. Her violence was more ferocious than her father's. *"I dunno how saved she is."* He muttered to himself. He picked at the blood under his fingernails and looked at the old man. "Besides, she didn't need no help with her captors."

"Oh now," Lucky chuckled and slapped Nate's back, "we all know the fates that would've befallen Miss Schaeffer without you aren't worth thinking on, but they would most certainly have come to pass."

He sighed. "I guess so." Reluctant to continue with the conversation, he heaved himself from the table. "I best get back to my duties."

Lucky nodded. "Of course, son."

Nathan proceeded towards Annie's tent to get her spare clothes and blankets. As he lit the lamp beside her bed, he noticed a new, beautifully illustrated picture. The vibrancy of the piece glistened in the lamplight. The artistry was both imaginative and somehow real. The familiar vivaciousness of her character, and the piercing magnetism of her eyes shone out in the image. How could the woman in that picture be the one he saw in that hovel?

He returned to his room with the belongings, as the team of caregivers headed out.

"She'll sleep a lot, I'm sure. E-especially now we've removed the pain for a while."

"Thank you, Doc."

Doc Carragher nodded and, for a moment, the ghost of his old self materialised. "I'll check on her in the morning, if you're intending to sit with her."

"I ain't plannin' on bein' anywhere else." Nate winced a smile, thanking them all once more. He placed Annie's items on the desk and pulled out the spare sleeping roll from under his bed, unravelling it on the floor beside her.

"Nathan?" Duke stood in the hallway. "How is she? I heard… Well, Maw was *careful* with the details, but…"

"She's alive," he shrugged, "and that ain't gonna change anytime soon. She's beat up but not… *broken*."

Duke patted Nathan's shoulders. "Good. Good news, my boy."

"Duke, I don't think you understand what happened to he-"

"She survived the Fitzgeralds." Duke stressed. "And she survived with only cuts and bruises."

"Only cuts and bruises?" Nate hissed. "The woman is only bein' held together by goddamn cuts and bruises right now!"

"All the more reason for you to let her rest up and focus on our next steps – getting some good funding back in the coffers." He slapped Nate's arm. "Don't get upset, son, you have Annie back. Now we can get on with our plans. Rest up tomorrow, then we'll all go to Boulderhead and take a little trip to The Gin House Hotel." Duke turned and made his way upstairs, oblivious, or unbothered by the glare that followed him.

"Nate…? Is Annie alright?" Mikey stood by the staircase with

Marie beside him, an apologetic look across her face.

Nate switched his expression to what he thought was a natural smile, walked up to Mikey and ruffled the boy's hair. "She's banged up, Mikey, but she's gonna be fine soon. Not like she's gonna let a bunch of morons best her in a fight, is it?

"No." Mikey huffed a sad chuckle as he looked at his feet. "No, I guess not…" He looked up and grinned. "I can't wait to hear the stories!"

Marie tightened her hand on Mikey's shoulder. "Best you don't visit her for a little while though, huh?"

Mikey nodded. "Well if she's knocked out cold, she ain't no fun no how." He gave Nate a playful punch in his gut and turned back to go downstairs. "G'night old man!"

"I'm sorry, honey. He got spooked. Annie got him inside and he feels kinda responsible for leavin' her." Marie shook her head and looked down the stairs after Mikey. "I told him not to be silly, but you know what he's like. Thinks that if he ain't doin' somethin' to help, he's hinderin'."

Nate nodded. He knew that feeling all too well. "It'll be alright. Once that kid gets told to shove it by Annie again, he'll be just fine. Goodnight, Marie." He returned to his room, closed the door with a sigh, and collapsed against the wall, sliding down to the sleeping roll.

Though his exhaustion was overwhelming, he couldn't sleep. So much had happened in such a short amount of time. He kept thinking about that first gunshot in camp. Neither he nor Danny had seen it happen, but it was loud. Someone close by had taken it, and from what he knew up to that point, no gun needed firing.

To distract himself, Nate pulled Annie's necklace from his pocket and looked at it. She had worn it constantly since they arrived in Arkansas. The filigree pattern on the front was elegant and had faded with age. The clasp on the side of the oval pendant was heart-shaped, and as he opened it, he stared at the image of a woman close in resemblance to the one beside him. Only, her expression had a natural lightness that Annie's did not. He closed the hinge on Elizabeth Malone and turned the locket over in his hand. An ominous message was scratched into the back, and Nathan hoped Annie hadn't yet been lost.

19

A Half-honest Crust

Nate watched over Annie throughout the night. He had been too restless to sleep, but too tired to fix the chain of her locket. Instead, to feel vaguely useful, he spent many hours checking on her; applying a cool, damp cloth across her forehead to help prevent a fever, or simply watched her for any sudden changes. Though she slept on, her face flicked and flinched with troubled expressions, like she was fighting against something. As the fringes of dawn reached the window of his room, his eyes closed.

When he woke, Doc Carragher was standing over the patient, assisted by Maw. They checked on the bandaging, and cleaned her wounds.

"Sh-she's healing very well. N-no infection to be seen."

"That's good news."

Maw turned to Nate. "Ye stay sittin' with this lassie, Mister Healey. Ye haven't slept 'n' there is hee-haw you're wanted for elsewhere."

He had no energy to argue, and looking at the bruised woman in his bed, he couldn't have agreed with Mrs. Hicks more. Duke had told him to rest anyhow. "Seein' as I'm confined to this room, could one of you haul me up off this damned floor? I need to get some movement back into these bones."

Doc heaved the aching man up and eyed him in a way only doctors can. "Did you get hurt in the rescue?"

His lucid and confident manner threw Nate, and he blustered a small chuckle of surprise. "No, Doc... Coupla bruises from some weak brawlers is all. Nothin' to run to momma about."

Doc nodded and escorted Maw from the room.

Before leaving, she gave Nate a rare smile. "I'll get ye some supper."

He must have slept almost fifteen hours as the sun was setting outside. No one had bothered him, still he felt he had wasted the day; he never rested guilt-free. With a stretch of his back, Nate took a moment to step onto the walkway that wrapped around the building's outer walls. It was as if camp had never been attacked, but the stiffness in his shoulders and the injured Miss Schaeffer in his bed were stark reminders of a day none had anticipated. Having to move to the woodlands of Arkansas because of snooping lawmen, then an ambush from Domhnall Fitzgerald's men caused something to gnaw in Nate. He needed answers. Duke and Lucky must have felt the unease too.

Once Maw brought him food, he sat at his desk and looked to tackle the broken locket chain with some small pliers Tanner kept for the horses. Despite the sleep he had already managed, he felt as unrefreshed as ever. He found fixing Annie's jewellery frustrating in the dwindling light, but he was determined to do at least one thing of use that day. When success finally came, Nate leaned back in the chair, let the pliers slip to the tabletop beside him, and shut his eyes.

The sharp light from the window was a rude awakening. His whole body had seized up from another night of sleeping upright. As he fought temporary blindness, Nate felt like he was being watched. He turned to see two green eyes smiling at him, framed in all manner of bruising.

***

Annie finally woke up to the weighty pain that cracked ribs, a blow to the head and a multitude of bruises gifted her. Her sleep had been filled with angry memories that left her almost as exhausted as she had been when she arrived at the Fitzgerald hideout.

The brightness of the room was jarring. She stared up at the ceiling of Nate's room, blinking to adjust to the light. Aware her torso was tightly bandaged; she gingerly tested the abilities of her limbs. Everything ached. Most parts stubbornly resisted any form of movement, punishing her with sharp pains if she tried. With great effort Annie twisted towards a low growl that rumbled from a chair at the desk. There slept Nathan Healey; legs sprawled in front of him, arms folded, and his head bowed. It looked like he hadn't changed or moved in days. The sunlight streamed through the window and surrounded him in a golden haze. Her locket dangled from his fingers, sparkling in the light.

Annie watched him for some time, his being there had a tranquilising effect, and she smiled while he snored on like a faithful hound. Eventually, the guard dog jolted awake and rubbed at his face.

"I don't see the point in your unrollin' a bed if you're gonna sleep in a chair the whole night."

Nate's expression was one of relief as he stretched and struggled to stand. "It's been *two* nights, Annie." He eyed her with concern. "… How are you?"

"I know what it must be like for a critter to get trampled by a stagecoach now." She winced as she rolled on to her back, coughing a short breathless laugh as she did so.

"You had us worried there for a minute."

"Really? An *entire minute*…? My, my, I must be losin' my immortal veneer."

"We'd just forgot what a stubborn ass you are. You've survived just to piss them Fitzgeralds off."

Annie grinned a wide, toothy grin. "Well, I ain't one to give bastards any type of satisfaction…" she looked up at Nate and pain flashed in her eyes, "but them boys gave it a helluva go." The two remained awkwardly silent for a moment. The weight of the events at Sugar Oak pushed heavily on them both.

"…Your locket's all fixed." Nate bent down to settle it at its rightful place around Annie's neck, careful not to aggravate her injuries.

Annie hated being dependent on anyone, but the care Nathan took with her was an unfamiliar comfort that she found herself welcoming. The man seemed capable of a gentleness she couldn't muster if lives depended on it.

"Thank you." She whispered, as he stood back up. "… It was only a broken clasp…"

He shrugged, working to avoid looking directly at the woman "Listen, we're all stayin' put for now. Duke thinks the Fitzgeralds know not to come play bandits again, 'specially as they've seen what you're capable of doin' to 'em…" Nate tensed. He hadn't meant to bring up Annie's destruction, in part because he didn't want it to become some great argument. Her flat expression told him to continue, "We got an idea to go earn some keep."

"Honest work, or thievin'?" Despite her bruised face, she was still able to give Nate a humorous, disdainful look.

"Honest… For now, at least." He ignored her short, wheezed laugh. "No point makin' things worse for ourselves right now, considerin' we got an invalid to look after."

"Very funny. So, then what?"

"I dunno… I guess build up some good trust with folk… Then abuse that trust…? Get ourselves a nice bit of money and disappear."

"All you Needham Boys plannin' on runnin' to a new state, huh?"

"All of us, Annie." Nate held her hand tightly and locked her gaze. "You ain't gettin' away from us that easy." He started to back out of the room and picked up his hat with a grin. "Not after the trouble you've put us through anyhow."

Annie stared at the door Nate just left through. She was unsure how many weeks she had before the gang felt they had 'a *nice bit of money*', and they moved to pastures new. She started to panic. She had never agreed to travel with them, nor thought she would be taken along in their tide; trapped and drowning.

The money Annie had would dwindle fast unless she could increase it gambling, and considering her last encounter in town, she would need a new card table.

"*Annie....?*"

"Come in, Clara." The door creaked open, and her friend's worried face appeared. Annie smiled at the sight. "I ain't never seen you look so scared, you alright?"

"I should be askin' you that." Clara came and sat on the edge of the bed.

"Well, I ain't dead, and I ain't crippled... Least not permanently." Annie gripped her side and heaved herself into a sitting position, grinding her teeth through the pain. "It's just bruisin' really. I can see outta both eyes so I'm guessin' it ain't *that* bad."

Clara smiled at her as Annie attempted an elegant pose.

"Prettier than ever, Miss Schaeffer." She said, tucking a strand of hair behind Annie's ear. Without warning Clara's expression dropped, and sincerity burned through her eyes. "... Did... Did they..."

"They kicked the crap outta me, Clara... *That's all*... They could've done a lot worse."

"It can't've been fun anyhow."

Annie knew a little of Clara's story from whiskey-soaked evenings at the campfire. She had felt helpless as a child seeing her mother getting forced upon by Fitzgerald's men before both her parents were killed.

Annie softened her voice. "I've had the crap kicked outta me my whole life... and more, too." She looked at the expression on Clara's face. The anger, disgust and humiliation her friend felt over her own experiences saddened Annie. "But I'm still here. You gotta keep goin'. Just got another filthy memory to carry with you." She gripped Clara's hand a little tighter. "*You just keep goin'*. That way they never win."

Clara coughed out a short sad laugh and nodded. "And we all know you ain't one for losin'."

"*Exactly.*" Annie grinned.

"I better leave you to rest. If Maw sees me in here, she'll throw a fit." She patted her friend's bruised hand and stood back up. "Get yourself healin', miss. The sooner you're fixed, the quicker we can get back to makin' you do stuff 'round here."

"So that's why you bothered me." Annie called. "Checkin' I weren't fakin' to get outta work."

"Of course." Clara laughed. "You can't get away from hard work here without proper cause."

The door closed leaving Annie to sit in her own concerns once again. She didn't like the idea of being classed as 'one of the gang'. Suffocations crept through her chest from being incarcerated in one room. She couldn't stay in that spot any longer. With a scream of pain, she managed to swing herself onto the edge of the bed, reach to a spare long-barrelled rifle, and set about using it as a rudimentary crutch.

Her first attempt was a failure, she fell to her knees trying to stand. Her ribs burned above her stone-like legs. But she was determined to make it to fresh air. Steeling herself, she gripped the butt of the gun, slammed the barrel into the floorboards, gritted her teeth and heaved herself upright.

She must have made more noise than she realised as Maw Hicks rushed into the room in a panic. *"ANNIE SCHAEFFER WHAT IN GOD'S NAME ARE YE DOOEN??"* She marched her way over to the hobbling lump. "Get back in that bed *right noo!*"

"No offence, Maw…" Annie grimaced breathlessly, "but you can shove that idea wherever you… *shove things*. Excuse me, I need some goddamn air."

Much to Annie's surprise, Maw stepped aside. "Wey, at least let me help ye." She strutted over to the door, which connected Nate's room to the outer walkway, and flung it wide open. Then, she dragged a chair onto the balcony, and waited behind it expectantly; arms folded.

Each step felt like hot knives in Annie's limbs. She rocked against the desk. "I fear I've been a little over-determined in my adventure today, Maw." She said almost defeatedly. "This spot seems as good a place as any to spend the rest of my days." The gun failed to be either tall enough or sturdy enough to provide any meaningful support to its owner.

"Ohhh I dinnae think so, lassie!" Maw shook her head strictly. "Ye want some *goddamn* air? There's plenty oot here, *Madam.* Ye ain't gonna go back on your word aboot shoving things now are ye?" She raised an eyebrow at Annie and twitched a sideways smirk from the corner of her mouth. "Stop bein' such a baby."

Annie took as deep a breath as her bound ribs allowed, braced herself, and hobbled onwards; crunching her teeth into her jaw to ignore the pain. After what seemed like hours, she lowered herself, most ungracefully, into the chair.

Maw brought her a canteen of water and wrapped a thin blanket around her. "You're doin' great, lass." She whispered and lightly rubbed Annie's shoulder before she left.

***

The smile from Nathan's lips fell as soon as he closed the door to his room. He headed to the camp's grounds lost in thought. There were so many factors about their current circumstances that made little sense. How had the Fitzgeralds known Annie even existed? No one knew about her until she appeared bruised and brawling on some dusty road in Mississippi a few months back. Even then it was Nate that recognised her from some distant memory. If his mind hadn't been as sharp, she would still be known to them all as Annie Malone. Then the sudden appearance of men by Onti Lake after she joined them concerned him. Someone had said it was the law, but no one knew for sure, the gang had been lost to lawmen since fleeing Missouri. Though news could travel, there had been no murmurings of The Needham Boys in Tinulca until the vault robbery. Then that gunshot from the mill…

"You gonna pour that coffee or are you just holdin' it for comfort like some long-lost love?" Clara's mocking pulled Nate out of his own mind and branded her empty cup in his face.

235

"It's been a long few days." He grumbled, pouring her drink.

"Looks like it." She eyed his dishevelled figure. "Danny was out like a light after he came back, said things were a little more… I dunno, *shockin'*… Wouldn't say no more beyond that."

"Hmmm." Nate lifted his cup to his mouth.

"How's Annie doin'?"

"She's okay, I guess. Pretty beat up but that just seems to have made her even more of a smartass."

"Well that is a relief then." Clara chuckled. "Wouldn't want somethin' like that to change her."

Never had a sentence been more apt or worrisome. Nate nodded silently, and Clara took her leave.

"Nathan!" Duke came marching over to him with Lucky in tow. "You good to go?" he stared at the mess of blood-stained, rumpled clothing and tutted. "You aren't looking in the best way, son…" he said, flapping a hand in the direction of Nate's shirt, "I mean sure we want to make an impression on people, but perhaps the *correct impression* would be wise."

Nate clenched his jaw. "My apologies, Duke, I guess livin' in a ruined buildin', and havin' to fight off more than enough assholes lookin' ta kill me, made me forget my *dress code*." He strangled the middle of his coffee cup as he drained its contents.

"Okay, look." Lucky stifled a smirk and stepped between them.

"The Gin House Hotel is *pleasant*. And, Nate, if we want work, we need to not look like butchers."

"Listen, I ain't about to get trussed up to-"

Lucky lightly closed his eyes and raised his hand; the signal he had used all Nate's life to quiet him. "You aren't getting *trussed up* for anything, Nathan. But for goodness sakes boy, you can't think that what you're currently wearing will be suitable for this?" Nate huffed. "I ain't got nothin' else. Anythin' I own is in my room. Annie's probably restin'."

"CHUCK!" Duke called without taking his eyes from Nate. "YOU GOT A CLEAN ENOUGH SHIRT FOR MISTER

HEALEY HERE?"

"Sure! Lemme go check!"

"Wha-?" Nate began protesting.

"You're a broad man, son. You'd rip the seams of the others' clothes. At least Chuck's will be wide enough."

"It ain't gonna cover my navel, Duke."

"Then wear your pants as high as they go, kiddo!" Lucky slapped Nate's arm and the Needham brothers started to walk towards the paddock. "Meet us by the horses when you're ready!" Nathan glowered watching the men snigger into the distance. He inspected the shirt that Chuck leant him; an itchy wool affair the shade of faded sand, with the thinnest, pale red stripes down it. *"Christ."*

After what seemed to Nate like a painfully long ride to Boulderhead in a shirt too short, and made from what felt like cactus needles, the three men hitched up outside the hotel. "Now remember," Duke pushed, "we're here to discuss *work*. We are men who can work protection escorts, but we want to be working as house guards. If the folks you speak to have nothing of note to protect, you move on."

Lucky and Nate agreed and, under Duke's instruction, the three men split up and stepped inside the bar. It was a hive of joviality. The pianist played upbeat tunes worthy of a music hall, while the poker tables were overflowing with men looking to waste their family money on chance. Thanks to their upbringing, the Needham men would have no trouble pitching the idea of a protection business, but Nate wasn't sure of his need amongst these types. Perhaps he was to be used as a prop - proof that Duke and Lucky had the goods they were selling. That thought darkened Nate's already low mood. He decided to make his way to the bar, silently dodging guffawing blowhards as he scratched at his shirt. He found a gap next to a cluster of young socialites, leaned onto the bar, and ordered an over-priced sipping whiskey. He winced into it as the gaggle of pretty young women and over-exuberant young men squealed in delight at some story being told by a softly spoken man in his late twenties.

The fellow stood at the centre of the throng. His well-spoken accent fresh from the Southern territories sing-songed from his throat. "I mean I'm sure it can be seen as my own fault," the suave gentleman chuckled, "when one is so frequently surrounded by *decent, elegant* ladies such as you fine women before me…" he flashed a cool smile at the blushing girls, "you forget that not all creatures are so… *Educated*."

Nate's irritation prickled with every word the man spoke.

"Personally, I blame these Suffrage Seekers. They keep filling the heads of perfectly *fine* women with notions of *political independence*. It makes them irrational. Just because they are old, haggard and unloved, they are looking for some way to be noticed and attended to by us gents once more." The man glanced at Nathan as he scoffed bitterly into his whiskey. "What say you, sir?"

"Nothin'." Nate looked at the amber liquid as he rolled it around in his glass. "I say nothin' at all." He had tried hard to ignore the nonsense the gent had been spouting. It seemed fruitless for his own endeavours. But the boy's thoughts on the opposite sex were naïve.

"*Women,* my dear fellow. You obviously *have* an opinion." The man's wolf-like eyes studied Nathan with smugness. "You look like a man with a history…. What are you in?"

"*In?*"

The young man laughed at Healey's blank expression. He started to dislike the fellow's ability to make him feel foolish.

"*What's your line of work*, good man? I can tell you aren't from this stuffed-shirt town. You a Rancher, sir? You certainly have the brawny roughness, and attire, of a man who has toiled in the outdoors for all his days… *No offence*."

Nate stood up from the bar and forced a stern smile from his granite expression. "I'm in protection." He growled. The young man and his friends seemed to respond knowingly. They congratulated themselves on their completely mis-perceived guess. He glowered at the polished upstart who sipped at an elaborate drink. "And you have the very barin' of a fella that ain't never worked a day in his life. *No offence.*"

The man spluttered a bellowing laugh at Nathan's observations, which cued the group to join in. "Oh magnificent! No offence taken *at all*, dear man. It's always a joy to meet someone who can tussle with the best of us." The handsome man offered his hand to Nate. "Luther Cowley. Heir to the Cowley Textiles empire. And you're right. I have had the great honor of being quite a pampered pup when it comes to avoiding labor."

Nathan grinned and took Cowley's small, uncomfortably soft hand, squeezing it harder than an average handshake warranted. "*Mister Cowley.* How good to meet you. Nathaniel Deleaney."

"*My,* that is a hand and a handshake!" Cowley gently massaged his crushed digits with awe.

"What was it you were sayin'?"

"Oh yes! I was merely wondering what your thoughts on these modern girls playing in politics would be. I sensed that you and I are at opposites in this discussion, based on your reaction moments ago. You seem like a well-travelled man, an old soul if you will. I can't believe you don't agree that it is improper for women to be acting like men. They are becoming so *unbecoming.*" He smiled at his little pointless wordplay. "So irrational and having such ideas beyond their measure. I profess I was the recent victim of women's so-called rights. A robbery at the hands of such a type befell me not one week ago."

Nate turned his whole body towards Cowley and leaned his hip casually against the bar with great amusement. He was eager to hear the victim's side of the story. "And you think this is down to politics?"

"*Indirectly,* yes. These bitter old spinsters are getting into the minds of the younger ladies, making them think they are entitled to act out in such ways. Leaving them to become childless loners themselves."

"You don't think that the woman just wanted your money?"

"Have you ever been robbed, Mister Deleaney?"

Nate found himself enjoying the company of this milksop immeasurably. "Not by a lady, no." He smirked.

"Of course, what am I thinking! Well, let me tell you. As thrilling as it may sound at first, there was something far more sinister to it than simply *"wanting my money"*. I fear she meant to humiliate me on account of my sex. You see, if she merely meant to take my money, she could have asked so very prettily, and we could have come to a gracious arrangement easily." Cowley sipped his drink and leaned in; his voice hushed conspiratorially. "And believe me, the siren in question could have taken *anything* she'd liked from me *had she asked prettily*." The boy winked, and Nate felt the glass creak in his increasingly tightening grip.

"No, Mister Deleaney. When a stray follows you to your room and proceeds to bludgeon you unconscious to raid it, takes your finery in the process, and leaves you as good as naked; tied to a bed for a maid to find, I would say it was nothing more than a fanciful opportunity to make a mockery of a good man. So, as a man who has obviously worked hard and traveled with many a different fellow, wouldn't you agree that there is an epidemic of hysterical menaces rising?"

Nathan sighed and lit a cigarette. "Mister Cowley, throughout my time on this earth I can advise you of only one thing. Women ain't never wanted to be tied to a fella like some lost child, and they ain't fanatical of bein' regarded as such." He exhaled a long line of smoke. "Now, I don't believe the reason for it is *politics*, but you best believe when a woman is tired of nonsense, they'll let you know it. And *some of them* just know the easiest way to steal everythin' off a man. From his heart to his britches." He raised his glass and drained it. "But, if you're in need of bein' protected from such wildness, may I direct you to the gentleman at the end of the bar." He pointed his empty glass in the direction of Duke. "He'll be able to arrange somethin' most suitable for your needs, I'm sure." Nate put the glass down loudly. "Have a pleasant day, sir." Tired and irritated, he left the impertinent fool to make his friend's acquaintance. Chuck's shirt stabbed at him, and there was a light draught from where it barely tucked into the back of his pants.

Nathan Healey had no more patience to give. Instead, he made his way out to Prynne, unhitched her, and headed back home.

***

As camp bustled below her, Annie gripped the locket around her neck. She had allowed the lessons her father taught her to overrule common sense – *never leave one to run, Annie. Unless you know they won't come back,* she heard Caley Schaeffer say. "Guess you didn't heed your own advice with them Needham Boys, Cal." She heard a creak of floorboards from Nate's room, Tommy was returning the maps from the rescue. Annie gave a light nod when he saw her.

"Alright, Miss Schaeffer? It's good to see you up." "As up as sittin' down can be, I guess." She twitched a smile as the man came to join her. "Worst thing about it is my legs work, but my ribs don't wanna cooperate, and bein' given tepid water ain't much of a comfort for healin'."

Tommy scoffed and leaned against the balcony siding, rolling a cigarette between his fingers. "You're a fine lass to have in a scrap, Annie, I told you you'd be needed."

"I fought stupid, Tommy." She sighed. "I ran off on my own to shoot some jackass that were leavin', and I got myself caught. I nearly killed three good folk for my trouble."

"*Four.*" He pointed to Annie.

"Yeah, well, this one's expendable."

"Here." Tommy lit and handed the rolled cigarette towards Annie, the fresh green of its contents peaked through the thin wrapper. "It'll help better than water or whiskey."

"Man, I ain't had hash in a *long* time." She said, inspecting the smouldering roll. "Where'd you get it?"

"I spotted Old Carragher enjoyin' them a few months back." Tommy winked. "He's pretty precious over 'em. I don't think he has much of a stash, so I grabbed a couple before he ran out." The mossy smell reminded her of younger days with the show. Its perfume wasn't dissimilar to the natural scent of Onti Lake. She inhaled with a painful struggle, held the smoke in her lungs for a few seconds, then slowly blew out. The change inside her was almost instantaneous. All the tension melted from the top of her head, out through her fingertips and toes. The pain across her upper body wasn't gone, but she no longer minded it. The sunlight fused with the humidity and campfire smoke to shroud the view in a warm, golden tone. She passed the roll-up back to Mr. Kelley.

"You know, there was a fella in the show for a while who smoked this stuff pretty regular. Didn't like a drink, but a smoke…?" She laughed. "He weren't fond on *sharin'*, mind you, guess it was hard to come by."

"What'd he do?"

"He was a trick roper, came up from Mexico to try and be a rancher. Hadn't figured on the fact folk weren't keen on Mexicans tryna make an honest name for themselves outside their own country. Smythson picked him up when he was buskin'. We had a double act sometimes. I'd have to try and shoot or throw knives through various loops he was spinnin'. I miss him."

"A good man, yeah?"

"To some, I guess." Annie shrugged. "Marcos liked to get hold of things that weren't his to hold."

"Ahh! He liked to rob fellas, huh?"

She raised an eyebrow. "If you call stealin' a man's woman *robbin a fella*. He liked a married lady."

Tommy laughed. "The fella liked a challenge!"

Annie shrugged. "It weren't no challenge for him; a handsome man with tanned skin and a foreign accent who did amazin' tricks with ropes?" She shook her head. "He liked 'em 'cause it were *easy*. God knows how many little Marcos there are runnin' 'round the country today."

"What happened to him?"

"He made a mistake." Annie took the cigarette back from her company. "He picked a crazy. There she was, front row, first night, and the night after that. He must've been good at appreciatin' the ladies. She convinced herself she were gonna run away with him and that they were in love. Told Marcos she'd left her husband. 'Course, her husband turned up, drunk outta his mind, and mad as hell." Annie looked sadly out at camp. "Aired all their nasty laundry in public. She told him she'd found a *real man*, that they were in love. Well, her fella didn't take too kindly to that and shot his wife on the spot. Then Marcos… Then himself."

"*Christ…!*" Tommy Kelley coughed out the cigarette smoke.

"Why didn't Marcos shoot the fella?"

"He was a pacifist!" Annie laughed hard. Her ribs complained but she didn't notice. "He didn't even own a gun! Goddamn fool."

The pair laughed uncontrollably. Down in the grounds, the figure of Nathan Healey was hitching his horse and marching angrily towards the camp, kicking at anything in his way. Annie and Tommy exchanged glances. She licked her fingertips and snuffed out the cigarette, handing it back to her friend as the sound of heavy footsteps thudded up the stairs.

"I best be goin'," Tommy raised his eyebrows towards the angry clumping, "I'll see ya."

He pocketed the joint and decided to take the scenic route to another doorway into the building, just as Nate stomped his way back to his room and crashed onto the bed, his thumbs buried into his temples.

"You know, Mister Kelley has some pretty good cigarettes that will mellow you right out." Annie called from the balcony. "Stole them off the Doc." Nate shot a glare towards her. The light of the afternoon glowed over her as she smiled a confused, bruised face at him. "Don't look at me like that, Mister Healey, I ain't the one that's got you mad."

"What're you doin' out there?"

"Not gettin' sat on by the looks of things. I won't ask if you wanna talk about it."

He took a deep breath, pushing the annoyance from his lungs, and joined Annie outside. "You takin' a watch from up here?" He joked, pointing to the rifle propped against the sidings as he dragged an empty crate to sit beside her.

"Only if imaginary bullets kill people." She scoffed. "It ain't particularly good as a walkin' stick neither."

"Guess you're sleepin' out here then."

"Very funny. But don't worry, I ain't gonna burden you further. I'm just workin' up the energy to get down those stairs."

"Are ya now?" He laughed. "You think you're gonna manage that, three days after havin' the shit kicked outta you?"

"I'm pretty sure I can slide down that banister if I can get a leg-up." Annie grinned. "But I ain't takin' your space no more, Nate. You need your rest. Even if I have to sleep in them stock shelves."

"You have to be *the most stubborn* woman I have ever had my misfortune to know." His eyes glinted as he gave her a small sideways smile.

"Yeah but you wouldn't change me for nothin'." She laughed and looked out towards the horizon.

"I guess not." He lit a cigarette. "I met your handsome benefactor today."

"Did you now?" Annie huffed with amusement. She didn't know if it was the effects of the joint, but she felt more content than she had in a while. Even the bruises started to feel like an affectionate ache. "And what did you think of Luther Cowley?" Nate flicked his eyebrows as he fiddled with the matchbook in his hands. "The man's an imbecile. How hard did you hit him, Annie? 'Cause there's gotta be good reason he's as dumb as that."

"Maybe his parents are brother and sister." She giggled. "He has money. Least he's got some comin'. Could be a good swindle but I doubt I'd be welcomed back with open arms."

"I dunno. He seemed quite animated over you, based on his re-tellin' of the renegade woman hell-bent on humiliatin' the male species."

"Maybe he figured me out after all." Her green eyes glinted in the afternoon haze.

Nate looked at her. All the bruising and scabs that marked her washed him in guilt. "I'm sorry you're stuck here all beat up. Things ain't been right for a while, but this was such a *mess*." He stared at his feet as his tired voice rumbled on. "You know, we never had it bad before. Not really... I mean, sure we weren't exactly always upright, but no one got hurt. Then Duke decides that he wants Madsen outta prison for somethin' that he should be locked up for...?" He shook his head. "I dunno. I can't understand how folks even knew *we* were here, let alone you... I'm sorry. You picked a real bunch of hucksters to hide amongst, Annie."

Annie twitched a sad smile at the man beside her looking toward the horizon. He shrunk into his exhaustion; concern strained at his face. He didn't appear to enjoy the work he did but understood its necessity.

It encouraged her to confide in him. "You know what I want beyond all else in this world? Four walls and a roof. All my own. Don't even need another room." She gave an embarrassed laugh. "I know it's simple, but I ain't never had that. It'd be out of town, *but not too far out*, maybe close to a river, I dunno. I'd be a Bounty Hunter or a Trapper or somethin', to pay any costs I have. And I'd live off the land, all quiet like."

Nathan let his mind drift into her vision. "Sounds like a pretty idea." He muttered.

Annie sighed and rested her head against him as they watched the sunset in silence.

20

Pointing Fingers

Late August 1893

It had been two weeks since Annie was retrieved from Sugar Oak. Despite a lot of contesting from Doc and Maw, she had insisted upon returning to her own lodgings to recover. She also wouldn't accept help while slowly shuffling down each dusty step of the mill on her behind.

"Y'know, it'd be a damned sight quicker if you'd just let someone carry you." Nate had said as he watched on, amused, at the bizarre choice of movement Annie had committed to. "I can do it." She forced through gritted teeth while the wooden steps splintered into her hands and her bound ribs argued loudly against her statement.

Now she had privacy and solitude again; able to hide in her tent from the looks of pity, even if its cover was in the stifling heat. The first week of recovery left her practically bed-bound, and being nestled back in her canvas home, she was practically invisible; people were too busy to think about her when she wasn't struggling out in the open. With almost hourly visits from Doc and Maw to check on her injuries as the only thing to preoccupy her through the day, Annie became very skilled in eavesdropping. Not that it was avoidable when living in a tent, unable to retreat from earshot. She started to learn a lot about the gang; far more than the group may have realised. The most apparent change had been between Duke and Lucky.

"There's no reason to look for a new spot. This is safe." Duke hissed at his brother late one night.

"How? How can you possibly believe that?!" Lucky implored.

"Look what happened not two days into living here! Those damned Fitzgeralds… They knew we were here. Knew soon enough to plan for an ambush. They knew about Annie! The Marshalls around here don't even know about her – she isn't on any wanted posters."

Annie stiffened. She, too, was unsure how the Fitzgeralds had connected her to The Needham Boys. She had been careful when touring Boulderhead after her run-in with their messenger, and she had been vigilant in checking she wasn't followed back to camp. She had done everything right.

"According to that uppity youngling, Cowley, in town, she's already made an impression." Duke huffed out what Annie guessed was cigar smoke.

"Regardless. Look what happened. That first shot taken, Duke. Then look what they did to her."

"And yet, here she is. Back in our fold." Duke's voice dropped menacingly. "Despite my reluctances about her. Despite what could now befall us because of Nathan's brainless moment of gallantry."

There was a chilled silence between the men. The world seemed to hold its breath. "… Duke… You can't be serious… She isn't Cal… She's a good wom-"

"She's a danger to us all! But, no one listens to me. Whatever fates are brought to us because of that woman, we are not moving. We have a good thing in Boulderhead. We can make some real cash. And if the Fitzgeralds realize we're still here, then we shall give them what they want."

"What?!"

"No trouble from them for years, now this? I shan't sacrifice us all for that bad omen."

Annie heard one set of footsteps boldly kick through the grass away from the swimming hole, and fade as they scuffed through the dirt towards the mill's entrance. She stewed over Duke's words as, out in the grounds, Lucky forced out a defeated sigh. Duke wasn't stupid enough to forget she was there; you don't turn a group of misfits into an organised gang if you have corn for brains.

The entire conversation had been orchestrated for her to hear, but why? Perhaps because he knew she could do nothing about it. No one would believe her, or side with her if she told them. Perhaps it was just so she'd remember her place.

"Well," Annie muttered to herself bitterly in the dark, "I guess you misjudge quite how stubborn I am, Mister Needham."

The second week of recovery saw Annie finally get the bandages removed from her midriff. Much to her relief, Doc told her she could take up gentle exercise. Mikey and Lucky had made a cane to support her weight when standing, and the teen used it as a bargaining chip to get her to teach him how to throw knives.

The cane itself was impressively crafted and as tall as she was. The two craftsmen had taken a large branch from a fallen hickory tree and managed to sharpen the end to a point that could be staked into the ground. The top of the cane was naturally flared from where the branch once joined the trunk. They had worked hard to carve out the middle of the flare into a rounded hollow which could act as either a resting place for her hand, or a shotgun barrel if the need arose. The density of the wood could also become an impressive weapon for knocking attackers out cold or putting a teenager in his place with a swift rap across his shins.

"I wished we'd never made that damned thing!" Mikey mumbled, rubbing at his ankle.

Annie grinned and forced her cane back into the ground. "But I am so *very* glad you did. Last thing I'd want is you bein' able to run rings 'round me with no way to trip you up."

Mikey smiled sadly and turned back to the targets, sighing as he flung the wooden knives half-heartedly into the ground. "… Y'know, Marie and Nate wouldn't let me come see you when you … *got back.*" Mikey's head dropped. "… It weren't 'cause I didn't want to. Said you needed rest." He kept his gaze away from Annie.

"Well, they weren't wrong." Annie knew the kid would never have handled how she looked upon her return.

"Did it… Does it hurt…?" His eyes were remorseful as he waved his hand towards Annie, "all o' that?"

"Shit, yeah it hurts, Mikey! I got kicked just about every which-way."

"I shouldn'ta ran inside that day… Shoulda stayed with you."

Annie wheezed a short, painful laugh. "Why? So you could get shot? You can't even fire a gun straight, I weren't gonna be the reason you'd be buried at fourteen."

"I guess… Well… The fellas do say, *"Heroes always die"*." Annie softened her gaze upon seeing the usually cocky teenager shuffle guiltily. "You did *exactly* what was needed. You raised the alarm. You kept everyone safe, and you musta bucked a trend, 'cause you were a hero to them that needed it."

"…I guess."

"Mikey, you shouldn't listen to everythin' them boys say. If they knew everythin', they wouldn't be holed up in a crumblin' old buildin' in the middle of a bear-infested forest, alright?"

"That's true." He smirked.

"Look. It ain't just heroes that die. We *all* go. There's no need to run into gunfights or prove your worth to these misfits. Best thing you can do is get outta this situation. Read your books, make somethin' more of yourself. These boys ain't even gunslingers, or bank robbers. Not really. They're just a bunch of buffoons."

"Old ones at that!" Mikey laughed and leaned against the tree trunk Annie sat on.

"There you go! Old buffoons that don't know how to be smart. If they did, we wouldn't be in this mess."

"Well, I'm glad you're in this mess with us."

Nate had been sure to visit Annie each evening since her abduction, even though he had been employed as Cowley's top minder by Duke, which kept him away from the mill all day. "Nathan is stretchin' himself thin. Always gettin' back here when he's done in Boulderhead. I've never seen him in camp this regular in a long while." The muffled tones of Dotty floated through Annie's tent one evening as the women sat by the fire to put the world to rights over a drink. "Regular as clockwork these days. Should just hold up somewhere in Boulderhead, instead of shamblin' back here every day."

"Aye, well, he's got somethin' worth comin' back fer now. That Schaeffer lassie is a goodun. He fusses hisself to the bone fer her, 'n' rightly so."

"You've changed your tune, Maw." Clara slurred. "I thought you called her *the rotten offspring of some degenerate*"."

Annie sat up and smiled at Maw's initial assumption.

"She's proved hersel' *ten times over*. She's a lass you'd want brawlin' with ye."

The trio hummed in agreement.

"At least Annie's proved that Nate still knows how to have a little fun." The women cackled at Dotty's observation. Doc Carragher shuffled towards Annie's lodgings to bring the daily poultice for her injuries. She had refused more modern, chemically induced tinctures, which Doc happily kept in stock for his own ends. So instead, he and Maw worked to create an old wives' concoction that had been used by frontier camps and cross-country caravans for generations. They mixed yarrow, hummingbird blossom, and sage with some oil to soothe her cuts and ease the pain of her bruising.

"You're healing well, M-miss Sh-Schaeffer. Though I wish you h-had heeded my concerns a-about s-s-sleeping in here."

"Now, Doc, I had no other option." She lied as he placed the bowl and a cloth next to her lamp.

"W-we both kn-know that's untrue." He smirked while taking a quick look over her injuries. Annie was always pleasantly surprised by Doc's abilities when he wasn't soused. His hands barely shook when he worked, though their tell-tale tremble would return as soon as he was satisfied with his checks.

"This is your last poultice." He said in an uncharacteristically forthright tone. "Apply it all, and rest up."

"Yessir, of course." She nodded sharply with a smirk on her face. "Doctor's orders."

Carragher smiled and left.

Within thirty minutes of her chat with Doc, Nathan appeared. *Like clockwork*, Annie thought.

"How's the cripple doin'?"

"I'll cripple *you*, Mister Healey, if you continue to call me that."

He took a deep breath. "I see Doc's been by."

"Indeed. And this is my last night smellin' like some kinda roasted turkey. How was your day, bein' nanny to that *little prince*?"

Nate huffed and sat carefully on the edge of her camp bed. "You know he don't do nothin' that warrants bein' looked after? The kid don't leave Boulderhead. Just wants to seem important enough for the need of *"Brutish Men"*." He sat tall and uttered those last two words in his haughtiest, most simpering voice. It made Annie laugh, and her ribs complain.

"Have you at least got some good information on future funds?"

"Duke does." He shrugged. "… I s'pose… I'm the *brutish man*, so I don't have the excruciatin' joy of sittin' in the cab and hearin' the swill pour from Cowley's mouth. I ride up front. Though the driver sometimes lets complaints slip."

"Well, you have a talent for bringin' the crotchety out in folk." Nate nodded and leaned close to Annie's face, checking her injuries in the lamplight. "Your bruises have gone that nice yellowy-green color now. Two more weeks and you'll look like you again." He lingered where he was, his face creased with serious study.

Annie smiled at him. "You needn't fuss over me you know. I'm a big girl, Nathan Healey."

"I know." His eyes shifted to meet hers, he smiled broadly and gently patted her cheek with his heavy, calloused hand. "G'night, Annie."

***

Nathan's travelling since first visiting The Gin House Hotel had been demanding, in part, by his own decisions. Duke had declared him the go-to for all Luther Cowley's escorting requirements. It was his job to ride out to Boulderhead each day, meet up at the coach house stables, and join the driver for a day of nothingness. Duke had frequented a couple of the journeys under the guise of keeping his customer happy and would ride along trying to obtain any useful opportunity for furthering the gang's fortune. At least, that's what Duke would say. To Nate it felt more like he was trying to get a seat at the table of the rich and awful.

All this dull work would have been manageable enough, but Nate's keenness to return to the mill each night racked up the miles he and Prynne were covering. His consistency in camp didn't go unnoticed by his friends, and they liked to point this out to him on every return.

To save his mare from exhaustion, and to alleviate some of the guilt he still felt over Annie's situation, Nate took Bessie on a few rides to town through the weeks. He was careful not to let the highly conspicuous creature draw too much attention. Luckily, a place such as Boulderhead was a hive of show-offs and so he found she blended in more than expected.

Considering Bessie was calm to the point of docile, and exceptionally intuitive when Annie rode her, she wasn't as keen on being commanded by someone else. It took great effort to convince the mare to move away from the camp's paddock, and though Nate was a strong man, the Percheron was determined to fight him when he tried anything but brush her. After much struggle, he coerced the beautiful beast into a partnership and found, despite her reluctance, that she was a cooperative, but stubborn horse.

"You've spent far too much time with that Schaeffer." He joked as they arrived back home one evening. "If you had a black mane, I'd be callin' you 'Annie Two'."

"Back again? You tryna start some kinda record?"

"Evenin', Tanner."

"You told Annie you been stealin' her horse and makin' it look difficult?"

"No."

"Maybe you can go tell her this evenin' on your *daily visit.*"

"You wanna get off your ass and feed these animals?"

"Oh they're fine!" Tanner grumbled, lumbering to his feet.

"You should lighten up! Least you got all your faculties still in workin' order. Fancy workin' a poor old man like me into the ground."

"*My heart bleeds.*" Nate dismounted with a wry smile. "You're welcome to take over my duties of sittin' on a hard coach seat in all weathers, for a soppy boy instead." He slapped Tanner's shoulder and made his way towards camp.

"*DUKE WANTS TO SEE YOU!*" Tanner called after him, "*BEST DO THAT BEFORE YOU GET SIDE-TRACKED WITH YOUR PATIENT.*"

Nathan waved his thanks and walked towards the house, stopping to look towards Annie's tent. He sighed and pushed himself forward.

"Why on *earth* should I be calm about this?! The idea of it is preposterous and dangerous for her."

Nate braced himself as he heard Marie bickering with Duke beside the red maple on the mill's lower floor.

"It's a good plan… The boy's all boast and no substance."

"And that's supposed to make me feel *alright about this* is it?! Whatever happened to gettin' her a job as a *maid* somewhere?" Marie was pacing back and forth with her arms folded. The scowl across her face was a combination of Annie's and Maw's. "The girl don't need to be part of some… *Half-brained scheme!*"

"It's *not half-brained.*" Nate noted Duke's exasperation as he reluctantly joined the pair. "… It was Annie's idea…! Tell her, Nate."

Nate looked at his friend with surprise. "Tell her what? What's goin' on?"

"The *ever-intelligent Marmaduke Needham,*" Marie spat, "is tryin' to convince me that Dotty would be perfectly fine to *whore herself out* for the good of this camp!"

"*What?!* And you're sayin' this were Annie's idea?" Duke sighed and sat on a crate beside the maple, running a hand across his brow in frustration. "She isn't *"whoring herself out"*. Nathan, you said that Cowley is someone drawn to a pretty face. You told me Annie was made very aware of that, correct?" Nate fidgeted as he thought about that boisterous upstart's manner, and cleared his throat. "That's what she said at first, But-"

"So, as Miss Schaeffer has indisposed herself, and Dotty currently finds herself inactive most days, I felt it would be a good chance to get her acquainted with young Master Cowley."

Nate felt the sharp glare of Marie burning into him, so he purposefully avoided looking in her direction.

Forced to be a regular attendee of Cowley's entourage he was well aware of the man's personality. "How would you go about introducin' her, Duke…?" He rubbed the back of his neck as if to bat away Marie's stares. "I mean, it ain't like we've mentioned any ladies lookin' to meet him, is it? And… I dunno… How would we keep her safe?"

Duke sat up and stared flatly at his friend. "Are you telling me the great Miss Schaeffer might be *wrong* about something?" Duke's question silenced the building. Nate had only experienced it once before, when first discussing Annie. He felt trapped.

"… I'm just sayin' that… Well, she didn't know much about him then. She knocked him out cold and robbed him. Dotty ain't exactly like that is she?"

"*Exactly!*" Marie flung her arms up in some premature celebration of support from Nate. Nate knew Duke's mind had been made up, and two against one in an argument against him never meant victory.

"She won't need to go in all rough. Annie isn't known for being *demure* at the best of times. And from the conversations I've had with Luther Cowley, that phase of desiring *feral women* has been knocked clean out of him. Quite rightly so."

Nate couldn't help but smirk at that. Annie most definitely

liked to ensure men reassessed their opinions of women when she was around.

Duke stood up, ignoring the huffs coming from his lover. "Nathan, I shall discuss it with Dotty this evening, and we shall meet you on your daily work tomorrow. You will happen to bump into us in town and introduce her there."

"*WHAT?!*" Marie's usually perfect complexion had turned puce, "I can't *believe* that you are gonna continue on with this ridic-"

Duke held up his hand and glanced sharply towards her before continuing his conversation with Nate. "I shall introduce her as my ward, and we shall have a most pleasant conversation with the boy."

Marie stormed out of the building in murderous silence, and Nate swallowed his own protests. "… If you think it's a good idea."

"Annie certainly did." Duke grinned. "I don't see why things would have changed."

Once Duke finished discussing the finer details of Dotty's long-term plan, Nate made his way towards Annie. The stifled, liquor-soaked giggles of Clara, Dotty and Maw stopped him as they spied his regular visit. He greeted them with a light smile and a wave of his middle finger before he knocked on one of the tent posts and stepped inside. The warm lamp light illuminated half of Annie as she welcomed him with a familiar grin.

The guilt for her predicament, and the fear he felt when he found her beaten and out of her mind left him awkward in himself; he had never felt this new twisting sensation in his gut for someone as he did for her, and yet he felt so completely unnecessary to her when he watched the way she survived.

Their conversation merely added to his guilt. This latest idea to use Dotty to infiltrate Cowley's family didn't sit well with Marie, which would quickly spread to the rest of the gang. He was sure that if Annie knew she'd been credited with it, she would have words.

As he went on to check her injuries, he became lost in thought. What would be the next point for them all weeks from now? They had always planned to make themselves scarce and live comfortably. The Bounty Hunter work was never going to return, and he wasn't going to be a decoration at the end of the Hangman's rope. His desire to avoid that had never been stronger than now, viewing the battered face of Annie Schaeffer.

He looked deep into her green eyes as she smiled in a way that could so completely disarm him. He thought about what her plans might be. She was always so close to disappearing, and he caught himself daring to think he might be able to disappear with her. They could get out of this, could start a life free of struggle. Something he had wanted since he was a kid. "G'night, Annie."

***

Tired of her confinement, Annie rose the next morning eager to see Bessie. Though her ribs still caused her issues when moving, she knew they would loosen if she powered through. She heaved herself up and struggled to change out of her nightgown, lifting it above her head was almost as torturous on her shoulder as her initial injuries had been. She forced her breath out through gritted teeth while she dragged a loose shirt and prairie skirt on. Taking a deep breath, Annie limped her way outside. The walk from her lodgings was slow and stiff, but with the support of her cane, she felt surprisingly comfortable in her movement. She beamed as she made her way towards Bessie. Not far off, Tanner was sleeping propped up against a horse trough.

"*My girl.*" she whispered, fawning over the mare. "I am so sorry to have left you." Bessie snorted with affection at the nose rub Annie gifted her.

"She's been fine." Tanner called from his seat on the ground. "Nate took her out a coupla times this past week. Not sure she liked it much." He joined her. "You shouldn't be out here, Missy. Though I know you ain't one for listenin' to folks."

"If I'm alright to stand, dress, and walk by myself, Tanner, I'm perfectly fine to come see my horse." She smiled at the old man. "'Specially after she must've had such a *frightful time* with that Mister Healey."

"That's a fine cane the fellas made for you." He nodded towards her gift. "I ain't never had somethin' so nice done for me, and I need it!"

"Well I ain't givin' you this one, even after I'm healed." She winked at the old man. "Would you be so kind as to pass me a brush, Tanner? I wanna give this girl a pamperin'."
"And how d'you fancy bein able to do that? You can barely stand up straight. Hobblin' about like some old witch."

"I know my limits… *to a point*." She shrugged stiffly.

The old man shoved a worn leather-backed brush at her. "Go on, then, do a deservin' job with one hand."

Annie steeled herself, forced the point of her cane into the ground, and attempted to lift the brush to Bessie's shoulder, trying to hide her grimace. Her injured, heavy-handed work was less than appreciated by the mare and Bessie side-stepped from reach with a disgruntled snort.

"Dammit girl!" Annie hissed as she buckled from the sharp dart of pain searing her ribs. She dropped the brush in favour of grasping the cane with both hands.

"I think that horse knows your limits better than you do, young lady."

Annie stayed gripping the cane to catch her breath. She glared petulantly at Tanner as he bent down to collect her discarded item and set about tending to Bessie instead

"Guess I gotta be bad if she's favorin' you over me." She sniped lovingly and watched the soothing motion of Tanner slowly and calmly brushing Bessie's mane.

It was odd for her to be outside, back in the company of anyone other than Mikey. No one had bothered themselves much to talk to Annie upon her return; all too busy working to their orders given out by Duke.

"…How were things after… You know…?"

"Them Fitzgerald's grabbed you?"

"… Yeah."

Tanner shrugged. "Other than the number of corpses we hadta throw into the woods, and Nate's actions retrievin' *you* puttin' Duke's nose outta joint a little, I'd say there was nothin' else to report."

"How'd they know where we were?""I think it's more a question of how'd they know where *you* were." Tanner stopped and stared at Annie with an unfamiliar seriousness. "They weren't here for no one else, Annie. Came 'specially for you." Annie frowned. "If they didn't know about you all, then why bring so many fellas to come get *me*?"

"You're a Schaeffer!" Tanner chuckled shaking his head and returning to Bessie. "I mean, sure *we know* you ain't half as scary as old Caley, but they didn't know that. Was probably just precaution. I mean, you're still a feisty spirit. You musta picked up a follower on your journey from Boulderhead."

"No. There's no way… I'm *certain*. And if they just wanted me, they coulda ambushed me far easier on the road." Annie pulled herself upright with a grimace and rested her hand on the top of the cane. "Plenty came here, Tanner. And that messenger talked in riddles like he was in on some big joke… Least, 'til *someone* shot his head off."

"Well, all I know is that Duke don't see 'em as a threat. And thankfully I don't need to pack up all them bags of feed again." He stopped grooming Bessie with a contented sigh. "There we go. Is this to your satisfaction, *your highness*?"

"As difficult as it is to admit, you did a far faster job than I could today." She smiled. "But don't go thinkin' you do a better job of it all the time."

"Oh I wouldn't *dream* of it." Tanner moved over to a small wooden box of grooming accoutrement. "Anyway, I can't stand here blatherin' with a cripple. I gotta fix up Atlas and Dove before noon." Tanner hoisted the ornate saddle usually worn by Duke's steed onto a spare hitch post and began to drag a dry cloth over it.

"Duke and Marie steppin' out?"

"Nope. Dotty's borrowin' Dove. Off to work on somethin' with that kid Nate's workin' for."

Annie tensed. "Does Nate know about this?"

"I'd say so, seein' as he has to meet them in town and start introductions."

A prickle of worry snaked over her skin. It had only been a mere suggestion of hers a few weeks back, and that was before anyone had any real knowledge of Luther Cowley. Nate knew Cowley better than any of them now; not mentioning this plan to her only told Annie that he was uncomfortable with it as an idea.

After hearing that whispered argument between Duke and Lucky a week ago, she was sure that this sudden decision was made to create more spite toward her. "Is she alright with this? I mean, who'll be keepin' watch over her?"

"How should I know?" Tanner flustered, obviously tired of the inquisition. "All I know is you're in my way and I gotta lotta work to do… You should be happy 'bout it. Not often Duke gives folks' ideas the time o' day, but he obviously liked this one o' yours."

"*What*? Who told you it were my idea?!"

Tanner sighed and slammed his hand on Atlas's saddle. "Maw. Mentioned it last night. Said she heard Duke talkin' with Dotty."

"… *Christ…*" A cold sweat formed at the nape of Annie's neck. She couldn't believe Duke thought any of this was a smart move, and no one seemed to question his decision about staying. "Somethin' ain't right in all this."

"Will you quit fussin'?" Tanner huffed as he dragged his sleeve across his sweat-ladened brow. "The only thing that ain't right is you hauntin' me with your presence while I'm tryna work." He stepped up to Annie and pulled the cane out of its position in the ground. "You've been sittin' stewin' in your bed for two weeks, buildin' all this worry up for no reason. Go rest. Enjoy bein' a lady o' leisure for once. Ain't that what you always wanted? Duke knows what he's doin'."

"*Oh I bet he does.*" She muttered darkly.

Nate woke early and hid in bed until mid-morning. It had been late when Marie managed to calm Dotty's worries down enough to get her to sleep. The muttered protests drifted up through the building, causing his own slumber to elude him. He stared at the same rot-stain on his ceiling for hours, trying to work out the best way to keep Dotty at ease as she played the part of the debutante. Dotty's role was simple; woo young Luther as per the requirements of polite society. Nate told himself that as long as she was ladylike and proper, Cowley would act as such. This would keep her well out of reach, and ensure she was always chaperoned. Eventually she'd be gifted trinkets and finery as small love tokens, worthy enough for the Needham Boys to make a good penny from. It really was a long game Duke wanted to play, and Nate just hoped their decision to stay put at this camp would be safe enough to see it succeed.

He grabbed some food and a coffee, while avoiding the glares being shot across the camp.

"It's lucky that woman ain't good with a gun." Clara shoved a freshly mended bundle of his smarter clothes into his arms and nodded toward Marie. "Though that look might be enough to finish you off."

"I don't see why I'm gettin' the daggers." Nate mumbled. "I ain't the one pushin' this ahead."

"You ain't the one arguin' against it neither." She huffed and crossed her arms.

"Ain't no harm gonna come to Dotty, Clara. Cowley's an idiot but he's an idiot bound by society..." He thought back to how Annie came to know him. "... Least as long as the proper introductions happen... Duke'll keep her safe."

"I'm sure he will if he wants Marie back on side." Clara smirked a little, "Ain't sure how long he'll last out bein' on her bad list."

Nate thanked Clara for the clothes and went back to dress for his day. From his window he saw Annie talking with Tanner and smiled at her unnaturally ladylike outfit.

Annie stomped her way back to her tent and braced herself for anything that may come her way thanks to Duke. She sat heavily on her camp bed and picked up her dog-eared copy of '*Treasure Island*' in the hopes that she would seem too busy to disturb. "You been to see Bessie?" Nathan filled the doorway to her lodgings, looking a little strained.

"I hear Dotty's comin' along on your little escapades with Cowley now." Annie snipped from behind her novel. "…Yeah, well, seems like a good idea to get started on workin' the rich idiots of Boulderhead seein' as we're stayin' here."

"Until you start robbin' 'em."

Nate laughed until he saw the severe look in Annie's eyes. He had become the permanent target for scowling at in camp, and it wasn't yet noon. "It ain't like we're gonna go in guns blazin'. This'll take a while." He shrugged.

"And Dotty is happy to be part of that?"

"She used to pickpocket fellas with Marie back in Iowa, ain't really no differen-"

"So Marie is goin' with you too, huh?"

Nate stared at Annie. She already knew the answer, and his mood grew rapidly more impatient for passive aggressive questioning.

"Look, this was your idea in the first place."

"Sure! I suggested someone might think about a *con* with the fella. I didn't think it'd be picked up without further thought… I didn't even think Duke would be interested in a suggestion uttered from the mouth of *that Schaeffer woman*." Annie could see Nate had doubts about the whole idea too; Dotty was like a little sister to him.

"Duke's got this. He'll be right by Dotty the whole time."

"I hope so." Annie put her book down. "Because it were my idea *as everyone seems to know now*. And I ain't up to fightin' off a whole group of angry folks if you're wrong."

21

Manners and Social Usages

Nate swallowed his concern and left Annie to meet up with his escort.

"You got everything, Nathan?"

"Sure, Duke." He got comfortable on a well rested Prynne and glanced over to a sullen Dotty. She was dressed in a pretty lilac dress, fidgeting on Dove. "You alright there, Dotty?"

"It's *Primrose* for the sake of Mister Cowley." Duke interrupted. "Isn't that right dear?"

"Yes, Duke." She sighed and forced a short smile at Nate. "I'm fine. Guess this was all a bit sudden is all."

"Let's get going," Duke continued, "we don't want to keep your *employer* waiting now do we, Nathaniel?"

The trio departed into the hazy afternoon towards Boulderhead. As planned, they would split up before the town's main entryway. Nate continued to Boulderhead's coach house stables, while Duke and his "*ward*" would partake in a light lunch and await the opportune moment to meet up with Cowley's private coach.

"Course them all end up the same, like a bunch o' no good ingrates."

"Uh-huh."

"Bin driven' coaches nigh-on twenty years now. They don't drop me nothin' in thanks."

"*Kids, huh?*" Nate's eyes wandered across the cobbled streets as he continued half-listening.

"*Him in there...?*" Walter, the driver, dropped his tone and pointed his thumb over his shoulder, "you know now. Less manners than a spoilt child. Just wanta show off his Daddy's dollas."

"What does his Daddy think of that?"

"Nothin much. At the end o' his life. Must be a hundred. Stuck in bed. Head all fogged..." Walter scoffed bitterly. "Not so foggy to forget how much a damn *misery* he be... still don't want folks like me in the house 'less it's maids."

Nate cleared his throat and shuffled uncomfortably. "... *Oh.*"

The pair fell into an awkward silence as the raucous merriment continued from the rich children they nannied. Though it felt like a lifetime, it wasn't long before Duke and Dotty appeared, stepping out from a small public garden.

"Hey, Walter, pull in here. I think I see my boss."

"Boss always close, eh?" Walter mused as he pulled to the curb and nodded to Duke. "Aftanoon, Sir."

"Well good day to you!" Duke beamed up at the driver.

"Walter! Why on earth have we stopped?" Luther Cowley whined from the coach.

"My fault, Mister Cowley." Nate jumped down from his seat and went to the coach's door. "Just saw-"

"Unless you saw a person or *persons* about to take my life, you do not get to dictate when or where one wishes to halt..." with a clench of his jaw, Nate stepped back as Cowley shoved his head out of the window and glared in the direction of Duke. His expression immediately softened as he saw a pretty, shy young lady beside the man, lightly fanning herself and averting her gaze.

"Mister Cowley."

Duke sauntered up to the man staring past him and turned on his casual charm. "I'm afraid Nathaniel here is trained too well to be comfortable passing me by. Even during workdays." He slapped Nate's back with a patronising firmness.

"No... No... Not at all my dear fellow..." Cowley's gaze stayed fixed on Dotty as he stepped out of the carriage to limply shake Duke's hand. He had completely forgotten his companions inside. "It is always a delight to see you Mister Taylor, and it seems the weather has been most joyful of your presence too."

Nate rolled his eyes at the whole misty scene.

"… Or should I perhaps connect the glorious sunshine to the appearance of this fine young lady you are accompanying today…?"

Dotty turned and smiled sweetly at the man. Nate saw that her eyes didn't share the sweetness, as she coyly stood beside Duke. "Ah! This is my magnificent ward, Miss Primrose Abernathy. She arrived in Boulderhead just yesterday." Duke jostled Dotty slightly.

"*Well*, speak to the fellow!"

"It's a… pleasure to meet you, Sir." Dotty cooed softly in a voice far more educated than her usual.

"Oh I must profess the pleasure surely is mine, Miss Abernathy." Cowley bowed deeply causing her to bluster a short, surprised giggle. "Mister Taylor, may I ask if you and your ward intend on staying around these parts for some time?"

"I do believe that is our intent, Miss Abernathy?" Duke stared intensely at Dotty.

"Oh, yes!" she found herself quite animated, "Mister Taylor has had nothing but compliments about this place. I am *most interested* to explore it."

"Oh, that is most excellent news." Cowley gushed. "I hope to see you again soon. But for now, I must depart your charming company and attend to some business of my own." He bowed once more, and Dotty gave a sudden playful curtsey, causing Cowley to laugh at her spirit. "My, Taylor! I should have known a ward of yours would have such good humor in all things as introductions."

"… Yes… *Indeed.*" Duke laughed nervously.

"Alas, I shall bid you one final *adieu*… Nathaniel! Would you be so good as to accompany me as a passenger in the cab?" Nate panicked. "Err... Well, Mister Cowley… I ain't sure there's roo-"

"Nonsense! Why, I know you are a man of great build, but we

can fit one more."

Nate could feel all the eyes on him. He reluctantly agreed, clambered into the cab and wedged himself in between two shocked looking fops. "*Gentlemen.*" He nodded gruffly as they grimaced, failing to get comfortable with Nate's frame pinning them in place. The final, long-winded goodbyes were uttered, and Walter continued their journey up to the Cowley estate outside of Boulderhead.

The three squashed men sat in disgruntled silence for some time as Cowley became lost in the fantasy of romance and courtship.

"Deleaney." Cowley sighed toward his own reflection in the window.

"Mister Cowley...?"

"How well do you know Miss Abernathy?"

"Err..."

"Is she spoken for?"

Nate wrestled himself free of the bony shoulders that pierced his arms, and sat forward. "Well, I know she ain't spoken for. Least I don't know of any fellas with professed designs on Miss Primrose." That wasn't entirely true, Tommy Kelley was more than attentive towards Dotty. It had proved useful to get him to do tasks around the camp when she was in view.

"*That is most interesting news...*" Luther Cowley's eyes narrowed in thought. "What is her standing?"

"What's her *what*?"

The other men tittered smugly as Cowley finally turned to look at Nate. "Oh my dear man, I sometimes forget your world must be somewhat less burdened with such matters as mine. *Her standing.* Is she of good stock?"

Nate began to sweat. Duke hadn't provided any specifics regarding *Primrose's* story. "I'm afraid I cannot say for certain. She is Mister Taylor's ward after all, I just work for the man."

"Hmm, yes of course." Cowley's mind drifted once more.

"Obviously she is a little *slight* in shape, but she is undoubtedly pretty. And such a sweet, *playful* innocence about her nature. One couldn't possibly mistake her for something other than a lady… May I ask you to be an intermediary for me to Mister Taylor? You must have some sway with the man to arrange another meeting?"

Luther opened a silver case and pulled a small business card from it. "Please. I have no need of you tomorrow. Use the day to pass this card on. I may be a *worthy* caller for Miss Abernathy." Nate sighed and took the card that sat on top of his day's salary.

"*Sure*. I'll see he gets it."

"You do that, good sir. Else, I will be concerned you have desires on her of your own."

The loud guffaws at Nathan's expense made him clench. It took all his might to wince a smile at them through his scowl.

The sun was lowering into a haze of gold when Walter turned onto the private road towards the Cowley House. Though Nate had accompanied Cowley home each working day, the outlandish grandeur of the building that loomed at the end of the gated driveway still amazed him. All white and gleaming, it stood two-storeys high, with four towering columns holding the eaves of the front porch, accessed by stone steps up to the front door. Lights shone from windows, giving glimpses into the large, tall rooms. His short conversations with Walter had given Nate hints about the number of residents and level of security, and what little information he had now gleaned about Cowley Senior meant the whole plan could well be quickened to the Needham Boys' advantage.

***

Through the afternoon Annie walked a small circuit of the camp's land, as instructed by Doc Carragher. The sun beat down on the swimming hole behind her lodgings, and there was a quiet bustle of activity around the mill from people busying themselves. Three of the men were out hunting or selling their '*finds*', Clara and Sam

Clifford were on watch. Doc had headed to a small town away from Boulderhead to try and peddle his sugar pills, and Marie and Mikey were sitting by the red maple in the shade of the building. They angrily argued over the pronunciations of words in the book Lucky had given them. Lucky was nowhere to be seen. Gripping her cane, Annie hobbled over to the pair to measure the level of animosity she had earned regarding Dotty's situation. "I'm guessin' the curse words you're both slingin' ain't in that book?"

The argument stopped immediately, Marie stood sharply. "What d'you want?"

"Just thought I might come give y'all a hand if needed…"

Annie spoke carefully, "… Ain't Lucky helpin' you?"

"He ain't wantin' to," Mikey shrugged. He drew lines in the dust with the edge of his boot, "been in as foul a mood as *madam* here all day." He winced as Marie clipped him across the back of the head.

"Where is he?"

"*Why?*" Marie pulled herself to full height and stood close to Annie. "Got more *bright ideas* to suggest have ya? Got one to ship Mikey off to some poorhouse, save on feedin' him?"

"… Well…" Annie smirked as she looked at the boy. "it might get him to do some hard work for once."

Marie shoved the book at Annie, knocking what little air her lungs could hold, and marched away.

"Think he went off with Doc." Mikey said quietly. "What's up with 'em all? Bunch o' miseries."

"Duke decided to employ Dotty on some errands that none of 'em approve of." She tossed the book back to Mikey and leaned heavily on her cane. "Apparently it's my fault."

"Your fault?!" Mikey snorted. "*My!* Considerin' you been a bed-ridden cripple since almost the day we arrived, you been keepin' busy huh?"

"It's amazin' what a person can accomplish when they really want to."

"I always thought bein' grown up meant answerin' to nobody. Livin' your life free o' folk's nonsense."

"*Yeah well, I thought that too, kid.*"

"Seems nonsense just gets worse."

"You want my advice?" Annie asked as Mikey escorted her towards the food wagon.

"Not sure," he chuckled, "is it gonna keep makin' everyone mad?"

"Probly. Nothin' worth sayin' if someone ain't got their back up over it." They stopped by Chuck's prep table and Annie picked up an apple. "No. My advice, Mikey, is to let everyone's nonsense stay their nonsense. 'Less they're willin' to hear you out, ain't no point in you forcin' sense into 'em. The truth always comes good in the end."

"I guess that's why you got so many friends." He slapped her shoulder and started to skip away. "Alright, loner, I'm offta cause my own nonsense."

"Don't be goin' far, laddie!" Maw shouted after him. "We dinnae need another to break oota jail." She turned to Annie. "That lad is hee-haw but a strain on my soul. More grey hairs since Lucky took him in than anythin' else I've dealt wi' in my life." She huffed a short laugh. "You're popular at the minute."

"Oh ain't I just?" Annie sighed.

"Ach, it'll be fine." Maw interrupted. "The lass isn't some waif, she can hold her own. She's just worried aboot Tommy."

"Tommy?"

"Aye!" Maw laughed. "Dinnae tell me ye didn't know they have designs on each other?!"

"*God damn.* If that's all she's gotta cry over…"

"Wey, Mister Kelley's had plenty o' time to grow up 'n' say somethin'." Maw sniffed. "The way I see it, it's his own fault if he's missed the boat." She nodded towards the figures of Danny and Tom Kelley thundering back towards the entrance, both with game on the back of their horses. "Danny took him oot to kill some things. Mind, I dinnae think ye should be in his eyeline for a while. He's still sulkin' after all."

***

Duke and Dotty appeared back at camp shortly after the return of the hunters. The whole event for them was quick; she had reluctantly accepted her role.

"Hey." Annie greeted Dotty as she dismounted from Dove and handed Tanner the reins.

"Hi Annie."

"I heard you'd been roped into some business."

"You *heard*, huh?" Dotty shook her head and walked towards camp.

"This weren't nothin' of your plans then?"

Annie shambled after her. "Listen. Sure, I met the guy. Thought he were an imbecile that we could trick some cash outta... I figured I weren't a likely option to pursue that myself after our meetin', so I-"

"So you served me up instead did ya?"

Dotty stood with her arms folded. Her petulant expression was like small child's.

Annie had to stifle her laugh at the figure facing her. "Look I didn't serve up nothin'. I happened to mention to Nate that someone could trick Cowley from his fortune as he's a simp for a pretty face."

Dotty looked quizzically at her. "That's all?"

"That's all."

"You didn't come up with the whole courtship thing?"

"Honestly Dotty? I don't think in long-term details for anyone but me. And I never really thought more on this idea after I mentioned it to Nate. No asked me more about it. And I can tell you now, once I had the soul kicked outta me by them Fitzgeralds, I weren't much interested in anythin'." Annie hobbled close to

Dotty and placed a hand on her shoulder. "I ain't a nice enough person to give anyone a second thought once I'm in trouble myself."

Much to Annie's amazement Dotty laughed and softened.

"Well, that part ain't much of a surprise. I guess I were put out at this bein' thrown at me. Duke ain't usually a man to involve me in things without the nod from Marie. One minute we're enjoyin' an evenin' 'round the table, next I'm summoned to Duke bein' told I'm to woo some young rich gadabout."

"He weren't… *improper* towards you, was he?"

"It was all a mess of nothin' I guess." Dotty shrugged. "The fella is a *boy* in a man costume, like all the ones with Daddy's money. I don't reckon he's gonna be anythin' of concern toward me, 'specially as I'm chaperoned."

"What's Duke got you doin'?"

"Young Miss Johnson here will await a response from Master Cowley with regards to a *courtship*." Duke came and stood beside the two. "And we shall take it from there."

"How?"

Struggling to hide the glower on his face, Duke forced a smile. "As planned. With the use of *proper social etiquette*, Miss Schaeffer. Something I am almost certain you have been a stranger to your whole life."

Annie raised an eyebrow. "I have my own code of conduct that ain't been dictated to me by some tenderfoot dandy if that's what you mean."

"*Exactly my point*." Duke turned his focus back to Dotty. "Come on, my dear, let's get you back to Mrs Bassett and calm her waters with regards to the day." He put an arm around his ward and guided her towards the mill.

The evening brought with it a strange awkwardness across the camp. Marie's demeanour remained frosty towards Annie out of pure principle, though she had been quicker to soften towards Duke. She and Dotty had taken up residence beside the main campfire, with Tanner absent-mindedly plucking out some half-melodic tune on the banjo. Tommy had chosen to take the night watch with Campbell Madsen to avoid everyone and stew in his own resentment. Chuck and Maw were playing Faro by their wagon, and Nate still hadn't returned from his work.

"I gotta say," Clara joined Annie at the rudimentary card table, handing her a beer, "there ain't many dull nights since you turned up here."

"It's a regular party wherever I am." Annie stretched her painful, stiff ribs.

"Danny was sayin' Tommy were like a bear with a sore head over this Dotty nonsense."

"Considerin' he acts like a rampant cur 'round anythin' in a dress I'm a little surprised."

"Ah well, the fella knows Dotty," Clara swigged from her bottle and leaned back, "knows what happened to her with that farm hand. He'd rather sit on the side of caution."

"It's funny how these fellas can stare into the eyes of a man before they beat him to a pulp but are so yellow when it comes to women."

The two laughed.

"Let's hope it stays that way!" Clara grinned as her husband joined them.

"What stays what way?"

"You bein' nothin' but a yellow-bellied sop when it comes to me."

"I ain't stupid." Danny teased, "you did shoot me."

"*Not on purpose*." Clara mumbled into her beer.

"*Exactly*." He jostled her and sat with the two. "Best to expect you're always about to injure me than not, 'specially now this one's got you throwin' knives."

"Speakin' of shootin' fellas, where's Duke?"

Danny flicked a knowing smile at Annie. "He's bickerin' with Lucky inside. All thanks to your bright ideas, Schaeffer."

"Jesus just lay off alright? It may have forgotten everyone's notice but I ain't exactly been *active* in this whole scheme." Annie fiddled with the top of her beer bottle. "… Is Lucky mad?"

"Not at you, Annie no." Danny's brow furrowed. "He ain't been happy with a lotta things since we got here. Stuff ain't sittin' right with him and Duke."

"What d'you mean?"

"Oh, they've always been at each other a little, it's the nature of bein' in charge I guess." He shrugged and looked at the table. "… But we hear them through the ceilin', arguin' at night sometimes." Clara continued softly. "Duke's goin' off decidin' things without him. Lucky ain't happy 'bout the way the roads are twistin' for us."

***

It was late when Walter dropped Nathan at the coach house stables to make his way home from Boulderhead. Knowing Annie was healing, albeit into someone that scowled at him, meant some of his guilt was alleviated. If the camp hadn't thrown her to the bears yet, he could take a moment to breathe.

He slowed Prynne and relished the freedom of being under the clear night sky. He had always enjoyed the peace of prairies, and it was so rare for him to have time these days; not needing to rush to or from errands. The stars shone brightly from a blanket of deep blues and purples as the white, moonlit flowers at his mare's hooves marked his way. Hopefully, he could convince Duke to speed up Dotty's courtship, and rob Cowley's wealth sooner than later. That would stop anyone from having further upset, and there would be a great haul to take if they could arrange a meeting of the families.

Life had become more complicated for them ever since leaving Missouri, but the latest run-in with the Fitzgeralds kept returning to him. So little of their sudden appearance made sense to him. They had avoided conflict for years, but there they were, with their unfathomable knowledge of Annie's existence, let alone her presence with The Needham Boys. The volume of men in that skirmish was a pre-planned decision. Then that gun shot. *"That gun shot from us..."* He muttered. Neither he nor Danny had seen who had fired it, but it was loud. It had caused all hell to break loose. No doubt a fight would have broken out eventually, he wouldn't have let those degenerates take Annie. Though her willingness to converse with that first messenger had put him on edge. He had momentarily thought she would go willingly with them, that she had agreed to escape. Until he witnessed her violence at Sugar Oak. He looked up towards the stars and sighed. "I guess this is why I keep busy."

The camp was still when he finally arrived back at the mill, and only Tommy and Madsen were up, taking watch.

"The prodigal son emerges from the darkness." Madsen goaded from his post at the front of the camp. "Here to bring a miracle which fixes folks' sourness are ya?"

"Short of slittin' your throat, Madsen, I ain't entirely sure how to stop folks from bein' sour." Nate dismounted and removed the tack from Prynne, thudding it heavily on a spare hitching post.

"So, who's deservin' of your attentions today? The Schaeffer or your family?"

"What're you talkin' about now?"

"Our great leaders, Healey." Madsen sauntered up to him. The orange glow of cigarette embers hovered in the darkness. "Seems that Miss Schaeffer can get under any fella's skin, *in every excitin' way imaginable*. They've been bickerin' like old wives all day over this nonsense she threw into the ring."

"Christ." Nate pinched the bridge of his nose and headed towards the mill.

"… I don't understand your reasoning, Duke!"

"You never have done, brother. I don't see why that would suddenly change your support in such matters."

"It's a little difficult to support your *schemes* when you so actively keep me in the dark about them. We haven't run around like this in years."

"How else do you expect us to make money now we're locked out of bounty hunting?"

"And whose fault is that, hmmm? That damnable bank job!" Lucky huffed. "Are you trying to relive some youthful rebellion?"

Nate walked quietly to the top of the building as the men continued.

"They knew us regardless." Duke snapped. "May as well get some notoriety beyond busting Madsen from prison."

"Oh and don't get me started on tha-"

The brothers turned to the door at the top of the staircase as Nate stood patiently. "Fellas." He nodded. "Everythin' alright?"

"Nathan, m'boy!" Duke marched across to him gleefully. "Are you only just getting back from Cowley's now? You must have had quite a day. Anything I should know?" Duke placed a thick, friendly arm over Nate's shoulders.

"Sure… Quite a lot actually…" he looked apologetically across to Lucky who slumped at the map-laden table. "He – errr – well he gave me this card. Says he wants you to arrange a meetin' with Dotty."

"Excellent!" Duke practically skipped over to the lamp on the table to scrutinise Cowley's information, ignoring his brother's scowl. "Anything else?"

"Cowley's father seems close to dyin'. Accordin' to the driver, the man ain't always sure how to breathe, let alone know where he is."

"So it sounds like we may have struck gold, gentlemen. This is excellent news all round, Nathan, thank you. We must find a time to make the next arrangements."

"… He gave me tomorrow off… Seems he felt I'd need the whole day to convince you he is worthy of her affection."

"Ohhh I am sure he is." Duke chuckled. "I'm sure he has more worth than we can possibly know."

22

Revelations

September 1893

The gang had been living in the crumbling mill for six weeks without further incident. As Annie's injuries had healed, she found her temperament more lenient towards the way Nate nodded along with Duke's choices.

She was placed back on watch duties, her first being with Tommy Kelley. It amused Annie to see the young man purposefully avoid her during their work together. She made it a game; see how close she could get to him before he would notice and move off again.

"That's a damn stupid thing you do, Annie!" He spat towards her. "It's gettin' dark. You could get shot, playin' the fool like that."

"Not by you, Kelley," she sauntered up to him, his gun still raised, "I seen the targets you miss. 'Specially in the dark." Tommy lowered the rifle and glowered. "Why don'tcha sod off, Schaeffer? Leave me to do me job, eh?"

"Are you still sore about this Cowley business? C'mon, Tommy, it ain't my fault the girl you have fancies upon is pretendin' to woo that fella."

"It's nothin' to do with that." Tommy stated with no conviction.

"Dotty ain't got designs on him, you know that. And Nate won't let anythin' happen to her."

"I suppose that's true enough." He relaxed. "You know she taught me how to pickpocket...? Course I had to change the technique a bit. Can't be flutterin' eyelids at rich fellas in bars now, can I?"

"Not with those looks, no." The two laughed as they walked together back to the front of camp.

"What about you, Annie?"

"What about me?"

"You're not crippled no more. What's Duke got you doin'?"

"This." Annie shrugged. "I can't work the Cowley job on account of our first meetin', and Duke ain't seeminly interested in pursuin' other financial avenues."

"So you're free of it, eh?"

"*… I guess so…*" her mind wandered as Tommy continued to patrol the camp's boundaries. She had focused so much on healing that she hadn't thought about how she was, essentially, a forgotten loose end. This could have been her out, if she hadn't been injured in such a foolish manner. Now, she was four weeks behind funding her exit.

She cursed herself for having become so entangled with the gang. Their lifestyle had snuck up on her, she'd become complacent. Looking back towards the mill, Annie thought about its occupants. From the way they spoke of years gone by, the last twelve months was far removed from their usual way of life. If this illicit path Duke was taking them on was so different, why did it sit so naturally with him?

She couldn't bring herself to steal the money the gang had accumulated; she wanted to keep her reputation clean. Her moral compass left her stranded. Maybe that was someone's whole plan. Annie stood by the front barricades, at the very spot where she was showered in the messenger's blood. His words still drifted through her like a riddle, they were purposeful but meant for another. Dawn would soon threaten the horizon. The soft noises of sleep hummed from the ground floor of the mill. She made her way over to Campbell Madsen and gave him a kick. "Get up." She shoved the rifle in his hands. "It's your turn."

"I see that Fitzgerald beatin' ain't softened your affections, Schaeffer." Madsen said gruffly as he heaved himself from his bed roll.

"Not even a *'good mornin', sweetheart'*."

"There ain't nothin' sweet about your heart, Madsen." She muttered on her way to rest.

Annie woke to the buzz of the departure of 'The Abernathys'. She dressed quickly and went to watch the spectacle unfold as Lucky and Marie stuffed themselves into the back of Doc's small merchant wagon. Nate stood close by with his back to her, laughing at Tommy fussing at his clothes, who only settled when Dotty came to his aid. The two had fallen into the typical trap of young love; choosing to believe that there was no reason to pursue the other.

To Annie's surprise, this infuriated Maw most of all who, though brash and forthright, was a fierce disciple of true love. "Wains never learn, they just wallow in heartache. It's ridiculous."

"I think Tommy's hand may be forced to change that decision." Annie mused as she and Maw stood watching the well-dressed game of sardines continue.

"How're ye feelin' now anyhow?" Maw eyed Annie with a mix of pride and judgement. "Ye've recovered well, lassie. Keen ta start helpin' oot again, I'm sure?"

Annie lowered her voice as Duke and Nate meandered close by. "Everyone's so wrapped up in this nonsense with Cowley there ain't much for me to do."

"Och! This willnee be forever." Maw chuckled lightly. "Now you're fightin' fit, Duke'll have ye runnin' 'round all over the lands fer him."

"*Hmmm.*" Annie watched Duke head back to the mill. She may well have to run throughout the lands because of Duke, but maybe not quite how Maw envisioned.

She turned her attention back to the matron and smiled stiffly. "As it currently stands that ain't required. *So*, I figured I might venture out and stock this place up with some good eats."

"Aye. Poor Chuck has been wrestlin' with all kind o' buckshot in them stews he's been makin' of late. You gettin' some *edible* meat would be a canny thing."

"Then it's settled." Annie slapped her hands together. "I'm off huntin'."

She collected her rifle and a small length of packing rope from her wagon, picked up her father's knife and slid it into her boot. Finally, she made her way to the paddock where Mikey was being harangued by Tanner trying to teach basic saddle maintenance.

"… Because some day you might wanna do somethin' with your life that ain't bein' a plague on my soul."

"You just want someone to do this for *your* lazy behind."

"Why you-"

"Fellas!" Annie interrupted before Tanner could chase Mikey around the paddock. "When you're done tryna spook the horses, you wanna help me saddle up?"

Tanner grumped off towards the saddle store as Mikey greeted her. "You escapin'?"

"Funny." Annie jostled him, and a pang guilt hit her. "I'm off to get y'all some grub."

Mikey's face lit up. "Huntin?! Can I come?"

"Please to Christ say yes." Tanner dumped the hefty saddle over Bessie. "Hopefully you can accidentally shoot him." Mikey stuck his tongue out at the man.

Annie tightened Bessie's tack. "I dunno. Ain't you got some lessons from Lucky?"

"Oh come onnnn, Schaeffer," Mikey whined, "the teachers've all gone to play dress up. And they ain't had a lick of interest in me since this Dotty business."

"You got a horse…?" Annie smirked at Mikey's pout. "Fine, kid." She tied the rope to the saddlebags and shoved her rifle into her saddle scabbard. "But I ain't handin' you a gun. And if we catch somethin' big, you're walkin' home while I ride."

"We'll see." Mikey winked and went to put his foot in Bessie's stirrup, hesitating as the mare towered above him. "… How d'I get in the saddle…?"

"*You* don't." Annie laughed. "But I'll give you a leg-up to sit behind me." She made Mikey reach as high as he could, then she and Tanner shouldered his behind; launching the boy up most ungracefully into the saddle.

"Christ! Feels like I'm on top a cliff!" Mikey tentatively shuffled back to sit on Bessie's hind quarters, which she grumbled about slightly, before Annie pulled herself up.

"Make sure you don't fall off. You'll be left where you land." She pushed her hat down tightly on her head, fixed the reins, and nodded farewell to Tanner before kicking Bessie onward. Mikey jolted and gripped the saddle.

It was some time before either spoke again. Mikey was too terrified to do more than concentrate on holding on, and Annie enjoyed the peace that gave her.

"Where're we goin' exactly?"

"The river. That should have somethin' worth bringin' back."

"I ain't never shot nothin' before." Mikey mused quietly.

"And you ain't gonna." Annie tapped at the rifle resting beside her leg. "This ain't somethin' you just pick up, Mikey. And I ain't gonna teach you. There's enough folk who can shoot in this world."

"Shoot *well*?"

"… *No*." Annie scoffed. "But well enough."

The pair took Bessie through a small forest trail. Following the slow babble of the river, they were led to a clearing where the river widened.

"This should do." Annie hitched up with a satisfied sigh. "Lotsa good hidin' spots, clear views."

"Thank Christ!" Mikey rolled onto his belly and slid off Bessie.

"I can barely feel my legs."

"Them boys really are lettin' you down in their teachins if they ain't even taught you to ride a horse."

"I can ride a *horse*." Mikey sulked as he joined Annie at the river's edge. "Just ain't never ridden a big monster."

"Keep talkin' like that 'bout my Bessie and you won't get

home." Annie drew the rifle from its sheath and pocketed some spare bullets from her saddle bags. "If you prefer, I could just hunt *you*."

"Funny ain'tcha?"

"When occasion calls f'rit."

The pair walked further down river and sheltered in the treeline. They hunkered down to avoid spooking potential game. "Now, the trick is to keep still *and quiet*." Annie instructed in a low voice.

"We might be here a while."

"*Perfect.*" Mikey hissed. "*My favorite ways to pass time.*"

Annie stifled a laugh as her companion huffed into a more comfortable position. The trees sang with gentle bird calls.

It wasn't long until Mikey started picking at the greenery around them, absent-mindedly tying fronds of grass and wild posies into a chain. "How comes you know how t'do this?" With an eye roll, Annie set herself back from her position.

"Smythson weren't a fan of spendin' money on eats, 'less it were for him. Someone needed to go find food."

"So they sent you?"

"Yup."

"*Alone??*"

"Sure."

"Weren't you afraid?"

"*No*, I can shoot." Annie chuckled and shuffled onto her stomach, readying herself again.

"…Have you shot a lotta… *things?*"

The hesitancy in Mikey's question wove tension through Annie. "I've shot my share."

"Don't… Don't it weigh on you?"

"Folks gotta eat, Mikey." Annie mumbled.

"That ain't what I'm meanin'."

"… I know…" She lowered her rifle. "Mikey, you know who

you travel with. Weren't that long ago you saw me out there fightin' with 'em."

"Yeah but they came at *us*."

"Every *thing* that I've shot in my time has been… *necessary*. Whether to feed folk or save lives." While they lay flat at the edge of the shadows, a small deer sniffed at the water's edge. "There's always a point you gotta choose what you do. Even if you think it ain't in your hands to make that choice." Annie gripped her rifle, her voice lowered to a whisper. *"But, as long as you're swift in action, that time is over quick."* She pulled the trigger on an exhale. In a blink, the animal lay still; its head floating in the river shallows.

The two pulled themselves from their hiding spot and walked towards the deer. Mikey's face whitened as he stared down at the lifeless creature and Annie sighed. "Don't mean you forget what you did, or what you did it to. But *sometimes it is necessary...*" She shook herself out of her memories, shouldered her rifle and looked at the boy. "Go on, make yourself useful and bring Bessie over. We have to work on luggin' this thing onto her."

***

Marie and Lucky were to act as 'Primrose's parents' once the inevitable discussion of matrimony arose with Cowley. Thanks to their reluctant agreement on the matter, the con continued quickly. With each town visit Dotty and Duke made to take tea with Luther, she would leave with glistening gifts, which the pair happily fenced for cash before leaving Boulderhead the very same day. Nate still endured the young man's company and had to field messages between the courting couple while earning a vague pittance for it. This left Danny with the arduous task of assisting Doc in his medicinal exploits, which brought him back with a black eye on more than one occasion. Clara and Maw had managed to get a laundry job for the Boulderhead Lawman uniforms. This kept them alert to any news regarding the gang.

Tommy tended to sulk more than anything else since Dotty's

involvement with Luther Cowley. As a formal invitation had been extended to "The Abernathy Family", Duke thought it prudent to use Tommy as their accompanying Valet. The whole plan was a monumental task. Marie, Lucky and Tommy would head out to a distant train station to provide the pretence of arriving in Boulderhead. Sam would be used as Duke's coachman, Madsen was to be left behind on watch with Clara, Annie and Danny. On the off chance that young Luther Cowley had been more observant during Duke's introductions at The Gin House Hotel, Lucky had grown out his moustache to a thick brush across his top lip. With an old comb, he applied a mixture of charcoal dust and water to his hair to distance his looks from his brother's.

Nate eyed the congregation with some amusement as they fidgeted at their clothing like children in church. Though he was as miserable in the get-up he was required to wear for his duties, it was far less flamboyant compared to the garments Tommy was forced into. Clara had managed to swipe a butler's outfit from a bundle of laundry she and Maw collected from the wash houses. The uniform consisted of a stiff, high-collared white shirt, thin bow tie, high buttoned waistcoat, black swallowtail coat, and grey trousers. He completed the look with a sheen of sweat beading from his forehead to neck.

"Well look at you," Nate teased, "from rags to riches in just a matter of hours."

"Ah get on with ya, ya gobshite." Tommy grumbled. "I look like I should be carryin' a coffin… Or bendin' over fer sailors."

"I'm sure if this is all done with early, you're welcome find your way to some docks and earn extra coin."

Tommy shoved away the arm Nate slung around his s houlders."I'm stewin' alive, and what're you doin' in all of this? *Nothin'*. Just sittin' on the top of that carriage lookin' like you're not covered in shite for once."

"Look, I have my own pains. I suffer that fool Cowley enough daily. This is different. You'll be invited to sit in that house with the servants." Nate jostled Tommy. "And you know full well how to *charm them soft souls*. They'll tell you everythin'. *Then*, when

Cowley calls on 'em, we'll be free to roam, and take some keepsakes."

"I tell ya somethin'," Tommy grumbled as the pair made their way to Doc's cart with empty travel bags, "we better get more than a bloody souvenir outta this. I'm not dressin' like an eejit for knick-knacks."

"I think you look rather dashin', Tommy." Dotty blushed as she watched the man faff at his coat sleeves. "Even if it is causin' you to look like you have a sickness." A small smile played at her mouth, and she handed him a cotton handkerchief to mop his brow. "Oh he's plenty sick enough." Nate laughed. "But she's right, Tommy, you're gonna need to get that under control, else they'll figure somethin's up. Maybe keep your head stuck out the train window to cool off."

Tommy thanked Dotty for the cloth and headed over to his companions, with a middle-fingered farewell to Nate.

"That boy best keep himself in line." Nate muttered to Dotty as the Abernathys left camp.

"You'll be there for that. He'll be sat up top on the coach at least goin' to the house, right?"

"True." Nate realised this would be Dotty's first visit to the palatial Cowley home. His heart sank as he remembered the story of her first love "... Dotty, has Cowley told you anythin' of his business? His land and such?"

"*Not really... Why?*"

"You know his family's in textiles dontcha?"

"... Sure."

"Cotton? *For generations?*"

Dotty's skin whitened with painful realisation. "... Oh."

"Now, don't think on it. Those in his service are paid, but... Well, I know the Cowleys favor a certain... *look* for their staff."

"*Duke never mentioned any of this.*"

"I know. I'm guessin' he wanted you to play along happily. But... I thought you best learn, before it's too late to keep your face steady."

"When's this all over, Nate? I ain't marryin' that fool!"

"It won't come to that, Dotty… Today's close to finishin' it. Duke'll wrap it all up."

"How, exactly?"

Nate had no idea. "In his own way, as always…" he gave Dotty a light hug. "Go on, now. Go get yourself somethin' to eat. Got a busy day ahead."

The rest of the gang had some time until their day started. Nate would meet Walter at the old plantation in the early afternoon before escorting Cowley to the station to meet Duke and Dotty. From there, everyone would head back to Cowley's home and discuss the matters of betrothal.

A frown crumpled across Nate's brow as he watched Duke wave off his friends. There had been no clear indication of how it would pan out, and he'd be damned if he was going to see Dotty married off to that rich idiot. "Duke!"

"Nate," Duke wrapped his arm around the man's shoulder as he gazed across the clear blue sky, "what a perfect day for this meeting."

"Uh-huh. And what exactly is the outcome we're hopin' for in all this?"

"Success!" Duke declared happily as the pair walked towards the swimming hole. "That man's father is as good as in the ground, and his son has no intelligence to understand the workings of business. He'll fritter away that fortune quicker than my brother at the tables. We will discuss the families' complimenting wealth, and our proposed dowry for the *delightful* Miss Abernathy. All the while you men'll fill those empty cases. After that we shall disappear."

Nate stopped. "… So, you plan on us movin' again…?"

"With the sum you boys can gather during this, we can all leave this godforsaken land, and on to brighter pastures."

"And, what? The law'll just forget about us?"

Duke winked. "They aren't looking for us in the North territories, Nathan."

"And what about Madsen? The fella's on the run!"

"Can't you just be happy that there will be enough money for us all? We can all ride off into whatever lands we desire." Duke gave a sharp, serious nod towards Annie as she stood conversing with Maw. "Alone or accompanied *if necessary.*" He flinched a smile. "Best get ourselves fixed for this show, don't want you to be late."

The two parted ways. Nate changed into his heavily starched collar shirt, strangling tie, and scratchy coat and pants. He hated every moment of it; from the impracticalities for riding, to the tight fit that already pulled at the seams from his broad build. He stood by his window, forcing his feet into the unyielding leather shoes.

He spied Annie, Tanner and Mikey making a spectacle of themselves trying to haul that kid on top of Bessie. He had only attempted cautious, civil conversation with the woman since the Dotty debacle; Annie's changeable attitude was far easier to wait out than force into changing. But seeing the nonsense in the paddock, he missed being a part of it.

Once dressed, Nate left for Cowley's. It was indeed a fine day; too warm to be messing about in such clothes, he thought, as the shirt stuck to his back.

There was an unusually rushed flurry of activity in the plantation grounds. Nathan paid it no further thought, assuming it was for the grand meeting, and pushed on towards the stables. One of the younger stable hands was there to greet him. "Afternoon, Mister Deleaney."

"Where's Walter?" Nate asked, dismounting, and handing the reins to the man.

"Not sure. Been a while. Prob'ly talkin' with Mister Cowley." Nate scanned the grounds. The staff's expressions and level of haste they moved with seemed to hold more worry than guests visiting his home should warrant.

"… What's goin' on?" the young man looked at him blankly.

Nate gesticulated to the hurried nature of their surroundings. "… Everythin' alright…?"

"Oh! Yes, sir…! You look a li'l warm, sir. There's some water right there." The man pointed towards a barrel and ladle. With nothing else to do but wait, Nate took the offer and drank deeply from the ladle. "Thanks. Everyone seems a little…" Nate turned and found he was alone. "… *Odd today.*"

It wasn't long before Walter hurried into view, fidgeting with his handkerchief when it wasn't mopping his brow. "Mister Nathe."

"Walter… What's all the fussin' for?"

"What're you talkin' 'bout?" Walter went to the pens for the coach horses and began to tack them up.

"There's a lotta ruckus today."

"*Sho is*." He muttered as he handed the reins of the first big coach horse to Nate. "Git that over t'the coach barn. I'll be there swift."

The walk to the barn only gave Nate more questions. He watched small pockets of house staff whisper and shake their heads. As he hitched the horse to the coach, Walter came up with the second.

"How's old man Cowley?"

"Oh, he fine. Nothin' gonna kill 'im off."

"Really…? I just thought that might be why all this-" Walter held up a hand and leaned forward. "Aaaalll kinda talk goin' 'round." He whispered. "Bad times they sayin'. Some kinda panic up north ways… Got Cowley worried."

"What panic?"

"Over his business. Might have ta sell up." Walter hoisted himself into the driver's seat and laughed heartily. "Might end up mo' poor than me!" Nate stared at the man trying to compose himself before leaving the barn.

Nate rested the shotgun in his lap. "So… What'll you do…? Any of you, should work dry up?"

Walter simply shrugged, pulled up outside the house, and waited for Cowley. "Hush now. No talk on this with none."

"… Sure…"

The ride to Boulderhead was quiet. Their passenger's weighted silence was only punctuated by the rumbling wheels of the coach. If Cowley was out of money, today would be far more urgent than originally expected, Nate realised.

The station was a sturdy structure on the edge of town. It boasted three platforms which snaked out from behind the building. Outside stood a cacophony of stagecoaches, delivery wagons, and travellers hurrying on foot. Nate was glad to have Walter traverse the mayhem. Their coach pulled in, and Nate joined Cowley as Walter opened his door for him.

"Wait with the coach, Walter, and be sure to clean it. I'm hoping to escort Miss Abernathy and her parents back in it and the current state of this vehicle is most unappealing."

"Yessir."

"Nathaniel. Accompany me to seek out your employer, won't you?"

Nate sighed and followed him into the din of bodies, pushing their way towards a chalkboard of arrival times.

"To the platform we go." Cowley chirruped and marched over the tracks to the central platform. Nate spotted Duke and Dotty at the opposite end, and led Cowley towards them with a loud, friendly greeting, to signal the pair to begin their roles.

"Ah! Mister Cowley, I am glad to see you made it in time."

"Yes, well, one shouldn't worry about punctuality when dealing with the reliability of A and M Railroad." Cowley stood beside Dotty and placed a kiss on her gloved hand, "Miss Abernathy… *Primrose.*"

"*Luther.*" Dotty feigned a coy smile at her suitor.

"I am most keen to meet your wonderful family."

"Mister Taylor…?" May I have a word…?" Nate faltered as the group stared at him with varying levels of astonishment. "Erm…

That is, if that's… amenable to *you*, Mister Cowley…?"

"Of course, dear fellow! Anything to spend unchaperoned time with my beloved."

Nate huffed an unenthusiastic laugh and moved away with Duke.

"What?" Duke hissed.

"Cowley's all but done."

"*What are you talking about?*"

"He's down to the threads on his back."

"How d'you kn-"

"There's commotion back at the house." Nate whispered hurriedly. "Pretty sure he's known a while, but things seem bad. Staff're makin' hasty plans. I reckon he only wants to wed *Primrose* for the dowry."

"*That sonofabitch…* You think his staff will take what's left before we get there today?"

Nate stared at his friend. "… *What…?* No, I-"

"Well, then." Duke relaxed. "No matter. Gives us an even better out. If the staff are all conspiring to take what they can, who will miss our take? We won't even be considered as culprits." Duke walked back to young couple leaving Nate staring on at the man's audacity.

It wasn't long before the Abernathy's train finally pulled into the station, and the welcoming party headed towards their weary guests in First Class. Dotty flung her arms around Lucky as any doting daughter would.

"Mister Cowley," Duke proceeded, "may I introduce to you, Mister Laurence Abernathy, and his *beautiful* wife, Rebecca."

"It is a *true honor* to meet the family that brought this magnificent creature into my most humdrum life."

"*Is he for real?*" Tommy appeared behind Nate, scowling. His shoulders rolled from struggling with a loaded station trolley.

"And it is a wonder to meet the fellow that has… *intrigued* my daughter's heart." Lucky shook his greeter's hand before bidding a hello to Duke.

"Oh! I thought we may have lost you, Dillon." Marie glared towards Tommy Kelley with a look that even had Nate check his behaviour. "Mister Cowley, this is our Valet, Dillon *Langer*." A small, devilish smile played at Marie's lips as Cowley greeted him.

"Mister Langer! How good of you to attend to your masters on this journey."

"Sir." Tommy nodded sharply and swallowed the annoyance at his newly christened name.

"Deleaney! Give Mister Langer a hand, won't you? Let's adjourn to our carriages."

Nate turned, took one of the empty cases and the two men walked behind the rest of the party as Cowley wittered on.

"Does the man ever take breath?" Tommy muttered.

"Not that I've noticed... *Langer*."

"Ah, sod off. I'm havin' a bad enough time as it is with this damned day... What's the old sods whisperin' about?" Tommy nodded towards Duke and Lucky who had dropped two steps behind the rest of the group.

"Somethin's up at the Cowley place. All kinda ruckus this mornin'. Dunno more on it but seems the walkin' Clap-Trap may be broke."

"*Broke?!*" Tommy laughed. "And he's still takin' a carriage to a big mansion. You and I have *very different* ideas on what it means to have nothin' Nathan."

***

"Jesus that took long enough."

Annie looked down at Mikey dragging his feet over the stream's bridge into the mill. "Quit your whinin'. I shared the ridin', didn't I? You weren't all that happy 'bout sittin' up here, neither."

"Funny that, bein' on a hulkin' beast surrounded by death not really bein' my thing."

They had a good haul of game for Chuck, thanks to Annie picking off a few ducks and rabbits before they headed back. Despite her threats, she had let a grey-faced Mikey sit in the saddle for a lot of the journey until he got over the reality of hunting. It had been a long day, and it was some hours since the pair finished what little food Annie had in her pack.

"*Gahd*, somethin' smells good." The aroma of cooking stirred action into the kid's muscles, and he lumbered quickly off towards the chuck wagon.

"I'll do this then, huh?" Annie hitched Bessie at the paddock and started to unload the small, manageable game as Tanner untacked Bessie.

"He came back unharmed, eh?"

"Sorry Tanner."

"Can't trust you to do anythin'." The man nudged her.

"Nice timin', Miss." Danny called. "All set to take over from me." He handed the rifle over to Annie and eyed the deer carcass on her horse. "I'm guessin' I'm takin' this for you?"

"Looks like it. 'Less your brother's back?"

The corner of Danny's mouth lifted with a small, knowing smile.

"*No, he aint*. Seems everythin' must be goin' well seein' as they ain't thunderin' back in here." He lined himself up with the back of the deer and pulled it onto his shoulder with a grunt. "You can keep an eye out for 'em now you're on watch."

"Who's on with me?" She called after him as he struggled towards Chuck's station.

"Madsen."

"*Goddamnit*."

The meeting of the families went as expected. They were given a tour of the grounds, and Nate noticed Tommy's struggle to keep his decorum in place whenever Cowley cooed at Dotty. Eventually, the important people retired to the drawing room, while their aides were escorted to the staff quarters in the kitchen. Sam was left miserable atop Duke's coach in the searing heat.

The tension amongst the staff was obvious, and their talk stopped abruptly as the men were seated at the work-worn table.

"You're Deleaney." One of the house girls filled two glasses with water and placed them in front of Nate. "Walter speaks kindly of you." She narrowed her eyes at his friend. "Don't know you though."

"Dillon." Tommy nodded and took a glass. "Pleased to meet ya."

"Huh!" The girl's eyebrows lifted. "Never thought I'd see a *mick* in Big House! *Really is the end of days.*"

"She can shove it up her end o' days." Tommy muttered into his drink, glaring slyly at the girl as she went back to her chatter. Everyone busied themselves with nothing, hurrying around with cloths in hands or polishing clean cutlery. They would jump at the clattering of food preparation from the kitchen and rush off when the bell rang from the drawing room.

"Broke, eh?" Tommy shook his head. "I gotta learn how to be broke like this."

"*Shut your hole.*" Nate hissed as he watched the last few staff scurry out. "Let's do this quick."

Annie gnawed on a stale chunk of bread while she leaned against the mill cogs at the camp entrance, trying to alleviate the throb in her feet. It had been a long time since she had to slog such distance on foot, and the repairs she had done on her boots were beginning to give way again. "*Another goddamn expense.*" She mumbled through the crumbs. Afternoon slid into early evening, and it wasn't long before she saw the silhouette of a coach. A pink-faced Sam drove into camp and reined in the horses as Duke leapt out of his carriage, a bloated case in his hand. "Folks, we are truly blessed." He dropped the bag with a metallic ***thunk,*** and two more cases joined it. Many of the gang cheered. Lucky stepped from the coach. "We need to divvy everything up fairl-"

"These spoils aren't going anywhere, brother. A celebration is in order!" Duke called out and the gang scattered into action, except for Nate.

Annie watched as he looked down on the loot and scratched at the back of his head; half smiling, half wincing. "Everything alright?"

"Yeah." He lied.

"…Did things get rough?"

"No." Nate sighed and looked at Annie. "No, I… I dunno." He thought about how they had snuck a lot of small shiny objects from the house in shifts, about how he had seen a few staff doing the same. He thought about Walter, and how he had told him to get more for the coach and horses than Cowley knew about when the time came to sell them. "Just glad it's over."

Annie nodded slowly. "Well, I'm sure Dotty's relieved." "Shit, she's done better than all of us. The size of the rock on her finger, she could buy Arkansas with it." Nate laughed awkwardly trying not to think too hard about the Cowley heirloom. "The man almost fainted when Lucky offered the dowry he ain't ever gettin'."

"Looks like this thing is done then." Annie sighed. "But I still got a watch to do before we all ride off forever."

Nate smiled as the sun haloed her, and suddenly he didn't worry so much about the swag at his feet. "Yeah. I guess you do."

Music and alcohol flowed freely. Gang members rifled through the bags like children at Christmas. Annie continued her watch around the back of the mill. The quiet gave her space to wonder if Duke would hand her a cut of the loot. She was already sure of the answer.

The sound of banjo strings twanged softly on the air, but something else hit Annie's ear; the low hum of voices in the trees.

Nate leaned against the card table, beer in hand, looking on as his friends celebrated what was soon to be their opportunity to start fresh. He thought about what Duke had said, about how they all could head North, go their separate ways. Maybe he and Annie could pool their take. He downed his bottle and went to look for her.

"So Lucky reckons no more livin' in ruins huh?" Mikey lumbered stiffly towards Nate.

"What the hell happened to you?"

"Been spendin' quality time with your lady."

Nate leaned back and folded his arms, the corners of his mouth curled upwards. "*That so?*"

"Fat lotta good it done me. Made me walk halfway home from huntin'. Wouldn't even lemme shoot the gun, and all I got to show is walkin' like you."

Nate huffed a short laugh and turned the corner of the mill.

"That makes you a man now, kid… *What's she doin'…?*" The two stopped and saw Annie creep slowly in the direction of the darkening woodland. "She seen a bear?"

"*Nah…*" Nate continued to watch as she prowled like a panther towards a kill. With the beer's encouragement, he grinned and nudged Mikey with his elbow. "*Let's go get shot.*" The sniggering duo mimicked Annie's stance and followed on behind her.

Clutching the rifle, Annie's eyes narrowed. She strained to hear the raised voices in the shadows.

"… You've been nothing but a thorn. I should've killed you long ago. You could've been *something*. But no. Your damned brother put a stop to that." She recognised that voice.

"I've been paying for that my whole life, Domhnall. Paying *you.*" She recognised that voice, too. "*Putting Kelley with you as collateral? Sending you what I owed…? I even got you a Schaeffer.*"

"You got me shit! How many men did that bitch put down, huh? And those two your fellas finished in Tinulca? The way I see it, you owe a lot more."

Something jolted at Annie's hips, and she swung blindly behind her.

"*Jesus,* Annie!" Nate stumbled backwards.

"What in damnation are you fools doin'??" She hissed.

"Makin' you shit your pants?" Mikey snorted.

"Get the hell outta here." She glowered, turned around and moved forward.

Her seriousness sobered Nate, and he rested his hand on the butt of his revolver. "Go on, kid. You heard her." Ignoring Mikey's protests, Nate ducked down beside Annie and waited.

"…Besides, you can't blame me for Miss Schaeffer's actions." Nate tensed. "I-is that-?"

"*Shhhh*." She snapped. The two got to the edge of the treeline and took cover. They could see Duke and Fitzgerald in the last beams of the day's light.

"You goddamn *knew* what she'd do to my boys. You betrayed me, you whoreson!" In a beat, Fitzgerald laughed bitterly. "I always said you had smarts. The way you could fix a robbery… You wanted to be in charge since we first rode together…But you got arrogant with it." Fitzgerald drew his six-shooter. *"And that doesn't win out, my friend."*

"DUKE!" That shout may have just saved his life. Duke turned towards it, and Fitzgerald's mis-shot bullet only sliced his neck. The moments that followed passed in what seemed like hours to Annie. She could see it all so clearly. The yellow of Fitzgerald's teeth when the victorious grin peeled across his face, the twist of his body with his arm aiming towards them. She felt a rush of air as the rifle was ripped from her hands, and the pull as each sinew of her body stretched beyond their means, from the tips of her fingers to her back foot. She launched herself to grab the gun back. She watched Mikey fumble with it, and she heard the soft *whip* as Fitzgerald's bullet landed between his eyes. Mikey's shout may have saved Duke's life. But that was all.

***

The camp was still. There were no more songs. The day's prizes sat ignored, glistening in the firelight. Worthless as tin in that moment.

They buried Mikey under a tree beside the pond with a keepsake from each of them. Annie had placed a playbill from her show days on his chest; one of the few things he would read without prompting. Nothing was uttered as they wrapped him in burlap and lowered him down the six feet. No one made a speech, no one sang a hymn. Lucky sat at the graveside, flinching as every shovel of dirt fell on the body. Finally, he couldn't stand it any longer and wandered away.

Duke had been moved into Marie and Dotty's quarters after being fixed up, thanks to some quick work between Annie and Doc to clean the wound and get it stitched.

The gang sat, listless, in the mill's grounds.

"… I guess we should get movin'." Annie stated. "*You* guess?" Sam Clifford threw the shovel down angrily and slapped the dirt from his hands as he tried to catch his breath. "*I guess* you shoulda been diggin' that hole. Shoulda been the one in it."

"We can't stay here." She looked around the glares from the gang.

"*You* can't stay here." Madsen growled. "Look what you've brought us. Lucky's nowhere, Duke can't be moved more." He stepped forward, cueing many of the others to close in around Annie. "You ain't *no one* in this gang. You've got no authority to choose *our* paths."

Nate sat at a table, staring at the bottle of whiskey in his hands. He picked at the embossing around its neck. Seething as he tried to make sense of what little he had heard, or remembered, before Mikey…

He drained the last quarter of the bottle, letting the burn of the liquid scrape his insides. He felt all the expectant eyes turn to him; it was unbearable. "She's right." Nate cleared the croak from his throat, and continued to stare at the bottle. "We shouldn'ta stayed after the last time. We can't stay now. Fitzgerald's injured, but he could come back any day."

Annie had managed to badly damage Domhnall Fitzgerald's main shooting arm as he made his escape.

Nate stood and walked away from the protests, away from the catcalls about why he agreed with Schaeffer and allowed the chaos to resume. The world had collapsed for them all. Each one grieved, and many blamed Annie for the way it all unravelled.

"*Maybe*," Danny shouted over the arguments, "we should get to thinkin' about our next camp." He scowled at Madsen. "We can't go back to Mississippi or Missouri. And it'll take a good week headin' west towards Oklahoma."

"Longer i-if we want to keep D-duke steady." Doc sighed, carrying his medical bag out from the mill. Annie wasn't so worried about that herself.

"So we hide in Arkansas." Danny said. "Quit your bellyachin'. Start doin' somethin' useful. And lay off Schaeffer." He looked sadly towards Annie who had remained quiet during the in-fighting, "… I gotta find Lucky."

23

Winds of Change

October 1893

The gang had settled into their new camp. Two weeks prior, the caravan had travelled slowly into Northwest Arkansas. Duke was transported carefully in the back of Annie's wagon, Marie at his side. There was an abandoned Indian reservation not far from Fort Onchuba, which Chuck recalled from his military days. It was far from any big, established towns. The shelter was sturdier than the mill had been, but smaller. Only a school room and chapel sat in the remnants of old, tattered tipis and small Christian burial plot, overlooked by a tall watchtower. Duke and Marie shared the school building with Doc, and Lucky shut himself away in the chapel.

Mikey's death had caused far greater change through the gang than predicted, splintering it into factions. Nate had been appointed the go-to for all things gang-related, despite his reluctance to step up to the role, and his connection to Miss Schaeffer casting doubt in some of the more sullen camp mates.

Annie hadn't ingratiated herself during that time. She refused to engage with the bitter taunts about what had happened, but Lucky's distance from both her and Nathan was tough to bear. Nate watched, crestfallen, as the man who raised him looked at him like he was a stranger. The weight of Mikey's demise pressed differently than Martha's murder had. Lucky had no fight left in him, nowhere to aim his anger. Instead, he retreated into himself, focused on keeping close to his recovering brother. It raised concern in Nate.

He hadn't discussed that fateful night with anyone other than

Annie. Even then, it was stilted, awkward exchanges. He didn't want to believe what was said, nor did he want to argue with her about something he knew she was right on.

"We need to divvy up the loot." Danny said one night as the Healeys sat together at the edge of camp. "Let 'em make their own way now. The longer we're all stuck here, the more likely you and Annie get murdered in your sleep."

Nate huffed out his cigarette smoke with a sad scoff. "How's Lucky?"

"*Breathin'*." Danny said. "You know you could just stop bein' a goddamn coward and find out for yourself."

"He don't wanna talk to me."

"Neither do I when you're mopin' like this, but that don't stop you harassin' me."

Nate had already tried with Lucky. Already looked to coax him out of whatever poison his mind swam in.

"There's been nothing but trouble these past months, Nathan."

"I know."

"*So much that shouldn't have happened.*"

"I know, Lucky bu-"

"Seems like Schaeffers always lead to death… You'd do well to distance yourself from such bad luck."

His heart had sunk, that wasn't Lucky's voice; it wasn't even grief talking. All it did was convince Nate that Annie's opinion of Duke was correct. He hadn't mentioned it to her, she'd only fight back; getting herself shot and burned out in the prairies somewhere. But as Duke grew in strength, his words would continue to twist among the rest. Nate couldn't have Annie square off with his entire family, it wasn't her fight. No one would win. Danny cleared his throat to cut through the silence and nodded towards the mass of canvas that was now Nate and Annie's combined lodgings.

"You two seem… close again."

"Hmm."

"She doin' alright…? What with everythin' goin' on these last few weeks. I mean, I know it ain't friendly but-"

"Danny… I'm gonna need your help with somethin'."

***

Despite so many of them turning on her, Annie continued with watch duties. She was under constant scrutiny whenever she walked through camp, just like her first weeks with the gang again. No one trusted her to be offsite, or left alone, yet they didn't much trust her with the rifles either. She didn't care, she didn't trust them at all.

Her quiet talks with Nate about the last night at the mill were rare, short, and bitter; he would end them abruptly. She was grateful for Danny and Clara, who suffered for fraternising with her. They would use watch handover as an excuse to talk more freely.

Today was no different. Annie watched Nate and Danny sit far off, deep in conversation.

"You know, for a woman that can dispatch a man quicker than a viper, you really need to work on lookin' less forlorn at that fella."

"I'm just worried for him is all. He ain't alright."

"He ain't never been right, Annie." Clara handed her the rifle. "But I think the way things've gone lately are takin' their toll." The pair stood in thick silence. "Well," Clara sighed, "I gotta head out for Chuck now. You need anythin'?"

Annie smiled bitterly. "P'raps some new knives. Think I might lose mine in some bodies before long."

"How about candy instead? Somethin' sweet seein' as you're so sour."

Annie bid her friend farewell and took off around the boundary. Under different circumstances, being situated on a hill, overlooking sprawling prairies and distant woodlands would be a welcome change; peaceful. The watchtower would have been claimed by Mikey the moment they arrived, probably finding a way to fling rocks or mud or any sort of nonsense at everyone below.

Annie's face dropped at that thought.

"Least you ain't gonna get a hidin' for that now." She mumbled with a sigh.

"I'm sure he'd appreciate that, if he could hear you, Schaeffer." The low, leering tones of Campbell Madsen crawled across her skin.

"Shouldn't you be on watch?"

"What d'you think this is?" He brandished his rifle at her.

"Yeah, well, we don't need two watchin' the same bit of land, do we?"

He stepped close to her. "Who says I'm watchin' the land?"

Annie glowered. "I'm sure you think I'm concerned about that, too, dontcha?"

"Now why would I want you to be concerned about me, Miss Schaeffer?" Madsen ran a hand over his moustache and let his eyes peruse the length of her body. "I told you I ain't had quarrel with Schaeffers. And I ain't never been a fan of *good, trustworthy girls*. And since you got here you seem determined to prove to me you ain't one."

Annie shouldered her gun, turned on her heel and marched in the other direction. She knew he was trying to cause a reaction. She knew he would get one if she stayed.

"You know they're splittin' that Cowley loot soon?" Madsen called after her.

"Your point bein'?" Annie heard him following after her.

"You ain't been contributin' much of late."

"Funny that, considerin' I were laid up for weeks broken and battered."

"Don't think you'll be gettin' a cut of this neither."

She coughed a bitter laugh at the obviousness.

"But I don't mind bein' a little benevolent." Madsen continued.

"Keep you right. A lady of leisure sat on that pretty behind of yours."

Annie stopped to warm her hands by the large campfire. "I can find my own way, Campbell. No need to concern yourself."

"Oh but I do, Miss Schaeffer. I can't see how Nathan Healey's recent attitude instils confidence in you. You need a fella that'll see you right, not some daydreamin' coward."

Annie felt the rage burn in her gut.

"You've been mighty ornery of late, Annie. I assume you ain't feelin', *fulfilled* in your duties as Leader's Mate." He closed in behind her. "Seems like my offer could be win-win.'"

Anger clawed from her guts to her throat. "What are you suggestin', Madsen, hmm?" She rounded to face him. "***That I should lie with you??! FOR YOUR BENEVOLENCE?***"

Madsen grew smug as a crowd began to gather. "*Everythin' gets shared, Annie. Anythin' anyone brings back to us.*" He leaned in. "And I don't recall you stumblin' into our camp yourself now."

"You are one *desperate* little bottom-feeder ain'tcha?"

"You need funds? I can fix that. Jus-"

Annie was consumed. All that had happened in the past weeks came to a head. The world around Madsen went black. She pulled her right leg back and swung with powerful, deadly precision into his privates. As he buckled, she brought her fist up and around to his nose, crunching it against her knuckles, her hand moved through his face.

"***IS THAT WHAT YOU HAD IN MIND, MADSEN, HUH?!***" She paced around him. Nothing else mattered beyond making him suffer in that moment. She was caught mid-attack; her arms trapped at her sides, and her legs a good inch or so from the ground.

"Annie! *For Christ's sake!*" Nate gritted his teeth as she struggled to be free of his vice-like hold.

"You should keep a tighter leash on your woman, Healey."

Madsen wheezed.

"I'M MY OWN GODDAMN WOMAN!!" Annie broke free and stood above the doubled-over man. "And you best stay the *hell* away from me, 'less you wanna mourn the loss of your *miniscule pecker.*" She powered past him towards the solace of her shelter.

***

"She ain't long for this place, Healey. Not if she keeps this up."

"How're you feelin' from that whoopin', Campbell? Need another?"

"You know her conduct ain't right."

Nathan smirked as Madsen tentatively dabbed the blood leaking from his nostrils. "I dunno. Her conduct always seems to be aimed at exactly the right person."

"You may think you're in charge right now, but Duke knows what goes on in his gang. And he's comin' back. She ain't protected with you no more. Best keep her outta sight if you want missy hangin' off your belt a few days longer."

Nate patted Madsen's bruised and bloodied cheek with a firm, patronising hand. "Fix your face, Campbell, you're lookin' uglier than ever."

He went to the tent and stood in the doorway watching the back of Miss Schaeffer as she angrily inhaled a cigarette before stubbing it out, nearly through the barrel her lamp rested on.

"I ain't apologizin'."

"I should think not, Annie." Nathan squeezed her shoulder warmly. "Though I think you should probably aim your foot somewhere that he uses more often next time. Make him more useless."

She turned her angry face to him, and he smiled sadly thinking about Madsen's last, real threat. "…You know, we ain't had a lotta peace lately. We should take a day."

Her face crumpled into confusion. "What're you talkin' about?"

He sighed. "Things've been… *busy* for both of us… I thought a break from it might be… I dunno… nice."

"Nice? We're in the middle of nowhere, where exactly are you suggestin' we vacation?"

Nathan sat heavily on the camp bed. "Doc mentioned a small town a short distance away. Says it's got some good places. There's a station not far from here. I thought maybe we could get the train down."

Annie's scowl made him uncomfortable. Her natural state was to be suspicious, and he was too tired to keep the charade up if she pushed much harder.

"Look, there ain't many options for entertainment in these parts. I thought you could do with steppin' outta camp."

He had no idea how right he was, she thought. "When precisely were you thinkin' you might have a gap for this? Ain't like you have a lotta free time."

"Tomorrow. Jesus, woman, can't you just let me do somethin' for ya for once?"

She thought about what he said. There was a station, and a chance to check her routes of escape. If she wasn't going to receive any more funds from the gang, she had no reason to wait around. She could scout this journey, return, pack, and be gone.

"Alright," she sniffed, "nothin' I want more than to get away from them gawkers anyhow."

Nate looked at Annie. How could he tell her she needed to leave? He slapped his thighs and stood back up, forcing what he thought was a natural smile across his face, and took the camp rifle from her. "I dunno 'bout you, but I ain't in any mood to see more fights break out today. Reckon it's safer for everyone if I take your watch."

***

It was a crisp, cold morning. Nate peered through a small gap in the tent entrance to check the activity. Those not asleep were

303

muttering in their small groups.

"Can I stop hidin' in here like some damned leper now?" Annie faffed at her outfit; a white cotton blouse tucked snugly into the waistband of a floor-length skirt which laced tightly above her hips.

"Yeah. C'mon, let's go."

They were both dressed well to blend in better with the townies at their destination; Nathan chose to wear the clothes he used as a coach guard. He marched, head down, behind Annie as she strode out from the tent with the same attitude as she had upon her initial arrival at Onti Lake. She stood tall, defiant almost, with her eyes piercing through the shadow of her hat's brim.

"I still don't see why we can't take both horses." She grumbled as she gave Bessie a loving embrace and a peppermint.

"I told you," he muttered, mounting up, "it's a sign you're comin' back if she's still here." Nate offered his hand to Annie who looked from it to his face and smirked, leaping effortlessly onto the back of Prynne unaided. She swung into a straddle sit behind him; her skirt trailing across the mare's back.

They headed out silently and it wasn't long before Nate felt Annie fidgeting and grumping to herself. "You alright?"

"No." She huffed.

"I ain't surprised." He looked down at her leg, her hitched skirts exposed it to the wind. "Why d'you think ladies sit side-saddle??"

"I feel… *naked*."

"Don't look how I remember it."

"Without my gun belt!" she playfully punched his ribs as she held onto him. "I don't like not havin' it."

"Ladies in polite society don't have guns, Annie. They have fellas do all the fightin' for 'em."

He smiled upon hearing a judgemental snort of derision coming from his companion.

They hitched up outside the station and Nate organised two

tickets and a stable car space for Prynne on the train waiting at the platform.

Once Prynne was settled, the two made their way to the carriage. Annie sat by the window and gazed at her surroundings. Small metal sconces dotted the sides, and each window was edged with a thick curtain. The slatted benches they sat on were held in place with wrought iron legs bolted to the floor. The dark-varnished wood of their passenger car creaked as other passengers boarded.

"This your first time inside a train, Annie?" Nathan scoffed at his companion as she looked around, wide-eyed.

"I've spent my life travelin' by horse and cart. Ain't had a need to sit in such luxury."

He eyed her with amusement. The Station Master slammed the doors and the whistles blew. With a hiss of steam, the train lurched forward into action, causing Annie to grab Nate's arm in surprise. He patted her hand. "Big strong woman snuffs out lives like a candle, afraid of a train movin'."

"You shut your hole, Healey, else I'll snuff out *your* candle." She shoved him lightly and looked at him. A strange wave of guilt hit her. All she had ever wanted was to get out from under others, to live for herself. So much of what happened to the gang had been because of her. Death followed her, and the moment she dropped her guard, it took another piece of her away.

Moving on had always been her plan, and the longer she had stayed, the murkier her life had become. She almost resented Nate for delaying it.

He didn't try to change the silence; he was battling with his own decisions. Annie didn't deserve to be deserted, but he couldn't think of another way to keep her alive. The thought of actually telling her to go was excruciating. He would sell what little soul he had left to sit on that train forever. But with every whip of the wheels on the tracks, they edged closer to the inevitable. He saw the concern in her eyes and tightened his hand over hers with a forced, reassuring smile, which she returned just as falsely. She let her hand drop from his and turned back to the window, lost in her own thoughts.

The train pulled into the town of Clifton Springs by early afternoon. The sun had broken through the clouds as the two stepped out onto the wooden platform.

"Alright," Nate looked up at the station's clock, "we got some hours for explorin'." He went to the stable car and retrieved Prynne. "Remember," he said with mock seriousness, "you're *ladylike*. So, no arguin' when a fella's tryna be nice." He mounted his mare and leaned over, offering his hand to Annie once more.

"You're really enjoyin' this, ain'tcha?"

"I have no idea what you mean." Nathan hid his entertainment behind clamped lips and pulled Miss Schaeffer easily onto his horse. "But you might wanna sit side-saddle."

Annie did as she was told, with only a small amount of blustering, and wrapped one arm tightly around Nate's midriff. The couple headed onwards.

The town offered small shops and a park. It was a twee affair that neither Nathan nor Annie felt classy enough to visit. It wasn't long before they found themselves in the less-developed part of town and relaxed when they saw the large brick-fronted stores were replaced with squat taverns that advertised gambling. Nate hitched up at one, dismounted and lifted Annie down.

"This is humiliatin'." She muttered at being placed lightly on the cobbles.

"After you, Miss." Nate swept his arm ahead of them for her to lead the way.

He watched from the bar for a while as Annie joined a poker table with an easily accepting group of players, settling in to play a few hands before finding her stride. He had never seen her play cards before. She always declined when in camp, stating (to a lot of guffaws) that she didn't want to add to her list of enemies when she took their money. Now, having seen how fast she accumulated chips, he was relieved she wasn't one to change her mind. He instead visited the blackjack table.

"Did you escort that young lady here today?" Nate's dealer asked.

"She seems expert at cards."

"I certainly came here with the woman at the poker table," he paid for his chips, "can't say how much of a lady she is." He mumbled to a few chortles.

After a little success, Nate cashed in what he had, and went back for a drink.

"I think we should be goin'." Annie said lightly as she joined him and counted the bills she had gained.

"You cleaned 'em out?"

"Course!" she folded the large bundle and nestled it safely between her cleavage and her undergarments. "*And* this pocket watch I just won tells me we're late for lunch."

The two didn't go far to find food. Choosing to stretch their legs, they walked Prynne through the streets towards a coffee house. Neither had eaten since the night before. Being out of sight and mind as much as possible at camp had been smart. With Annie's winnings, they treated themselves to almost everything on the menu. For the first time in a while, they sat laughing and talking, unburdened by reality as the sun dwindled.

"You know, them fellas were mighty impressed with your card playin'."

"Not the ones at my table." Annie scoffed.

"No one offer to escort you to their rooms then?"

"Not this time, no."

The heavy, solemn cloud of life hung over them as they made their way towards the train. Nathan pulled up beside the small ornamental park opposite the station. "We got some time, let's wait a while." His voice was quiet and thick. He jumped down from the saddle.

"Alright." Annie sighed and slid from Prynne, landing heavily. The time had come.

"Y'know, I find it odd that folks dig up land, only to put grass and flowers back on it, but it's kinda nice." Nate said as they sat at a bench.

"I'm leavin, Nathan." Annie said softly. He turned sharply to look at her, and she smiled, placing her hand on his arm. "It's alright. This weren't never meant to be permanent. I always told you I'd be out your way once I was back on my feet. And thanks to that card table I am."

He sat dumbfounded as her words worked to embrace him.

"Annie-"

"I know I've outstayed my welcome ten times over," she was calm as she looked at the greenery, "'specially recently." She shrugged. "Now I can get gone right away."

His insides lurched, *right away?* Annie was resilient but this was ridiculous. "Annie it ain't that easy. They ain't gonna just wave you off. We need to do this slowly." He knew that wasn't true. He knew it could be quicker if they were smart, but he needed a week, just one more week.

"*We?!* Nathan, I ain't gettin' you involved further, there's no need. I ain't unpacked half my wagon. I can get gone in hours, leave the tent behind. No one'll know."

'Well, that ain't happenin'."

"Duke is healed." She said flatly. "And he knows I heard somethin' that night. You think he's gonna let that slide?"

"You saved his life." Nate argued weakly.

"And…?"

And nothing. Nate had nothing. She was right, and he worried how much Duke remembered. Wondered if he saw Nate before he blacked out. "Me and Danny hav-"

"You're bringin' your brother into this?" Annie's glare softened when she looked at him. "Nate, the less folks involved the better. I don't need you doin' this for me."

"I ain't told Danny why we're doin' this, just how we get you gone… And I ain't lettin' you get outta that place on your own, Annie. We dunno how connected Duke is with…" He faltered; he still couldn't say it out loud. "Fitzgerald's got men everywhere." He looked at the woman beside him. "Me and Danny'll tell Duke we're out to find him, bring him back to answer for what he did.

We're takin' you as your cart can carry more for the journey." Annie blustered. "Ain't no one gonna believe that! Why make it more complicated?"

"Because you have the biggest, most obnoxious wagon and there's no other way to get you out without questions… We gotta try." Nate took a breath. "I want answers, Annie. I wanna know how long this has really been goin'… Duke won't be the one to tell me… We'll ride towards Sugar Oak with you, then…" he stopped again, clearing his throat. "… But you're gonna need to be careful packin' your belongins; folks're always watchin' now. It'll have to be slow, at night, and when Clara or Danny are on watch."

"What's gonna happen to you if we do this plan?"

"What d'you mean?" Annie didn't elaborate. Her look told him to grow up. "…I'll be fine." He muttered. "Don't worry about me."

Annie sighed and turned back to blossoming flowers. "I ain't the person you think I am." She said.

Nate laughed in disbelief.

"I ain't worth this fight and struggle."

"Don't be stupid, Annie."

"When we met, I weren't runnin' from Smythson. Didn't give him an opportunity to chase me. Not unless he rose up from hell, and I don't think he had that in him to do." She exhaled a mirthless laugh.

Nathan thought about the scenes at Sugar Oak. "Well, I guessed that."

"I didn't end him quick neither. *But it was pretty.*" A strange, wild stare flickered across her eyes before she turned to him desperately. "I've lost count of folks I've put down, and I ain't sorry 'bout any one of 'em. That's why I ain't worth this fuss." Nathan's brow furrowed. "Would they've harmed you?"

"I guess…" Annie looked down and thought back to some of the worst. Then there was that 17-year-old kid; her first murder.

"Well then." He sighed, hoping to leave it at that.

He wasn't listening to her. "But I were happy to do it… *I*

enjoyed it." She pushed. "And that's the problem..." she gripped his hand.

"I remember every second of all of them. I remember those Fitzgerald killins, and if I could, I'd do it over again, all the same, only slower... You are not to worsen your life for someone like me."

Nathan studied her face and smiled. Her green eyes were wide, determined to have him give up on her. Her face was laughably serious with a jaw clenched so tightly her lips pursed. He let her dig her fingers into the top of his hand as he placed his other on top of hers. "I was there, Annie. I saw what you did to those fellas. I had to put one of them outta his misery. I ain't forgotten. D'you really think you'd still be around if I thought for a moment you were trouble?"

"Nathan, you ain't listenin'-"

"I certainly wouldn't be happy to lie beside you." He laughed lightly, stood and looked back to the glow of the station lights bleeding into the dusk. "Looks like we missed our train." He lied. "Maybe we should find somewhere in town tonight."

24

"**A**lright, this'll do." Nathan sighed and slowed Prynne. "We can't risk goin' much further, else we'll hit Fitzgerald country."

The week leading up to Annie's departure had been rough. Nate had spent his time trying to get through to Lucky who now sat in a dark spiral. He and Danny told Duke their plan to capture Fitzgerald and use Annie as transport. Duke waved them off with little questioning, which raised further concern.

The three had journeyed northeast in silence and arrived at the fork he had planned as a meeting point when retrieving Annie from her captors.

Annie stepped down from her wagon. "Thank you, Danny." She reached up to shake his hand. "You look after yourself you hear me? Don't be takin' nonsense from that lunk over there."

He took her hand in both of his. "If you say so Annie."

"Give my love to Clara."

Nathan handed Danny his reins and dismounted heavily to retrieve something from his saddle bag as Annie gave Prynne one final nose rub. She kept one eye on him, but he wouldn't look at her.

"Well…" Annie stepped back. "Best not keep you fellas any longer. You got a job to do." She turned and made her way back to Bessie.

"*Annie.*" Nate's voice was nothing more than a whisper. "I'm gonna find you. Once this is done. I promise." He walked over to her and reached forward with a bundle of notes in his hand. "Take this. I don't need it."

"Nate I ain't takin' this from you."

He smiled. "Stop bein' so damned stubborn for once and take it…. Look after it for me. I'll come get it when I find you." Annie stared at him. She knew he wasn't coming back when they left this place, and this gesture was him knowing it too. She took his hand and squeezed it before removing the notes from his fist.

"It all better be there when I see you next." He joked. She huffed a shaky laugh, nodded, and folded the large roll of bills before placing them awkwardly into her blouse; that familiar trait of hers.

"Here." she pulled the watch that she had won in Clifton Springs, from her pocket. "Somethin' to remember me by. In case you forget."

Nathan opened the silver casing. The smell of her perfume rose from it, and the inside was lined with the painted fabric from her tattoo gauntlets. "Oh, there won't be no forgettin' you, Annie Schaeffer." He nodded sadly and closed the watch, running his thumb across its filigree pattern. "I'll see you, Miss." He tapped the brim of his hat as his voice cracked, and he turned to leave. Annie reached for his wrist. She knew the chance of him returning was non-existent, that his promise was something he said out loud to try and make it real. She wouldn't allow herself to become a regret for him when his final day came. They stared at each other; too stubborn or too afraid to say the words.

"Thank you for everythin'."

"Annie I-"

"Be safe, Nathan Healey." She whispered, placing a soft hand against his cheek as he put his own on her waist. He looked at her and went to speak again, but found no voice. What good would his words have been to her then? They would only leave them bereft of what could have been. Instead, he let instinct take over and pulled her to him, taking one final, deep, desperate kiss from her lips. He moved his hands to Annie's face to take in every detail of her skin; its warmth, the scent of her perfume, the lightest touch of her hair as it brushed his fingers through the breeze. He relinquished her mouth with a heavy breath, rested his forehead on her own. "I'll find you, Annie." Forcing himself to let go of her, Nate walked backwards to Prynne, trying to capture the final sight of her for as long as he could. Eventually, resigned to his duties, he pulled himself into the saddle, and took the reins from his brother. Without looking back, he kicked Prynne on, and rode away.

The men traveled for some time before Danny spoke. "You alright, Nate?"

"Sure." A gruff voice replied. "Let's get this done."

Annie waited until their silhouettes were less than specs on the horizon. "Well girl," she patted Bessie, slouching in the seat of the cart, "guess we're headin' east."

25

Reunion

September 1894

TO: N. Deleaney,
The Mission.
April 1894

Nathan,

I hope this letter finds you. I have sent copies to many places I felt you might be.

I headed to New York in search of my family. It took most of my coin, and some weeks, but I did indeed find them. They have a show. Sally is now in charge (and quite a fitting role it is for her too!). I was errand runner. It is more taxing than performing in many ways, but preferable. I must say the winter months are not the season to reside there. The weather was as treacherous as I imagine the mountains would be. We stayed together, all crammed into two rooms hardly a bed between us. I nearly pined for the days in that tent. You would have truly hated it, dirty, full of people, and not enough room to stand let alone sleep. I was always concerned for my health.

The statue in the Hudson was a sight to behold, however. Quite a spectacle she was, looming.

I couldn't bring myself to stay in the city. Bessie was kept in stables far away, and the cost of keeping her safe during the terrible storms left me with so little. When the city thawed, the two of us made our way West to Pennsylvania. I found work in a town called Snow Rock, I can't seem to get away from that damned stuff! I am working at the Tavern Saloon. Thanks to my way of upsetting uppity folks, they employed me as protection for the girls. Now every fellow wanting a nice

time must be quizzed by me first (as you can imagine they aren't too excited about that part). It pays poorly but they provide food and lodging.
If by some small miracle you do find your way here, ask for Annmarie. I'll be waiting, with that cash of yours. Ready to buy you a drink with it.
Annie

He folded the letter with a sigh and placed the envelope in his pack. It was almost five months old, and nearly a year since Annie left the camp. She couldn't have waited around, despite having a job and lodging, she wasn't the type. At least it was a place to start. He rolled his shoulders and mounted his horse. It was a long journey to Pennsylvania, perhaps he could treat them both to a rail ticket.

Annie sat at her usual spot in the Tavern Saloon, feet up on a small desk with a view down over the staircase. She had a cup of coffee on the desk and held a broad newspaper. There had been a break in the weather. Muddied roads were being given a chance to dry out. Sharp morning sunshine streamed through the saloon windows; Fall was closing in.

Mornings were boring. Most locals knew better than to cause trouble losing arguments with Annie, and workdays didn't trade much in carnal requirements, not until lunchtime. The only activity was the same old tunes coming from the piano downstairs.

He hesitated as he pulled into Snow Rock. Unfamiliar towns caused him to check the layout; an instinct left over from the Needham days. He kicked on and made his way down the main street towards the saloon. There was no sign of a white Percheron.

"Get some rest." He cooed to his horse as he dismounted, and headed inside with the hope of news of Annie's whereabouts.

"Excuse me?"

"Good Morning, sir! What can I get you?"

"I was lookin' for an Annmarie? She work here?"

The barman looked at the man cautiously. "She doesn't *work* here."

He scowled. "I don't follow."

The barman fidgeted. "Well, sir, I mean Miss Malone works here, but she isn't, erm… *obtainable*."

"Obtainable?!"

"*She isn't for hire.*"

"I can imagine she ain't!" he laughed. "I ain't lookin' to hire her, I figured she might like to see an old friend."

Behind her paper, Annie could hear muffled conversation from the bar. She didn't think much of it; none of the girls were up yet anyhow. The customer might have wanted a liquid breakfast.

"Miss Malone…?" The barman appeared at the top of the stairs.

"Whaddya want, Mister Williams?" she asked from behind the newspaper.

"There's a gentleman asking for you downstairs."

"Have you told him I ain't on the menu?"

"He knows that, he…"

She sighed. As kind as Williams was, she had to do a lot of unnecessary leg work when it came to giving men a hiding.

Still hidden behind the paper, she continued as heavy footsteps clumped up the stairs. "Well *tell him* that if he's here to dispute the way I handled a disagreement, he can come back later. I ain't in the mood to shoot him right now."

"Hello Annie."

She knew that voice, one she thought she would never hear again. She lowered her paper just enough to peer over the top of it.

"It's good to see you." He rumbled.

"*Well I'll be damned...* Daniel Healey as I live and breathe. What're you doin' here?"

"Lookin' in on a friend." He smiled softly and she walked around the desk to embrace him.

"You happened upon one of my letters I'm assumin'?"

"That's about the size of it."

"How's Clara?"

"Fine. She's back home."

"Home? Look at you all grown up! And Nathan? He with you?"

Danny shuffled. "Look I ain't travelled this far east to have you ask about my brother. What about a drink, huh?"

"Sure. Make yourself comfortable," she gestured to her desk,

"I'll go grab somethin'." She marched off downstairs.

Danny became very aware of eyes twinkling at him. He cleared his throat and nodded to the scantily clad women close by.

"*Ladies.*" Then sat and lit a cigarette.

A girl slid herself onto the corner of the desk as Danny reached for the newspaper. "How d'you know Annmarie? You aren't from here. Least none of us have seen you before… You her lover?"

"*Christ no.*"

"What, then?"

He squirmed in his chair, Annie seemed to have trained these women to be as brazen in their questioning as she ever was. He felt an oppressive shadow envelope him; the girls of the saloon surrounded the desk.

"You better not be fixin' to rile her, Mister. I've seen what happens to those that rile her."

"So has he, Cassie." Annie's voice parted the sea of faces and she smirked at Danny cowering in his seat. She nodded towards him. "Let's talk in my office."

Without hesitation, Danny stubbed out his cigarette and launched himself from the chair, hurrying past the abundant flesh on show.

He followed Annie to a room towards the back of the saloon. "I gotta say, I didn't think you were here at first. I couldn't see Bessie anywhere."

She shoved the tray into his hands and pulled a key from her pants pocket. "I got her a spot in the stable. I don't get paid much, but it's enough to keep my girl in some care." She unlocked the door and ushered him inside. "After you m'lady."

She studied Daniel Healey as he slid past her into her room. Whatever had happened over the last year had matured him. He seemed stronger and obviously more assured.

"Clara sends her best." He placed the tray on Annie's walnut coffee table and groaned down into his chair.

Annie nodded and uncorked the whiskey.

"… So, how're you findin' bein' a Brothel Madam?"

She grinned and raised an unimpressed eyebrow. "How'd you find havin' a black eye?"

Danny laughed with a warm, familiar tone. "I know that ain't what you are."

"Look, I just beat up the fellas that beat up the girls."

"Perfect. Might as well get paid to do a job you were doin' for free for years."

"Well, quite." She sniffed proudly and raised her glass. "Your good health."

Danny reciprocated, taking slow sips as Annie stared at him. "So… You goin' by Annmarie Malone for good now?"

"Where's Nathan, Danny?"

He froze, gripping the glass.

"What happened after I left you boys?"

Danny placed his drink on the table and sat back in his chair.

***

"There's only two of us." Danny pushed. "How the hell're we gonna survive this?"

"We'll be alright." His brother said flatly.

The pair dismounted at the edge of Sugar Oak and tied their horses. The place was eerily silent.

"I don't like this, Nate."

"Then stay here." Nathan pulled the lasso from his saddle.

"Look, I know today's been hell, but you gotta get your head outta your ass. This is the Fitzgeralds for Christ's sake!" Danny stopped as his brother stared at him; he looked tired.

"D'you trust me?"

"Course."

"So quit whinin'." Nate muttered and turned back towards the ghost town.

Though they were cautious, there was no need to be. The place was deserted, except for one solitary figure at the centre of Sugar Oak. Domhnall Fitzgerald sat by a campfire, his right arm bound in a sling. He looked finished. "You're later than I expected." He called.

"Had some business." Nate walked towards the old man. Danny hung back, clutching his rifle. *"Nate! What're you doin'?"*

"Duke dead?"

"Nope." Nate continued forward.

"Course he isn't." Fitzgerald muttered. "I am sorry about that kid, though. Always a shame to end them young."

Nathan stopped, causing Danny to raise his gun.

"Tell that brother of yours to relax." Fitzgerald whined and stood up. "I'm not running. I'm even unarmed." He pointed to his mangled shooting arm. "Quite literally!" he laughed a cold, bitter laugh. Nate took to walking again and unravelled his rope. "Ah c'mon now Healey, is there really any need?"

"You got a horse?" Nate asked.

"Of course I have a horse; you don't think I'd send the boys away along with that do you?"

"After the week I've had I ain't sure what to think." Confusion welled up in Danny. "Nathan! What the *shit* is goin' on?" He waved his gun between his brother and Fitzgerald.

"Danny, we're takin' him in. Just as I told you."

"Where the hell is everybody?"

"I sent them off, son!" Fitzgerald said as he let Nate tie his free wrist. "Told them another old gun would be taking over."

"I don't…"

"Go get his horse." Nate sighed, nodding his head towards the silver dappled Arabian.

The men travelled slowly back towards the Needham camp. Domhnall Fitzgerald's good arm was tied to his saddle horn, his horse was led by the Healeys.

"Wish we'd gagged him." Danny muttered to his brother as the old man ranted about nonsense with Duke and spat obscenities about Annie.

Nate kept them riding through the night. They didn't stop until they reached a point in the road that split into five directions, with a large oak tree in the centre.

"You aren't lost are you boys?" Fitzgerald goaded.

"Danny, go on ahead. Get Duke to meet me here. I'll wait with Fitzgerald. Last thing we need is everyone makin' this a side show back at camp." He reached into his saddle bags and passed his brother a letter. "Read this when you get back. *Alone.*"

"Alright, but-"

"Do as it says." Nate's voice was stern, teetering on threatening.

"*Alright.*" Danny said warily. "I'll see you back there."

"Go on, Danny."

***

Danny picked at the arm of his chair in the thick silence of Annie's room. Piano keys tinkled in the distance. "I did as was asked. Sent Duke up towards Devil's Compass… Then I read Nate's letter." Annie swallowed and stared towards the window. She could guess what it had said. "Then what?"

"I did as Nate told me to do. I got me and Clara gone. Got all of 'em told. Only Lucky, Marie, Madsen and Clifford refused to leave. I waited up at the old fort. Kept watch usin' the rifle scope."

"And did he? Did Duke return?"

"No."

Annie winced a bitter smile. *"Course he didn't..."* she swirled the whiskey in her glass before throwing it back in one go. "And what of Cowley's trinkets? You get your cut?"

"Some, but far less than there shoulda been." Danny muttered. "There were no time to look for Duke's things before we thought he'd be back."

She turned to Danny. "And what happened to Nathan, Danny?"

He shook his head. "Annie, I- I'm sorry." He watched as she rose from her chair and paced with unnerving calmness. "... I don't know..."

A look washed over her like nothing Danny had seen before. She raised her glass high above her head and threw it with full force onto the floorboards, shattering it into dust.

"Jesus Christ!" Danny was up out of his chair.

"That damn Needham! That *bastard!* He's gone. Gone with everythin'. Took it all. *May God damn him!"*

She stalked around her room, shaking her head. "Shit, that asshole really played the long game, took you all for fools." She stopped and gripped the back of her chair. Her feral stare cut through Danny. "But I bet he ain't figured you'd come lookin' for me. And I bet he ain't figured I'll hunt him." Her knuckles turned white.

"Hunt him and destroy it all."

26
Epilogue

"So, we're to sit here until Marmaduke trots on by?" Fitzgerald fidgeted in his saddle. "I hope we've got a picnic."

Nate dropped from Prynne and hitched her to the five-point road post. He stood close to Fitzgerald. "How long's this been goin'?"

"What? Duke's flirtation with betrayal?" He smirked at Nate.

"The man lives in a nest of snakes dear boy."

Nate clenched his jaw and paced. "You're lyin'."

"Why? Because you want me to be?"

"YOU'RE *LYIN'!*"

Fitzgerald laughed at him again. "Marmaduke Needham is only interested in bettering his self. Stole from me, tried to give it back as debt repayment."

"He did that for Lucky."

"He did that for himself!" Domhnall spat. "He took everything. Always planned to as soon as he realized he couldn't vie for my position. His *failure* of a brother just gave him an excuse."

Nate grew hot. "Lucky Needham is not-"

"Lucky Needham was, is and always will be a *weak* and *pathetic man.*"

Nate roared. He grabbed Fitzgerald's leg, wrenching him from his saddle, his arm still tied to the saddle horn. A great wheezing wail came from the old man as his good arm detached from his shoulder, leaving him half-dangling like a marionette.

"Duke… Duke has worked for us… his whole life… Sent Kelley as an offering of loyalty."

Nate looked at him. "Tommy knew?"

The old man whined a tired, breathless laugh. "Christ you're slow... No!... Thought he was playing spy... Duke sent him as a sacrificial lamb."

Nate turned away, leaving the bastard dangling. "I really thought he was one of us… Until that *Schaeffer whore*." Fitzgerald grinned at Nathan's sudden halt. "He played an ace with her."

Nathan walked over to the Arabian and calmed it before untying the rope, letting Fitzgerald fall limply to the ground.

"She could've been our golden goose…" Domhnall slumped, breathless. "Except she's a stubborn bitch…" his eyes rolled up to Nate towering over him. "Wouldn't even take a fucking."

***

Nathan Healey sat with his back against the road post, swigging at a bottle of whiskey. He looked at the oak tree where Domhnall Fitzgerald swung.

He didn't remember looping his lasso around the man's neck, or when he threw the end of it over the thick tree branch and pulled. But he knew it was after he'd given him a beating. Waiting at Devil's Compass for the Devil himself, and it wasn't long until Duke appeared.

Nate stood as the man dismounted and eyed the dead Domhnall Fitzgerald with vague indifference.

"Daniel told me to meet you both here. I didn't realize that you would already give him his day in court." Duke's hoarse voice croaked out. Forever changed by the bullet, it held a steady malevolence. It fitted him now, Nate thought.

"Weren't this what you wanted?" He growled.

"I suppose." Duke shrugged. "Get him down for goodness

sake, Nathan."

Nate lumbered across and unwound the make-shift noose, letting Fitzgerald hit the ground like the sack of shit he was.

"Though he was wanted alive preferably, he'll still be of value as he is."

"For who?"

Duke shot him a withering look.

"Funny." Nate continued, walking back towards Duke. "I never understood the need for law when a fella confesses everythin'."

"Yes, well…" Duke's eyes narrowed.

"That Fitzgerald's a real bastard… But he sure sang pretty." Duke's smile darkened. "I should've taken more care with you as a kid, Nate. That brother of mine made you soft-headed. You can be so *infuriating* at times."

Nate's hand hovered close to his pistol.

"Happy to rob and blackmail when I conjured up some *moral obligation* around it, happy to kill a man if he wronged you first. *As long as you had an excuse.*"

His teeth clamped down hard.

"But put some supple-skinned delight in your path, and you're as worthless as a whore with the clap. Getting notions of *doing good. Ideas of heroics.*"

The searing pain hit him before he heard the gunshot, and Nate collapsed, gripping his gut.

"What was it I always told you, Nathan, hmm?" Duke stood over him as he convulsed in panic. "*Heroes always die.*"

As the sound of Duke's horse melted into the horizon, Nathan Healey sat with his back against the road post, his vision fading. Waiting at Devil's Compass for the Devil himself.

About the Author

E.J. McKenna is a freelance writer in the UK with a great interest in American History, and a degree in English and American Literature with Creative Writing from the University of Kent.

At the end of 2023, she co-created a creative writing app (InkWritingApp) for people of all ages to improve their writing skills in a fun, relaxed environment.

Born and raised in the UK, but a lover of traveling, she has a fascination with all social history across different countries and cultures. One of her favourite historical periods is the Victorian era, especially with United States history. "The juxtaposition between the established countries of Europe, and the new world of America is fascinating to me. So many people trying to survive harsh frontier life, while trying to continue the uptight decorum of Victorian society."

A huge advocate for feminism and human equity, her writing centres around determined female protagonists in traditionally male roles, tackling the perceptions of women in history. Her strong female protagonists go out of their way to change their society's expectations for the fairer.

Learn more at

www.thehistoricalfictioncompany.com/hp-authors/e-j-mckenna

Acknowledgments

Despite having written an entire novel, and never being short of things to say, an Acknowledgement page is certainly a challenge for an awkward Brit.

However, this is quite similar to novel writing, as the struggle of knowing where to start is seemingly as real here as Chapter 1's opening lines. Nevertheless, we shall prevail!

I guess we should go in order.

Firstly, to my mother who was the first person to read that initial scribble, before the first draft was even formed. Thank you for your belief in my story, seeing the diamond through the rough of that early work, and for sharing it with other family members (despite my request not to!), because you were proud of what I was producing.

To my father, who quietly approved of my creativity. Thank you for patiently listening to too much back and forth about the book, its constantly changing status and learning the steps to publication alongside me.

To my fellow writers in the weekly writers group all the way back in 2020. Your support, conversations, and presence on those zoom meetings kept me motivated to keep pushing onward, it also kept me sane in a very insane time.

To my two assistant writers, my cats, who would sit on the arm of my chair for the eight hours a day I was typing away. Sadly, my chief assistant is no longer with us, but she lives on in the Biloxi name of Onti Lake.

To my Beta Readers, friends and family who provided amazing support, advice, great feedback, and historical guidance. Without you, this novel would still be a WiP, or an under-edited long fiction on AO3.

To my editor, Claire Selishta at Quill and Scrolls. Your hawk-like scrutiny of my work, alongside your love for Annie and ongoing championing of the book has been nothing short of heroic. You deserve a medal, or at the very least, a very large biscuit.

Lastly, to my amazing partner in crime, madness and all things; my husband James. The Nate to my Annie. Thank you for the support, the funding, the ability to cook every meal when I was in the 'writing flow', and for constantly pushing me to bring this story to life, even if you're waiting for the screen adaptation to fully know what happens!

Thank you for loving this era as much as I do, and for being excited for us to visit amazing historic American towns (even if you complained about the heat in Tombstone).

Your patience, care, humour and enthusiasm are a constant in my life, and for that I will forever be grateful. Here's to many more adventures together!

Emma x.

www.historiumpress.com